I0600761

Demons, Devils
&
Denizens of Hell
Vol. I

A Horror Anthology

HellBound Books Publishing LLC

A HellBound Books LLC
Publication

www.hellboundbookspublishing.com

Printed in the United States of America

Demons, Devils
&
Denizens of Hell
Vol. I

Compiled and Edited by P. Mattern

A HellBound Books Publishing LLC Book
Houston TX

Dedication

This mighty tome is dedicated to all of the thoroughly talented authors who have entrusted us with their darkest imaginings so that we may entertain you, Dear Reader, with tales from the deepest recesses of the Abyss.

Also, the biggest, most heartfelt thanks to P. Mattern, superlative wordsmith and possessor of boundless energy – without you, Dear P, this book may never have happened.

ON WRITING HORROR

A Foreword By
P. Mattern

I don't really believe any author sets out to write horror—horror chooses US, and it is a dark anointing that transports both author and reader into the nether realm of our greatest fears.

Fear is arguably the strongest and most deeply felt human emotion. No other emotion reaches inside of us, grips our entrails with an icy hand and twists them. Nothing else releases so much adrenalin and causes our heart to feel as if it is pounding out of our chest.

Although stylistically horror can shape shift into many forms, I am convinced that gore, psychological thrills, deviant behaviors and plot twists and turns that the reader doesn't see coming are hallmarks of great horror. A horror story should be like something jumping out at you after an inexplicable chill causes the hairs on the back of your neck to stand on end.

There is always a forewarning, but few choose to heed it, and that is where the real fun begins.

Horror captures universal themes of shock, futility and the awful knowledge we have long suspected: many of the monsters we grapple with in our nightmares are, in fact, real. Real horror has teeth, fangs and claws.

Horror written in short story form has the daunting task of making a lasting impression in a condensed arena. Every word must be chosen with a surgeon's skill, every detail designed to make a lasting impact.

All 23 of the authors participating in the HellBound Books' *'Devils, Demons and Denizens of Hell'* Anthology have gathered to drag you down into the bottom of the soul, where the dark ooze of your most primal fears resides. We are trying to scare you, far beyond your having to leave the light on to sleep. We want our exquisitely woven nightmares to follow you into the morning like a hangover from Hell.

If we are doing our job, they will.

P. Mattern

Demons, Devils
&
Denizens of Hell
Vol. I

YOUR TABLE OF CONTENTS

The Lair   **13**
Tania Hagan
The Haunting of Prosperity Inn   **34**
Lily Luchesi
Walker County is Small and Smith
Lake is Deep   **65**
Jay Michael Wright II
Slouching Towards Bethlehem   **93**
Ken Goldman
The Purification Process   **108**
Sergio "ente per ente" Palumbo
Depraved Collective   **126**
Emery LeeAnn
Circus Be Damned   **146**
Crystal Barnard
Face of an Angel   **172**
James H Longmore
The New Recruit   **197**
Toneye Eyenot
Son of Mestopheles   **201**
James Richardson
Tainted Revenge   **225**
Lori Fontanez
The Threshold of Hell   **241**
Marcus Mattern
Eye of the Needle   **258**
Lance Tuck
The Arthrogens: a New Breed   **288**
L. Ashby
I Dated Satan's Girlfriend   **305**
P. Mattern
Insatiable Hunger   **322**
Elizabeth Cash

Dark Land   **337**
Bryan A. Tann
Holtby   **359**
Elizabeth Zemlicka
Careful What You Wish For   **385**
M.J. Sutton
Icarus Ascending   **409**
Thomas S. Gunther
Coven of Ignorance   **426**
Feind Gottes
The Rats   **459**
Nik Kerry

Other HellBound Books   **489**

THE LAIR
By
Tania Hagan

The hideaway was easier to discover than he had anticipated. But Rev stalked them for the better part of a year, just to be sure.

Of course, he had his suspicions earlier. The week he started his job in this town, he noticed something was off at that particular location. It was subtle, but almost glaring to a man with his experience.

As a postal carrier, he could keep his eyes wide open, looking for places where large groups of them might gather.

He hit pay dirt when he spied the inconspicuous, one-story, brick building at the end of a country road. Maintaining his watch on the place, he saw them coming and going until he was certain of their true nature. He almost couldn't believe his luck when he roughly estimated their numbers. There were at least two-hundred of them.

They interacted mostly with each other, but sometimes they spent time with one or more of the keepers.

Not after next Friday, he thought. Their reign of terror would be over and he'd be the hero.

Halloween was such a perfect day to slaughter demons. It was a little personal joke for Rev and he almost wished he had someone to share it with.

But he'd been alone for many of his forty-six years. Sure, he'd had his share of somewhat serious affairs with various women. He even had a kid out in Arizona who he didn't visit often enough.

Personal relationships weren't really the problem. He wasn't a social butterfly by any means, but he did just fine with people in general.

He simply longed for the camaraderie of other hunters, especially now. He ran into a couple of them ten years earlier. They were a father-daughter team who were far more badass together than he'd ever be on his own. With his help, they managed to banish demonic entities from three innocent victims.

That was the easier task—exorcising their rotten souls from living human beings. It was especially rewarding when the host was still alive after the procedure.

This looming mission was different. He would end up with a body count this time. He wasn't sending the souls back to Hell as he had before. Instead, he was going to kill the bastards outright while they were in their *own* bodies, before they could inhabit any unsuspecting mortal. There would be nothing left of them to return to Hell, or to anywhere else.

Only fellow demon hunters would understand. It seemed no one saw the true nature of the demons, at least not with this bunch. The rest of the town just went about their own business, with the monsters cavorting right under their miserable noses.

To make up for his lack of kinship with other hunters, Rev recorded all his thoughts in a plain, leather-bound diary. The simple act of writing it all down made him feel as if he was sharing his plight with someone.

His methods, his plans, and his research about the special shotgun shells were all in the book. At the back of his mind, he knew he was also making a how-to manual for anyone who might take up his mission later.

If he didn't make it out alive, there was always the diary.

Rev dug his fingernails into his palms to shake off the thought.

This will be a triumph, not a tragedy.

He leafed through the diary and swiftly scribbled a few notes into a previous entry. He didn't want anyone reading this to make any mistakes about the demons' physical characteristics, even though their description had baffled him at first.

These creatures, in their true form, were much smaller than anyone would guess. They were about one-third his size. Unfortunately, their slight build had fooled thousands of hunters who came before him. These poor idiots had underestimated the demons' powers when they got a good look at their size.

Every one of those saps had gone to their grave, and probably to Hell because they didn't know what they were up against.

Morons.

Rev stood upright and glanced into the mirror that was mounted behind his foyer table. He absently ran a hand through his thick, completely white hair.

"Reverend," all his friends had called him when he was in his twenties. The title had a lot to do with his first name, "Reveland." But it was clearly fueled by the fact that he was prematurely gray at twenty-five.

He had his father's chiseled jawline, which only added to the distinguished reverend look. For the most part, people considered him handsome. These traits allowed him to quickly gain the trust of others over the years.

He only wished he had met more hunters along the way. They were a dying breed and he sometimes feared he was the last of them.

Stretching and cracking his knuckles, he paced back and forth in the hall for a few seconds before he stepped into the kitchen.

His shiny Remington shotgun laid across the small, circular dining table. Next to the weapons, a pile of homemade, specialty shells waited for him.

He knew the twelve-gauge weapon packed a punch. But the size of the impact didn't really matter much. In fact, he didn't plan to get up close and personal with these demons before he shot them.

It was the contents of the bullets that would really make the difference.

He sat down and picked up a shell near the top of the pile. After holding it up to the light for a quick inspection, he slowly brought it to his lips and kissed it.

The moment felt almost religious.

Reverend, indeed.

"You kids have to make Papa proud, now." He patted the pile and wiped away a tear. "Dear God, don't let me down. The future of Humankind depends on us."

***

Rev's heart pounded as he neared the lonely building at the end of the winding road. He was driving his usual postal vehicle, so he knew he wouldn't be scrutinized as he approached.

Hell, no one would look at him twice when he hopped out of the truck and marched right up to the door.

Except, this time, he wouldn't go near the front door, where the mail slot was located. Sure, he had mail for the handful of human minions who occupied the premises. But, today, they wouldn't get a single envelope.

He sucked in a quick, sharp breath as he thought about how he would take care of the people who might try to hinder his mission.

He'd have to shoot them too. Not that it mattered, though. They were here for the sole purpose of guarding the creatures. They had it coming to them. Still, he found some comfort in the fact that his weapon wouldn't really damage them much. He would fire those shots in order to get them out of his way, so he could get on to his intended targets.

Under his government-issued jacket, he wore a heavy vest filled with a hundred rounds. It was enough to take down half of them, at least.

He shrugged off the coat as he reached for the handle on the back door. The keepers had no idea the latch was broken on this basement entrance. But, Rev knew all about it. He had counted on it.

For a fleeting instant, he considered turning away.

Go around to the front of the building.

Deliver the God-forsaken mail to the brainwashed mortals. The keepers will be none the wiser.

Take some time off work. Head to Flagstaff to visit little Billy.

Let someone else tend to this mess.
They'll never even realize you were here.
No!

Even if the keepers didn't figure out his plans, the demons would surely know. They probably already knew. They'd taunt and torture him the rest of his life, and undoubtedly into the afterlife.

He'd be doomed by a momentary act of cowardice.

It was now or never.

It was Rev or no one.

As he entered the first darkened hallway, he aimed his already-loaded shotgun. There was no sign of demons in the hall, but he heard their squawking, shrill voices nearby. And they seemed to be approaching his location quickly.

Trying to control his heavy breathing, he flattened his back against a painted, cinderblock wall. Through his t-shirt, he felt the chill of the cooled, underground bricks.

Suddenly, they appeared from an adjoining hallway. There were six of the monsters, walking together and speaking among themselves in their high-pitched tones.

"Bam!"

He fired the first round into the demon at the head of the pack.

The creature spun on its slimy little heel and fell to the floor.

"Bam!"

He hit another, and then another.

By the time he had emptied the gun of the first set of rounds, a couple of the bastards had scattered. Their disgusting squeals resonated through the halls, but he didn't care.

Rev dived into a stairwell which he knew led to the main upper level. In the distance, he heard human and demon cries as he reloaded his weapon. The far-off noises were loud at first, but they quickly became muffled. He knew they were going to make it difficult for him to locate them, but he had confidence in his skills.

As he turned the corner, he almost ran into one of the monsters who had been crouching in the upper doorway to the stairs. They liked to hide in the shadows, waiting to pounce.

The thing looked up at him, almost as if it was challenging him. The creature wore a grotesque clown mask across its face.

How fitting, Rev thought. He always knew clowns and demons were somehow connected.

"Bam!"

He shot the demon through the fake clown eye. It cried its squeaky cry and fell over dead.

The upper hall was empty, as he had expected. He was sure the keepers would be busy protecting the demons by now and they would make it as difficult for him as they could.

Difficult, but not impossible.

He shuffled down the hall, opening closed doors here and there, to no avail. If they were hiding in any of the rooms, they were well hidden.

Rev spun around as a door opened and closed behind him.

To his surprise, one of the human keepers stood in the hallway, staring at him with unblinking, blue eyes.

The woman, an attractive brunette in her thirties, raised her arms out on either side of her small frame. He smiled as he saw one of the miniscule demons shrink behind her.

19

"Bam!"

The shot hit the keeper in the gut. She grabbed her midsection and fell forward, landing on her face.

A whole throng of creatures had been hiding behind her. They started to slither away as Rev took aim again.

He hit three of them instantly, but the others disappeared as he reloaded.

"Damn!" Rev shouted to the empty hallway.

He leapt over the human's body as he jogged in the direction where the demons had dispersed.

Somewhere, ahead of him, there was a commotion and a cacophony of unknown words. It didn't sound like the piercing cries of the creatures, or like the human wails of the keepers. Somehow, these new voices sounded more organized and ominous.

He considered the new development for only a second. His work was far too important to stop and ponder the meaning of anything.

To his right, another keeper scurried across a narrow corridor. This woman was older and plumper than the other one.

But, much like the first keeper, she was tailed by a bunch of screeching monsters.

"Bam!"

"Bam!"

"Bam!"

Three of the demons fell before he fired at the human.

This time, he reloaded quickly and slaughtered four more.

When he was satisfied that he had killed all of the beasts in the woman's care, he proceeded to jog down the main hallway again.

As he rounded the corner at the end of the hall, a single tiny demon stood facing him.

It looked up at him with its beady eyes. The thing didn't appear to have an ounce of fear in its putrid little body. In fact, he could have sworn it smiled at him.

"Piss off!" He shouted as he raised his weapon.

But, something wasn't right. This creature was grasping a disturbing and peculiar item in its fat little hand.

Rev hesitated and moved his head away from the shotgun so he could get a better look.

The beast lifted both arms towards him. Grinning wildly now, it held the pink, fluffy teddy bear in the air as it started to speak.

"Hi," the demon said, seemingly unfazed by its eminent execution. "What's your costume?"

No, Rev thought.

He wiped his sweaty face with his free hand and took aim again, dismissing the horrifying but momentary thought.

"Bam!"

The demon fell, just like all the others.

Too late, he noticed the tall, menacing figures a few yards behind the dead monster. The pair of them were clad all in black, except for the few letters in white print adorning their breasts.

Were these some sort of dark keepers from Hell he didn't know about? They certainly didn't belong here, and nothing he had researched prepared him for their presence.

Rev stood upright and took aim at them, but they were faster than him.

"Tat-a-tat-a-tat," the weapons of these new beings sang out in unison.

Pain seared through every inch of his body. Then, everything went mercifully numb.

He realized he had fallen to the floor, but he had no memory of how he got there.

Time ticked by endlessly, but he knew it was really standing still, as his last lucid thoughts looped over and over again through his mind.

The damned teddy bear.

Could it be?

No.

It has to be a trick. They're so good at that.

It's no trick.

Look at what you've done.

You were the only monster here today, Reverend.

He made a wretched attempt to raise his head off the ground. He knew he had to fess up to the shameful truths he finally recognized, but he also knew it wouldn't matter to anyone but himself.

Maybe God would listen. Maybe He would care.

"Dear Lord, please forgive me," Rev sobbed a second before his world went dark.

***

Police Chief Dan Tomczak scratched absently at the dry flesh on his bald head.

He stared at the pile of papers in front of him. It was already creeping into the early evening hours and he had barely sorted through half of the reports on his desk.

Never, in his thirty years on the force had he witnessed such a deplorable crime. Tragedies like this one happened to other people, in faraway lands. It couldn't possibly happen in New Antioch.

Yet, inexplicably, it did.

The plain facts seemed to be ripped out of the headlines.

At nine-o'clock that Halloween morning, a gunman entered Angelwood Elementary through an unsecured basement door. He proceeded to shoot nineteen children and two teachers before the Swat team managed to gun him down.

It was all too much for this sleepy, Midwestern town.

It was definitely too much for Tomczak. He was planning to retire in the next two years. But, given the nature of this nightmare, he felt obligated to stick around for his people. Someone would need to be here to help them heal properly.

"Are you ready for your speech, boss?"

Tomczak jolted upright as the woman asked the question.

"I'm never ready for these things, Hester. Who the hell would be?"

The deputy took a seat in a faux-leather rolling chair in front of the chief's desk.

Despite the situation, he glanced up and smiled at her.

Hester Chapman was not only his most trusted deputy, but she was also one of his closest friends. They had graduated college together and joined the department the same fall.

Over the years, they had both moved up in rank steadily, but he ended up as Chief.

He knew Hester didn't mind, though. She had intentionally taken more than the expected time off with the birth of her son, so her path to promotion was interrupted. Her boy always took precedence over her aspirations in law enforcement.

But he had great admiration and respect for her decisions.

While Tomczak was also a family man, and he and his wife had two beautiful adult girls, Hester outranked him in that area. Her husband and son came first, where he focused at least two-thirds of his waking hours on his career.

"I didn't mean to startle you when I came in." She laughed a little and leaned forward to examine some of the scattered paperwork. "Don't be so jumpy, Dan. It's not a becoming trait for a police chief."

"Sorry, Hester. This disaster sort of crumbled my nerves-of-steel façade."

"Ah, it's not a façade. You're just rattled." She picked up a thick stack of field reports and flipped through the pages. "Besides, this whole thing could have been a lot worse, you know."

"Worse? How the *hell* could it have been worse?" He realized he had snapped at her, so he softened his tone. "I apologize, Hester. I guess I *am* a little shaken. Pissed off, for sure."

"Well, don't be. The perp is dead and gone."

"What about the victims? Have you heard any more news out of Saint Benedicts?"

Hester settled back in her seat. She unclipped her shoulder-length blonde hair, twisted it, and reapplied the plastic clamp.

"That's the bright side I'm trying to get you to see, chief. We've had no fatalities, except for the bad guy."

"Everyone is still stable?"

"Yes. They are. Some are better than stable. Most have been released, as a matter of fact."

"What about that six-year-old boy?" Tomczak sifted through his paperwork again until he found the report he was looking for. "Zachary Polson. How's he doing?"

"It looks as if he's going to lose his right eye." Hester paused and took a deep breath. "He was shot at close range and the impact alone caused the damage."

"Dear God." Tomczak planted his elbows on his desk and laid his head in his hands.

"But, all the rest of the children have superficial wounds, Dan. The majority of it's just cuts and bruises. One kid had a dislocated elbow. Another has a broken wrist. Sadly, a few of them were knocked temporarily unconscious, probably from shock."

"And the adults who were shot?"

"Fine. They are *fine*." Hester pulled out a notepad from her jacket pocket. "Ava Dunn is pregnant—three months along…"

"And you're sure she didn't lose the baby?" Tomczak's heartburn acted up as soon as Hester reminded him of the pregnancy. He grabbed his bottle of antacid and twisted the top open.

"You really haven't read the latest information, have you boss?" Hester shot him a silly smirk.

He *had* read it. He read as much as he could get to between the phone calls and the officers interrupting him as he tried to focus.

Maybe Hester *should* have been Chief.

"I've read it, deputy. Just humor me."

"Well, if you read it, you'd know Mrs. Dunn's baby is as healthy as can be. The teacher did get the wind knocked out of her, though. She also broke her nose as she hit the ground. Her husband plans to be here tonight for the press conference."

"And, the older woman?"

"Delores Jackson. Yes, she has a concussion. And she now owns a pair of shattered glasses." Hester shifted her own wire-rimmed glasses, wrapping them more securely behind her ears. "Like I said, we're lucky, all things considered. It could have been much worse."

"The only luck we've had here today is the fact that the son-of-a-bitch used regular table salt in his shotgun shells. Even rock salt might have caused a few fatalities, at least with the closer-range shots." Tomczak stroked his salt-and-pepper goatee as he allowed himself a brief chuckle. "The ballistics guys say each and every one of the rounds were handmade."

"Yeah. They found some kind of batshit-crazy manifesto in the perp's house." Hester paused. "You did look at that, didn't you?"

"Yes, Hester." Tomczak rolled his eyes and moved some papers aside on his desk until he found the thick, stapled packet he was looking for. He thumped the top of it with his fingertips. "The evidence room was kind enough to make me a copy before they secured it."

"That's impressive." Hester nodded and winked. "You'd think you were the boss around here, or something."

"Yeah, well, because I'm the boss, I have the authority to hand this over to you." He scooted the document across the desk, in Hester's direction. "Go ahead. Interesting reading."

"No thanks." She smiled mischievously. "The boys down in Evidence made sure to print a copy for Robinson and me too."

"Well, what do you know?" He chuckled heartily this time. "That means they think the two of you actually get some work done around here."

Tomczak knew better, but he liked to tease his old friend.

"In this case, I think I've actually done more work than my aging chief." She laughed along with him.

"This guy—this Reveland Markus Kingston…Shit, what a name for a would-be mass murderer, huh?" He flipped the pages in the photocopied book. "Apparently, he was a postal carrier."

"That doesn't surprise you, does it?"

"Well, they do have a bad rep, but this one appears to be squeaky clean, at least as far as his record goes."

"So? What about it?"

"Nothing. It's just that I'm surprised by the entire thing, I guess." That wasn't the whole truth, but it was all Tomczak could explain at that moment. He didn't even know where he was going with the thought. "I mean, you wouldn't know he was such a model citizen if you read this rambling diary here."

"That seems to be the MO for a lot of psychopaths, Dan. Just look at Dahmer."

"Dahmer only pretended to stay out of trouble. This guy really did. Except for his preoccupation with demon hunting—whatever that is—he behaved like a regular guy."

"Um…until he shot up an elementary school, boss."

"Yes, but he did it with care."

"With *care*? Sorry, Danny Boy, I don't follow."

"Then pay attention."

"Right. *I'm* the one who needs to pay attention here."

"The thing is, he knew the salt wouldn't kill any human being, unless he was right in their face when he fired."

"Well, he was almost in that Polson kid's face when he shot him in the eye." Hester partially covered her mouth with her hand and spoke through splayed fingers. "That poor little angel."

"He thought the boy was a demon, so it didn't matter how close he got to him. His only goal was to blast them with the salt, which he assumed would kill a demon on contact."

"I read that part in there." She nodded to the book in Tomczak's hand. "It looks as if there are different schools of thought when it comes to demon hunting. One major theory is that they can be obliterated with salt. Hence, the salt rounds."

"And can they?" He glanced up at his friend, not really knowing why he was asking such a ridiculous question.

"How the heck should I know? Round me up some demons, and we'll give it a try." Hester stood up and stretched. "All I *do* know right now is that we have that press conference in forty-five minutes and you're the fool who has to address the media."

Tomczak also stood.

"You'll be there to back me up, right?"

"What, in case the reporters all draw their guns?" She punched playfully at his ample belly.

"You know what I mean, Hester. In case I forget some of the crap I have to say."

"I'll be right behind you, chief." She saluted him and turned on her heel towards his office door. "Just bring some notes, okay?"

"Got it." He moved back behind his desk as Hester exited the room.

The stack of reports in front of him seemed to have grown since Hester had walked into the room. He decided there was no way he would ever be able to fully understand this mess.

Moving forward, he realized most of these families would need counseling and support during their grief. No, they hadn't lost any children, but, perhaps, the children had lost their innocence.

He pushed piles of paperwork aside until he got down to the folder with the kids' photos in it.

As he glanced at their little faces, which were obviously poses from last year's class photos, he smiled.

Yeah. Maybe, they'll be okay.

He rubbed his weary eyes and took another look. When he did, something subtle caught his attention.

All nineteen children were clearly unrelated to each other. Every one of them had different facial features, different skin tones, and probably even different nationalities.

But, somehow, they all had a unified look.

He blinked repeatedly and looked again. He couldn't put his finger on exactly what it was, but it was definitely *something*.

The chief glanced up at his closed door, almost wishing Hester would walk through it again. She'd tell him he was losing his mind and smack some sense into him.

On a hunch, he pulled out another folder his men had also retrieved from school records. This one had group photos of every classroom.

Once again, he looked at face after tiny face. They were entirely different, yet exactly the same.

Impulsively, he snapped both folders shut and returned them to the bottom of his unruly pile of documents.

That retirement was looking better and better every second.

***

Seven-year-old Hailey Ferguson wiggled restlessly in her hospital bed at Saint Benedict. She clutched her old teddy bear to her chest as she tried not to bother messing with her aching, bandaged shoulder.

She brought the toy to school as part of her costume. Her mother dressed her as a baby for Halloween. She wanted to be a superhero, but her mom insisted that she looked so adorable made up to look like an infant.

But now, they had taken off her sticky, blood-spattered, footed pajamas and made her wear a stupid hospital gown instead.

She heard the adults saying she would be able to go home in a few hours. All her friends who were hurt were probably going home tonight too.

Maybe not. There was the one who lost his eye. He might have to stay a while.

They called that one, "Zachary," but she knew him as, "Zaesuhr."

It didn't matter. She couldn't have cared less about what his parents named him.

She also didn't care much about his eye. Hailey knew he'd only have to strengthen his other eye until it could do the work of two. He might even grow a new one, but the adults didn't need to know that.

Over the past few hours, she overheard a lot of talk.

Most of them fussed and worried about the minor injury to her arm. But occasionally, they said things that were valuable to her. Things they didn't want her to hear.

That very bad man was one of the topics of their hushed conversations.

She tried to control her facial expressions when they talked about how he loaded the shotgun shells with salt. In the end, she figured it was better for her to just close her eyes and pretend to nap while they discussed such things.

Now, since her parents had gone out of the room to get some coffee, Hailey could make any expression she wanted.

She grinned from ear to ear. A little giggle escaped her mouth and she stifled it with the stuffed animal, in case anyone was listening to her through the closed door. It tasted salty, thanks to him.

Salt?

She laughed again at the thought.

"There's my princess." Her father peeked his head in the door, carrying a tall paper cup.

"Hi, Daddy." Hailey beamed as the man sat on the edge of her bed.

"I'm happy to see you smiling." He handed her the cup as he spoke. "Don't tell the doctor, but I snuck a milkshake up here from the cafeteria."

"Vanilla?" Hailey sat up straighter in bed and moved the bear aside before she clapped her hands.

"You bet it is." He deposited his coffee on a side table.

After a few sips, Hailey laid her shake on the rotating tray near her bed.

"Daddy?"

"Yes, kitten?"

"Did the bad man die?"

When he didn't answer for a second, Hailey thought she had said something wrong, something out of character.

Crap.

31

"Yes, honey. He did." Her father picked up her milkshake and handed it to her again. "But, Mommy and I don't want you thinking about terrible things like that. Okay?"

"Okay, Daddy," she lied.

"All we want you to do is focus on getting better." He smiled and patted her knee. "The doctor says the hurt on your shoulder is just a little bruising and a few scratches. We might even get to some trick-or-treating tonight. No matter what, you'll be in tip-top shape in a few days."

"I'll be fine because that mean man used salt in his gun?" She already knew the answer to her question.

Her dad seemed to hesitate again. His mouth hung open for a second as he blinked repeatedly at her.

"Yes, Hailey." He softened his voice to nearly a whisper when he finally spoke. "I'm sorry you heard us talking about that, sweetheart. But, yes. You're going to be okay because the bad man used salt."

Hailey clenched her teeth around the straw and offered her dad a wide smile. She hoped he would think she was beaming about her milkshake.

Apparently, the shooter had wholeheartedly believed the ancient rumors about the usefulness of salt. Thankfully, such stories were little more than fairy tales.

Hailey finished her drink and handed her father the empty cup. She leaned back on the pillow and pretended her eyelids were getting heavy.

"You go ahead and get some rest, Hailey." He pulled the hospital blanket up to just below her injured shoulder. "When you wake up, it'll be time for Mommy and me to bring you home."

"I love you, Daddy."

"I love you too, my sweet angel." He leaned forward and kissed her on the top of her head.

Salt? Ha! Hailey thought blissfully as she laid there with her eyes closed.

She had smiled at the shooter when he held the weapon up in front of her. It caused him to have doubts. She knew it would.

She smelled him coming. She smelled the salt, even when he first entered the lair.

Now, if the idiot would have used Platinum pellets…

Well, that would have been unfortunate.

What is that line from their precious little book of lies?

Oh, yeah. "Suffer the little children…"

THE HAUNTING OF PROSPERITY INN

By

Lily Luchesi

Investigator Jamie Parker met Doctor Christopher Luffy when she took a case at his practice. Of course, that case involved long-dead patients and a lot of skepticism from Chris, but Jamie did her job and did it well.

Her job? Paranormal investigator and medium. She had been born clairvoyant, clairsentient, and clairaudient. Her curse? She had always been haunted by the hurt, disturbed, angry, and plain old evil spirits. She had performed her first exorcism when she was just ten years old, when her family's new apartment proved to have a dark shadow hovering about in one of the bedrooms.

Ever since then she used her God given gifts for good, helping friends, churches, and even businesses with their spirit problems. She didn't think of charging for her services until she saw that there were entire TV shows dedicated to fake ghost hunters who didn't even have any abilities.

Realizing that she could make a living for herself while helping people, she became a CEO and COO of her own company by the time she was twenty-one, and now, at thirty, she was known the world over for her skills.

She did not go on talk shows, write books, make a TV show, or any of that. Occasionally she'd get interviewed by a newspaper or a blog, but that was about it as far as publicity went. She believed that the truly skilled, as she was, didn't need to prostitute themselves for attention.

It was Chris' nurse who had contacted her about the haunting in the newly renovated medical building. Chris was suspicious and distrustful of her at first, but when she saved him from having his energy drained by the vengeful spirit, he began to be a believer in what he couldn't see.

It was also how he fell in love with the strange, beautiful girl covered in tattoos who could see the dead.

They shared an apartment in New York City, not far from his practice. He spent his days helping sick children, and she spent hers burning bones in cemeteries and splashing holy water over haunted buildings that had had bodies buried in their basements.

One day, neither of them had work, so she was lounging in one of his robes, reading a book, while he was idly surfing the web. Comfortable. Safe. Not like their respective jobs, where death held dominion.

Chris' phone rang, and he went on the balcony to take the call. He was gone for a few minutes, so Jamie stuck her head out the sliding glass doors to see what had happened. "Everything okay?"

He put the phone to his side and said, "Remember Geoff Stryker?"

"Your old friend, the one you met when you studied abroad in London? Of course! We attended his wedding last year. How's he been? The Facebook front has been quiet," she said.

"You want the good or the bad?" he asked.

"Oh no!"

He smirked. "Amanda is pregnant. It's a girl, or so they say."

"Aw, congratulations," Jamie said. "Now, what's the bad news?"

"Well, do you remember that she and Geoff left the medical profession to open that inn in Vermont? They did, three months ago. It's been a huge success...but there's a problem with the property."

"Asbestos?" Jamie guessed.

"If only. In three months, three people have died. All of them with these strange bruises, all of them wrinkly...even a twenty-two-year-old man. It's not normal, and Geoff thinks that this might be your kind of problem," Chris explained.

"Put him on speaker."

"Hello, Jamie. I'm sorry to have to converse again under such circumstances," Geoff said, his accent smooth.

"Yeah, so am I. What happened?" Jamie asked. "Oh, congratulations on the baby, by the way."

"Thank you. Well, it started three weeks ago. The first death. It was a woman of about forty, staying with us for a weekend because she was snowed in. We were pretty packed full that weekend, in fact. Only one room was open. Anyway, when she was supposed to check out Sunday afternoon, she never showed at the front desk. So Amanda went to check on her. The door to her room was locked, but we have master keys to get in in case of emergency. When she opened the door...she smelled cinnamon. You know, how old mummies smell when you go to the museum?

"Amanda pulled back the covers on the bed to see the wrinkled, hollowed out shell of our guest. She had bruises - finger marks - along her jaw, as if someone had pried it open with their bare hands. Her corpse creaked as the coroner took it away. Creaked! Her eyes were sunken; her lips were nearly invisible...it was horrible.

"The bobbies - oh, I mean police - they investigated us, but obviously, they could find nothing wrong. We were in the clear, but still quite disturbed.

"And a week later, the second death. He was an elderly man, I'll admit, so the police thought nothing of it when he passed. Natural causes. Amanda and I noticed the similarities, though. The extremely sunken eyes - they were blackened, I swear - and the cinnamon smell. A corpse only eight hours old does not smell like that."

He took a breath, and Jamie could tell he was mentally gathering his wits for the next part of his story. It was obvious he'd had quite a shock.

"The third victim was just two days ago. A young man. Staying here to pass the night before finishing his trip to Maine to see his grandparents. He was nice, even chatted with us over the fire, like inn guests always do in stories. When he didn't come down the next morning...we knew. We just instinctively knew.

"I went into the room, not Amanda. I didn't want to stress her out, because of the pregnancy. He was prone in the bed, the covers off as if there had been a struggle. His eyes were so sunken in, I wasn't sure he even had eyeballs anymore. His mouth was wide open

- the jaw completely distended. No jaw should be able to open that wide. His skin was dry and wrinkly, like the others, and there had been those same finger marks on his jaw.

"No human is that strong, and no illness could cause that kind of decomposition. Plus, all doors and windows were locked from the inside, so there could not have been an intruder. I explained to Amanda what it is you do, and she told me to call you."

After that long-winded explanation, Geoff sighed. Jamie was trying to picture the things he had described, but failed. "Amanda was right: this does sound like my kind of problem. I can be there by eight tonight, not counting any traffic I get into. This could be a simple blessing, and I can be home for breakfast tomorrow."

"You'll really take the job?" Geoff sounded surprised.

"Of course. I'll be there soon," she promised.

Chris took the phone back and said, "Prepare the room for two, Geoff. I think I might be able to be of use and get the police to back down. ...No matter about work, it's a weekend, and I only go in for clinic duty as a volunteer. As long as I'm back by Monday morning, it's fine. See you both soon."

He hung up and saw Jamie smiling at him. "You're worried about me."

"What? Worried about you?" Chris laughed. "I wouldn't waste my time with that. With what you do, my worrying is the equivalent of a politician telling the truth: there's no point."

"You're an ass. Do you really think you can help keep the police at bay so the inn doesn't get shut down?" she asked, going into the apartment to pack an overnight bag.

"Sure I can. I assisted the NYPD in a few murder cases before I met you. I have a good reputation," he said, folding a few things into a small bag.

They got into Chris' car and drove over to Vermont. The views were gorgeous, as fall was just beginning, and the leaves were starting to turn. Autumn was Jamie's favorite season: cool weather, pumpkin everything, Halloween, and of course the gorgeous views you got when you lived on the East Coast.

"We should take a vacation here," she commented. "The views are so lovely. I can imagine them in the daytime."

"You should see Italy in the autumn," he replied. "I went there once. You'd love it."

She looked over at him, his blue-green eyes, his soft lips, pale skin. She wondered how on Earth a strange girl like her got fortunate enough to have a man like him. She had always thought she'd be alone, or maybe with someone else who did what she did for a living. She never expected to have a normal life...well, normal when you left out her profession, anyway.

They arrived at the inn earlier than expected, and the sight of it all lit up, nestled between the orange and red trees, warm and inviting, was breathtaking. Chris had questioned Geoff and Amanda's choice to leave the medical profession to open the inn, and now Jamie could see that even he understood why they did it.

Geoff and Amanda were sitting on the porch, talking and sipping tea with two guests who had apparently not been scared off by the deaths. It was a cozy scene, but Jamie could sense the uneasiness in both the Strykers' auras, and in the house itself.

"Definitely haunted," she told Chris as they got out of the car.

"You can tell already?" he asked, getting their suitcases. "We haven't even been inside yet!"

"I know, but the vibe the house gives off is making me feel a bit ill. It's a deep-seated darkness. I'm glad you had the presence of mind to bring more than just a night's worth of clothing. We might need it. I wish they'd had me check the place out before they bought it," she said.

"Well, I highly doubt that they had thought about evil spirits when they were scouting locations," he commented.

They walked up the front steps and Geoff gave them both warm hugs, followed by Amanda. They made a cute couple: both blonde and petite (even him), with childlike means and warm hearts. Jamie noticed that Geoff really looked the part of an innkeeper with his checked pullover sweater and collared shirt.

"Would you excuse us for a bit?" he asked the couple on the porch. "These are some friends come to stay, and we want to see them settled in."

They walked into the inn, feeling the warmth from a fire in the grate. The room was comfortable and warm, very homey. If only the vibe of the building matched the vibe of the Strykers' decor.

"You have got one evil ghost...at least, I hope it's only one," Jamie commented when they were all alone. "This inn is gorgeous, but the vibe of this place spoils the effect you guys created."

"You can tell already? Oh, no, that's bad, right?" Amanda said.

Jamie nodded. "I need some background on this building, and also photographs of the deceased. If possible, Chris, do you think that you can get me in the morgue to see the newest corpse?"

"I can try," Chris replied.

Geoff went behind the front desk to get what she needed, saying, "You know, Jamie, I thought being a paranormal investigator was more like *Ghost Adventures*, not *Law and Order*."

"An investigator of any sort has the same basic needs to perform their job properly. I used to say that Sherlock Holmes had it backwards: in my type of investigation, you need to eliminate the possible, and then whatever remains is the truth." She bent her head over the photos and article about the building. It had been a convalescent home in the 1920's. The sick, the elderly, the addicts, and the mentally ill all stayed there to get better. Some died before that happened.

"Do you have a list of all the patients that died here?" she asked.

"No, but I bet either Chris or I can get it," Geoff said. "Let me send an email."

"Has anyone, yourselves included, seen anything? Heard anything? Felt anything? Smelled anything? Cold spots, creaking floors, water going too cold or too hot, water being turned on and off at odd hours, the stench of sulfur, the feeling of being watched?"

"Wow, that was quite a list!" Geoff laughed.

"I feel cold spots quite a bit," Amanda said. "A few times upstairs. I figured maybe it was a breeze because this is an old place after all. And we wouldn't notice creaking floors: they all creak, and we're never empty here."

"I saw a woman once, on the balcony of the room the last guest died in. I blinked, and she was gone. I thought I was imagining things. And there have been a few times I swear I was being watched. Always upstairs, though, near the bedrooms," Geoff said.

"Good. At least we know that the ghost is a woman, and she only stays upstairs. It makes my job easier." Jamie flipped the photo of the inn in the twenties over and let out an involuntary shriek. The photo below it was recent, of the first deceased guest. Her dark brown hair was dried and wispy around her nearly skeletal head. Her skin was sallow and sunken, wrinkled everywhere. The eyeballs were resting in what looked like two black craters. The lips were colorless and pulled up, exposing her gums and teeth. The bruises on the jaw were made by slim fingers, and the jaw was certainly quite distended. In fact, it had been pulled so violently that it was completely dislocated.

"What the fucking fuck?" she said. She'd never seen anything like this. It was as of the woman had been drained dry of...everything. Blood. Saliva. Muscle. As if there was nothing left but literally skin and bones.

Chris was just staring at her. "I don't think I've ever seen you scared."

"I've never been scared. Not once...until right now," she said, turning the picture face down. "You don't have a normal ghost by any means, Geoff. I can try and ward the rooms so your current guests will be safe, but I don't know how well it will work. I recommend you three sleep down here tonight, just in case."

"And you?" Chris asked.

"I'm not going to sleep if I can help it. I'm going to banish this thing."

"With what?" Amanda asked.

Jamie held up her bag. "Holy water. Latin prayers. Burning sage. I'm going to use my entire arsenal if I have to."

Amanda gave her an unexpected hug. "You don't know how much this will help us. I've been so scared."

"I know. And fear isn't good for the baby." Jamie patted Amanda's already showing stomach. "I'm not going to let everything go to Hell on you when you've got so much to look forward to."

Geoff cleared his throat. "And what about your fee?"

"My what? Geoff, don't be an asshole. I'm not charging you guys. You're like family to Chris, which means you're family to me, too." She smiled. "Now, what you can do for me is get to work on that dead patient list."

"If I wasn't so grateful to you, I'd be offended at how you're treating me like a gofer," he said, doing some clicks on his computer.

"I'm going to ward the rooms. Glad I always carry along more things than I usually need." The three of them watched as she walked up the wooden staircase, determined as ever to rid the world from the darkness.

****

Chris leaned against the desk, his head in his hands. "I'm worried."

"About Jamie?" Amanda guessed. "Or about us?"

"Of course I'm worried about you both. However...Jamie is not just a ghost hunter, or exorcist, whatever she calls herself. She's a daredevil. Her favorite program is about two ghost hunters who die repeatedly 'for the greater good'. I don't want anything to happen to her because she was reckless. This isn't TV." He opened his suitcase and put a box on the desk.

"Oh, my stars…" Amanda leaned over and saw the beautiful diamond ring in there.

"This is what was going on this weekend, had you not called," he explained.

"Should I apologize?" Geoff laughed. "Hopefully she'll get this done quickly, and you two can finally take the plunge like we did."

Chris walked upstairs to see what Jamie was up to, and he saw her drawing strange symbols at the doorways, windows, and on all thresholds in the hall with white chalk. "What's all that?"

She didn't turn. She had told him she could sense auras, so he was sure she had known he was there. "They're to keep evil spirits out." She had also taped palms that had been bent into crucifixes above each doorway. He watched as she bent back into her duffel and took out a holy water font.

"Tell me, does the Catholic Church actually let you in, or do you pay churchgoers under the table to smuggle you this stuff like drugs?" he asked, grinning.

She looked up and said, "If I wasn't praying, I'd tell you just what I think of your jokes. Go back downstairs. I'm almost done here."

He walked down the stairs, but not before he saw a worried look pass across her face as one of the taped palms fell to the floor. He thought that the tape just hadn't been strong enough, but it was apparent that she thought more of it.

Downstairs, he took out his phone and called an old colleague of his. When he had been a resident, another doctor had gotten into some trouble, and Chris had risked his job in order to help his friend. The colleague was now doing well, and still owed him a big favor. It just so happened that he worked in Vermont, in this very county as the coroner.

"Dr. Franklin, this is Dr. Luffy, from Bellevue," he said when Franklin picked up the phone.

"Oh, hello! Good to hear from you. How've you been?" Dr. Franklin said.

"I'm well. Tell me, do you recall saying that you owed me a favor in return for helping you out after that little 'vodka in your Sprite bottle' incident?" Chris asked nonchalantly. "If you do, I am in Vermont and would like to collect on that favor now, please."

"Of course," the coroner stammered, embarrassed. "Whatever you need, just ask."

Chris grinned. He knew that that incident would come in handy. "You know those mysterious deaths at the Prosperity Inn? I need to have a colleague of mine see the latest corpse. Also, I'd like to check the body myself."

"Um, sure, no problem. It would look good to get your opinion on it, too. You are one of the most respected doctors in New York. When can you get here?" the coroner asked.

"When do you open in the morning?"

****

Jamie had been spending sleepless nights in abandoned mansions, old cemeteries, mausoleums, and even an asylum since she was sixteen. Never had any of those places given her the willies like Prosperity Inn was giving her. Geoff and Amanda's own quarters were on the first floor, so they normally slept away from the spirit. Finding accommodations for Chris had been a bitch, because no one wanted to have the paying guests seeing him sleeping in the lobby.

So, Geoff had decided to pretend the library was closed for the night and had Chris sleep on the sofa in there. Jamie, as she had said, was not going to sleep. She was going to try and spot this ghost and banish it this very night if possible. She'd had a very good vibe about this weekend, something good was going to happen, and now that vibe was gone ever since Chris had answered Geoff's call.

God had given her these gifts to help people, of that she was sure, but it was getting to the point where she wanted to have downtime. She wanted to spend her nights in bed with Chris, not wandering the unseasonably cold halls of a haunted inn. She wanted a balance between the deadly unbelievable life she had always lived and the safe confines of a new reality she had found with Chris.

Besides, this inn was overly creepy. She had dealt with evil spirits that she was convinced were demons. She had exorcised people of all ages. She'd faced off with murderous ghosts before. So why was this ghost so different?

She held her flashlight tight, careful that her shoes made no noise on the wooden floors. She didn't want to disturb the few guests that were vacationing there for the weekend. To have them questioning her presence could mean the end of the Strykers' business.

Unlike ghost hunters who did not have any preternatural abilities, she did not use EMF meters or heat-sensing cameras. If a ghost wanted to show up on film, even a Polaroid would do. And she was her own EMF detector.

The halls of the inn were not too vast, so it would not tire her out to walk about all night. She turned down the east hall, the one where the first and the last dead guests had been found, pondering if she had time to go and get another cup of coffee from the kitchen when it happened.

It was not like the films, where the flashlight started flickering and she could see her breath in cold puffs. It was more like a goose walking over your grave.

Her entire body stiffened as the hairs on the back of her neck rose. She saw her arms were prickled with gooseflesh.

"All right, who are you and where are you?" she asked. She found that ghosts who did not appear right away were sometimes more coherent at speaking than showing. Proving that point, she heard a girlish chuckle, but it was dry, as if someone with a sore throat or allergies was laughing.

She turned slowly in a circle, observing every nook and cranny, searching for the spirit. Her skin was getting colder by the minute, and her black bangs moved in a light breeze. The fingers holding the flashlight were tingling with the sudden cold.

"Find something funny, do you?" she asked, her voice never betraying the shudders that were wracking her body. She was a professional. Why was she so scared? "Why don't you tell me about it?"

The chuckling changed pitch, becoming a low whine. Had this been any "normal" person, they would have soiled themselves at that sound. Jamie gripped her crucifix that she always wore around her neck. It was made of iron and she blessed it with holy water daily to keep her protected. She was still trying to convince Chris to wear one as well.

"Hungry."

The word was not so much spoken as it was hissed through the very walls. It sounded like it was coming from all around her. "I have news for you: you're dead. You can't be hungry. Why are you here? Why did you never cross over?"

The breeze got stronger. She noticed some of the framed art prints that Amanda had hung were starting to sway.

"It's not fair."

She jumped, turning to where the voice came from this time. Nothing. "What isn't fair? Maybe I can help you. Talk to me."

Silence. The breeze seemed to still, but that didn't mean that the spirit was gone. Jamie had seen many instances where it meant that the spirit was gearing up for an even stronger attack. The dead hated and envied the living, always wanting to trade places with them.

"You're pretty."

She turned again, certain that the voice was coming from the dead end of the hall. She stepped closer, holding her crucifix before her.

"Why is my appearance important?" she asked it, fairly certain that the ghost was a young woman by the sound of the voice. Ghosts could imitate sounds and voices, so nothing was certain. She walked slowly, before she found herself stuck. It was as if someone had superglued her shoes to the floor. That had happened before, so she wasn't as worried as she should have been.

Before her eyes, the ghost began to materialize in front of her. The air began to shimmer as the form slowly took shape. It started from the feet up. Bare feet, small. Extremely thin and pale legs leading up into a hospital Johnny. The Johnny was once white, but it was grey and decayed now; ratty. Thin arms that looked like no more than bones hung at the sides, the hands like thin, white spiders splayed.

The body beneath the Johnny was also painfully thin. This girl had been very ill when she was alive. The neck was like a toothpick. So far, she looked like the corpses she left: thin and papery, made of no more than skin and bones.

Her hair was dirty, stringy, and as unhealthy as her body. It was such a light blonde it looked white, and just hung there, with bald patches in her scalp. Her face was the most frightening part of her. Sunken, skeletal, with deep hollows in the cheeks and eyes. Her lips were dry and so thin they might not have existed at all. They were spread in a grimace that revealed yellowing, rotted teeth. Her eyelashes and eyebrows had fallen out or had been plucked out. The eyes themselves were sunk into the deep crevasses that surrounded them. They were colorless, like her hair. Her pupils were constricted, and it looked like she had cataracts. Her skin was greyish as well, like she had already been a corpse long before she had even died.

Cancer, Jamie guessed, feeling sorry for the girl. But a painful death did not allow her to remain here and murder innocent people. This had to stop, tonight. Despite her fear, despite the seriously dark vibes she was getting from the ghost, she had to make it cross over.

"Go," she said. "You don't belong here anymore. It's time to cross over, and then your mortal past will be just that: the past."

The ghost cocked her head, eyes widening even more. "You don't...deserve..."

"What? What don't I deserve?" Jamie asked, not expecting what was going to happen next.

"You don't deserve to live!" the ghost cried, and quick as lightning she shot across the floor, floating a few inches above it. She moved fast, but to Jamie it happened in excruciatingly slow motion. Her hair flew behind her, as wispy as her form. Strands fell out as she moved. Her eyes became nothing but large black holes with two white pupils, staring at Jamie and making the hunter feel like she was staring into Hell, and it was not fiery, but dark and cold: a void of black nothingness. Her teeth were bared and the lipless mouth opened in an unearthly shriek that shattered the glass on the paintings. Her ghastly visage and outstretched hand was the last thing Jamie saw before she passed out.

****

Chris could not sleep; he was too worried about Jamie. So he stayed up, perusing the library. It was impressive, and Jamie had commented that she could happily live in that room for the rest of her life. He had rarely had the time to savor the written word thanks to his job, but Jamie's books took up one entire wall of their apartment. She loved to read, everything from the classics to modern horror and poetry made their way to the shelves.

He spotted some of her favorite books, noticing that her lifestyle didn't make her shy away from the macabre in fiction. He picked up one of her favorites, an Edgar Allan Poe collection, and sat down, sipping a cup of tea. He smiled as he read "The Murders in The Rue Morgue", recalling her saying that Dupin might be the original, but he was coarse and idiotic when compared with Holmes. She had been so indignant, and so cute, that at that very moment Chris had known that he was madly in love with this strange girl, and that he would marry her one day.

As he was reading, he heard a loud thump and glass shattering above him, and he immediately jumped from the couch like he had a spring beneath his bottom. He ran so fast he made nearly no sound as he dashed up the stairs, terrified of what he might find. To picture Jamie like those mummified dead bodies made his heart trip and his nerves shake.

When he saw her body slumped on the floor, surrounded by broken glass, he felt his heart in his throat. Bending down at her side, he felt for a pulse. It was a bit too fast, but she was alive. No sign of mummification or injury. He checked her eyes, and felt her head. Everything seemed okay with no evidence of concussion. He picked her up, holding her tightly to him, as he walked down the stairs and placed her on the couch in the library. He knew he needed to wake Geoff, to make him clean up the broken glass, but right then he just wanted to watch Jamie breathe, to reassure himself that she was all right. He had feared the worst, and was quite shaken up.

There was a knock at the library door, and Geoff walked in. "Is everything alright? I thought I heard something moments ago."

Chris quietly explained how he had just found Jamie passed out in the hall, and Geoff went to go and clean up the broken glass. Chris hoped that he would be okay up there by himself. He would have gone with his friend, but he refused to leave Jamie, who had fallen into a deeper, more natural slumber. He moved her hair away from her face and noticed that there were bruises like finger marks on her jaw.

His breath got short as he realized how close she had been to being killed. Whatever that thing had done to those poor guests, it had tried to do to her.

****

Jamie's head was foggy. Had she been asleep? Why? She sat up, realizing that she was in the library of the inn. She tried to gather her thoughts. She recalled wandering the halls of the inn to find the ghost, and then...she had found it.

She remembered it's strange words, it's rage. It's face. Lord, that was one thing she wished she could forget!

"Hey, Jamie, are you okay?" Chris said. She rubbed her eyes to get the sleep out of them and saw him, bending over her. "What happened last night? I found you on the floor, and all the glass was broken."

She leaned her head back and he immediately went to look in her eyes. "I hit my head, right? Damn it, she got away!"

"Who got away?" he asked.

"The ghost. I saw her last night," she said. "Does Geoff have the list of patients yet?"

"Whoa, first things first. I need to be sure you're okay, and you need to eat something. Then I think I have a way for you to get some more information," Chris said.

She stood up, not dizzy, thankfully. She was shaken up, however. This was no longer a random ghost haunting. This was personal. No ghost had been so direct with her before, or threatened her wellbeing. She wanted it gone, partly because she was ashamed to admit that the thing had frightened her. Being scared was new, and she found that she didn't much like the feeling.

"I'm fine. I can see, no dizziness, no aches except for my neck from sleeping on this couch, and I want to get on with this. I'm going to take a shower." She smiled, gave him a soft kiss, and went to the room the Strykers' said that they could use to wash up.

Getting out of the shower, she went to the mirror to put on her makeup and nearly fainted again: five distinct finger marks were on her face, in the exact same places as the victims'. The ghost had tried to get her, too. She gripped the sides of the sink so tightly her knuckles turned white. She had been so close to being yet another victim. She had been on the edge of death.

She tried to calm her breathing. After all, she had survived. It meant she had another chance to send this bitch right back to Hell where she belonged. Now, however, she needed to be even quicker: she might not survive the next encounter.

After she dressed, Chris gave her a cup of coffee. "If you're so insistent, let's go to the morgue now. The coroner owes me a favor, and he's agreed to let us come look at the latest body."

She kissed him more enthusiastically. "You are the best!" They went to the lobby, where Amanda was manning the desk while Geoff was with the guests, being a charming host. "Hey, did Geoff get that list yet?" she asked her.

"No, he gave the task to me. Working on it now. It's hard, because records that old are sometimes not catalogued in a computer system," Amanda replied. "Is there anything you can give me to narrow down the search? Chris said you saw the ghost last night."

"I did." Jamie stepped up to the counter. "She's young, probably not even in her mid-twenties. Blonde. She was very ill. She looked emaciated, and claimed she was 'hungry', which leads me to think that that was why she took so much muscle, fat, and blood from the victims. She's eating their very life force to feed her unearthly appetite."

"You know, I didn't need your macabre observa-oh!" Amanda looked up and saw the bruises that were not quite covered by Jamie's makeup.

Jamie waved a negligent hand. "I know."

"Tell me you and Chris had too rough sex last night and that's not what I think it is!" Amanda said, her blue eyes wide.

Chris blushed, while Jamie said, "I wish. Don't worry, I'm going to get rid of her."

Amanda hugged her. "I am so sorry we're putting you through this."

Jamie smiled. "Part of the job. See you later."

They got into Chris' car and he drove into town, which was very quaint. A great vacation spot for sure, but it was very haunted.

There are hauntings like what you see in horror movies: evil spirits who do awful things to humans, and then there are hauntings that are much more placid. This was an old town with a lot of history. Their dead liked to hang around, and they could cross over anytime they wanted without any help from Jamie. She loved towns like these. They felt safe, with all these pleasant spirits around, watching over the living.

They went into the medical building, and Chris showed an ID, saying that Dr. Franklin was expecting them. They were ushered into an elevator and rode down to the basement...the morgue. Jamie hated seeing dead bodies. She saw both ends of the spectrum: the living and the dead. Seeing the empty vessels of those already passed on made her feel uneasy. It showed death as cold and empty, when in reality she knew that it was anything but.

Dr. Franklin was a middle-aged man who had the face of one who had been an alcoholic. Jamie could read his need in his aura: he would forever crave a drink, the one thing he could never have. It was like how the spirit wanted food, when she had appeared emaciated and starving when she was alive.

Chris made introductions, and she could tell that the coroner was a bit taken aback that Chris' "colleague" looked so...unprofessional. Jamie dressed how she wanted to, despite her choice of clothing making her seem less than professional to most people.

"Have you performed the autopsy yet?" Chris asked.

"No. I was going to last night, but figured you'd want me to wait till you were here," Dr. Franklin replied.

"Good thinking. Jamie, put on a mask. I doubt the body will have any pathogens or any noxious gases inside, but best to be safe than sorry in this case," Chris said, pointing to one of the drawers. He went to another drawer and got out gloves and another mask.

"Your so-called colleague isn't happy that you want to assist on the autopsy," Jamie murmured.

"How'd you - oh, never mind. Maybe not, but I need to see all of this first hand, so he needs to suck it up and deal with it," Chris replied.

Jamie stood to one side as the doctors moved the corpse to an operating table. She judged that, from the way it was handled, it could not have weighed more than a hundred pounds. They put it on the table and Jamie could smell that papery, cinnamon stench that she did acutely remember from visiting the Egyptian exhibit at the Field Museum as a child.

Dr. Franklin pulled the sheet off the body, and it took considerable willpower for her to not gasp. Seeing the body in a photograph was one thing: in person was an entirely different horror. By then, the eyes had been removed and the lids were so thin, the tape they used to close them would not stay, so she was gazing into those deep hollows. The distended jaw was monstrous to say the least, a great gaping maw that looked like it was eternally screaming in horror and pain.

The photos had only shown the faces, but now she could see the emaciated torso. Its skin was sticking to its ribs. There was not an ounce of fat, and she was reminded of the Holocaust, how those in the concentration camps looked before death.

"So, why are you interested in this? You know the police think that those two who own the inn killed this guy, right?" Dr. Franklin asked.

"I've known Geoff for twelve years: he's no murderer," Chris said. "We're looking into it to disprove the police."

"We?" The older doctor looked at Jamie, who pretended not to notice. "Hey...aren't you that girl who rescued those kids from the house in Rochester?"

Jamie looked up. "That would be I," she replied.

"You're some kind of ghost hunter, like those guys on reality TV," he continued.

"Big difference: I can actually see them, and I'm not an attention whore. Now, I don't want to hear your skepticism. I did not come here for that. I came here to find out just what happens to the victims when the ghost gets to them. So, please, carry on." Jamie crossed her arms as Chris and the coroner began to cut into the body.

She could hear the scalpel dig into the dry skin and hit bone. Minute particles of dry skin flew up like dust. She watched as Dr. Franklin and Chris just stared at each other wide-eyed. "What is it?"

Chris looked up. "The body is empty. It is, quite literally, skin and bones."

****

"It eats the victims' bodily fluids and fats," Jamie said. She, Chris, Geoff, and Amanda were sequestered in the library.

"You're joking, right?" Geoff asked.

"Saw it with my own eyes," Chris said, shuddering. "Jamie said the ghost was hungry. It's eating the victims to feed itself. Why?"

"I think I know why." Amanda handed Jamie a piece of printer paper. "I believe I found our ghost when she was alive."

Jamie took it. There was a grainy, black and white photograph of a pretty blonde girl who was painfully thin. The article was an obituary in the local paper.

" *'Nineteen-year-old Hannah Hoff, daughter of the mayor, died on November first, 1944, at Mercy Rehabilitation Hospital. Miss Hoff suffered from self-harm and an eating disorder. She succumbed from the disease in her sleep. There will be no service, as her family has chosen to have her cremated'*," Jamie read. She looked up. "Good job, Amanda. This is her, and now it all makes sense, why she eats people's fat and why she looks the way she does."

"Here's something else. Something...a bit more disturbing." Amanda handed over another paper. It was a news report about the convalescent home, after Mayor Hoff had made an inquiry against his daughter's death. Jamie again started to read aloud.

"Mercy Hospital has been closed down permanently, due to findings the local police have released as to their inhumane treatment of patients. While electroconvulsive therapy is a very modern technique and has been proven to work in patients, it was discovered that the way in which the staff at Mercy was performing them incorrectly and too frequently for the patients' health. In the case of Miss Hoff in particular, they found that the electroshock therapy had been the cause of her death. Miss Hoff had entered the facility because of her eating disorder, which also caused heart problems. The electricity made her heart stop.

"It was also found by the coroner that Miss Hoff had been force fed, with her jaw repeatedly pried open and food forced down her throat. It caused permanent damage to the musculature, and her jaw would have had to be wired shut had she lived.

"Emotional abuse was also reported by various sources after the police made an inquiry."

"Mother fucker," Geoff gasped, wiping sweat from his forehead. "How awful!"

Chris sighed. "This is all really sickening, but that doesn't mean she gets to stick around and kill people. Jamie, can you make her cross over using this information?"

Jamie nodded. "I can, but I am going to need some help from you guys."

****

That night, Geoff helped her clear out a room, and she was going to pretend to be a guest, asleep. Hannah had tried to kill her once, and failed. Now Jamie was certain that she'd try again, and this time she would be prepared.

In case things started to go south, Chris and Geoff were there to rescue her if necessary, and Amanda was ready to call the hospital. She prayed it would not come to that. She'd never had this much trouble with a spirit before.

The room was dark, save for the moonlight streaming through the window. She'd kept it open so she could see better. The religious wards weren't keeping Hannah out because Hannah wasn't technically evil. She was lost, confused, and angry. Jamie would first try to get her to cross over. If that didn't work, she'd have no choice but to dispel the spirit the next day, dissipating it from existence.

She laid in bed, covers pulled up to her chin. In one hand was the cross-shaped holy water font, and in the other was a short iron bar, in case Hannah got violent once again.

A little after midnight, she heard the wind whistle past her, and the low crack of the window glass. The room gradually began to get colder, and she felt her eyes water and nose run from the sensation. Hannah's malevolence filled the room.

The ghost materialized directly above Jamie, her ghastly face mere inches away. Jamie slowly opened her eyes, ready to talk, but Hannah screamed in rage, her face contorting into that Hellish mask again. The shriek made Jamie wince, and her head was fuzzy from hearing it.

"You don't deserve to live!" Hannah screamed, her voice cracked and gravelly. When she yelled, her jaw also distended like those she'd killed.

Jamie swung at her with the iron bar, making her temporarily disappear. Jamie scurried out of the bed, thankful she didn't get caught in the covers.

Hannah appeared in front of her, head cocked at an odd angle, and jaw hanging slack. Those dark caverns stared at her accusingly. Jamie got to live. Jamie wasn't sick. She wasn't being electrocuted every day. Her jaw wasn't pried open with metal bars.

If ghosts have enough energy, they can become corporeal, completely solid on our plane. With what she had done in the past three weeks, Hannah had more than enough energy. Jamie was thrown across the room, her back hitting the wall nearest the door. It was only out of desperation that she didn't drop her things.

Hannah's bony hand was on her throat, and the other was trying to pry at her jaw. Jamie swung the iron again, and it hurt the ghost enough so that she could run out the door. She needed to put space between them, so she could get rid of her.

Jamie turned around in the hall, and didn't sense anything. Hannah's presence was gone, and she hoped that she would reappear soon, so she could banish her. She should have known to be careful what she wished for, as Hannah came behind her, grabbing her tightly around the waist and neck.

"I didn't deserve to die!" she screamed, and Jamie felt her hands digging into her skin. She heard her T-shirt rip, and felt sharp pain in her side. She was bleeding.

Jamie swung her body around, thankful that, despite the unearthly power the ghost had, she was still barely ninety pounds and could be moved easily. Jamie felt her body growing weak. Hannah was already beginning to drain her, and she needed to act fast if she wanted to live.

Hannah threw her weakening body against the railing of the staircase. She flickered as she moved past some of the warding that was still up in the hall, and appeared again in front of Jamie. The grip on her jaw now felt like steel: it was forcing it open despite her best efforts to get the ghost off her.

Downstairs, Jamie could hear Chris and Geoff's voices, and gauged how far from the bottom of the stairs they'd be. When she heard them getting closer, she did the most daredevil move she'd ever performed and rolled herself down the steep stairs, and it worked: Hannah let her go!

She hit the bottom, but was cushioned by Chris, who had seen her going down and waited there.

"My God, are you okay?" he asked.

Jamie was dizzy. She was bleeding. However, she was not giving up. Using him as a support, she stood up, uncapping her bottle of holy water. She could sense the darkness that was Hannah's tortured soul, and was prepared to combat it.

She was not prepared for Hannah to go after Chris. One second he was right next to her, and the next Hannah was holding him against the nearest wall, pressing her vile hands against his jaw. His spiritual strength was not half of what Jamie possessed, and she could see his life energy being taken through his mouth. His aura itself was being transferred to Hannah.

Jamie was incensed, seeing the man she loved being hurt. She was unsure if she could get Hannah off him, but thankfully Amanda appeared as a distraction.

At the sound of her feet pattering on the floor, Hannah looked up and her distended maw seemed to be trying to smile. As she dropped Chris to the floor to go to Amanda, Jamie knew this was her last chance.

She stood up and started to sprinkle the holy water over Hannah, and the ghost shrieked as if it were being hit with acid. The sound made glass shatter and Jamie swore she was temporarily stricken deaf. Her very spirit ached at the sound. It was pure pain. Despite this, she started reciting the only prayer she knew to be one hundred percent effective, as she kept sprinkling the holy water.

"*Sáncte Míchael Archángele, defénde nos in proélio, cóntra nequítiam et insídias diáboli ésto præsídium. Ímperet ílli Déus, súpplices deprecámur: tuque, prínceps milítiæ cæléstis, Sátanam aliósque spíritus malígnos, qui ad perditiónem animárum pervagántur in múndo, divína virtúte, in inférnum detrúde. Ámen.*" [Short prayer to Archangel Michael*.]

At the end of her prayer, she had used up quite a bit of her energy. It takes a lot of spiritual life force to do what she had just done, and she slumped against Chris by the wall, as they both watched Hannah's spirit fade away.

Amanda slumped back, fear seeming to strike her boneless. Geoff ran to her side and held her. Jamie felt Chris' arm hold her, being careful to avoid her wounds, which were thankfully slowing their bleeding.

"Jamie, is that it? Is she finally gone?" Geoff asked, cradling his wife.

Jamie was silent. Something isn't right, that little intuition in the back of her mind kept saying.

However, Hannah's spirit was gone. She couldn't feel her anymore. So, what was it?

"Jamie?" Chris asked, his voice trembling. Bruises were already forming on his face.

Before she could say anything, Amanda gave a little yelp that was somewhere between surprise and pain.

"What is it?" Jamie asked, her heart already knowing what her mind refused to recognize. Hannah was a girl who wanted to live again. She wanted to steal others' life force in order for her to be alive. Of course…

Amanda looked up, smiling. "The baby kicked!"

Saint Michael the Archangel, defend us in battle, be our protection against the malice and snares of the devil. May God rebuke him we humbly pray; and do thou, O Prince of the Heavenly host, by the power of God, thrust into hell Satan and all evil spirits who wander through the world for the ruin of souls. Amen.

***

Lily Luchesi is the award-winning author of the bestselling Paranormal Detectives Series, published by Vamptasy Publishing. She also has short stories included in multiple bestselling anthologies, and a successful dark erotica retelling of Dracula.

She was born in Chicago, Illinois, and now resides in Los Angeles, California. Ever since she was a toddler her mother noticed her tendency for being interested in all things "dark". At two she became infatuated with vampires and ghosts, and that infatuation turned into a lifestyle. She is also an out member of the LGBT+ community. When she's not writing, she's going to rock concerts, getting tattooed, watching the CW, or reading manga. And drinking copious amounts of coffee.

WALKER COUNTY IS SMALL AND SMITH LAKE IS DEEP:
A Tale from the World of Talon

By Jay Michael Wright II

Tommy drove towards Duncan Bridge with what felt like a dragon trying to claw its way out of his belly. His hands trembled as they clung tightly to the steering wheel. Every pair of headlights he saw he *just knew* was a police car. He'd been lucky so far. None of them had been. Lord knows if they pulled him over, he'd be spending the rest of his life in prison.

He reached for a cigarette and shakily put one in his mouth. His hands still carried the coppery smell of blood. He's taken two showers and scrubbed his hands at least eight times, but nothing could make that smell go away. There had been *so much blood.* He had no idea how much blood there would be. It had been like a crimson ocean had poured out of their bodies. He thought, *I just should have drowned in that blood. It would have made my life so much easier.*

He pulled onto Duncan Bridge and killed his headlights. There didn't appear to be anyone in sight. His spirits rose. *I'm going to get away with it. I'm actually going to do it.*

He got out of the car and unlocked the trunk. Once again the smell of blood slapped him in the face. *My God! How much blood can these two have left?*

He took the giant red duffel bag out of the trunk and set it on the ground. He then took some chain he had kept in his shed and wrapped it around the handle four times before locking it into place with a padlock. He took the other end and attached it to a masonry brick as he cursed his ex-friend Stephen.

"Fucking asshole! I never did like you anyway."

He grabbed the duffel bag by the handle and the chain and carried his little homemade package to the edge of the bridge and tossed them over the edge. He stood there in the dark listening. When he heard the Smith Lake waters splash, he smiled weakly and aimed a middle finger down at the black waters below. He whispered, "Fuck you, Stevie. You got what you deserve."

He walked slowly back to the trunk as his eyes began to well up with tears. He stared at the black duffel bag setting there for what seemed an eternity. "God damn it, Stacy. You just had to go do it, didn't you? Six years together and *this* is how you end it. My fucking best friend, Stacy? *Really*? Of all the dicks in Jasper, you just had to jump on his?"

He unzipped the duffel bag and shouted, "Look at me when I'm talking to you!" The severed head wrapped in cellophane had one eye open. It seemed to be looking up at him, mocking him even now in death.

"I loved you, Stacy. I gave you everything and you repaid me *like this*? I broke my back working two jobs just to give you the fucking house you always wanted, and you couldn't even keep your Goddamn panties on for me. Fuck you, bitch!"

He zipped the duffel bag shut and repeated the same process he had gone through with Stevie's bag. When he was done, he dragged her to the bridge's edge and tossed her off the side. He heard the water splash and whispered, "Rot in Hell, bitch."

"Actually, people don't rot in Hell. They're tortured, agonized, maybe even tormented, but they don't rot." The voice startled Tommy so bad, he nearly pissed his pants. His heart raced in his chest and he broke out in a cold sweat. This was it. He was going to prison. He just knew it.

He turned to find a debonair fellow wearing a solid white suit standing there smiling rather pleasantly. Terror grabbed Tommy by the balls. A witness, he couldn't afford to have any witnesses.

"What are you doing here?" Tommy asked as he inched toward the car. There was a gun in the glove box. If he could just reach it, there'd be *three bodies* in Smith Lake instead of two.

The man casually twirled a cane and continued smiling. "Oh, I was just out for a stroll when I came across this lovely scene. I've got to admit it, Tommy, you surprised me. I never thought you had it in you."

"Wh—what are you talkin' about?" He moved a little closer to the car as a bead of ice cold sweat slithered down his spine.

"What am I talking about? Why, what you did to Stevie and Stacy! Killing them was one thing, and no one would blame you. After all, you *did* find your best friend balls deep in your girlfriend's ass. Who wouldn't have killed them? But cutting their bodies up with a chainsaw, wrapping them in cellophane, and dumping them into the lake. Now that, my boy, takes some real initiative!"

Tommy felt absolutely numb. "How…how do you know that?"

The man laughed. "I know a lot of things. It's part of my job. I've been watching you a long time, Tommy, and I do believe you're ready for the big time."

That's all Tommy needed to hear. He yanked the car door open and almost yanked the glove box off its hinges as he grabbed his revolver. He fired three rounds straight at the man's chest, but all the fellow did was twitch a little bit as he was hit. The man looked down at his suit and frowned.

"You put holes in my suit! Do you have any clue how much it costs to dress this good? This is a custom fit, tailor made silk suit from Italy. These aren't just some rags you pull off the rack at JC Penney. You're lucky I like you, Tommy. I've damned people for less than this."

Tommy lowered his revolver. His hand shook so horribly that he dropped the firearm to the ground. He couldn't believe his eyes. He thought perhaps he had gone completely mad.

"Who are you?" Tommy gasped.

The smile returned to the man's face. "Oh, where are my manners?" He bowed quite formally and added, "Mephistopheles, at your service, but you can call me Meph—all my friends do."

Tommy backed up until he was right against the edge of the bridge. "What the hell are you?"

Meph pursed his lips and tilted his head to the side, as if in deep thought. "*Well*, some would call me a Demon. Personally, I prefer the term 'Fallen Angel.' It has a nice ring about it. Wouldn't you agree?"

Tommy was frozen with fear. "What do you want?" he blurted out.

Meph smiled mischievously. "You mortals and your questions. You're such a curious lot. One of the many reasons I love you all so, but it's not about what I want. It's about what *you* want. Let's be honest here, Tommy. Stevie may have been a lowlife piece of shit, but he was a lowlife piece of shit with some *very* dangerous friends. How long do you think it'll be before they put two and two together and realize that you were the one to kill him? Walker County is small, Tommy, and Smith Lake is very deep. How long do you really think it'll take them to find you?"

The Demon's words rang true, but Tommy was in shock at what he had seen. He simply couldn't wrap his mind around the fact that a Demon, something he didn't even believe in, was standing right in front of him.

"What's the matter, Tommy? Too in awe to speak? Yea, I get that a lot, but if you think I've thrown you for a loop, wait 'til *the others* show up."

"*The others*?" Tommy replied in a high-pitch squeak.

"Oh, yes! Why, you've got about half of Hell looking at you right now. Two murders, cutting the bodies up, chopping off Stevie's dick and shoving it down his own throat before wrapping him up in cellophane—*those* are the things that will get Hell's attention just like that." The Demon snapped his fingers.

"You're about to be recruited by some of the nastiest of the nasty, and most of them lack my charm and charisma. You can either work for me, or you can let the others try to recruit you." Meph dropped his voice to a whisper. "Just between you and me, some of those guys are complete savages."

Tommy had heard enough. It was time to retreat. He picked the revolver up off the ground and ran to the other side of the car. As he pulled away, he heard Meph scream, "Call me if you need me!"

When Tommy got home he was a complete wreck. He emptied his pockets, and to his surprise, he found a white business card with shiny gold lettering on it. The card simply read: "Mephistopheles: Here to help when you need it." Tommy ripped the card into four pieces and threw it in the bathroom garbage can. He wanted nothing to do with *anyone* who claimed to be a Demon.

***

Tommy sat watching the Alabama-LSU game, trying to forget the previous night's events: the murders, the weird guy in the white suit, *everything*. He snacked on chips and talked to the television. "Oh, c'mon, Saban. Run the God damned football."

He sighed and scratched his Pit-bull Jackie behind the ears. Suddenly, the dog stood up and looked the direction of the hall. She began barking like someone was there, but Tommy didn't see a thing. "What is it, girl?"

The lights went off and Tommy had a chill that felt like it went all the way down to his bones. The hairs on the back of his neck stood up and his gut was telling him something wasn't right. Before he could stop her, Jackie was off the couch and running down the hall, barking up a storm. She disappeared into his bedroom and her bark turned into a whimper.

"Jackie? What is it, girl?" Tommy was off the couch and stumbling in the dark down the hallway. He found his bedroom and the lights flickered back on.

Tommy froze in place. Jackie was nowhere to be found, but on his bed, was something that gave him the urge to puke. Stacy's mutilated corpse was laying there and written in blood above the bed were the words, "Nice job."

Oh my fucking God! This can't be real. I tossed her into the lake.

The somber sounds of a harmonica being played behind him made Tommy get goose bumps. He spun around to see a skinny dark haired man standing there. His clothes were from another era and he had incredibly somber eyes. The man looked up and said, "Ya did a nice job cutting her up, mate. I couldn't have done a better job myself. Just got one question for ya: you gonna eat that? No point in wasting good meat." The man smiled and chuckled to himself. "Brings a whole new meaning to the term 'eating her pussy,' doesn't it?"

Tommy spun and grabbed a lava lamp off the dresser. He turned with every intention of smashing it over the man's head, but he was gone. He looked back at the bed, and Stacy's body had vanished along with the bloody message on the wall.

Tommy walked over and sat down on the bed. *Pull it together, Tommy. It's just your imagination running away with you. It's all in your head.* He kept repeating it over and over, as if that would make it true. *It's all in your head.*

He heard glass shattering in the hallway bathroom and without thinking ran to investigate. He found the sliding door to the shower had been broken into three large pieces. He stood there baffled. *What in the fuck?*

He turned to leave and saw a message written in lipstick on the mirror. It read, "Good luck at the interview, baby. I love you so much." There was a heart drawn beneath the message and it was signed, "Stacy."

Tommy reminisced. *I remember when she wrote this. She wasn't even living here yet. She had spent the night and went home before I woke up. She left this message for me on the mirror.*

He slowly reached out and placed his hand on the mirror. He lowered his gaze and fought the urge to cry. *Damn it, Stacy! Why'd you have to go and fuck things up?*

He looked up and was horrified to see a pale man in a robe standing behind him in the mirror. The man's eyes were sewn shut and when he smiled he revealed row after row of razor sharp teeth.

Tommy let out a scream, spun, and jumped up on the sink with his fist ready to strike, but there was nobody there. *What the holy Hell?* He gasped for breath as his heart felt like it was going to beat out of his chest.

He slid down off the sink and tried to calm his nerves. He looked back at the mirror and the message was gone, replaced by the stitched together corpse of his girlfriend Stacy staring at him. Her flesh had turned a sickly blue color and she appeared to have already started decaying.

The corpse in the mirror said, "What's the matter, baby? Not happy to see me? I still love you."

Before he could move, she reached out of the mirror and grabbed hold of his head. She leaned out and planted an open mouth kiss on him. Maggots poured from her mouth into Tommy's, along with a salty, viscous fluid he couldn't recognize.

She retreated into the mirror and Tommy started gagging. The maggots wiggled their way down his throat and lodged themselves there. He couldn't breathe and almost immediately he began throwing up. He vomited until he thought he couldn't possibly vomit anymore.

He looked up into the mirror at Stacy's corpse who was smiling coyly. She wiped a white, milky substance from her lips and giggled. "Sorry, baby. I guess Stevie left that in my mouth the last time he saw me."

Oh, my God! That was…

Tommy discovered that he was wrong. He could vomit some more. He punched the mirror, shattering it and cutting his hand to shreds, before hitting his knees and hugging the toilet for what seemed an eternity. By the time he was through, his abdominal muscles were sore from all the heaving they had done.

He sat there, the burn of stomach acid eating away at his throat, and tried to catch his breath. When he finally could talk, he said, "Fuck…this…shit."

Tommy pulled himself up to his feet. His entire body ached and his right hand was dripping blood at an alarming rate. Not having the time to mend the wound properly, Tommy ripped the bottom half of his t-shirt and wrapped his hand. He grimaced as he pulled the knot tight, but his fear overwhelmed his pain. He wanted out of that house and he wanted out of it *now*.

He stumbled down the hallway, still dizzy from all the vomiting. He was weak and lightheaded, but as soon as he found his car keys he was making his exit whether it was safe to drive or not. He forced himself all the way to his kitchen table and cursed as he found his keys were missing.

Oh, come the fuck on!

He frantically searched to table, shuffling newspapers and advertisements that had come in the mail from one side to another. The keys *just had* to be here. This is exactly where he left them.

The lights flickered off and on. Out of the corner of his eye, he saw shadows moving on their own. They twisted and contorted into different shapes—some almost human, others in the form of creatures straight from the nightmares of his youth.

He dropped to the ground and crawled to the cabinet that he hid his revolver in. Making sure the gun was loaded, he backed against a wall as the air around him grew ever colder. In no time at all, Tommy could see his breath forming as visible vapor in front of him.

He shivered uncontrollably as the cold chilled him to the soul. The lights flickered out again and the entire house shook as he heard a hissing sound coming from the end of the hallway. He wanted to run, but his legs were paralyzed with fear.

He did a double take as a pair of red glowing eyes appeared at the end of the hallway. He could barely make out the thing's silhouette as it started slithering towards him. His heart beat like a war-drum as the thing started speaking in a deep, raspy voice. "Come with us, Tommy. You belong *with us*."

Fear turned to rage as Tommy raised his firearm. With every round he cursed, getting louder with every shot. "Fuck you, motherfucker! Die! Die! Die!"

Its eyes faded to black and the lights came back on. Whatever had been in the hallway was nowhere to be found. Tommy sat there trembling, his sanity holding on by a thread.

You're losing your fucking mind, Tommy. It's the guilt. You can't live with the guilt. That's all it is. You've lost your mind.

The sound of his keys jingling snapped him out of it. On the kitchen counter to his right was a little impish creature, no more than two feet tall and solid grey. It had a long hook nose and a pair of tiny horns adorning its head. As it flapped its tiny bat-like wings and wagged its pointed tail, it dangled the keys for Tommy to see, like it was taunting him to come and get them.

Moving slowly to not scare the creature away, Tommy raised his revolver. He whispered, "That's it. Stay nice and still." He fired off a round, but the creature ducked low and the bullet shattered the kitchen window above the sink. The little imp ducked out the window making a sound that made it seem it was laughing at Tommy.

You're not getting away that easy, asshole.

Tommy was to his feet and flung the sliding glass door open that led to the back deck and the swimming pool. The imp was perched on top of the privacy fence with its back turned. Tommy raised his revolver and shot the creature straight through its back. The imp vanished in a puff of black smoke and Tommy's keys fell helplessly to the deck.

For the first time since this ordeal began, Tommy smiled. He ran to the other side of the pool to retrieve his keys. Just as he reached them, something snagged his leg, and Tommy crashed face-first to the deck. He laid there, groggy and seeing double. He placed his hand on his forehead and felt the swelling already forming a goose egg.

"Son of a bitch," he gasped as he climbed up onto all fours. He grabbed his keys and suddenly the whole world started to spin. He heard a pair of female voices that seemed to be coming from everywhere and inside his own head all at once.

"Look, Persephone—a new play toy. Isn't he just divine?"

"Why yes, Priscilla. I think he'll do just fine."

Tommy tried to clear his head as he snatched his revolver and climbed to his feet. *It's just in your head, Tommy. It's just in your head.*

"Won't you come and play with us?"

"It's so nice at the bottom of the lake."

"We have your girlfriend with us. We could all be one happy family."

Out of the corner of his eye, Tommy kept seeing flashes of a pair of teenage girls. They were identical twins, dressed in matching formal dresses and drenched from head to toe. Their long black hair helped hide their faces as they started mockingly singing as the encircled him.

"A tisket..."

"A tasket..."

"The twins are out..."

"Their caskets."

"Drowning souls..."

"In swimming holes..."

"Of everyone..."

"Who passes."

Tommy covered his ears and screamed, "Get out of my head!"

He looked up and one of the twins was standing right in front of him. She asked, "What makes you think we're just in your head?"

He raised his revolver and fired, but he was all out of bullets. The twin tilted her head to the side and said, "Tsk, tsk. Don't you know to save the last bullet for yourself? Suicide is the easy way out. You really should look into it sometime."

The girl pushed Tommy and he fell into the deep end of the pool. He started sinking to the bottom when he felt two pairs of hands grab hold of his legs. Their fingernails dug through his pants and cut into his flesh. He kicked frantically to get away as he could still hear the girls' voices in his head.

"Get him, Priscilla!"

"Won't you stay with us, Tommy? We have such wondrous things to show you."

Tommy kicked himself free and swam for the edge of the pool. He popped his head out of the water and gasped for breath. Before he could do anything else, one of the twins was on his back. She wrapped her arm around his neck and pulled him back under.

"Nuh, uh, uh. We're not done with you yet, Tommy."

He found himself at the bottom of the pool, fighting one of the twins off his back while the other twirled around and laughed. The way they moved in the water didn't seem natural. They seemed to float through the water instead of swim through it.

Tommy threw an elbow and knocked the twin on his back loose. The other twin throttled him and growled, "Don't you hurt my sister!"

Tommy's lungs burned from lack of oxygen and he knew he had to get away from these girls as quickly as possible less he drowned. He shoved his fingers into the eyes of the twin holding his throat and she cowered away and began crying.

This was his chance. Tommy kicked like he had never kicked before and came up gasping for air. He pulled himself up on the deck and turned just in time to catch one of the twins emerging out of the water. He placed a boot in the middle of her forehead and she sank back down into the water as everything turned quiet.

Tommy kept expecting one of the twins to leap out of the water like the ending of the first *Friday the 13th*, but thankfully it never happened. He laid there, coughing up more water than he thought humanly possible. He then caught his breath and cursed as he realized his car keys were laying at the bottom of the pool. As badly as he needed them, there was no way in Hell he was going back in that water.

Fuck it. I'll walk.

He climbed to his feet, grimacing as every step made the scratches on his legs burn that much more. He opened the gate and started limping down his driveway. It was about a quarter mile to the road, but if he was lucky, someone would be passing by and give him a ride out of this nightmare.

He was about halfway down the driveway when he rounded a curve. He froze in place. There was a girl with red curly hair standing there, holding a gas can. After all he had seen, he didn't trust anyone, no matter how harmless they looked.

He took a step back. "Who are you?"

The girl ignored him, instead twitching her head from side to side as if she was listening to something. "Can you hear that?" she asked.

"Hear what?"

"Condie's voice off in the distance. It's like a feint whisper on the wind. She's calling out to me. She wants me to go home with her."

The girl popped the lid off the gas can and Tommy's heart started to race. "Hey, now. Whatever you're thinking of doing, let's talk about this."

The girl smiled mischievously. "There's nothing to talk about. I'm finally going home."

The girl poured the gasoline all over herself as Tommy began to shake. When she pulled a lighter from his pants, he all but started crying. "Honey, whatever you're about to do, don't. Please, don't."

The girl smirked. "You act as if this is a bad thing. I'm going to finally be *free*."

She struck the lighter and her entire body went up in flames. She stood there a moment, seemingly unaffected by the fire that now engulfed her. She screamed out, "Condie, I'm coming home!" and fell to her knees.

Tommy heard movement to his left and he spun to see the man with the harmonica from earlier casually propped up against a tree. The man smiled and gave a nod of his head. "Nothing quite like a weekend barbecue, is there, Tommy? You got dibs on the ribs, or can I just help myself?"

Tommy started backing up. He pointed his finger at the man and screamed, "You stay away from me!"

The man staid put and calmly shrugged his shoulders. "There's no point in running, Tommy. Don't you get it yet? You're already in Hell. You just don't realize it yet."

As the smell of burning flesh and hair turned his stomach, Tommy turned and ran back towards the house. Again, he shouted, "Stay away from me!"

The man laughed and called out, "Run, run, as fast as you can! You can't catch me! I'm the Gingerbread Man!"

Tommy limped back to the house as fast as his legs could carry him. He was delirious with fear. Every shadow hid a face. Every sound was something coming to get him. He would do anything to escape this nightmare. He remembered one of the twins' words and wished he still had his revolver and a bullet.

He'd happily end it all if this madness would just fucking end.

He propped against the car and ran his hands through his sweat drenched hair. He didn't know what to do or where to go. He certainly didn't want to go back in the house, and he'd be damned if he went anywhere near that fucking pool again. He stood there, too afraid to move, and too afraid to stay in one place.

Branches snapped behind him and Tommy closed his eyes and started to cry. *Please just be a stray dog in woods...please just be a stray dog in the woods...*

He slowly turned and said a little prayer as he faced the direction of the sound. The trees outside his house were absolutely covered in ravens. There must have been hundreds, maybe even a thousand of them, all staring in his direction.

What the Hell?

A small silhouette started to move in the shadows. It stepped forward and Tommy was terrified to see a porcelain doll mask staring in his direction. The dark-haired girl wearing it was barely five feet tall. The black and red dress she wore was in tatters and the hatchet in her right hand gleamed in the moonlight.

Holy fuck! What in the name of God is that?

The tiny girl raised her hatchet at Tommy and the ravens all sprang into action. Tommy ran two steps before they were on top of him and he fell to the ground. Talons tore into his flesh and pointed beaks pecked at his eyes. He knocked the ones he could away, but it felt like a half dozen were tangled up in his hair, bringing blood with every strike. He laid there, covering up to protect his eyes, until—just like that—the assault ended.

He uncovered his face and looked up to see the girl in the porcelain doll mask standing over him, her hatchet held high overhead. He was too tired to run, and too tired to fight. He covered up and waited on the end, but nothing happened. He moved his arms just enough to peak out and he saw the fellow with the harmonica standing over him.

The chap said, "Man, you are having the king of all shitty nights, aren't you?"

Tommy grabbed hold of the man's pants legs and found himself laughing and crying at the same time. "Just kill me," he begged. "Just make it stop. Please, just make it all stop."

The man shook his head. "Sorry, mate. I'm just here to initiate you. Speaking of, you ready for the bonus round?"

The man punched Tommy square in the nose and everything went black.

***

Tommy slowly came to. His whole body ached. He had bruises and scratches from head to toe. He had been put through the ringer and things were only going to get worse.

He tried to move but couldn't. He realized he was tied to a chair in his living room and that's when he fully came to his senses. He started rocking the chair as he tried to get loose. Unfortunately, he wasn't having the least bit of luck succeeding.

He looked up at the man who had hit him and snarled, "What are you going to do to me?"

The man shook his head. "I'm just here to observe. I'm not going to do a thing to you, but if I was you, I'd be worried about *that guy*."

Tommy heard heavy boots walking on the floor behind him. The boots circled to his right and a man in a black trench coat and a gas mask came into view. As soon as Tommy laid eyes on him, he was picking up his weight and bouncing the chair in the other direction of the man.

"*Whoa*, what the fuck is this?"

"Hello, Mister Tommy. It's time to play some games, no?" the man in the gas mask said in a thick Russian accent.

Tommy watched in horror as the man unrolled a black canvas pouch that contained a countless number of deadly looking tools. There were scalpels, hammers, knives of all shapes and sizes. It was like a sadist's dream collection of play things.

Tommy's heart began to race. Cold sweat slithered down his spine as he watched the Russian inspect each tool one by one. Out of desperation, Tommy tried to negotiate. "Come on, guys. Can't we talk about this?"

The Russian laughed. "Yuri came to audition for job. So, Yuri is going to audition, show off what he can do, see how many ways he can make you scream."

Tommy tried to pull free, but his arms were bound too tightly to the chair. He began to cry as Yuri picked up a hammer and approached him slowly. "Did you know there are two hundred and six bones in the adult body? And breaking even the tiniest of them, like for instance, the tip of the pinkie—"

Yuri slammed the hammer down on the end of Tommy's little finger and Tommy screamed out in agony. "—can cause incredible pain to the victim but not threaten their life at all?" Yuri stood in front of Tommy and then leaned down to whisper to him. "You see, we are not here to kill you. We are here to practice the art of suffering. I am the artist, and you, you are my canvas."

Yuri looked over his shoulder and asked the man with the harmonica. "Faust, did you bring the music I asked for?"

Faust smirked. "Yes, sir. I've got it right here."

"Would you mind playing it for me? It sooths my soul to hear Tchaikovsky when I work."

The music began playing and Yuri began to almost dance as he circled Tommy. "Aw, Tchaikovsky, the 1812 Overture, one of my personal favorites. What other composer would be so bold as to use a cannon as an instrument? Only a *true Russian* would do such a thing."

As the music built, Yuri picked his shots. He slammed the hammer into Tommy's ribs. "Another glorious spot that causes such pain. With every breath, you will feel the reminder of what I have done to you."

Tommy was crying so hard, he could barely breathe. "Please, for the love of God, please let me go."

Yuri looked around the room and shrugged his shoulders. "God? There is no God here. There is only pain. Now, where were we?" With another blow, Yuri shattered Tommy's knee cap.

"God fucking damn it!" Tommy cried. "Oh my God! I'll do anything you want! Just please fucking stop!"

"Stop?" Yuri asked. "Why, we've only just begun." He put away the hammer and retrieved a surgical scalpel. He straddled Tommy's lap as Tommy did the best he could to lean away.

"Stop moving, comrade. I was taught to handle the scalpel by one of the best. Oh, Marcus, if only he could see me now. I will not lie, Mister Tommy, this is going to hurt more than a little bit."

Yuri covered Tommy's mouth and started slicing at the base of the nostrils. Tommy's entire body shook as the shock of what was happening to him set in. Every nerve in his body seemed on fire and for a moment he almost lost consciousness.

Yuri finished and tossed Tommy's nose to the floor like a discarded piece of garbage. "Look, comrade, I cut off your nose to spite your face."

As the blood gushed into Tommy's mouth, he started rocking the chair back and forth violently. His entire body trembled with rage and he frothed at the mouth as he barked like a wild animal. "So help me, God. When I get out of this chair, I am going to fucking kill you! Do you hear me? I'm going to rip you to fucking pieces and skull-fuck whatever is left of you!"

Yuri looked at Faust and laughed. "I like him. He has a belly full of fire. I can see why your associate has an interest in him."

Tommy continued to rock the chair. "Let me up, you cocksucker!"

Yuri folded his arms and sighed. "Comrade, you take this all too seriously. This is just business— nothing more, nothing less."

Gravel popped outside as headlights shone through the living room window. Faust looked and smiled. "Looks like we've got company."

"Company?" Yuri asked. "Well, the more the merrier."

There was only one person Tommy could think of who'd be visiting him this time of night: his mother. If he had to die, so be it. It's not like he didn't deserve it, but his mother was a saint. She had raised him all alone since the age of eight and he never went wanting for a thing. He might deserve this abuse, but she didn't.

"Please, guys, just let her go."

Yuri laughed. "Let her go? This silly little man still doesn't understand the game we play, does he? Strigoi, will you kindly greet our next guest."

From out of the shadows walked a man nearly seven feet tall. He looked to be as wide as the side of the house and had muscles where most people didn't even have places. Tommy started to shout a warning to his mother when Yuri covered his mouth. Tommy could only watch as he heard the screen door open and his mother step into the living room.

"Tommy, I brought some leftover—"

Strigoi had her by the throat and lifted off the ground in a matter of seconds. With one flick of Strigoi's wrist, Tommy heard his mother's neck snap. Out of disgust, Strigoi slammed the woman's corpse down on the coffee table, shattering it. "Little woman is frail," the giant man remarked.

Tommy stared down at his mother's lifeless corpse and tears rolled down his cheeks. "Oh, mamma...mamma, I'm so sorry. This is all my fault."

The house shook and plaster fell from the ceiling. Tommy coughed uncontrollably as a piece of plaster landed on his head and turned to dust. His eyes burned and the open wound where his nose had been was on fire.

Faust walked up, patted Yuri on the shoulder and said, "That's our cue to go."

You could hear the disappointment in Yuri's voice. "Time to go? But I have hardly begun. I haven't even ripped his fingernails off with pliers yet."

Faust folded his arms. "You came here to audition for a job. Well, I've seen more than enough. The job is yours."

Yuri held out his arms like he was about to hug Faust. "Comrade, that's all you had to say! Strigoi, gather our things and let's leave this puppet to his game."

Yuri and Strigoi exited out the front door while Faust threw Tommy's mother over his shoulders. Smiling, he said, "No point in wasting a free meal." He walked up and patted Tommy on the shoulder. "Okay, kid. Main event time—time to make it or break it. Good luck, mate. See ya on the other side."

Faust pranced out the front door and Tommy was left all alone, tied to the chair. He had no clue what was coming, but he had a bad feeling about it. He struggled against the ropes that bound him, but still they wouldn't give an inch.

Well, shit. How do I get out of here?

The lights started flickering on and off again and Tommy felt sick. Everything went dark and he began to tremble as the shadows on the walls began to move. He screamed out, "I don't want to play anymore! Game's over, everyone! Just pack it up and go home, okay?"

His desperate pleading did no good. The shadows continued to dance around him and noises started coming from the end of the hallway. He saw the same red eyes from earlier and panic washed over him. He tugged with all his might at his bindings until the chair fell backwards and broke into multiple pieces.

Freeing his hands, he worked diligently to untie his legs as something gigantic slithered down the hallway straight for him. The lights flickered back on and once he saw the thing coming for him he doubled his efforts.

It was a sickly bluish grey color and had two pairs of arms which it used to drag behind it a long serpent's tail. The thing hissed and opened its mouth wide, revealing snake-like fangs and rows of sharpened teeth.

"Thomasssss," it hissed. "It'sssss time for you to join usssss."

Tommy untied his legs and leaped to his feet more from fear than actual physical ability. He backed against the wall as the thing kept slithering towards him. "Look, pal, I don't wanna join *anybody*."

It moved closer. "Too late for that, Thomasssss. You opened the gate. You sssssumoned usssss, sssso we came. Hell isssss a beautiful place. Sssssuch exquissssite agony. Sssssuch glorioussssss pain. Sssso many wondersssss to show you. Come my child, and take my hand."

Tommy shuffled down the wall and kicked over his old softball aluminum bat. He quickly armed himself and found the courage to strike. He swung for the fences and connected against the creature's temple. Its head whiplashed to the side but quickly snapped back into place, its fangs now fully on display.

It swiped with one of its clawed hands and Tommy nearly tripped over the kitchen table as he moved away to avoid it. The thing slithered closer and Tommy took several swings that missed trying to keep the creature at a distance.

Rising up like a cobra getting ready to strike, it said, "You will pay for your insssssolence, little mortal."

Tommy reached up and smacked the creature in the mouth, knocking one of its fangs out. Tommy laughed madly as he swung over and over, eventually knocking the creature flat of its back where he proceeded to attempt to flatten the thing's skull.

He screamed with every wing of the bat. "Fuck you!" *Whack.* "Fuck this night!" *Thud.* "And fuck Hell!" *Crack.*

The creature was now completely still. Tommy took a few steps back and collapsed to one knee out of exhaustion. He panted heavily and then laughed. "Yea, motherfucker. That's what you get for fuckin' with someone from Walker County."

The thing suddenly sat up. "You bastard! Look what you've done to me! I offered you a place in my kingdom and thisssss is how you repay me? I will eat you alive!"

The creature lunged at him and Tommy was down the hallway as fast as his exhausted legs could carry him. He knocked pictures off the wall, he turned over tables, any and everything to put something between him and whatever that thing was.

He slammed the bathroom door behind him and locked the door. He stepped away slowly as the entire side of the room with the door shook as the thing tried to beat its way inside. Cracks started forming in the door and Tommy began to cry again. He readied himself and held the bat ready to strike at anything that came towards him.

Part of the door broke away and the creature reached one of its arms inside, clawing madly in Tommy's direction. *Oh my fucking God,* Tommy thought. *I'm gonna die in here. Why didn't I just take that guy's offer when I had the chance? Why didn't I...*

It suddenly dawned on Tommy. *His card! It's in the trash!*

Tommy tossed the bat down and dropped to his knees. He turned the bathroom trashcan upside down and started searching for the four corners of the card which he had torn up.

Goddamn it! I know they're in here! Where are they?

Another piece of the door broke away and the creature stuck its head inside. It started reaching for the door handle to unlock the door and Tommy began to tremble uncontrollably. *Damn it, man! Come on!*

He found the top left corner of the card as the creature reached the doorknob. He found the bottom right as the thing unlocked the door. The top right corner he found as the door swung open and the monster howled at the top of its lungs.

Oh, my God! Where's the last fucking piece? It's got to be here!

Tommy found the last piece of the card as the creature lunged out at him. He placed the four pieces together and closed his eyes. He screamed, "Whatever you want! I'll do it! Just come back!"

Silence.

Tommy sat on his knees trembling, afraid to open his eyes. Slowly, he forced them to open, and sitting on the commode rather nonchalantly was the man in the white suit.

Mephistopheles smiled and gave a tip of his hat. "What are you doing down there? Bathroom floors are simply filthy."

Tommy looked up and his bathroom mirror was no longer shattered. On top of that, his hand was no longer cut up and bleeding. In fact, as far as he could tell, he wasn't hurt even in the least little bit.

"What…what happened?" Tommy asked.

Mephistopheles smiled. "Sounds to me like you had a rough night, but you've come to the logical decision, my boy. Working for me doesn't sound so bad after all, now does it?"

Tommy shook his head. "No. It doesn't."

Mephistopheles helped Tommy to his feet and opened the bathroom door which was now in one solid piece. "Come on," the Demon said. "Let's have a look around."

As Tommy entered the hallway, he asked, "So how does this work?"

Mephistopheles smiled. "Tommy, have you ever seen *The Godfather* movie? It's kind of like that. One day, and that day may never come, but I will ask you to do a favor for me, and you'll do it. Understand?"

Tommy nodded. He entered his living room and everything was back in its proper place. There was no broken chair. There was no broken coffee table. It was like the whole night never happened.

Jackie, his Pitbull, ran up and started jumping on Tommy. She licked his face as he laughed. "Jackie! You're okay!"

The phone rang and Tommy jumped from being startled by the sound. He looked at Mephistopheles, who was smiling pleasantly. The Demon said, "Jumpy, jumpy! Go ahead, answer the phone."

Tommy slowly reached out with a trembling hand and answered the phone. "Hello?" he said in a shaky voice.

"Hey, Tommy! It's your mom. How are you doing?"

He thought about what he had seen earlier and the panic came back to him. "Mom? Are you okay?"

"Yes, son. I'm fine. Why?"

Tommy glanced over at Mephistopheles and replied, "No reason. I love you, mom."

***

Mephistopheles poured himself a strong drink and said, "Yes, Faust. You did a wonderful job."

Faust smiled. "So, when do I get paid? When do I get my *real* harmonica back?"

Meph took a sip and replied, "Well, there's one problem with that. The current owner is being a bit difficult."

Meph handed a picture to Faust and Faust all but growled. "Nicky! After all these years, he still has it." He looked up at Meph with begging eyes. "So, when can I go up top and get it? I owe this guy a world of pain. You owe me this. You promised me."

"In due time, my friend. Trust me, it's all part of *the plan*. Now take everyone else their payments and thank them for me. They did a *wonderful job* scaring little Tommy right into my clutches."

Faust gave a reluctant nod and exited the room, closing the door behind him. Meph took a seat on a leather sofa, took a sip, and stared directly…at *you.*

"Hi there, reader," he said, giving a little wave of his fingers. "I know what you're thinking. 'Is he really talking to *me*?' Why *yes, yes I am.* You think I don't realize that I live in that little electronic device of yours or on the pages of the book in your hand? I know *exactly* where I am. After all, how do you think this 'Wright' fellow got published in the first place? *He knows* what deal he made and *he knows* what he owes me. He gives me life, and I give him a small piece of fame. A fair deal, if you ask me."

He took another sip. "And you're also probably wondering, 'Did that handsome Devil really set up that whole night just to get Tommy to work for him?' Well, guilty on both counts. You see, all's fair in love and war, and there's a war coming, people. Pawns are needed to move the other chess pieces where they need to be, and that's where I come in."

The Demon smirked and then sighed heavily and shook his head. "There Wright goes, calling me a Demon again. He bloody well knows I prefer the term *Fallen Angel*, but he *just insists* on calling me the other. If he keeps this up, I may have to renegotiate his deal, but I digress.

"So, where was I? Oh, yes. The war. You see, I help move pieces for both sides. I make sure things happen *just the way they're supposed to*. I help bring order to the chaos. It's what I do, and I do it well.

"So, dear reader, if there's anything you ever need, just say my name, and I'll be there. I'm the man who can make all your dreams come true—" He smiled wickedly. "—*if you're willing to pay the price*."

"Now, if you'll excuse me, it's almost time for the Rocky Horror Picture Show at the Alabama Theatre and I have a Vampire named Nicky and a pretty little damsel named Sadie to go and fuck with. Until next time, reader. Ta-ta."

SLOUCHING TOWARDS BETHLEHEM
By
Ken Goldman

"And what rough beast, its hour come 'round at last. Slouches towards Bethlehem to be born?"

William Butler Yeats
- The Second Coming (1921)

Nights at Saint Bartholomew's the silence seems different. After the last visitors depart the raw chill of the hospital's stillness is something you can feel inside your bones. Conversation at the nurses' stations - assuming there is conversation - reduces itself to whispers. Occasionally you hear the wheels of the orderlies' carts that drag along tiled floors of sterile corridors, their echoes clattering down long fluorescent tunnels. Sometimes a staff person laughs, one of the night nurses maybe trades insults with the interns. Laughter quickly becomes smothered past midnight and mostly there is this cold and steadfast

93

silence. The quiet sometimes gives an illusion of peace, but the institution's tranquil facade is anything but peaceful. Those who work the graveyard shift at Saint Bartholomew's know better than to trust the stillness

***

Lycanthia Mamuwalde broke the night's silence in a big way. The young woman barreled down the corridor striking Dr. Joseph Keller full throttle as the obstetrician completed his 11:00 p.m. rounds. Despite the enormous weight she carried inside her belly she somehow had managed to outrun Rosalie from pre-admissions who chugged sluggishly behind.

"You the doctor? The man I 'sposed to see for my baby?" Tugging at Keller's lab coat Lycanthia spat her words at him, then sucked at air she found difficult to breathe.

Rosalie caught up with the girl whose haggard coffee colored flesh glistened with sweat. She could not have been more than twenty, and Keller knew that she was already well into her third trimester. He would be willing to lay odds that her short breaths were not only owing to the marathon race she had just run down the hospital corridor, but also because her enlarged uterus was already preventing her lungs from reaching full expansion.

"I'm sorry, doctor," Rosalie huffed at him, an exhausted Brahma bull snorting for oxygen. "This woman just pushed right past the desk."

A formidable belly protruded through Lycanthia's frayed coat, as if what lay within the fetus inside her might at any moment kick itself free and tear open those oversized buttons itself. With an elbow shot that narrowly missed the receptionist's ribs, the girl turned on Rosalie screeching like a cheesed off panther.

You step back an' lay offa me, bitch, 'les you be pullin' back a stump 'stead o' your han'! You hear me talkin' to you?"

Clutching the full expanse of her stomach the girl fell to the floor still shrieking. Keller unbuttoned her coat and examined beneath the shabby housedress she wore. She had already started her contractions. The dilation of the woman's cervix confirmed she was in the final phase of the latent stage of labor. Her baby's head would be moving into the birth canal any moment, and once that happened everyone present could dispense with the formalities.

Keller reached for Rosalie's clipboard and handed his pen to the young woman now squatting at his feet doubled over in agony.

"Just sign this form now, okay?" he told her. "We'll fill in the details later. Let's have a look at you first?"

She stared up at the physician suspiciously. Still puffing mouthfuls of air into her cheeks she managed to scribble her name. Keller glanced at it and handed the clipboard back to the receptionist.

"Okay, Rosalie?"

The woman's eyes fused with his. He knew what the receptionist was thinking.

And fuck the horse you rode in on too, doctor.

"Fine," she answered without smiling.

***

Keller found the young woman a gurney. There was no point in placing her in a bed, not in her advanced condition. Her amniotic fluid sac had already ruptured. She had broken her water, and the doctor feared sufficient staff would be unavailable on short notice to handle the contingency of a breech birth. Before an orderly arrived to help move the expectant mother, Keller had rotated the fetus through external manipulation into a head downward position. Knowing nothing of his patient's medical history he could allow no margin for error because Lycanthia Mamuwalde was going to deliver her baby within minutes.

"Lycanthia, just nod your head, okay? Are you taking any drugs?"

His answer came in low moans.

"Are you on drugs, anything prescribed or not?" he repeated, posing one question after another when he received no response. "Medication for allergies? Can I talk to the baby's father - ?"

"Ain't no father here to talk to. And no, I don' put no shit like that into me!" the woman finally screeched. "Look, you just do what you got to do, all right?"

Keller trotted alongside the gurney trying to determine the young woman's pulse and heart rate on the run, struggling to accomplish this through the clatter of the litter's wheels and the mayhem of Lycanthia's recurring shrieks. He allowed the orderly to roll the gurney ahead while he stopped at the nurses' station, then shouted his orders at two unnerved floor nurses to find the RN and to get Head Nurse Eloise Hatcher's ass double-time into the delivery room. He tried again to measure Lycanthia's heart and pulse rates on the delivery table, performing an insane clown act while trying to switch between his forceps and his stethoscope. Unable to get a good reading he turned to the matter at hand.

It was not an easy birth, particularly for a team of two, but coaching the young mother through the event became blessedly simple. Although she had informed him this was her first child Lycanthia knew what to do. The OB and his nurse's usual words of encouragement seemed almost extraneous.

There was not much blood flow, significantly less than the usual amount as if the woman had arrived exsanguinated. But chronic iron deficiency anemia was not unusual during a pregnancy, and that could theoretically translate into the liquid's relative absence. Low blood cell counts were routine because of the increased menstrual flow during pregnancy, and the nutritional requirements demanded to support the fetus could diminish bleeding during childbirth.

Right up to the moment of delivery Nurse Hatcher raised not an eyebrow. Such was the woman's style. Had she discovered Lycanthia's fetus gorging itself like a tick on its own mother's blood, the RN would probably have reacted the same. As Saint Bart's oldest registered night nurse Eloise conditioned herself to the oddities of her midnight routine. She would not have cared had Keller shown up in the delivery room wearing only his jockey briefs and a smile.

There seemed no immediate danger of malpresentation. Lycanthia's contractions were almost perfectly rhythmic. Still, the fetus did not pass easily through the cervix on its way to the outside world, judging from the woman's shrieks of agony. Keller could see the baby's head emerge covered with the thick gelatinous goo of its afterbirth.

Lycanthia let rip one mighty scream.

For a heart stopping moment the baby's head lay wedged inside the opening. Keller looked at it, looked at it hard. Eloise's mouth fell open and she flinched at what she saw. The nurse's reaction, as minimal as it seemed, corroborated her silent agreement that something was very wrong.

At first the tiny head appeared misshapen. Two sharply pointed bones emerged goat-like through the flesh of its skull. The piercing protrusions must have shred through the mother's vaginal cavity like a weed whacker.

"Push! That's it!" Eloise shouted, wiping the perspiration from Lycanthia's brow. "Take a deep breath and push with all you've got!"

"Up yo' ass, bitch! Up yo' ..."

Hatcher remained undaunted.

"Push! Push!"

"... yo' ass! Dammit! Oh, Fuck! Fuckfuckfuck!"

"It's coming ... Give me one more ..."

"Pugh! Pugh!"

Women were always unpredictable during childbirth, at times amusing but often terrifying. Some laughed hysterically like maniacs, some lost complete control and cried. Others spewed venom at absent fathers or swore invectives at God Himself. The extraordinary joy of childbirth made strange bedfellows with its horrific agony.

"Puggghhh! Eeeeeeeeeyooooooooooo!"

Shrieking, Lycanthia wrapped both hands around Nurse Hatcher's neck, squeezing at the tendons in the woman's throat with long and bony fingers.

Keller could not free his hands, and unable to let the emerging child slip from his grasp he could do no more than stare at the choking woman.

"Jesus, Eloise! Are you all - ?"

The nurse's eyes bulged like an insect's before she finally tugged herself free, her legs buckling. Falling to her knees, Hatcher remained on the floor coughing and sputtering, trying to get her wind back as Lycanthia continued to wail. She collapsed gurgling thick mouthfuls of mucus.

"I'm all right!" Hatcher managed to croak at Keller. "See to the baby!"

Most nights this part of the birthing process remained routine. Keller would pass the newborn to his nurse, Hatcher cleaned the child, and she would dutifully hand it back to its mother. The procedure was systematic and efficient, requiring a few minutes once the baby arrived. Tonight had proved anything but routine, and Keller knew Eloise was in no shape to hold a newborn infant in her arms. He would have to scrub the child himself. The task promised to be far from pleasurable, judging from what the OB had extracted from Lycanthia Mamuwalde's womb.

The squirming monstrosity was the ugliest baby the physician had ever birthed. Even before he had sponged clean the membranous gunk of its afterbirth, Keller knew he had delivered some form of gargoyle with hardly any discernible resemblance to a human newborn. Its flesh felt gritty and it festered with hundreds of pinhead boils. Hanging loosely like a poorly tailored play suit, its skin clumped in pink jelly rolls at the joints. Ulcerous patch quilt strips covered the infant's entire body resembling the flaccid flesh of someone grizzled with age.

Worse was the newborn's liver and onions stench that came undiluted through Keller's face mask, a powerful reek like those patients in the last sickening stages of terminal cancer. The physician had not smelled anything as foul outside Saint Bartholomew's morgue.

Drenched in ruddy gore clinging to it like peppermint candy, the dripping face seemed too sentient for a human infant. Its black eyes first squinted, then bulged open enabling the small creature to become immediately aware of its surroundings. Studying its environment, it did not blink beneath the operating room's bright overhead lights. The newborn's stare fell on the face of the man who had delivered it. Cackling belligerently at the obstetrician, it tried kicking free from the doctor's grasp.

For one insane moment Keller felt a rabid desire like none he had ever experienced. His stomach knotted with shame at the thought, but still he could not dismiss it. In his mind's eye, he pictured himself grabbing the newborn by its legs, slamming it head first against the wall of the delivery room, and splattering its brains inside its skull like bloodied mashed potatoes before Lycanthia Mamuwalde - or anyone else - even had the chance to see it.

"You have a boy," he announced instead, aware he had uttered the words without the usual accompanying enjoyment. Keller felt no desire to repeat himself.

Lycanthia's baby squealed with fear or fury, Keller could not determine. It struggled in the physician's grasp as he sponged off the remains of pulpous matter. Unable to restrain it, he approached Lycanthia. The woman pulled herself upright on the delivery table reaching out for her child, and the creature wriggled from the physician into its mother's arms. With no hesitation, the young woman bared her breast and the newborn drank from her with an animal-like fervor.

"Don' you cry. Hush now, baby. Your mama's r'at here," Lycanthia whispered to it, undisturbed by the monstrosity she nourished. She drew her lips to its forehead and kissed one of the small protrusions of bone, singing softly to the infant in words neither Keller nor Eloise understood.

"Y'ai 'ng 'ngah, YOG-SOTHOTH, H'ee - L'geb, F'al Throdog, UAAAH..."

She sounded like some B-movie voodoo priestess working her evil spell, a Cajun witch rattling her collection of bones and spilling her powders above the head of a fiendish horned devil doll.

Gurgling with delight the baby stopped crying that instant.

"What's she singing?" Eloise Hatcher asked, her voice still raw.

Keller could only shake his head.

"It isn't Jingle Bells."

Suckling the child, Lycanthia turned her attention to the pair who had delivered it. Her lips pursed as if the young mother were about to hiss more of her contempt at the two. Instead she smiled a broad, purple gummed grin aimed directly at them, then muttered a profanity that seemed as incongruous as it was absurd.

"M'face to ..."

Keller turned toward Eloise. The nurse stared incredulously back at him.

" ... M'face to yo' ass ... M'face to yo' ass ..."

He heard Lycanthia say the words like an obscene epiphany. The woman burst out laughing but quickly caught herself, throwing her hand to her mouth like a little girl who had inadvertently uttered a bad word. She whispered to the newborn as if mother and child together shared a furtive secret.

Keller had no doubt they did.

He knew something else with as much certainty.

Theirs were not going to be the night's only secrets shared at Saint Bartholomew's.

2:47 a.m.

Inside the small incubator the child its mother had secretly named 'Phisto seemed to sleep. Its eyes remained closed, its breathing soft. The newborn lay on its stomach isolated from the other infants in another room, and for this moment a casual observer not seeing its face might have whispered "How adorable!"

The child did not sleep. It waited.

The infant's instincts were already sharp. It knew what it wanted and whom it wanted. A langsuyar quickly perceives its emotions, its needs.

The isolation.

The fear.

The thirst.

This last instinct told the creature what it must do.

The incubator containing it seemed not much larger than the small being inside, but air piped into the enclosed chamber was rich and made breathing easier. Although heat provided from the lamp within was a bother to a creature preferring the cold, the humidified oxygen supplied the male infant with strength more than ordinary air would have.

The langsuyar easily pushed the lid open and raised his small head above the glass. He sniffed like a rodent, tracking his mother's scent. She was not far off.

Instinctively he understood the most danger lay in these next few moments. Discovery would no doubt mean death to the unfortunate one who chanced to find him here.

He lay inside the heated incubator and waited for his mother.

3:02 a.m.

Lycanthia, fully awake, climbed from her bed. She, too, sniffed the air and recognized the scent. Her son was in a room at the far end of the corridor. She knew the ass wipes who ran this place had separated her child from the other infants. They had placed him in a holding room where the morning visitors would not see the wailing freak she had produced snarling at them from behind the glass of the nursery among the other children. In their foolishness the doctor and that wrinkled cunt had inadvertently acted wisely with the langsuyar. A nursery was hardly the place for a creature surviving on the blood of infants.

The bitch in the starched whites had also been incredibly shitheaded to believe she could sedate one like her. You don't sedate one already dead.

Lycanthia pushed the door open and examined the long corridor. The girl at the nurse's station was the only one on the floor, and engrossed in her magazine she did not seem a threat. Perhaps if Lycanthia were very quiet ...

"I'm comin' for you, child," she whispered, astonished at tears that blurred her vision for the first time in as long as she could remember. Wiping her nose on the cheap rag of the hospital gown they had given her, she stepped out slowly, progressing barefooted and spider-like along the wall of the corridor. The woman prepared herself to tear out the throat of anyone who stopped her.

No one did.

Lycanthia pushed open the door of the patient care room. Excepting the glow from the incubator the room remained completely dark. This was good.

She lifted the lid, pleased to find her infant awake. It reached for her and she cradled the langsuyar close to her chest, rocking it while chanting his name just as her mate had instructed her, precisely as the ceremony demanded the dark messiah's birth be announced throughout the night of his delivery.

Mephis-to you is ... Mephis-to you is ..."

3:17 a.m.

... M'face to yo' ass ...

Inside Dr. Joseph Keller's office the obstetrician turned to Eloise Hatcher.

" ... that chanting the woman did? You ever hear anything to beat that? And the little ditty about 'My face to your ass.' Jesus, talk about a gonzo night here."

Eloise looked quizzically at him. "Lycanthia said that? I wasn't sure."

"The moment I pulled that gargoyle out of her. What do you suppose that particular remark was all about?"

Eloise frowned, and took a long swig from her coffee cup.

"Damned if I know." She got up to leave, but turned toward Keller. "Damned if I much care."

Alone at his desk Keller stared at Lycanthia Mamuwalde's signed admissions form, the one he had spent ten minutes talking Rosalie into giving him.

"Amen to that," he mumbled.

He shoved the form inside his drawer and locked it.

3:46 a.m.

Lycanthia cradled her child alone inside the nursery among a dozen sleeping infants. No hospital staff member had seen her enter. It would not have mattered very much had anyone discovered her inside, but it would have been decidedly inconvenient and no doubt messy.

This part was not going to take very long assuming the child's instincts kicked in quickly. The young mother expected they would, that she would be gone from Saint Bartholomew's with her infant long before daylight. Still, the most essential act remained. Her mate had commanded it, and it was the reason her demon lover had selected Saint Bartholomew's above the others for the birth of the vampiress' son. Tonight indeed would prove itself a night of firsts.

"You th' chosen one, 'Phisto," Lycanthia whispered to the child. "Th' one chosen from all th' rest. Mephistopheles tol' me so hisself, the one you named for. Do you know who your daddy is? Do you, little one?"

The langsuyar examined his mother's grin and reaching playfully for her face gurgled something in unintelligible baby talk. In the few hours since its birth the child had grown six inches larger and its horns had almost fully emerged, small but complete. His senses too had come wholly alive. He knew that here there was nourishment for him. The newborn smelled infant blood and licked his lips.

"The in'cent blood of the lamb is what you need now, 'Phisto, like your daddy says. And the lamb is what we got here, jus' waitin', layin' asleep here before us, waitin' jus' for you ..."

She searched the name tags on the beds and carried her son to an infant fast asleep among the rows of slumbering newborns. The langsuyar already showed elongated fangs as it stared down at the soft pink neck of the sleeping child wrapped inside a blue blanket to show that it was a boy. The name tag on the small post indicated the baby's name was Andrew Christopher, just as her mate had told her. This was the one she wanted.

The new savior slept in no manger this time. No wise men stood by to offer gifts for little Andrew, no holy virgin warmed him at her breast. There was only the baby boy sleeping alone inside his tiny crib at this darkest and most silent hour of the night, the newborn king unheralded and unknown.

"This one's all for you, child, all for you," Lycanthia said. "You gon' to be th' one someday, and that day comin' real soon."

She smirked at the thought, her sharp teeth glowing in the dull light of the nursery. No star of Bethlehem shone tonight as little Andrew Christopher entered the last minute of his short life.

Lycanthia lowered the creature slowly, allowing her own newborn King to share the tiny crib with the sleeping little boy inside.

"Mephisto ... yo' ... is..." she chanted softly.

The young mother grinned as she watched her son drink.

####

Ken Goldman is a former Philadelphia teacher of English and Film Studies, and he has taught courses on Horror and Science Fiction in Film & Literature. An affiliate member of the Horror Writers

Association, Ken has homes on the Main Line in Pennsylvania and at the Jersey shore depending upon the track of the sun and his need for a tan. His stories appear in over 860 independent press publications in the U.S., Canada, the UK, and Australia, and over thirty of Ken's tales are due for publication in 2017. Since 1993 his stories have received seven honorable mentions in The Year's Best Fantasy & Horror. He has written five books: his anthologies of short stories, YOU HAD ME AT ARRGH!! (Sam's Dot Publishers), DONNY DOESN'T LIVE HERE ANYMORE (A/A Publishers), plus an e-book, STAR CROSSED (Vampires 2 Publications); and a novella, DESIREE, (Damnation Books, reprinted by eXcessica Publishing). His novel, OF A FEATHER, was published by Horrific Tales Publications (UK) in January 2014, and his upcoming novel, SINKHOLE, is due late summer 2017 by Bloodshot Books. You may find many of Ken's stories online and at Amazon.com. Stop by and scream hello.

Amazon.com site:
http://www.amazon.com/Kenneth-C.-Goldman/e/B004QVWTTE

Goodreads:
https://www.goodreads.com/author/show/3054969.Kenneth_C_Goldman

Google:
https://plus.google.com/110939908295908428356/posts

THE PURIFICATION PROCESS

By
Sergio "ente per ente" Palumbo
Edited by Michele Dutcher

The island was an immense greenish jungle thriving with plantations, breadfruit trees and lush scenes that had remained unchanged over time - some buildings of which were believed to date back to the original ancestors, around 700 A.D. The area was dotted with a few sacred temples hidden throughout the dense vegetation, retaining the true authenticity of early Polynesia. This was the usual panorama that came to mind when most people thought of this place, or arrived from abroad for a vacation. Huahine – which was actually two islands… - was in French Polynesia, in the Pacific Ocean. The name itself was a variation of the local word *vahine* (woman), presumably referring to a mountain resembling the outline of a pregnant girl — a symbol of the island's irrefutable fertility, or so the locals commonly thought.

With a population of about 6,700 residents, it measured 10 miles in length, with a maximum width of 8 miles, and was made up of Huahine Nui (Big Huahine) lying to the north and Huahine Iti (Little Huahine) to the south. The islands were only separated by a few hundred yards of water and joined by a sand-spit and a small bridge built to connect the two areas. There was also air transportation available via the small Huahine airport, located on the northern shore of Huahine Nui.

Generally speaking, the natives enjoyed a quiet lifestyle and the only deviations from their routine were brought from Sunday morning markets that were full of tasty fruit and colorful produce. Tourists came from many countries, too, and they repeatedly visited the islands and enjoyed popular water activities like diving, horseback riding, sailing and fishing - the same as they loved the hotels and resorts present in the area.

However, *there were other things*, things apart from the men and women who vacationed here, that came to this place and were uninvited guests nobody really liked or had ever asked for. Those 'guests' arrived here from the unearthly Realm of the Dead, and they wanted to remain here. Therefore, they had to be dealt with appropriately and not looked upon carelessly, both to protect the area from those evil souls, and to save the few unlucky people who chanced into such evil, endangering their lives and their minds because of those insidious presences that could easily ruin everything.

Purotu was one of the best women involved in this unusual activity who had ever existed on Huahine, and was good at accomplishing such uneasy things. Many thought she would soon become the most experienced and skilled female *tahuna* in that field. This was in spite of only being 44-years-old, outdoing and getting ahead of all the others who had previously followed the same path and had practiced that sacred job for much longer.

There had always been widespread belief in ghosts in Polynesian culture, some of which persisted today. After death, a person's soul would normally travel to the underworld, but some could stay on Earth, if they preferred - or were forced to do so. In many Polynesian legends, ghosts were also actively involved in the affairs of men. Some of those presences might cause sickness or even invade the body of ordinary people, and those had to be driven out through strong local medicines, in a few cases. Or a person could ask for the help of a *tahuna* like Purotu, of course, if you wanted a permanent result in the end. Polynesian shamans had always followed the way of the adventurer, which was a healing path based on love and cooperation, and their activity was highly respected.

Ghost sickness, as that curse was also called in these lands, took two forms: possession and strange behavior, where the victims talked with the voice of a dead person; or obstructed healing caused by an evil soul. The best way to treat the few patients who asked for her help was, as the woman had learned over the course of all her life, to use a few strong-smelling plants such as island *rue* or *ti* leaves which were also commonly positioned at the corners of the home to keep ghosts from entering property. Sometimes it was even necessary to resort to reasoning with the ghost, if a serious possession had occurred, but doing that made the outcome more uncertain, and exacting.

What she had been taught from her slightly-oversized teacher, named Akolo, who had been the renowned appointed *tahuna* before her coming of age, was that the important thing was to keep a strong mind and a strong heart, too. It was also important not to ask for things you couldn't handle, or to make other stupid wishes like 'I'd really like to know what it feels like to be dead', because, according to tradition, things like that happened. "It's always best to be a little afraid," Akolo had once told her. And Purotu still kept a clear recollection of those words.

The slender, swarthy woman had never imagined she might become a *tahuna* when she was very young. It was Akolo's son who was supposed to replace him when the time came, *and not just a young girl*, but things had gone in a different way, as a matter of fact. It was as simple as Purotu being gifted for such an activity, as it had been ascertained afterwards, and Akolo's son simply wasn't. So it had been her duty to follow her teacher's suggestions and training until she had become what she was today.

As that practice was a sort of religion, many people reasoned that there was no place for sorcerous practice in the modern world, because science required evidence and her work couldn't provide any. But the *tahuna* like her believed that all things had a life force of their own - as if they were alive - and so they weren't interested in what others thought of their activities. After all, regardless of the many religions that were known and followed, that ancient belief wasn't ever meant to disappear among the locals; instead it co-existed beside all the others.

"What am I going to face this morning?" the woman asked himself, as she studied the body and the behavior of a very young individual whose family had asked for her immediate help. They told her that a ghost had inhabited their son's mind for a few days and they wanted the female *tahuna* to make the presence leave their son's body. Of course, their conclusions were just suppositions, as only a true shaman might discover if such an opinion was true or not. It was not something that could be considered common knowledge or a common experience, and the locals might think that something unusual and unearthly was going on, but they simply couldn't confirm it by themselves. Only the examination of a woman like a true, powerful *tahuna* could reach that conclusion and then try to solve the serious problem.

Once Purotu had put her broad-nose past the wooden door of the house in typical local architectural style she had been invited into, situated on a raised rock platform, she had quickly passed through the first two rooms that were supported by four large ironwood posts. The roof was thatched with leaves, and the building appeared to be decorated with braided fiber—sennit lashings and intricately woven mats. Cultural tradition also required some dried leaves be placed on the floors initially and then covered with finely woven rugs which added extra softness and comfort.

The dark-skinned boy with wiry black hair, named Oroiti – a name meaning *Slow-footed* - who was presumed to be object of such an unusual possession proved to be, undoubtedly, strange and his movements were unpredictable, fast and pointless. He did not eat, didn't drink and didn't speak - although all those symptoms might have been due to some other illness. In that circumstance, some completely different plants and remedies would be necessary in order to treat him... But it was his slight paleness, along with his lost look and the insensitiveness she saw that made the *tahuna* sure that it might really be an evil ghost that was causing those signs. And, if that was true, she already knew what she had to do, undoubtedly.

So, yes, the woman was all for measuring the overall appearance and behavior of the subject and that information told her dark eyes exactly how the boy's body and mind had been affected by possession.

Purotu asked the very attractive woman with incredibly full lips and a very wide waist who was the owner of the house - her husband having died a few years ago - to leave them alone, and the *tahuna* removed the colorful shirt she wore and started dancing around the boy. With only her colorful shorts on, her dark curly hair floating about like weak branches pushed by invisible gusts of wind, she began violently shaking to such a point that a person might have thought *she was the one who was really in the hands of demons now...* Then, she stopped, opened the worn leather hold-all he had brought along with her, and rummaged around inside of it for a while.

After having performed that short-period preparatory commencement, an overheated Purotu knew that she was ready to start the true ritual and she needed the right ingredients to be used, undoubtedly. The first thing she did was take a sip of '*awa*' from a small bottle, as that was a ceremonial beverage widely taken before the start of important meetings and events, even in the field of the unearthly arts. Reports that the drink was mildly intoxicating were not incorrect although a *tahuna* commonly used it as a stress-reducing agent, and it even proved useful as a headache remedy, most of the time.

Then the woman paid homage to the ancestor mountain and to the ancestor river, before addressing all the other geographical features that were reputed to be the same. Two plants were soon positioned on the floor before the boy: the first one was *lau'akau* and the other plant had dark leaves, its true origins being a secret that only the practitioners of unearthly arts like her knew. By means of those, she began making an intricate pattern, and then she cut them into pieces. They were immediately laid out facing direct sunlight, and Purotu respectfully rolled them into larger 'wheels' about one foot in diameter. Using a very large shell, she positioned the remains of the leaves per the widths required for the completion of the desired ritual. The thinner they were the more difficult and valuable the result was, because perfectly treating such thinner parts took longer and needed more skill. This tradition was something unbeknownst to the common population, and was only known to the *tahuna* like her, of course.

At that point, Purotu prepared to dance again, and in a matter of minutes her gestures and her footwork became more and more violent, intense and unbelievable, while she closed both eyes. Her hair was tousled about another time, and all her body appeared to be shaken by strong blows that continuously and vehemently beat against her chest, arms and back, until all the room seemed to change and a strange, dark smoke covered part of the walls, the wooden furniture and the floor itself. The face of the woman had beads of sweat now, and her expression looked lost, though not as confused and lifeless as the boy's.

By means of that unusual dance, the *tahuna*'s mind was struggling to enter the target's being, and was also trying to get to his true self to help him and heal his unearthly illness. There was no other way to remove the unholy invader he had been subject to.

After many difficulties, the woman made it, in the end, and her thoughts finally reached the other's mind.

The *tahuna*'s thoughts were like a brilliance, a powerful sun that began dispersing all the smoke being around, a mist that turned to a grayish shade - *a manifestation of the very evil matter the unwanted ghost was made of* - and she brought the boy's mind to the present time. Then Purotu opened his eyes again a checked it all out.

Now Oroiti seemed to have acquired again his right complexion, and his look didn't appear to be lost or confused anymore. "Where am I?" the boy asked. The female *tahuna*'s tries had gotten to the point; the sacred ritual had been perfectly performed, as a matter of fact, though it had required most of her strength and power, of course. Purotu calmed the boy down and held his hands, smiling, and it was a sincere smile that opened wide on her face, indeed.

About ten minutes after that, the *tahuna* was collecting all her belongings and tidying her curly hair, before putting her shirt on again and taking leave of the two residents. "Thank you for your help! Now Oroiti is finally safe and has come to his senses!" The woman kept expressing her most sincere and heartfelt compliments for what she had achieved, and for freeing her son, and she was also giving her many fruits, groceries and other gifts while showing her appreciation. "Thank you, thank you great powerful *tahuna!*"

Purotu nodded in acknowledgement and bowed in return, thinking that she would prefer to receive a true, passionate kiss from that attractive person instead of fruits, even though the *tahuna* perfectly knew that she was not a lesbian as she was; then she turned, heading for the door, although her arms were clearly not large and strong enough to bring out all the goods she had been provided with. It was the other woman herself who picked up what had already fallen to the floor and helped her in making her way out.

*****

The call Purotu received in the morning, two days after her last job, surprised the *tahuna* and saddened her as well. It seemed that Whetu, the first son of Vainui, who was a wealthy female merchant living in town, had started showing some signs of possession and her presence was immediately requested. This looked strange, as another case occurring just a few days after her previous performance was undoubtedly unusual. But it was the name of the woman that astonished Purotu herself. She had known Vainui – who was just a little older than she was - since he was 13-years-old and she would never have imagined that one day she would be asked to give help to her son. Well, she would never have thought of becoming a *tahuna* in the years to come either, as a matter of fact, but that was precisely what had happened after all...

Other than that, she had always been secretly in love with Vainui, but she was straight and got married one day, therefore she could never love in return someone like Purotu, who was a lesbian, certainly. This just didn't diminish her interest in her friend, of course.

Vainui's luxurious abode was positioned along a pleasant stretch of sandy beach on the northern outskirts of town, and it did not take her long to reach it. When she arrived, she looked at the place and immediately recognized its peculiar features. That was a magnificent traditional house with beautiful gardens that would certainly please all the lovers of exotic plants and flowers, be they from abroad or be they local.

Once she had been welcomed inside and once she had given a big hug to her acquaintance, the *tahuna* said that she needed to be left alone and, as soon as she was taken from the entry room to the bedroom of the son, she closed the wooden door behind her and started examining the skinny boy, whose appearance looked completely different from her mother's slender though muscular build.

After just one look, there was no uncertainty that Whetu was experiencing some sort of possession, and there was no reason to wait any longer, as she had to act quickly. After searching her hold-all, she found the things she needed and put them on the floor at her feet before starting what had to be done.

The usual preparation was immediately completed and, after drinking the traditional '*awa*' from her small bottle, she started addressing the features that were reputed to be the ancestors of everyone living on Huahine before turning her attention to the ritualistic dances. Again this morning, the *tahuna* put in the right place on the floor the sacred leaves properly cut, and she saw the unholy smoke assembling and rising around her and the boy, and then it became lighter and much weaker than it was at the beginning. It was vividly dissolving and the evil ghost that was behind it all was going away with it, or so it seemed, exactly as Purotu had been hoping for deep in her heart, of course.

The ritual was now over, and her most difficult duty of the day had been accomplished, probably. As the woman was tired, and still shaking because of everything she had gone through that morning, another thought crossed her mind. She didn't feel the usual sense of freedom inside, the same pleasing impression she usually got at the end of her task. But it was what the female *tahuna* saw in the skinny boy's eyes that made her feel uncertain and then very worried. That strange brilliance she noticed in his irises: **that lost look was there again**. How was it possible? *There was something wrong, what was going on?*

When Purotu turned to the door of the room that was now open, the *tahuna* saw Whetu's mother waiting outside, and she didn't see any sign of worry on her face. On the contrary, there was a wide smile on her lips, or was it a smirk, a sort of evil smugness. All of this was very unexpected. Then, Vainui stepped into the room and spoke to the shaman. "Well done, my dear friend. You made it! Now his body is in order and everything is alright!"

The *tahuna* didn't want to abruptly displease the female merchant, but she didn't have the time to reply or to express her many doubts, as the other woman resumed talking. "We've been waiting for a long time for someone like you. We've been looking for a woman who happened to be endowed with great power and who might use it in connection with the necessary knowledge of herbs, plants and leaves to accomplish the required rituals. You see, experience and study aren't everything in this field, as without the proper strength and innate gifts anyone needs to delve deeper into the unearthly realm, no definitive outcome could be ever possible. A person might try his whole lifetime, but the prerequisite power to control and rule over such strong energies is not something that is given to everyone, and not even the most famous *tahuna* of this village ever got those gifts, as a matter of fact. But when you were born, we watched you growing up. So, we did it right when we decided to wait for the moment you were ready, more skilled and experienced. Because we knew we needed you, and no one else would do. And with a goal in mind, of course!"

"You...? What is this foolishness, Vainui?" Purotu asked her old acquaintance with a very surprised look, her eyes wide open as she had already understood she was now facing something unprecedented. "Who are you really? *And what are you talking about*?"

"*We* simply means me, and all the other ghosts of the Realm of the Dead that have been waiting for our chance to come back to Earth, to enter the kingdom of living beings again. Whoever else might we be?" was the plain reply she got.

"Are you saying that...? No, it's not possible!" Purotu cried out in disbelief. "How did you enter the body of my beloved Vainui, and how did you manage to stay in her for all this time, without anyone noticing you, not even me? She was an old acquaintance of mine, I know her well and she was always respectful of our rituals, but here you are!"

"The answer is simple: it was Vainui himself – the woman that you love so deeply- that accepted it. She had gotten ill, months ago, and there was no cure that would allow her to be healthy again, she was well aware of that. So, what she wished for was simply to free herself. She wanted to leave this world once and for all, with its many sufferings, meaningless days and flawed thoughts. And I came here to be of help. You see, she was weak, tired of living and that is when we can easily enter a human's body and never be noticed." All of this had been said in a low voice that seemed to come from another place, not truly being of this Earth.

"So, you did this! And how did you...?"

"You mean, how did I get to remove her soul without raising suspicions, without harming her body or changing her overall appearance? Oh, that's why I had her being undergo a purification process with the aim of completely get rid of her soul and letting mine enter, easily, silently, entirely, so I could remain attached to her mind now and forever. You have to purify someone from his true self, and turn his mind into an empty space before another ghost can finally go in and reside - that's the important thing. But you must have his permission, and that's rare, undoubtedly rare. The rest will follow afterwards, and you must simply pay attention, pretending to be a common individual. You must never show off any sign of possession and just behave normally. Not an easy task, but this is something an evil creature like me can do in order to accomplish a much higher purpose…"

"What is that? What are you aiming for?" the *tahuna* inquired of the other.

"We needed a new purification process, something we can't get in the afterlife and we wanted to apply that process to all the other objects of our interest, turning them into receptacles. They would all become new minds where we could enter and stay. But we couldn't do this all by ourselves, and we couldn't rely only on the few who call for us to come, like Vainui. But your powers, your strong rituals can make our goals possible, regardless of the will of the human target! You are the woman, the most powerful *tahuna* who ever lived in this country, much better than your teacher, Akolo, ever was. With your help, we see a lot of opportunities ahead of us!"

"My help?" Purotu looked very worried.

"Your help, sure thing - even though it will not be something you will be giving us willingly. But you will do as we say, in spite of what you think of our plans because there is nothing you can do to try to oppose us!"

"How…when?" the *tahuna* exclaimed.

"You see, your very efficacious rituals can really remove an evil presence from someone, as your job usually demands that you do - to completely heal a man or a woman. However, in doing so you also temporarily remove the soul of the one that you are treating, along with the presence from the Realm of the Dead. Probably it's something you never noticed before, and you would never find out unless I told you. Be that as it may, that is exactly when one among us needs to enter that body, the one which is empty at that time. At that moment, there is no evil ghost anymore, and no other soul of a living individual around, only a place to be filled with the presence of another deadman that is waiting somewhere nearby!" The creature that had once been Vainui had replied in her usual unearthly tone.

"What the hell? How did you figure all this out?"

"Well, we discovered it by chance. One night we were watching you, cursing you for the perfect results on earth you were getting at removing our kind while healing humans. We were incapable of stopping you, and we deeply hated your teacher who taught you how to do that. Then, we noticed it: an unexpected opening in the mind of the person treated - an incredible passage to Earth no presence had ever imagined before. Actually, I saw it first, and from that moment on everything changed. That unexpected opening was a hope for our evil purposes, a way out from the Realm of the Dead for all of us, maybe."

The young *tahuna* remained silent for a while, without even daring to look directly at the other. She felt dejected, deceived and defeated.

"And, as the first member of my family meant to forever receive the soul of one of us, the Dead, and lose his own, I chose Whetu, the elder son of Vainui, the woman who willingly let me enter into her body and completely rule over it. You know, the boy's name means 'star', and he will be the star guiding us all into a better future, a new existence, here on Earth, among you, the humans! And that will continue until we replace all the rest of the living beings among the locals, starting from this small place."

"You will never succeed!" the other burst out in anger, wildly.

"You can't stop us! If it's true that you are the most powerful *tahuna* who ever lived, and we know that this is correct, and if you yourself can't remove me from the body of your friend Vainui, then how do you plan to send all of us back to the unearthly Realm of the Dead? You know you simply are not allowed to do that. But there's something worse than that, from your point of view, possibly…"

"That being? What gibberish are you talking now?"

"I can't enter into your body. You're a *tahuna*, and a very powerful one. No ghost can throw your soul out of your body, it will never happen, I can grant you that for sure! Moreover, this only means that you are going to be the last one who will maintain your mind and your true self, while the world you live in will inexorably change, day by day, and all the people living here will soon become ours."

"I will fight you! And I will stop you all…" Purotu objected in a fierce way.

A terrible laugh filled the room, coming from the other individual, from the being that was once Vainui's son. "That's precisely what we are expecting you to do! We know that you'll never stop trying to heal people, and you'll never give up hope of removing a bad ghost from the body of a local. And every time you attempt one of your rituals, you can be certain that one of us will be waiting there, trying to enter the body you're treating, and through it he will get to Earth. By way of that one, another ghost will also arrive in your world and in doing so he will come to stay. A lot of Dead will come to this place more times than you could ever imagine. I am sure you'll never stop doing your best, but you must know that we will be nearby, ready to get inside looking for the right opportunity. Your best effort will also be our best!"

A sequence of laughs started being emitting from the mouth of both Vainui and Whetu who stood in the house, and that tone almost pierced through the *tahuna*'s body as if it was an otherworldly noise no one could ever dare to resist. It was at that moment that Purotu turned to the front door and started running away, trying to make her way out - but that cruel twang kept ringing again in her brain and pervaded all of her being. *There was no way to make it stop, to silence it once and for all…*

Purotu might escape that place, go wherever she wanted, run as fast as she liked, but she would never remove that deadly impression from herself. The same as the woman would never change what she truly was: a *tahuna* bound to her duty. But whoever thought that her gift, her power, would one day be reputed to be only a curse? Who would have believed that it would be the means that would lead the worst evil into ruling over them all?

As the woman was hurrying, the words of her old teacher came to her mind, like a faint voice in the darkness. "The snake when about to be killed looks but does not escape…" That was true, she knew it. But should she only remain to watch the oncoming ruin, and accept the destiny she was going to bring to their islands? *What could she do when she knew all her future wins might possibly be turned into bloody defeats, much to the satisfaction of her unearthly enemies?*

THE END

Sergio is an Italian public servant who graduated from Law School working in the public real estate branch. He has published a Fantasy Role Playing illustrated Manual, *WarBlades,* of more than 700 pages. Some of his works and short stories have been published on *American Aphelion Webzine, WeirdYear, Quantum Muse, Antipodean SF, Schlock! Webzine, SQ Mag,* etc. and in print inside 32 American Horror/Scifi/Fantasy/Steampunk Anthologies, 52 British Horror/Sci-Fi Anthologies, 2 Urban Fantasy/Horror Canadian Anthology and 1 Sci-Fi Australian Anthology by various publishers, and 22 more to follow in 2017/2018.

He is also a scale modeler who likes mostly Science Fiction and Real Space models, some of his little Dioramas have been shown also on some Italian (scale model) magazines like *Soldatini, Model Time, TuttoSoldatini* and online on American site *StarShip Modeler, MechaModelComp,* on British *SFM: UK* site and *Italian SMF.*

Some Sci-Fi/fantasy/Horror short- stories by him in Italian have been published on *Alpha Aleph, Alpha Aleph Extra, Algenib, Oltre il Futuro, Nugae 2.0, SogniHorror, La Zona Morta, edizioni Lo Scudo, Antologia Robot ITA 0.1, Antologia Il Segreto dell'Universo, Antologia E-Heroes,* etc.'

The Internet site of his Model Club *"La Centuria":* www.lacenturia.it

Michele Dutcher, aka Bottomdweller, lives in a carriage house in Old Louisville Kentucky with her border collie – Daisy Dukes. She has a BS degree in Elementary Education from Indiana University with minors in theology & sociology and has been writing Science Fiction stories for about a decade. She edits all the first drafts of Sergio's short stories.

DEPRAVED COLLECTIVE
(The Shattered Souls of Hell Chronicles)
By
Emery LeeAnn

Chapter 1

Cecily knew she was in trouble when her mother's voice woke her from the fitful sleep she was in. She hadn't laid eyes on her mother since the day her mother had banished her from the house and had the farm hands chain her ankle to the pole in the barn. Shifting her swollen belly to an upright position she glared at the woman.

"Did you come to apologise for what you have subjected me to?" Cecily ground out

"Apologise?" Her mother looked at her like she had three heads "I came to take care of your problem you brought on our home" she glared at her daughter.

"The problem I brought?" Cecily couldn't believe her ears. "Your husband raped me, impregnated me and then you hired men to not only imprison me but to violate me as often as they can get it up!" she screamed.

"Watch your filthy lying mouth". Her mother spat at her as she slapped her hard across the face, slicing her lip open.

Cecily kept her mouth shut, her baby was kicking up a storm, and she was uncomfortable enough on a daily basis with her limited activity. When she went to her mother the next day after her stepfather had raped her, her mother called her a liar and locked her in her room so she couldn't tell anyone else. After two months passed she woke up vomiting profusely, screaming for her mother's help. Her mother came in and cleaned her up and put her back to bed for the night. The next morning her mother was making her pee on a stick. It was confirmed she was pregnant. Her mother had stormed out of the room leaving her alone until late that night, then she was taken out of her bed by men she had never seen before, dragging her out to the barn where they shackled her ankle to the pole. She had been there for six months sleeping on the floor, eating whatever slop they deigned to give her, using a bucket for the bathroom and a garden hose for cleansing and being the men's personal play toy. The depraved things they did to her body were disgusting at best.

Now at eight month's pregnant, Cecily could barely hoist herself up off the floor. The men were there watching the exchange between her and her mother. Her mother nodded at them and one of them unlatched her chains. The others lifted her to her feet having to hold her up since she had taken to staying on the ground more these past few months as the chain gave her very little room to move.

Walking her outside she saw their big mare standing under the moonlight. It was a beautiful sight bringing tears to her eyes. All she had seen for the past six months was the inside of that musty barn and the putrid horrible farm hands. All four of them abused her repeatedly. Then to add insult to injury, her step father walked around the front of the mare holding the bit in his hand. Smiling broadly at her he waved and blew her a kiss. Before she knew what was happening they were hoisting her up on the horse's back. At first she felt a glimmer of hope, if she could only get away, the nearest neighbour was thirty miles to the south, then she saw the smirks on their faces and knew they had a much more malevolent plan.

Her stepfather handed her the bit, rubbing his thumb across her hand making her want to vomit. Cecily glared at him before she noticed him pulling the pistol out of his pocket. He smiled again "Have a good ride Princess. I will be here to welcome you back after that monster is gone" he pointed at her belly. Raising the pistol by the horse's ear he shot a single shot into the air. That loud crack spooked the animal to take off at a pace so that Cecily could barely hold on.

This was their plan! They wanted to kill her baby. She hated the father but she had grown to care about this creature that was growing inside of her. The horse was out of control running through the trees, causing her belly to severely cramp and all Cecily could do was hold on for dear life. They came up by a huge oak tree and the horse's hooves managed to get tangled in the thick vines that surrounded the ground around the mighty tree. The mare not knowing what else to do but buck, threw Cecily off her back onto the unforgiving ground. Landing hard on her back, she heard her bones breaking, the pain in her abdomen was excruciating. Her last coherent thought was revenge.

Unadulterated pure revenge.

Chapter 2

The Goddess Lilith was on the third level of Hell when she felt the pull of the soul that had just died. Normally she didn't feel the pull so her curiosity was piqued. Walking up through to the top level, she created a portal in the huge oak where she felt the tug. Trees were Mother Nature's gift to the Universe so they provided help to every realm, which made them the perfect conduit for a portal.

Walking through the portal Lilith noticed the carnage on the ground. Glancing to the side, she flicked her wrist at the soul keeper who nodded and kept Cecily's soul in limbo waiting for more instruction from the Goddess. The young woman was laying broken on the ground with the babe expelled beside her. Lilith placed her fingertips on the babe's forehead first and saw only pure light which meant the child's soul was accepted in heaven, there was nothing she could do to change that. She moved over to Cecily's body and touched her forehead. The light that washed through her body shook the Goddess to her core. This is who they had been looking for, this was their missing link. She reviewed in her mind what Cecily had done to be banished from Heaven, and saw it was the promise of revenge in her heart that kept her from being joined with her child. Lilith shook her head. The moment a mortal dies, their soul instantly went to Heaven to be judged and the majority of the time they were kicked to Hell. Mortals thought the devil was the bad guy. If they only knew she thought absently. She walked over to the soul keeper and took possession of the floating soul. Going to the portal, she brought Cecily into Hell

When a soul steps onto the realm of Hell, they become physical as if they are back in their bodies. It's like a reawakening of sorts. Lilith was excited but knew she wasn't allowed to sway Cecily's decision and unfortunately, she knew Lucian would give her the choice of her future. They needed her to stay so desperately but she would keep her mouth closed and let the girl make her own mind up.

Chapter 3

Cecily stared at the ethereal woman standing in front of her. She was mesmerised by her beauty. Looking around she saw dusty caverns and what appeared to be isolated huts hidden by huge rocks. The temperature was warm but not uncomfortable. She glanced shyly at the woman.

"Am I dead?"

"Yes" Lilith confirmed

Cecily ran her hand over her flat stomach. "And my baby?"

"In Heaven"

"So I am in…" Cecily trailed off

"Yes my dear. You are in Hell. My name is Lilith"

"As in the Goddess Lilith?" Cecily inquired

Lilith smiled feeling the link grow stronger with each step. She knew the girl had more questions but she needed to get her to the bottom level safely to Lucian.

"Yes and I am honoured you know of me. Now we must hurry and when we reach the bottom level I promise everything will be revealed to you. Stay close to me. It can be very dangerous here" She grabbed Cecily's hand and started the trek down to the lowest level of Hell.

Cecily stayed close to the Goddess feeling safe for the first time in her life. It seemed there were multiple levels and as they descended, each level was dustier and hotter than the last. She kept glancing around at the eyes peering at her, but never coming close.

"Flauros move aside" Lilith said abruptly to a demon like creature who had jumped down in front of the pair blocking their path.

"She has no protection markings" The demon hissed.

"Do you challenge me?" Lilith stood her ground hoping no one else joined in - one or two she could handle - a whole pack, she wasn't so sure….

He seemed to mull the question over. "No I do not Mistress, but she is a rare treat so I would advise to not leave her unmarked or the next time I may not be so generous".

Waiting until he scurried off, Lilith breathed a deep sigh of relief. She did not like fighting with her own, however if necessary she would. Taking the girl by her hand she realised it was only going to be worse the farther down they went. They managed to get down the first five levels relatively unscathed which in most part was due to the respect the demons held for the Goddess.

There were seven levels of Hell. Each level you descended was hotter, dustier and more uncomfortable. Depending on your sin, depended on which level you were placed. The worse your sin, the lower your plane and the less resources you were afforded with harder work expected from you. Each level had its own demons. The demons were free to travel from plane to plane, some moving all around and some would pick a certain level to reside on. There were gatekeepers at every entryway so no soul could leave the level that they were placed. Except for the top level, once a soul was placed on their level, they were there for eternity.

On the sixth level was the alchemy lab where the creatures from nightmares were made came from. One such blob like creature was called a homunculus. These blob-like creatures had huge front teeth and attached to a soul to chew on them for hours on end. Not for any reason, just for the alchemist's entertainment. There were several decrepit alchemists on level six. They even gave Lilith the creeps and she was the mother of all demons. These little guys had green skin, sharp razor pointed fangs, black beady eyes and a head full of black oily knee length hair. She shoved Cecily under her robe when she walked past their lab, she did not want them to get their greasy mitts on her. They loved torturing fresh souls.

Cecily wasn't sure what was happening but knew if the Goddess was hiding her, there must be a good reason. She tried to shrink into herself and stay as small as she could, not wanting to cause trouble for her or Lilith. Each level they walked down was more stifling then the last. Not overbearing but it was definitely warm! She gasped when she felt a claw grab at her ankle. Lilith jerked her out of the hold and they both ran to the next level. Her ankle was throbbing but she was slowly realising that she needed to be thankful it was still attached!

Finally reaching the seventh level, Lilith slowed her pace down. She glanced back at the blood trail the girl was leaving by her injured foot. "Are you too injured to walk?".

"I am ok" Cecily assured her.

Lilith brought the girl through the cavern walking briskly trying to hide her excitement. This frail young girl was the answer to their dreams. Now just to get Lucian to believe it. He had been let down so many times he had stopped believing in the ancient scrolls and the prophecy of the collective with all its power and that it would ever come into play.

The girl showed no fear, fierce need for revenge fuelling her spirit. Trying to hide her smile, Lilith presented Cecily to the King of the Underworld.

Chapter 4

Cecily looked at him and her mouth dropped open. Never had she seen a man, no that's not quite right, a creature, no, hmm a God of such magnificence. He was absolutely, undeniably the most beautiful specimen of a male species she had ever seen. His burnt red skin was sexy as hell. He had two horns that came out of the top of his forehead that curled inward, almost like a ram's, he must have stood over nine feet tall with a sculpted body that could rival any shit-brick-house (she had to stifle a giggle at that one), his face was, well perfect. Black eyes that looked like they could pierce your soul and sensual full lips that held so many possibilities. His muscular arms ended with nice large hands that had long black pointed fingernails, his legs, well they were oddly unique. Starting out as normal muscled legs until the knee where they turned into legs that went into hooves. And god save her she thought it was sexy as hell. Again, at that thought she stifled a giggle. Realising he had no clothes on, her eyes zeroed in on his very well endowed cock that was hanging over a nice set of heavy hanging balls. He was huge! And he had a tail! Sexy. As. Fuck! Snapping out of it she realised she was just drooling over the devil.

"Yo…you are Lucifer" Cecily stuttered.

Lucian rolled his eyes. He hated the name the angels had given him and how the mortals had picked it up and ran with it. "My actual name is Lucian" he replied in his deep baritone voice.

"Please forgive me your Holiness" Cecily squeaked out.

Lucian looked at Lilith and they both bust out laughing. Cecily looked confused. Were they making fun of her?

"We are not laughing at you little one, it's just there is nothing holy down here. Please just call me Lucian".

"Wait did I say that out loud?" She looked confused.

Lilith looked chagrined "No we can hear what you are thinking".

Cecily turned as red as Lucian's normal colour. "So you both heard what I thought when I first saw him?".

Lucian winked at her. Cecily wanted to crawl under the rock by the cavern. Lilith laughed "I thought the same thing honey. He is one hot piece of meat".

Lucian shook his head. "Ok Lilith explain why we are here instead of doing our duties today".

"Master she is the one!" Lilith started excitedly "She will complete the collective and our power base will be forged. The war is brewing and we do not have time to wait. She has pure vengeance in her heart. She belongs with us" She finished triumphantly.

"She must have a choice" Lucian said softly knowing he was hurting his consort with the words. Sending her a message he told her she did good and he was proud of her, earning him a radiant smile from the Goddess. When they had combined their essence with each other, they had awakened new powers that had been foretold in the prophecies. Speaking to each other in their minds was one.

Cecily was confused once again. War? What choice? Why was she special? Was she able to get revenge? She would play her part if the people who destroyed her paid for what they did. She looked at the two of them knowing they heard her thoughts and she didn't need to say a word.

Lucian nodded his head "First your choice. It is not common knowledge to mortals that Earth is the middle ground between Heaven and Hell. I am offering you the chance to put your soul into another body on Earth so you can live your life out as you should have been allowed to. Your memory will be erased from this life. It is kind of what you consider reincarnation. Clean slate. Then you may have a chance to be reunited with your child in Heaven."

"No. If I do that then that means no revenge and I won't be able to help you. Right?"

Lucian tilted his head and studied the girl. He did feel the connection but he was not going to get his hopes up. "Why does that matter to you if you help us or not? What about your child?".

Cecily stared at him intently. In her heart, she knew she could never leave this place. She had felt so connected and in touch with herself as she did with these two. She would serve them to eternity if it would put a smile on his face.

"My child was not conceived of love. My only wish was to protect it which I failed to do, however I believe his soul will be protected now so I am at peace with that. Now I need a new purpose. Please let me serve you and help you" with that Cecily kneeled down in front of him.

Lilith watched the scene unfolding in front of her. She knew this was the answer they needed. She looked at Lucian and smiled and raised the girl up. "You will not be serving us little one, you will be serving by us, as one power base".

Cecily nodded trying to understand the power base part, looked at the pair of them and smiled wiping a sheen of sweat from her brow. There was the small matter of her revenge.

"I do not forget" Lucian responded.

She was never going to get used to that. She watched him in awe as he swirled his fingers and conjured up two beasts that she had only seen in comic books.

"These two hellhounds are at your service. They belong to you now to do your bidding. You are not physical on the Earth plane but they are. May I touch your forehead so I can see what transpired? It is ok to object" Lucian inquired.

She simply thought yes and he walked over to her putting a huge hand on her forehead. She could feel him in her mind scrolling through her memories. His expression never changed. When he was finished, he wiped his thumb across her forehead and she instantly felt a sense of calm. The hounds whined until she placed a hand on each of their heads.

"May I make a suggestion?"

"Of course" she replied.

"Send your hounds up to kill them. I can send some of my top-level demons with them. I know who they are, they will not get away. When they arrive down here, I will give you free reign with them for eternity" Lucian said satisfied he came up with a solution that would solve her problem and keep her with him. He wasn't sure after being allowed in her mind and her kneeling, which was sexy as fuck and something he planned to have her do more of, he could let her go even if she wanted to and contrary to popular belief, he gave choices.

Cecily thought that over. On the one hand, it kept her here happy at last for the first time but on the other hand, she wanted them to suffer like she had. She felt arms circle around her from behind and heard the Goddess whisper "Let us take care of you, beautiful" Cecily had never felt so loved and accepted.

"Ok" she whispered as the dogs stayed at her side growling viciously wanting to take care of their new master.

Lilith summoned Ravana, Asmodeus, and Orusula to their dominion. Cecily was shocked as the demons all started to come at her only being held off by the hellhounds. Lilith ran in front of her to explain before Lucian burnt them all to bits.

"I gathered you all here for a mission. There are six mortals I need slain on Earth. Their souls belong to Hell. Along with these two hellhounds, I am asking you three to do this mission for me".

Ravana, who was a demon king, kept glaring at Cecily who couldn't seem to stop staring at the demon's head as it kept morphing into multiple heads. Asmodeus, one of the seven princes of Hell, who was very sexy kept his mouth shut and head down not wanting to anger Lucian. Orusula, whose demon shape was that of a humongous pig, wasn't so smart. He snorted and charged at Cecily only to be grabbed by Lucian and have his body ripped in two by the devil's bare hands.

"Don't ever fuck with what is mine" Lucian ground out as he crushed the sow's face with his hoof.

"She isn't marked" Ravana muttered.

"What? You dare question me?" Fire was flaming around them.

"No Sir of course not" Ravana finally looked panicked "I was just stating the fact that she does not carry any of your markings".

Cecily looked between the group. The power that roiled off Lucian came in waves threatening to suffocate her. She felt herself falling to the ground when his strong arms scooped her up, keeping her from landing face first in the hot sand.

"Could you call your dogs off before they tear me apart?" He asked sounding pained.

Cecily looked over her shoulder and saw the hounds trying to tear chunks out of Lucian because he was keeping them from her. "Fluffy and Bunny!" She shouted "Down!" The hounds let their grips of his skin go and walked over to the wall waiting on their next command.

"I create your killer hellhounds and you name them Fluffy and Bunny? Really?" He looked like he couldn't decide if he was aggravated or amused.

Looking at the creatures in question, they had saliva mixed with the Dark Lord's blood dripping down their fangs. They stood about four feet tall and were snarling at everyone but her. She smiled at them.

"Are you ok?" They both asked each other in unison. Their connection was already showing which could be fatal for Cecily if he did not mark her soon. Putting her back down, Lucian turned to the remaining demons.

"The Goddess will open a portal for you to go to Earth to find these six individuals. The soul keeper will bring you back into this realm with their souls when you are finished. Do your mission and then come back. The war is brewing; I do not want to lose you needlessly" Lucian gave his orders.

Asmodeus finally spoke up "No disrespect my King, but why should we risk our lives in the mortal plane for that?". His disgust was evident as he pointed at Cecily.

Lucian's anger was palpable "That" He bit out growing darker by the minute "as you so eloquently put it, is the third to our triad. With her acceptance, the Collective will be complete and we will actually have a power grid that may stand a chance in this upcoming war against Heaven".

Flames were coming out of Lucian's mouth he was so angry at the insolence so Lilith decided to take over. "You will be avenging your new Princess of Hell. That is why you should gladly risk your life".

Cecily stood there with her guardian dogs not at all sure what to say. She was to be a Princess? She was so ordinary. The King of the Underworld and The Goddess made perfect sense but where would she fit into all of this? Without knowing what was happening, Lucian had grabbed her up again and pushed her behind him in a protective stance. Her hounds were right beside her. She peered around his broad body and was shocked at what she saw.

The demons, along with what looked like several dozen others, had dropped to their knees to pledge allegiance to the new Princess. Lilith smiled and put a calming hand on Lucian.

"Please forgive us and tell us what instructions you have" The prince asked.

After clearing out the other demons, it wasn't safe for too many people, the group sat down to decide the best methods of elimination. The hounds could rip their throats out, or better yet for the men, their groins but Cecily wanted them to pay for the depraved acts that were brought upon her. An eye for an eye.

"I am the prince of lust. I could gladly do to them exactly what they did to you" Asmodeus smiled enjoying the thought a little too much for Cecily's taste.

"I want them to suffer as I did. I trust you both to do what is needed and what you believe is necessary. Take enough time to make it hurt but not so much it endangers you" Cecily pleaded.

"And your mother?" Ravana asked.

"Make her watch the torture of all the men, including her husband then let my dogs rip her to pieces".

Cecily walked the hounds over to the demons and whispered in each animal's ear giving them her instructions. Satisfied she walked back over by Lucian.

I will be back my love, Lilith sent to him in his mind and took the group on the trek up to the top level.

"Please tell me about the marks everyone is talking about" Cecily asked when they were alone.

"They are marks of protection. Once marked it will show your standing in Hell. You will carry my protection so you never need to worry." He assured her.

"When will you do it?" she asked.

"It will hurt" The look of sadness on his face overwhelmed her. She walked over to him and shocked him climbing on his lap. Being courageous wasn't her strong suit but his lips were calling her name. She stuck her tongue out and licked his bottom lip causing him to sigh. Before she knew what was happening he had taken control and was devouring her mouth with the most passionate kind of kiss she had only read about in books.

Chapter 5

Lucian's whole body was tense. He was filled with so much desire for this little vixen. Staring down at her flushed face, she was breathing so hard just from his kiss. Furiously undressing her, he was sure he ripped an article of clothing or two, he didn't care. He just needed to see her perfect flesh.

Cecily couldn't catch her breath. When he started ripping her clothes off, she almost orgasmed from that. She knew her desire would be evident when he felt how wet she was. Aw holy hell he was putting that tongue on her nipples. His tongue was so warm and add the tips of his teeth scraping across, she moaned out his name.

Lucian was so hard he thought he was going to explode. He was too large for her to take right now. It would take time and the connection for her to be able to sheath him. He flipped her over on her hands and knees rubbing his erection on her clit stimulating her. She screamed out from the simple ministrations and he watched in wonder as she had her first orgasm in his arms.

Cecily felt a hundred different emotions and none all at the same time. She had never felt so good. She had just recovered and she felt Lucian's thick finger slide inside of her. He added a second one stretching her a bit but the pain soon turned to immense pleasure. She was riding his fingers while feeling him exploring her body with his tongue, his other hand, and at one point she was positive he had brought his tail around to squeeze her nipples.

Lucian felt her pussy clamp down on his fingers as he found her spot deep inside her. She was absolutely beautiful writhing all over him. He needed to cum and he needed it now. Hoping he wouldn't frighten her he fisted his cock with one hand and pumped the shaft fiercely to relieve the pressure.

Cecily was a big bowl of dreamy bliss. She turned around to tell him and saw the most erotic sight. He was pleasuring himself. She watched with wild abandon, turning herself around to get a closer view.

Lucian couldn't stop if he wanted to. He hadn't expected her to turn around and watch him. That made him harder if possible. Within minutes he was spurting white jets of cum all over himself. Ready to get up to wipe it off, he never expected Cecily to start cleaning him with her tongue. She paid special attention to his balls nipping at them when she was done.

"I love your balls" She said lazily still holding them in her hands.

Trying not to chuckle he said, "I see that".

He felt Lilith walk in and turned around to smile at his consort inviting her to join. Dispensing of her clothes, she walked over to join. Cecily was adjusting to the situation better than they would have ever hoped for. The power was humming in the air so strong Lilith felt it caressing her body. Not waiting she climbed in the middle of the couple, reaching out to slide a hand on each of their chests spreading the lust pheromones she emitted.

Lucian growled and grabbed his Goddess and thrust his tongue in so deep in her mouth she didn't know where she began and he ended. "Bend over" He commanded.

Lilith grinned and turned around to gladly stick her ass up in the air for him when she noticed Cecily looking lost. Reaching her hand out she brought her over lying her down on her back kissing her softly on the mouth. Cecily gasped at the sensual kiss the Goddess had given her. She was now laid in front of the her, legs splayed wide open as the Goddess was offering herself to the Beast.

Lucian was about to cum all over himself when he saw Lilith dip her head in between Cecily's legs. Cecily's gasps of appreciation brought him almost over the edge. He rammed into the Goddess taking no prisoners staring Cecily in the eyes. All three of them were like a well-oiled machine moaning and moving in time. Cecily almost lost it completely when she felt herself being impaled and realised it was his tail. Holy shit his tail was a fucking genius! She heard him snort and realised he could hear her thought. She could feel her inner walls clamping down and all the sudden Lilith bit her clit, Cecily exploded on them both. At the same time Lilith was riding Lucian's cock and they were climaxing with her. Cecily thought the orgasm must have been earth shattering since her body seemed to go into a stasis and there were colours streaming everywhere through her mind. When she finally came down, it seemed like hours later and when she opened her eyes, everything looked surreal.

Lucian and Lilith could feel the power flowing through them. The transformation was complete. The three of them now had connected and the prophecy had come true and the Collective's Power was one to be reckoned with. Cecily however was transformed and at first they were unsure her small body could handle the immense power that now swirled through it. Neither one imagined the changes that would overcome her. When Cecily finally woke up, her once ice blue eyes were now coal black orbs, her blonde hair had grown another twelve inches and had turned a dark violet shade. When she stood up on wobbly legs, that was the most remarkable change, she stood two feet taller than her previous five-foot frame and she was covered in Lucian's protection markings.

Remarkable Lucian thought. She is breath-taking Lilith sent back to him.

"Thank you" Cecily replied.

Lucian gasped. You can hear us? Cecily nodded and smiled. Lilith clicked her fingers and instantly she and Cecily were covered in silk gowns as the demons came back with Cecily's hounds and the condemned souls.

Lucian stood in front of the souls at his full height while they whimpered back. "Kneel before the Depraved Collective! When you come before the King of the Underworld, The Goddess and mother of all demons Lilith and the Princess of Hell, you always kneel!" He bellowed so loud that flames shot from his mouth. They instantly dropped down to their knees.

"Cecily I will assign them to their space for you if that is ok my Princess" Lucian looked at her.

She beamed at him nodding her head as her mother looked at her slack jawed realising it was her daughter who was the new Princess. "Yes my Liege, Thank you".

"Take all the men to the torture room and the woman to my fiery pit" He ordered Asmodeus and Ravana

Fluffy and Bunny ran to Cecily's side happy to be back with their master.

"Tonight is for celebration. Tomorrow we start to plan and prepare for this war we know is coming" Lucian grabbed their hands and took his women properly, again and again.

The End

Emery LeeAnn lives in Ohio with her family. Besides being addicted to coffee, she is a true believer that variety adds spice to your life. Writing in every genre gives her the variety she craves. Her characters like to invade her mind every hour of the day usually waking her up in the middle of the night. Loving the dark and gray side of things, she is exploring her passion with the written word. There are many wonders to come from her in her twisted Wonderland… stick around you may find you enjoy her special brand of torture

Facebook:
https://www.facebook.com/authoremerylee13
Goodreads:
https://www.goodreads.com/author/show/16160108.Emery_LeeAnn
Amazon Author Page: https://goo.gl/dCi8Q6
Twitter: https://twitter.com/EmeryLeeann

CIRCUS BE DAMNED
By
Crystal Barnard

Marley looked over at her best friend with a serious glare in her eye. They'd known each other since kindergarten, so Jake was used to her looks and eye rolls by now. "I cannot believe I let you talk me into coming here. This place is a serious freak show!"

"Well duh, it is called 'The Freak Show,' you know, Mar. Come on, you can enjoy one night of fun with your best friend before you move, can't you? No more whining, now, let's go."

Marley looked at Jake, who had so nicely dragged her to this hell on earth he called a 'circus'. The place looked like it should be condemned, seriously. The building was falling apart, and they were lucky the walls hadn't fallen in yet. Moss covered the walls and not to mention the stench of rot that seemed to waft from every corner of. How was this place still running?

They stuck to the back roads, driving for an hour to get there, and so far, Marley was not impressed. Begrudgingly, she followed her friend to this warehouse looking, moss covered old building to see what the fuss was all about.

Pictures of clowns lined the outside of the place. Their freakishly smiling faces and grinning toothy stares that called to every bone in her body to run away. In the middle of those were pictures of balloons, and laughing kids all over the walls, streamers and glitter had been splashed in the oddest places; as if to try and make the place feel cheery, yet none of this made her feel more comfortable being there.

They made their way to the tall oak doors, where an extremely disturbing clown holding a floppy, deflated balloon, stood smiling and waiting for them. His hand moved in a queen like wave, fingers held together as that toothy grin from the posters, stared back at them. Jake approached the window off to the side and purchased their tickets.

Marley leaned in close to Jake's ear, "Um, have you noticed how there is like, nobody here except the extremely depressing, creepy clown? I mean, where are all the other customers? Where are the people who live here? I have yet to see one person even as much as look out their window." Marley was starting to freak out a little, but it was true, since they had been here, nobody had been seen at all.

Jake tried to calm her down. "Mar, relax, it's ten at night. Maybe everyone is just sleeping. This place is open late, so most likely they've all seen it before and we are the only ones here. It works out even better though, now there's nobody to get in our way!"

He chuckled but it did nothing to make her feel better. As they were walking towards the large doors the clown jumped in front of them, shocking Marley and making her stumble backwards. Her skin crawled as he thrust his hand towards her, clutching the string of the deflated balloon as if it were a prize.

Finally, it looked her right in the face and opened its mouth. "Have as much fun as you can, dear, it will all be over much too soon"

Its breathe was horrible, smelling like rotten food and something Marley couldn't quite place. Slapping a hand over her mouth, she pushed past the clown as fast as she could, her free hand grabbing for the door and pushing as hard as she could, her shoulder pressing against it for assistance. The worn, brass handle creaked under her hand as she pushed against it and rushed inside, Jake laughing and following closely behind her.

The first thing she saw made her jump back so fast that she slammed her back into the doors, making them slam shut. When she realized what she was looking at, she felt silly. It was a rusted old mirror covered in mud and dirt, and what made her jump was her own reflection.

Jake laughed beside her and took hold of her arm, leading her forward to enter the hallway.

"God, why are we even here, Jake? I mean seriously! This place is giving me the complete creeps!" Marley felt like she was being zapped with a joy buzzer. It felt like a million bugs crawling over her flesh at the same time, raising goose bumps along her arms, her hairs standing on end. She had a feeling this place was bad news, and just wanted to get it over with and go home.

Jake gave her what she called his 'serious' look. Eyes narrowed, lips pressed tight together. It usually meant she was going to get a lecture, so she braced herself for the coming words. "Marley, you are always so suspicious of everything. Why can't you just have fun? I mean it's only a carnival. What can go wrong?"

Marley let out a deep sigh and took his hand, following him down the narrow hallway to whatever monstrosities lay ahead waiting for them. The hall began to narrow the further they walked, as they were slowly pressed closer together, Marley just figured this was all part of the 'fun', so to speak.

They continued to walk further until they came to a dark room, only a sliver of light streamed across the floor from a crack in the right-side wall. Looking around, Marley could barely see her hand in front of her face. She was starting to get nervous when suddenly, the lights flashed on. In the center of the room was a large sectioned off area and in the middle, was a two-headed sheep.

Marley had to laugh at how nervous she was over something so silly, but just as she started to relax, the damn thing moved. "What the hell?????" Marley shrieked, gripping Jakes arm so tight she was leaving half-moon welts in his skin from her nails. She heard Jake gasp as he saw it too, but it was his reaction after, that shocked her.

"Oh, that is too cool…. it's automated, isn't that neat, Mar?"

Automated? She hadn't thought of that. Of course it would be! It was probably set to move the minute anyone stepped in the room, making it more realistic. "Oh God, I freaked out. I thought it was real! God, that scared me." Marley said, her voice still a little shaky.

She walked closer to the sheep, but when it started moving towards her in return she decided she'd had enough of this room and pulled Jake towards the door.

The soft bleating of the sheep, trailing to silence as they made their way out.

As they walked through the hallways, she looked at the walls, covered in light up boxes with things inside them. Small and large, they all had some kind of freaky insect or animal inside.

One had a snake with 2 rattlers; another had a bat with the wings in gold. Marley was starting to think things might actually be normal here until she saw the next box. Inside this box was the freakiest thing she had seen so far. It was a small kitten, but the worst part was it had huge paws and 3 eyes. Small wings were jutting out from its back as if it was going to take off any minute.

Black fur coated its body, with a tail that ended in spikes.

Her eyes widened in shock as she looked it over, her mind tried to focus, force her to believe it was fake, but something pulled at her. Some part of her mind that was starting to think this place was more than they thought.

"Jake, do you see this?" She asked him, her voice laced with fear.

"Sure, isn't it neat? Do you think it's real? Or did they make it that way to look cool?"

Jake's laugh did nothing but fill her with dread, something was not right here. Marley kept moving along, the light up boxes getting weirder and weirder. Finally, she had enough when she looked in the last box and all she saw was red. The glass was broken, as if someone has smashed it in and taken whatever was inside, cutting their hand in the process.

The smell of copper assaulted her nose as she looked closer, trying to figure out if it was something that broke out, or someone that broke in to steal whatever monstrosity had been in the box.

Why would someone steal anything from here? She couldn't help but wonder what had been in the box that was so interesting, but the nameplate had been ripped off, so there was no way of knowing.

Making her way further, her anxiety reached a new peak, as the walls and ceiling seemed to narrow in on her. Marley finally found her way out which led into yet another big room with a sectioned off center. She grabbed Jake's arm and yanked him forward, pushing him into the room ahead of her, just in case.

Things seemed to be harmless, as it were. In the center of the room was a rocking chair, and in that chair, was the oddest-looking doll Marley had ever seen. It looked like a small child, but had horns protruding from the sides of its head, and the legs looked wrong; bent the wrong way, almost backwards, like some sort of goat child. Marley had to laugh at herself, thinking how ridiculous that sounded. Yeah right, goat child? Where the hell had that come from? She watched way too many horror movies.

She started to walk towards it, but when the chair started to rock and the head swiveled sideways to look at them, she caught sight of the eyes. Black hollows, as if the eyeballs themselves had been plucked out, and only the shells left behind. Marley decided she wanted nothing more than to get the hell out of the room and pulled Jake forward.

"Geeze, slow down, Mar, or we are going to miss the whole thing!" Jake complained, while rubbing his arm. "I swear, you almost pulled my arm out of the socket back there!"

"I'm sorry Jake, but I swear it moved, and it wasn't automated. Nothing happened until we got

151

closer, then the chair rocked and the damned thing turned its head right towards us as we walked. The eyes…the eyes were gone Jake. How are you not seeing any of this? Something is seriously not right with this place!" Marley was losing it now and just wanted to leave, but it was clear that was not going to happen, as Jake seemed to be loving it here. So, she did what any good friend would do. She sighed heavily, letting her shoulders sag, and followed him through the doorway to the next area.

To be honest, what could go wrong? That's what she kept repeating in her head, over and over, the same words playing across her mind like a broken record. Maybe if she repeated it enough, she'd actually start to believe it herself.

The next few rooms were nothing big, a few dolls; a raggedy Ann, a couple baby dolls in strollers, some more mirrors and the same boxes all along the walls. The same trinkets and fake, misshapen creatures in every lit-up box along the wall. Nothing that unsettled her or stood out as spooky, but Marley was still on edge. Something was still tugging at her, telling her that something was wrong. She couldn't shake the feeling that something very bad was going to happen.

This place just did not sit well with her, and suddenly she started to smell something off. It smelt like mold but stronger. Her nose scrunched up and she gagged, as the smell drew closer. It almost surrounded her, as if something…or someone…was walking around her, wearing the stench as a cologne. It was an almost, acidic smell. Sour, but at the same time, deeply pungent. There was just something in the air that set her off completely. The hair on her arms stood on end, goose bumps raced across her skin as well.

There was a slight chill in the air as if someone had opened a window, yet the room was a complete box.

Marley rubbed her arms and looked around her, she saw nothing out of the ordinary, and yet she could not shake that eerie feeling. She decided just to stick close to Jake and ignore it. Maybe things would calm down and everything would all be alright.

The next room was actually something straight out of a horror movie, dark and mysterious. The lights flickered on and off, making everything seem even spookier. There were gravestones all along the floor leading from one door to another, and what looked like open plots behind some of them. Leaves and garbage was thrown all over the place. The smell that she'd gotten earlier, hit her like a ton of bricks. Shoving her hand in a pocket, she grabbed the hem of her jacket, yanking it up to her mouth and breathing into the material, praying it would stop some of the smell.

Well, that explained the bad smell, but what about the chill? The leaves and stuff were blowing around the floor, as if there was a wind; yet there was no window at all, they were in a complete closed off room.

Marley grabbed Jake's arm and tried to pull him to the door but he wasn't moving. She pulled a bit harder, afraid of hurting him but nothing. Marley was starting to panic, what was wrong with him? "Jake, what the hell is wrong with you?" Marley yelled.

He suddenly snapped out of whatever it was that held his attention and turned towards her. "What? Sorry, I didn't hear you. I was captivated by how real they made this all look! I swear I thought I was in a real graveyard for a minute." Jake chuckled at how real everything seemed to him.

Marley thought she was going to be sick. How in the hell could he find this funny? They were standing in a place that looked like a bona-fide graveyard with open plots and he was laughing. She had had more than enough of this place and was ready to leave, if only she could convince Jake of that, and find the way out.

As Marley was searching for the next door to move on, she saw something in one of the open plots. Looking closer, she could swear she was seeing the eerie clown from the entrance, but looking closer it was just a doll. A very gruesome look alike doll that smelled just as bad. That same sinister sneer was painted across its face, the balloon tied around one hand as if an exact replica of the clown outside, just smaller. Shivering, Marley rubbed over her arms again, before reaching for Jake.

Marley grabbed Jake's arm and pulled him from whatever trance had him staring into the gravesite. As they rushed back to the hallway and out of the ominous room, far away from the doll, Marley finally started to feel the chill leave her bones.

Not that the hallway was any better, but at least she couldn't see that doll. The halls were lined with more boxes, only these ones were different. These ones didn't have cute little oddities in them. These had body parts.

Marley was getting wigged out now. Some of the boxes had eyeballs, and others had fingers. At some point, she even gave up trying to figure out what random body part has been squashed into the boxes. She kept thinking to herself, What the fuck is this place? She had to get the hell out of this nightmare and fast. "Jake, this is so messed up. We need to get out of here now!"

"Seriously, Mar, you are freaking out over nothing. It's all fake! Really, do you think they would still be in business if this stuff was real?"

Marley wasn't sure what was real or fake any more, and she really did not want to sit around waiting to find out. As if she had spoken in her head too soon, the chill disappeared completely, being replaced by pure heat. She was finding it difficult to get a deep breath into her lungs, without the acrid stench or heat, filling her lungs and making her heave. If she didn't know any better, she'd have thought they had left the fairgrounds completely, and stepped into Hell itself.

As they came up on the next room, Marley could swear she heard laughing. Not a good kind of laugh either, but the kind that sent fear straight through to your bones. The kind of fear causing you to want to curl into a ball with your flashlight and teddy bear, eyes squeezed tight as if you could make whatever bad thing it was, disappear by counting to ten. It was as if the room was in surround sound, and the laugh was filling up the entire space. It filled her with fear and a feeling of death. Nothing good could ever come from a laugh like that. It was reminiscent of nails scratching on a chalk board.

They kept walking, since going forward seemed to be the only way out of the hell hole they were in. Every step she took increased that sense of foreboding. Marley couldn't shake the feeling that something ominous was in store, and the laughing over the speaker was not helping to make things any better.

She could have sworn she was hearing whispering too. Like someone was trying to tell her something but she couldn't make out what the voice was saying. This place was insane, and she would be damned if she was going to get caught here a minute longer than she needed to.

"Ok, Jake, listen. We must finish here and get the hell out of here. I really do not like this place. Please, can we just go?" Marley looked her friend straight in the eyes and begged for all she was worth. Jake sighed deeply, and then nodded his head.

Finally, all they had to do was find the way out and she would be free of this insanity. They turned a corner into the next room and Marley's stomach fell to the floor. Clowns were everywhere in the room. Dolls, littered the floor from one end of the room to the other. Their beady eyes stared at her with faces all painted up like a crack whore on a bad trip. Their lips, bright red as if they had been sucking on blood all day and night.

God, how she hated clowns. Why was it always clowns? It wasn't until she got further into the room that she noticed him, it was the clown from the entrance. His orange hair was bunched up and filthy, with leaves stuck all in it and clumps of mud and dirt.

He was holding something in his right hand. From a glance, it looked like a red balloon, but when she looked closer Marley could see it was bright red cotton candy, at least she hoped it was. She didn't really want to get close enough to him to find out otherwise. She grabbed Jake's arm and pulled him so fast into the next room she was almost positive she had dislocated it this time. Cursing, Jake yanked his arm from her grip and rubbed at his shoulder, his eyes locking to hers as an angry frown crossed his face.

"Marley, what the fuck, seriously, are you ok?"

"No, I am not ok, Jake! This place is really fucked up, and that clown is seriously freaking me the hell out! Did you see what he was holding? This place is insane!"

The laughing started again and all Marley could do was stop dead in her tracks. It sounded so loud this time, as if it was right in the room with them, whatever it was.

She grabbed her ears and tried to block it out, but it was all around her. That damn cackling, as if a pack of hyenas were in the room and dying of laughter. Not to mention the millions of nails being dragged across the chalkboard. Her skin crawled with shivers at every noise.

Suddenly, the room began to fill with the most disgusting odor Marley had ever smelled. It was rancid and over powering, making her cough and choke. She took a deep breath and gagged. "What the fuck is that smell?" she asked, covering her mouth with her sleeve. Not that it was doing much good.

The room smelt of, God only knew. It had the smell of a dirty bathroom, mixed with a bar room floor complete with vomit and spilt beer. It only became worse the closer to the middle of the room they got.

The smell of rotten eggs joined in the mix, something acidic and almost copper like, had her eyes watering, and her throat closing off. She didn't dare drag a deep breath, afraid of tasting, whatever the hell it was in the room.

Marley dared to look up and almost got sick herself on what she saw.

The room was once white, or she thought it was white. Who could tell through the red splattered all over the walls? Or the chunks of what could only be described as meat hanging off walls and other things and strewn all over the room?

She couldn't stop gagging, and yet, she also couldn't stop looking around. She had a really bad feeling that this was not part of the show. She looked around for Jake and panicked when she couldn't find him.

Her eyes scanned the room, not daring to move from where she stood, just searching everything and everywhere her eyes could see, her voice strained and panicked as she screamed repeatedly. "Jake where the fuck are you? Seriously! I am freaking out here, please answer me!"

Marley was really scared now. She couldn't get away from the smell, and now Jake was missing. What the hell was going on?!

She started to walk slowly around the room trying to see if she could find out where the smell was coming from, and everywhere she turned, it only seemed to get worse. By now, Marley was in complete panic mode. She was sweating so much her shirt was soaked through, and her stomach was killing her from the gagging and heaving she was doing from the smell. Her stomach felt like an empty pit, and everywhere she turned, she was trying as hard as she could, not to step on or in something, that looked even remotely out of place. Not that that was easy in this room.

Worst of all she was terrified something had happened to Jake.

Suddenly, the lights went out and Marley stopped, frozen in place. Her breath stilled in her throat, her heart hammered against her chest like the rapid beat of a drum. She gripped her chest, as if wrapping her fingers, imaginarily around the organ, could make it silent, hushing her location from anyone, or anything, in the room.

She was afraid to move, hell, she would have stopped breathing too if she thought it would help her stay unnoticed. But she wanted to stay alive more.

That horrible laughing continued, her ears burning with the sound, as she focused on slowing her breathing, swallowing back the whimpers of fear that threatened to leak through her lips.

The laughing was getting closer, and now she could hear the voice again too. It was whispering things, and as the sound grew louder and closer she could make out what it was saying. The words weren't comforting, if anything she was terrified. Every syllable crept along her skin like pure terror. Her arms littered with goose bumps at every word spoken.

"Told you to have fun didn't I, little girl? I told you it would all be over soon, and now it will be. Are you ready to have some real fun?"

What the fuck was that supposed to mean? Marley thought to herself. "Who are you and what the fuck do you want with us?! Where the fuck is Jake, what have you done with him? Please…let us out of here, I promise we won't tell anyone." Marley screamed into the air, her voice squeaking out as fear coated it, the high-pitched sounds bouncing off the walls.

She almost prayed she was going crazy and was hearing things. Damn near wished that this was all just in her head, even as the heat in the room heightened, breaking a light sweat across her brow as the voice answered her, "I want to play with you. Have you ever wondered what you look like…from the inside? Want to find out?"

The voice drifted off and suddenly the room was filled with a booming laugh. It shook the walls and filled Marley with complete dread. This was not what she had in mind for the night. God, all she wanted was one last night with her best friend, before she moved. To have fun again like they used to. She never imagined their last night together, would be pure Hell, literally if the heat and stench in the room was any indication of where she truly was. Never the less, she had to find Jake, stay alive, and get fuck out of there. No matter what it took.

Squaring her shoulders and biting back the fear in her gut, she began looking around for anything that could be used as a weapon, I mean, this was a freak show place, there had to be something in here she could use, right?

That was when she saw it. There was a doll in the corner and it was holding a knife. She just had to hope it was real and not a prop.

Marley made her way over to the doll and quickly took the knife from its hand, prying open the tiny fingers. The damned thing had it gripped tight, as if it too, was afraid of whatever the hell had them locked up in here. Lifting the knife, she ran a finger along the blade before testing it on the doll to make sure it was real, her lips curled at the corners as it sliced through the rubber arm.

Marley watched the arm fall to the floor and couldn't help but smile wider. God, she hated clowns.

She tucked the knife into the waistband of her pants being extremely careful not to cut herself, and started to make her way to the next room, carefully avoiding everything unsavory looking on the floor and walls. She didn't know what she was going to find in there, all she knew was that she had to find Jake and then get the hell out of there, alive.

As soon as she turned the corner the smell overwhelmed her. The room was pitch black, not even a strip of light came through the cracks. Not to mention it reeked of rotten meat that had been left out in the heat too long. There was a sweet hint to it as well, kind of like, sugar, that had been soaked in honey. It was unlike anything she had ever really smelt before and she never wanted to smell it again.

The gagging returned, her throat convulsing over and over, nothing leaving her but dry heaves, but it was enough to make her eyes water and her chest ache with the actions. She covered her mouth with her shirt and walked further into the room.

As she stepped blindly through the room, her feet bumped into something and a low groan filtered to her ears. Leaning down she felt around for what it was, her hands were getting all wet and sticky. She didn't even want to know what it was all over the floor. Hearing the groan again, she turned her head towards where it was coming from. Keeping her voice low she called out softly. "Jake? Jake, is that you?" she whispered.

When the groan came again she could have sworn she heard a faint yes and quickly made her way towards the voice. She couldn't move as fast as she wanted to because there were things all over the floor, in all shapes and sizes, blocking her way. Her feet kept bumping into things as she moved; kicking them and hearing them roll across the floor. She didn't want to think of what it could be; she just prayed it wasn't another doll...or possible worse.

As soon as she got to where the groaning was coming from, she knelt down and felt around, finally coming to what she hoped was his shoe. When she felt it move, she knew he was still alive.

Moving her hand quicker, she followed his leg up stopping at his ankles. It felt as if he was tied up, but who the hell would have done that? Marley took the knife out from behind her and very carefully cut the ropes at his ankles, then trailed her hand up to try and find his wrists. Sure enough, they were bound too, so she slowly cut through them as well, freeing him, careful not to nick his flesh.

"Jake, it's ok I'm here and I am going to get us the hell out of here, but I need you to stay here till I can find a way out. I promise I will come back for you!" she whispered to him, hoping he would be ok if she left him alone.

A soft groan was the only response she got as she pushed herself up.

Finally on her feet again, she started walking into the next room, being very careful of where she stepped to avoid tripping and landing on her ass.

The last thing she needed, was a welt on her ass, as well as being caught by a deranged clown. Once again, her head whipped around, trying desperately to search in the dark, as that damned laugh sounded off again.

The laugh was so close now. It was as if it was coming from the next room, along with the rotten meat smell that was seriously overpowering. Her nostrils were getting plugged up because of it, and she could taste it in her mouth. It tasted like pennies and mud. She had only ever tasted this once before when she had cut her lip. Remembering that, Marley suddenly had a very awful feeling about what she would find in the next room.

As soon as she entered the next room, a feeling of dread was all over her. Her body felt heavy, and her eyes were starting to droop but she knew she had to stay awake. She fought herself to keep going; she knew she had to get them out of there, no matter what happened.

Standing there, she felt something on her legs. Slimy and cold. It was wrapping itself around them trying to trip her and knock her down. Marley kicked out with one foot, catching whatever it was and making it squeal.

The sound grated her nerves, it was as if she'd kicked an animal, but it sure as hell didn't feel like one.

Without warning, whatever it was, lashed out at her leg, and she felt something sharp rake across her calf. The next thing she knew, something warm was dripping down her leg. She could only assume it was blood, the scent of copper hitting her nose confirming what she thought. No sooner had this happened that she felt a hand on her shoulder, and another encircle her waist.

Her body went completely still, her heart pounding, breath immediately going shallow in fear. She could smell his breath as he leaned forward and all she wanted to do was vomit. The smell was so horrid, as if he had been eating dead rats and gargling with blood.

Panic set in and Marley tried to twist away, she tried to fight and get free, but his hold was so strong. His arm wrapped tighter around her waist, the hand at her shoulder slowly making its way to her throat, fingers teasing over the main vein.

"Mmm, I like when they fight," he jeered. "I told you it would all be over soon."

His hot breath slunk across her flesh like a warm brand; shivers crawled along her arms, making her tremble.

Marley struggled with all she had; her hand finally wriggling between their bodies, gripping the handle. When she was finally able to reach the knife at her back, she slowly took it out, trying not to make any sudden moves. The lights suddenly came back on and what Marley saw made her head drop forward vomit spewing from her mouth, adding to the already mess on the floor.

The room was stacked with bodies. Every corner of the room had at least ten bodies in it, all decaying and all propped up as if they were at a party. Hats placed on their heads, and noise makers shoved between their lips, as if at some kind of macabre birthday shindig. Marley couldn't help but tear up. All those lives, lost, all because they wanted to have a little fun. Well she would be damned if she was going to let this continue. This had gone on long enough. Mustering all the strength she could find, Marley lunged herself forward, taking the clown down with her, and managed to loosen his grip from around her waist.

The second his hand loosened, she wrenched his fingers with her other hand, the scream ripping from his painted mouth, as the pain lanced through his hand.

Pushing herself to her feet, she quickly jumped up and ran. She had no idea where she was going; she just knew she needed to put some distance between them to get the upper hand.

She saw something, walking towards her on the filthy floor that made her freeze. It was so small, and if she hadn't been looking she would have missed it. It stopped right in front of her to make sure that she saw it. It looked like a puppy. Small and fluffy, with big bright eyes that blinked up to her as if it was lost, only there was something seriously amiss. It's nose, or what looked more like a snout, was twisted and it looked almost as though the teeth were on top of it. Instead of paws it had feet with claws, resembling the talons of an eagle, long and extremely sharp. That must have been what cut her before, but what the fuck was it?

"Do you like my pet?" the clown taunted her, his voice almost parent like, as he spoke of the bundle of razors and fluff on the floor. "He used to be all cooped up in a box in the hallway, but there was no way I could leave him like that! He's just a baby! How could anyone want to keep him locked up in a box for show? He needed room to play, to feed!"

Marley suddenly remembered the light box on the wall, the one that was smashed. So that was what was in it. "Well, he certainly does look well fed," Marley responded. "But, too bad it won't be alive much longer!"

Having said that, her head turned towards the creature, her lips curling up as she growled low. Immediately it took off, it's little claws scrambling for purchase in the floor to move quicker. Marley took off after the thing managing to catch it by its back paw and smashed in into the ground. Hearing a pop, she watched its head lurch forward, blood splash all over her and the floor, it's legs kicking with a high-pitched shriek, before finally stilling in her hand. It's head and neck going limp and hanging forward; in that moment, she knew the thing was dead.

She heard a loud scream mixed with a roar from behind her, too terrified to look back.

Marley tried to take off again, only to fall on her face as the clown reached forward and grabbed her ankle, slamming her face into the ground.

"You really fucked up now, girl! I loved that little guy, he was my bud! Now you have to pay for killing him!"

Marley tried to roll over, but was pinned, the heavy weight of the clown bearing down on her, making it hard to breath. All she could think of was getting free and gutting this fucking clown like a fish.

The weight of the knife in her hand, and the feel of the handle, reminded her she was still holding the blade. She had been knocked down, yet somehow managed not to lose her grip. The clown had yet to realize she had it. She knew she just had to wait for the right moment, needing to get onto her back so that she could use it. She just had to wait.

Feeling something wet on her face, she realized the clown was licking her. "My God you taste good. It seems such a shame to waste such a tasty meal by letting you rot here."

She scrunched her nose, that foul stench of death floating around her as his rancid tongue again, licked across her cheek.

The clown slowly started to get up. He grabbed her arms and started to pull them towards her back, pain marring her face as he tugged one way, and she tugged the other, trying to keep the knife concealed. Finally wrenching hard enough, she managed to get her one arm free, slicing upwards with the blade. He jumped back letting go of her other arm as the knife slashed through his outfit and into his stomach.

Marley whipped around and watched as red blossomed on the clown's outfit, quickly spreading in size from a small patch to coating half of his gut. His face twisted in anger, as he bellowed loudly lunging forward, reaching for Marley. She took a huge step back, almost falling over, but managed to catch herself and stepped away quickly, the blade still clutched tightly in her grip and held in front of her, ready to swing again.

She turned around so fast that she almost lost sight of him. However, out of the corner of her eye she saw a blur and whipped in that direction. Raising the knife, she brought it down, just as his hand reached forward. He screamed so loud that the windows shook as the knife cut deep into his wrist, severing his hand. Marley watched as it fell to the floor and she kicked it away from her with disgust.

Now the clown was really pissed off and lunged towards Marley who was trying to figure out what to do next. She turned and tried to run but something tripped her up and she went flying into the pile of bodies in the corner. Marley gagged as they fell around her, blood dripping down her arms and face, cold and sticky.

She tried to get herself up, but her hand fell into one of the dead, breaking through the skin and sinking into the stomach. Marley screamed as she felt the insides ooze through her fingers. The smell was overwhelming her, making her want to vomit, though nothing came from her heaving and gagging. She wasn't even sure what she was feeling; it felt like her hand was in a bowl of rotting spaghetti and meatballs.

She yanked her hand free, blood and debris flying everywhere. Reaching for the floor, her hand slid around, as if on a slip and slide, until she finally found a dry spot to get herself to her feet. The whole time the clown was looking wildly around the room trying to find her, his face twisted in pure rage.

Marley tried to make her way quietly out the door but something touched her leg and she squealed out loud, quickly slapping her hand over her mouth before instantly regretting the move. The clown whipped around, anger all over its pasty white face, drool dangling from his lips as he roared maniacally.

She tried to run, but he was faster than her. He was on her in a heartbeat, dropping her to the floor under him. She tried to squirm away, but he was too heavy on top of her. Doing the only thing she could think of, she twisted her arm around, and still holding the knife, slashed it across his throat.

His blood was warm as it ran down her arm, the spray from the gash covering her chest and face. She closed her eyes, forcing her mouth shut, despite the burning urge to scream. She heard him gasp as he took what were to be his last breaths, then his body twitched and fell on top of her. Red crimson blood ran down her body and onto the floor. She was covered in it, but all she could think, was that it was over and she was glad.

Getting herself up off the floor, she tucked the knife back into the back of her pants, where it was before and with blood dripping all over the place, she wiped her eyes with the bottom of her shirt, clearing her vision as best she could, before taking off to find her friend. It dripped down her face, covering her hands and chest as she ran as fast as she could back to Jake. She had to make sure he was ok and both get the hell out of there.

"Jake, are you ok? I'm coming! It's over! I stopped him!" She called out. She returned to the room she left him in, but there was no sign of him at all! Only a large pool of blood and what looked to be a mangled body of a small animal that had been butchered, chunks were in a pile making it look like some sort of oddly plated meal. But no sign of Jake at all, just a smear of blood in a trail leading through a hidden door.

Marley followed that trail, slowly pushing the door open. Hearing it creak loudly, she slowed her movements, not wanting to be seen or heard. Making her way through the opening, she could see a small light and heard moans. She knew Jake had to be somewhere close, but was afraid of what she might find. Finally entering the room, she saw what could only be described as sheer horror, every child and adult's nightmare.

The room was completely red, streaks of every shade splattered all over the walls. Jake was slumped in a corner. Blood was gushing out of his wrists and chest, and standing in front of him was the ugliest clown she had ever seen. His face was painted in green and red with tiles on it to look like scales. Bright red hair fanned out around his head making it look like he had been wrapped in blood red cotton candy. His teeth looked razor sharp, pointy and dripping with blood and flesh.

He smelled like something that had just come out of a barge filled with garbage and fish guts, rancid and decaying. Black wings spread out from his back and in his hands, he held a human head dripping blood. The flesh was ragged around the base, as if he had just been snacking on the damned thing.

There was no hope for Jake, he was gone. As a tear came to her eye she knew this thing had to be stopped so nobody else had to go through this again. She looked around the room, being armed only with a knife she knew she had to think bigger. She had to finish this, once and for all. She saw a gas hose in the corner of the room and remembered the lighter in her pocket from their bonfire last night.

Marley crept over to the corner, trying to be as quiet as possible so the thing wouldn't notice her at all. When she made it to the hose, she used the knife to puncture a hole in it. Hearing the gas hiss out, she knew there was no way she was getting out of here alive. She had accepted that fate. If these things were stopped, it was all for the best.

She stood up and proudly made her way back to her fallen friend when she heard the growl behind her. The thing had finally noticed her and was making its way to where she stood. Her smile stretched from ear to ear as she knew it would never make it to where she was and pulled the lighter from her pocket.

Quickly striking it, she laughed as the flame appeared and the room took on a bright orange glow. The last thing she heard was a shrill shriek as the thing was overcome by flames and turned into a huge, titian ball of light.

The stench of burning flesh was the last thing she smelled before the entire room filled with flames and smoke, taking everything with it.

Hours later people stood around the remains of the building as the police and firefighters tried their best to make sense of what had happened. Nobody knew anything, and no evidence was found to prove if it was arson or not.

The only trace of anything having been there was the small lizard like footprints leading off into the woods. Even now, if you looked really hard at night, you could see the red eyes peering out from the trees and you could hear the shrill shriek of something crying out for what it had lost.

***

Crystal Barnard is a woman who loves anything paranormal. She especially has a fascination for Vampires and Werewolves and often considers herself an Alpha Female. Having grown up surrounded by the horror genre and having to deal with her own twisted and gruesome thoughts, she often found herself sitting down and writing.

Living and growing up in Ontario, Canada, she often finds herself in wooded areas, feeling more at home than anywhere else. Her stories tend to run on the paranormal side, but also have been known to hit very graphic horror right down to the last eyeball falling out and blood spattered walls.

At the young age of 39 she is enjoying her time writing and spending time with family and friends, and yes, that includes those who turn furry and go bump in the night. Her childhood was normal like anyone else's, with the exception that her grandfather had a habit of waiting until the quiet parts in a movie and scare her. This went on till about age 8 and then her mind took over on its own and what would normally be gory and sickening to most is what she thrives on.

Most people find the monsters scary, but not Crystal, she pretty much has them over for dinner to discuss techniques and helps them with their ideas; needless to say, dinner parties are never a good idea.

FACE OF AN ANGEL
By
James H Longmore

John Johnson blinked the rain from his eyes and let out a melancholy sigh as he walked along the cheerless sea front arm in arm with his wife. His mind serenaded itself with the few lines of an old Morrissey song that he could remember after well over thirty years; something about trudging over wet sand and having your clothes stolen - a perfectly depressing song that seemed to fit his day so far to a tee.

Squinting out to sea, John studied the foam topped waves that jostled their way inland to flop on the sodden sand, and tried to recall the happy childhood memories that their soothing sound conjured.

Gray, bloated clouds were rolling in from the chilled waters of the Atlantic especially, it seemed, to discharge that unique species of fine rain that could find its way beneath even the most waterproofed of clothing and was apt to leave a body chilly and shivering. Mirrored beneath the low cloud's swollen bellies, the sea rolled muddied and listless against the litter-strewn beach.

John's wife, Crystal, struggled to stay in step with him as he strode along at his usual brisk pace, her chin rested on her chest to keep the clinging rain out of her face.

Truth be told, John had forgotten just how miserable Blackpool was at this time of the year. Then again, the west coast of Northern England was miserable pretty much any time of the year, let alone mid-October. John was surprised that in just forty-six years his mind had rose-tinted over that small fact.

Even the world-famous tower - the poor man's Eiffel - was not spared the harassment of the nebulous white mist that clung to its upper steel structure like myriad sleeping ghosts. Although, despite its grim surrounding, John thought that the tower remained proud and erect against the chilled air, like an elderly war veteran at the Cenotaph.

Down on the beach, the deck chairs were piled up and hunkered down for the winter beneath flapping, green tarpaulin, and the overly optimistic purveyors of donkey rides sought shelter next to their shivering, sad-faced charges. Most of the beach front amenities were closed up against the promised onslaught of winter, although a modest number of pubs and amusement arcades remained open; there remained a workable clientele for those particular amusements all-year-round.

John couldn't help but muse on just how much his daughter back home would love all of this. She was entering her *Goth* phase (which John still thought had come a little prematurely, but Crystal had assured him was just part of the girl's blossoming and her own way of dealing with what had happened. That, and Addison was obviously advanced for her age) and loved all things dark and disconsolate. The thought made him sad inside; his baby girl had metamorphosed seemingly overnight from all things pink and Disney Princess, to black bedroom walls with finger nails to match and music that sounded like the sound track to a 1970's Dennis Wheatley movie.

The last of Blackpool's bona fide holiday makers had retreated once school resumed and the cooler weather took a hold in September; smiling, wholesome families with two-point-four children and blue-collar careers who crowded the beach with noise and sand castles and frolicked in the sea no matter how frigid and murky it was. It was those same carefree-for-two-weeks families who filled the bed and breakfast establishments that were the backbone of the Blackpool economy, queued to see the end of pier variety shows, and merrily frittered away their hard-earned into the slot machines come evening time.

Sadly, this late in the year, the town was almost exclusively the realm of the drunken, raucous bachelor and bachelorette parties that it attracted like flies around something freshly dead. As a stark testimony to the nocturnal debauchery such soirees elicited, the gutters along the sea front road were awash with discarded 'L' plates, lackluster plastic tiaras, torn sashes - '*bride*', '*official bridesmaid*', '*mother of the bride*' - and used condoms that clung to the curb stones like sickly, stranded jellyfish.

This was John's first trip back to his native England since he'd moved out to the States a dozen years ago; his wife's first trip anywhere out of her native Maryland – ever. Never ones to stray far from their native country, the Americans.

It was also their first vacation since Declan, who

would have turned six come Christmas Day.

It had been the thing of every parent's nightmare, the kind of thing that you don't think you could ever live through. One minute, little Declan had been happily playing upstairs with his big sister, the next there came a heart stopping *thump-thump-thump* as his small body bounced down the stairs.

As quickly as that, John and Crystal's son was gone.

Within the precious few seconds that it had taken John and Crystal to get to Declan, he'd already died at the foot of the staircase and had looked for all the world like a crumpled, broken toy. His neck had twisted pretty much all the way around to face backwards and there was a surprised look on the beautiful face that had always reminded John so much of Crystal. There had been very little blood, just the tiniest trickle from his one nostril, nor any snapped limb bones and to John it looked as if he could have simply turned his boy's head the right way around, pat him on the behind and send him on his way to watch Big Bird and the gang.

Only, life isn't quite like that.

Addison Johnson was a smart kid (as well as having the advantage of being a doe-eyed blonde and cute as a button - John had known from the second he'd been presented with her at the hospital that she'd grow up to seize the very best out of life) who knew full well that the safety gate at the top of the stairs was supposed to be kept shut at all times, for the safety of her little sibling. And just this once, she'd forgotten to close it behind her, a simple, honest – but ultimately devastating - mistake.

But, as devastated as they had been, it was impossible for John and Crystal to lay the blame for such a tragic accident on a seven-year-old. So, the Johnsons had taken the easy route and blamed each other.

And themselves.

On more days than not now, John could almost convince himself that he'd gotten over what had happened that fateful morning, and he figured Crystal was well on her way there too. But then there would always be the days that he knew that no, no he hadn't; there were some things in life that you were just never supposed to get over.

When he'd gone ahead and booked the trip to England without telling her, John had informed Crystal in a way that she couldn't say no. He'd paid for the tickets, organized the itinerary and told his wife that she simply *had* to visit his home land, and especially this wonderful place of his childhood vacations. Cold, miserable seaside resort holidays were, after all, as great a British tradition as the Queen and queuing.

Crystal had agreed, with some reluctance, to leave Addison with her Mother, a last resort since their regular sitter had let them down at the last minute. It had been an annoyance at the time, for sure, but a freak gas explosion that leveled the poor girl's entire apartment complex and killed six people could hardly be considered Stacey the Sitter's fault. John and Crystal had decided not to tell Addison about the accident until after they got back from their trip, as the girl had grown quite fond of Stacey over the past couple of years. They also briefed Crystal's Mom to keep her Granddaughter away from news reports about the explosion, and about how they still hadn't found Stacey's head.

Despite that particular tragedy, which brought

back a whole slew of unhappy memories for the Johnsons, Crystal had conceded that yes, they probably were long overdue for some alone time. And so, after a frantic scrabble to organize her passport in time - she'd never had/needed one - John had introduced his wife to the unique delights of Great Britain.

Once they had visited with John's small family and handful of friends (the *obligated* part of their trip, John called it), he'd driven her northwards to Blackpool, away from the cynical tourist trap that is *London Town* that Americans love to visit and think they've seen all of England.

Now, though, plodding through the litter-strewn streets and drizzling precipitation with his visibly fed-up wife, John was forced to admit that Blackpool had fared far better in his childhood memories than it had in real-life. Perhaps he'd have been better off leaving them there?

"I'm sorry, babe." John said as he slipped an arm around Crystal's slim waist. "Not quite Disney World, is it?" He made with a light laugh.

"It's okay, Hun." His wife's voice was muffled against her chest. "I wasn't expecting ninety-eight and hundred percent humidity." She returned his laugh to let John know that all was well with Mrs. Johnson, despite outward appearances. "In fact, I'm finding it most fascinating to see what you Brits consider a good vacation."

"It doesn't rain *all* of the time." John protested, although he had to admit that it pretty much did just that. "When the sun comes out, Blackpool is the best place in the world." He wasn't even convincing himself by this stage.

"It's fine, sweetheart, honestly." Crystal finally

turned her head to face him. Her bright blue eyes sparkled and danced behind her rain-speckled glasses, and a beautiful half-smile played on her lips. "This is part of who you are, of what made the man I love." She kissed his nose. "And looking at those donkeys, it makes sense how come you wound up with that ex-wife of yours."

They giggled together, and John was forced to admit that yes, at least one of the threadbare beasts huddled down on the beach did truly bear more than a passing resemblance to the first Mrs. Johnson.

And John remembered all over again just why he had fallen so helplessly in love with her Crystal the first time he'd laid eyes on her.

John Johnson - hated that name, a product of unimaginative parents - had been on solo vacation in the US following his spectacularly messy divorce from the erstwhile, donkey-faced Mrs. Johnson. He was ending the trip on the East Coast, and it was on a chilled and drizzly day not a million miles away from this one, on the Chesapeake Bay, that he'd bumped into his future second wife.

He had vowed never to remarry - ever - and meeting someone other than for a casual one or two-night stand was the furthest from his agenda than one could have imagined when the fair-skinned, flame-haired Crystal Whitsell had blazed into his life.

John had been on the guided tour around the Chesapeake Bay Decoy Museum, more to get himself indoors until the rain eased off than for an interest in how the locals lured ducks to an untimely death. Unable to resist, John had cracked a joke about how the real museum was probably hiding in the reeds across the way and his attempt at humor was met with an almost universal silence amongst the group; this he chalked up to the whole Americans/lack of irony thing. There was, however, one exception to the stony-faced quiet however, that exception being the Ms. Whitsell.

She'd laughed at his joke with such gusto that at first John had thought she was breaking type and being ironic; but then she'd flashed him a smile that made his heart melt and knees go weak and it was very much love at first sight for John and, as it worked out, for Crystal as well.

John had never returned to the UK. He'd spent the remaining days of his vacation mostly horizontal with Crystal in her ranch house bedroom, and when his two weeks were up, he'd simply married the gal and stayed Stateside.

Hard to believe that ten years had flown by since then. John had acclimatized himself nicely to life in America; enough to have formed a circle of good friends who all '*love the accent*', to write cheque as '*check*' and not get overly annoyed when the spellchecker on both his laptop and 'cell phone chastised him for putting a *u* in *color*.

"So," Crystal sniffled loudly and broke John out of his reverie. He could see that the end of his wife's pretty, button nose was practically glowing red in the chilled air. "Are you going to feed me, or not?"

"Has the seaside air made you hungry, my love?" He smiled.

More like the fact that I'm freezing my balls off." Crystal returned the smile. "But you don't have-"

"Exactly." Crystal gave her husband a playful elbow in the ribs.

They giggled together, and the familiar pattern of an old, shared joke served to lift their spirits.

John then realized that he was hungry. Most likely

the power of suggestion, coupled with the fact that they had missed breakfast at the bed and breakfast - the landlady, Mrs. Staniforth, a sharp-faced, humorless woman, was quite the stickler for punctuality and they'd stayed in bed an extra five minutes for a morning quickie. A third option for John's rumbling stomach could easily have been the heavenly smell of hot cooking oil that wafted along the street and tugged on both his nostalgia and his taste buds.

"Remember I promised you traditional British fish and chips?" John said. "Well, it doesn't come any better than Blackpool fish and chips." He grinned.

"Sounds good to me." Crystal sniffed the air and the scent of frying food made her mouth water. "As long as we can sit down, my feet are killing me." She'd seen people walking around eating fish and chips out of what appeared to be newspaper and she didn't fancy that much.

John promised her that yes, they could sit down, and lead her towards the door of the nearest fish and chip restaurant which stood invitingly open not fifty feet or so away. The restaurant was named *The Fish Plaice*, a supposedly clever play on the latter word; although, as Crystal would point out later, with a plaice being a type of fish, the name pretty much boiled down to *The Fish Fish* and she failed to understand how that was supposed to work. Again, the American/Irony thing.

Once seated, Crystal took off her glasses and dried the drizzle off them off with a paper napkin.

"You really weren't joking when you said this was no frills, were you?" She eyed their table with its plastic tablecloth and old, tarnished *Sheffield Steel* flatware. She glanced over at the take-out counter where a steady stream of damp, bedraggled people were buying steaming piles of fish and chips - French fries to her - that were bundled up in what had turned out to be real newspaper. She shuddered to think of the countless health and safety implications of consuming newsprint.

"I'm sorry, sweetheart; would you like to go someplace else?" John apologized. There was disappointment in his voice. "I think there I saw a sushi place open near the B and B."

Crystal smiled her smile that could light up any situation, no matter how dark.

"I'm just teasing, babe." She said. "This is absolutely perfect." She reached out and placed her cold hand on top of his across the table.

"What can I get you?" a gruff voice broke the moment.

John and Crystal looked up and were greeted by the unsmiling, lined face that belonged to their waitress. It appeared that she was the *only* waitress in the place (*Plaice?*) and John found himself eye level with her unfeasibly large, sagging breasts and name badge that read '*oris*'.

"It's supposed to say Doris, but the D wore off." She explained. "And Mr. Patel won't replace it until next season." She offered a half smile and tapped her order pad with a stubby pencil to signal the end of the pleasant chitchat.

"I'd like the fish and chips and a cup of tea, please." Crystal spoke up and her ever-sunny disposition brightened even Doris's dour countenance. Was that the trace of a smile on the old girl's lips?

"And for me, too." John added.

"Peas?" Doris growled.

"Yes please." Crystal said.

Doris snorted and looked down her nose at the

American. John allowed himself a smile, it was kind of fun - albeit sadistic - to see his wife finally on the receiving end of what he had to put up with in her country. It had been the longest time before he'd quit saying *alumin-i-um* and asking for chips with his food and getting a packet of Lays.

"Boiled or mushy?" Doris asked, glanced at John. Was that a raised eyebrow?

"Mushy." John chimed in. "You'll love them, my dear." He added upon seeing Crystal's grimace.

Doris nodded and stomped off, as if customers ordering food just about ruined her day, every day.

Crystal had learned the hard way to mistrust her husband over weird British delicacies after the black pudding he'd introduced her to two nights previous. Especially so now, since he'd not disclosed that the main ingredient was pig's blood until after she'd eaten a belly full and declared it delicious.

"Ooh, look." Crystal exclaimed. She peered through the rain-spattered window. "They have a palmist's."

John sighed, careful not to show his exasperation. One roll of the eyes, or a sigh was all it would take to break the good mood between them.

Crystal's obsession with all things spiritual had begun with a psychic reading back in the day when Addison had been running around in diapers, and had reached fever pitch after their son's death. More recently, Crystal had either calmed down with the whole thing, or had got better at hiding it from her husband who she knew to be, at the very least, skeptical.

Crystal had always been a believer, the more *spiritual* person of the two of them. She'd never embraced a conventional religion like those Bible-thumping, praise-be-to-Jesus types, but she was certainly more in tune with the new age spiritualism movement and firmly believed in *'there must be something after we die'*. So much so that, over the years, Crystal had habitually paid visits to palm readers, psychics, tarot readers and the rest; searching for anything that would give her answers to the questions she didn't know how to ask.

She still had the recording of that first reading. It was on a cassette tape of all things - John had scoured the local thrift stores for one of those old-style player/recorders just so she could listen - and re-listen *ad infinitum* - to that tape. And she'd even insisted that John hear it at least the once.

To be fair to the psychic guy, he was obviously good at what he did. He'd nailed most of Crystal's particulars without giving away the fact that he was doing what all good mentalists did well and was simply reading her body language and feeding her loaded questions. He'd managed a spot-on guess about the Johnson kids, although it was probably not too difficult to guess that a married woman of a certain age would most likely have children, but to get the gender and ages exactly right? Even John had been forced to admit that that seemed to be more than just a stroke of good luck. After hitting that nail on the head though, the guy on the tape went down in John's estimation somewhat.

You have a daughter.

Again, a fifty percent chance of getting that one.

She has the face of an angel.

What parent doesn't think their little princess is just the cutest thing on God's green Earth?

And the mind of a devil.

What!?

Who the hell says *that* to a parent? Sure, Addison had all the makings of being a handful, she already ruled the roost with her manipulative, often petulant behavior. But then again, what little girl didn't?

The reading had ended abruptly after that, and Crystal never made her husband listen to the recording again, never even mentioned it, although John knew that she still played it from time to time.

After that reading, John thought that Crystal had seemed different around her daughter. It was a subtle change that John had hoped only he - and not Addison - could pick up on, and on occasion he would catch the feeling that in some way, his wife was wary of the girl.

"Two fish and chips." Doris plonked the utilitarian, white plates in front of the Johnsons. "If you want a bap instead of bread, it's a pound extra." She grumbled. "Each."

John assured the waitress that no, they wouldn't be requiring baps whilst at the same time suppressing a smirk at the word for bread bun that his childish generation had hijacked as a euphemism for breasts.

"Can we go?" Crystal asked him. "After we've finished eating - this." She peered down at the thickly battered fish and mountain of fries before her as if it had just beamed down from an alien mother ship. She poked her fork at the spreading puddle of mushy peas that soaked into her fish and looked like lumpy snot or something Linda Blair threw up. "I'd love for us both to have a reading."

"I can't see why not." John was truthful here. With all the best will in the world, he genuinely couldn't think of an excuse *not* to visit the palmist across the street, as much as he detested the idea. Crystal had him cornered.

"Awesome." She smiled, and John was pleased to

have made his wife happy, even if it was only because he really had no other choice.

John peered with some trepidation across the road at the palmist's gaudy shop front, hoping against hope that it would be closed for off-season. But no, the garish, red and yellow neon sign that declared *Palm's Read, tarot, fortune's told* shone bright and illiterate through the drizzle. Above the flickering neon, a fading, hand painted sign declared - *Gypsy Rose*.

Really?

There was a small, grubby window adjacent to the narrow doorway. It was adorned with frayed, crocheted silk curtains, thus completing the cliché that had been a seaside town staple since the mid-1800's. Just one more way to extract money from gullible holiday makers on their way to the pubs, slot machines and bingo.

John dug into his food like a workhouse kid. He tried his best to hide his initial disappointment that the fish was a flat, lackluster fillet of haddock and not the thick, flaky cod of his childhood - hadn't he read that cod were on the endangered species list now? Even so, it did taste good swimming in malt vinegar and nostalgia, accompanied by soft, doughy bread and mushy peas.

"This reminds me of that dip at Charlotte's wedding." Crystal ventured. "I thought *that* was guacamole, too." She held a small sample of the green mush to her mouth, gave it a tentative prod it with her tongue.

John took great delight at his wife's introduction to the dish he'd grown up with. God only knew what the stuff had been at her sister's wedding reception but it was neither peas nor guacamole; although he was surprised that she'd remembered a small detail such as the dip over the embarrassment of the ceremony itself.

It had been an ostentatious church wedding, even though it was Charlotte Whitsell's second marriage. Daddy, it turned out, was good friends with Reverend Hopkins and had pledged the equivalent of a hospital wing to the Restoration Fund.

John had not wanted to bring the children along in the first place - Addison had just turned four, Declan one - because he had planned to get himself hopelessly drunk at the free bar at the lavish country club reception. Sadly, he was expertly overruled by Crystal who had informed him that Charlotte had absolutely *insisted*.

The ceremony had started off well enough but they'd barely taken their place behind Crystal's Mom and her ginormous hat (John could remember wondering just how many birds had died to decorate the hideous millinery) when Addison had begun to grizzle.

Crystal had attempted everything in her power to placate the girl, even the dreaded, last resort pacifier she'd not had since she turned three, but the low growl of her daughter's grizzling had quickly degenerated into a full-blown wail.

John would remember vividly to his dying day the marrow-chilling looks from everyone in the church as his daughter's screaming echoed around the high, vaulted ceilings. It felt to him as if two hundred people - the normally serene and mild mannered Reverend Hopkins included - were simply willing him and his family to just curl up and die.

Then Addison had thrown up.

Not only all over her own mother, but down the back of the mother of the bride and all over the poor unfortunates who sat either side of the woman.

Of course, Crystal and John had been mortified beyond comprehension at Addison's display; by the sound of the ear-splitting, guttural screams that came out of their daughter, one would have expected her to have projectile vomited pea green soup. But no, it was half-digested, rancid milk and the Denny's pancakes Addison had wolfed down for breakfast.

The Reverend Hopkins, who was on his way over to ask - no doubt most politely - that the Johnsons take their screaming child outside so he could continue with the wedding vows, caught some of the thick, gray vomit globs on his cassock and John had mused that it looked had as if Addison was *aiming* it at him.

Declan, thankfully, had been far too young to be embarrassed by the episode, or to remember it.

John and Crystal had had no choice than to remove Addison from the church, and the ceremony itself was delayed an hour whilst Crystal's Mom changed outfits and the Reverend Hopkins slipped into non-vomit stained vestments.

John recalled that Addison had stopped crying almost as soon as they stepped out of the church and into the spring sunshine, much to the relief of his frayed nerves. He'd driven Crystal and the kids back to the hotel where they washed up, changed clothes and decided to sit the ceremony out and plan their apologies for the reception.

As it turned out, John and Crystal's shame amongst the Whitsell family had been short lived as Charlotte's marriage hadn't actually lasted all that long; what with New Hubby doing jail time for beating the crap out of his bride on their honeymoon.

Charlotte had been left severely brain damaged and with matching detached retinas by her husband's uncharacteristic and - as far as the police could tell -

unprovoked attack. Now, the poor woman wiled away her days in a private clinic muttering to herself about dark, sinister things that skulked in the periphery of what remained of her vision. John could remember all too clearly the one - *only* - time he'd paid his sister-in-law a visit.

"*There are evil things waiting for us in the shadows.*" She'd told him.

John, keen to soothe, had asked. "Which ones, Charlotte?"

She'd looked directly into his eyes and John had seen the spark of who she had once been and she'd whispered, "*All of them.*"

With hindsight, and a not immeasurable amount of cynical superstition, Addison's outburst in the church had seemed to John to have been a portent, like a black cat crossing one's path, or the unfortunate sighting of a single magpie. So much so, in fact that when (due to an unfortunate oversight by the wedding photographer) he and Crystal had received their copy of the wedding album, John had half expected to see sinister things lurking in the background of the pictures.

But no, just happy, smiling faces oblivious to the impending fate of the happy couple. And Addison's angry, screaming face in the cool gloom of the church.

"Yeah, what was that stuff?" John said. "It tasted worse that Addison's throw-up." He grinned at Crystal; saw the familiar - and much loved - wrinkles at the corners of her infinitely kissable mouth.

"You know I don't like to think about Charlotte's wedding." She said. "I've never been so embarrassed in my entire life." That smile again. "Although it did stop my parents talking to me for three years.

Pretentious asses."

John reached over the table and held his wife's hand.

Crystal had only recommenced communications with her family shortly after Declan died.

They ate in silence awhile, each lost in their own private thoughts. John studied his wife's reaction to the congealing pool of bright green peas on her plate and it looked like she was enjoying them. That or she was at least putting on the pretense of enjoying them.

"We should check in with home." Crystal broke the silence. "Make sure everything's okay."

"It's six in the morning over there." John reminded her. "Addison won't even be awake yet, and you know what your Mother's like if she doesn't get her full eight hours." John shivered as he pictured his Mother-in-Law asleep in his and Crystal's bed, having refused the guest bed because she said it was too lumpy. John had had to bite his tongue on that one, no matter how much it rankled, theirs was the bed in which he made love to Crystal, in which they had made two children together.

Crystal's Mom had, with some cajoling, agreed to house-sit as well as mind Addison; Crystal's proviso at not cancelling their trip was that the house was not left empty and Addison stayed home to be in familiar surroundings. Her mother - Janice - had finally agreed, albeit with some reluctance. Of late, she seemed to have caught some of her daughter's wariness around Addison, especially since the colored pencil incident the girl had been involved in at school.

John wasn't sure exactly why that had disturbed Janice so much. It wasn't as if it was Addison's fault and the school had said that the other kid would be okay; the doctors had saved his left eye and there'd been some great advances in artificial eyes in recent years. In the end, John put it down to Janice's advancing years and lingering upset following her husband's untimely death at just sixty-two.

John glanced at the fob on his bunch of keys that he'd rested on the table, an old habit as his growing clutter of keys tended to dig into his leg if he kept them in his pocket.

The fob had a picture of Addison on it. She was all broad, beaming smile, flaxen hair the color of morning sunshine, perfectly round cheeks, a tiny snub nose, and those deep, dark, browner-than-brown eyes that sometimes and in a certain light would appear black. John often found himself contemplating his daughter's photograph, more so since Declan's passing, and reflecting upon how little she looked like him, or his wife. So much so, that he and Crystal would sometimes joke that there must have been a mix-up of babies at the hospital.

There were occasions, though, where John thought that Addison looked a little like her Mom, and times that Crystal would make comments; *she has your pout, John,* or *she's just like her damned father.*

Declan had been different again, the absolute spit of John, so much so that John thought it was sometimes like looking in a mirror.

At that moment, whilst it was nice to be away and having a break, John realized that he missed his daughter terribly.

"Well, I think it's beaten me." John declared and pushed his plate an inch or two towards the middle of the table for emphasis.

"Me too." Crystal said through a mouthful of fries. "That was really good."

"Despite appearances to the contrary?" John

laughed.

"I even ate some of that fake guacamole stuff." Crystal sounded proud of herself, like a kid who's forced spinach down for the first time.

"I knew you'd like it." John said. "We should buy some cans to take home."

"Don't push it, buster." Crystal flashed him that smile again.

John slurped down the tepid brown liquid in his tea cup.

"Ready to go see the tower?" He asked

"After we go see Madam Rose." Crystal reminded her husband.

As if he'd *really* forgotten.

The rain had eased up some by the time they stepped back outside, although the sky remained ominously swollen, as if the clouds were about to birth something vast and monstrous. John had settled up with Doris, argued a little with Crystal about her making him leave a five pound tip - *that was almost eight bucks*, he'd protested - and ushered his wife from the restaurant.

They had to wait a minute or two for a sparsely patronized tram to rumble by and then they were across the road, through the narrow door and into the eerie - if somewhat hopelessly clichéd - realm of one astonishingly ancient, gnarled Gypsy Rose.

"Welcome!" She cried in a theatrical, non-specific eastern European accent. "I was expecting you."

Of course she was, John mused, how could she not be? He recalled an old cartoon he'd seen a long time ago in which there was a sign outside a clairvoyant's premises (not entirely dissimilar to this one, it had to be said, despite being an ocean away) that declared *'Closed due to unforeseen circumstances'*.

John smiled and stepped forward, his nose wrinkling against the heady scent of incense and naphthalene.

"Come in, come in, sit down." Gypsy Rose beckoned them into her cramped, ill-lit parlor. She pulled up a second chair and motioned for John to plant his ass on it. As he did so, Gypsy Rose lead Crystal by the hand to a rickety wooden chair opposite her own.

Gypsy Rose - and John seriously doubted that she was a true gypsy, or that she was actually named Rose; more likely she was from some inner-city council estate in Manchester and was called Edna - settled herself down and stroked the crystal ball that sat in the center of the small, square table.

"It's ten pounds for a reading, ball, palm or tarot." Gypsy Rose told them. Her phony accent slipped a little and John caught the undercurrent of a twang that could have come from the opposite side of the Pennines. "In advance."

Crystal fished through her wallet and handed over what she hoped was a ten-pound note and nothing larger. It was difficult to tell in the poor light, but that was probably the point of the half a watt bulb that swung gently over the table. John was about to crack a smart one about how it was supposed to be *cross the lady's hand with silver* and not bank notes but thought better of it.

"Palm please."

Crystal held out her hand, palm up, across the table.

Gypsy Rose cast a cursory glance at John, as if daring him to say something that would spoil the ambience. To John, it felt as if she *were* reading his mind, that she'd made some kind of connection with his psyche and knew what he had almost said. The thought creeped John out, the very idea of someone like Gypsy Rose skulking around inside his brain made John feel queasy.

John met Rose's eyes with his and sank back in his chair, suitably chastised. She'd got him at it now, with all her psychic mumbo-jumbo; anymore and he'd be begging her to read his palm too.

"You have had a troubled life thus far." Gypsy Rose began her shtick. "I see both tragedy and loss." She stroked Crystal's palm and traced the lines with a crooked finger. "But I also see love. A true, lasting love. You are a lucky lady." She looked up at Crystal's trusting face. "The man you are with now is the love of your life." She continued. "But not your first love."

Wait, what?

John sat forward in his chair.

"Your first is a love that runs far beyond our plane of reality and nestles deep within your soul. It is a love that has always been within you, a love that grows stronger with each passing day."

John made ready to be offended but checked himself. The old charlatan had seen the skepticism in his face the second he'd walked in and this was her giving him a metaphorical - or should that be *metaphysical*? - slap down.

"Can you tell me what my future holds?" Crystal slipped all too comfortably into the mystic-speak.

"Of course I can, my dear." The psychic said with the lightest of chuckles. "Your lifeline is a long and healthy one." She traced what John assumed must be his wife's lifeline with the gnarled finger. "And where it crosses here, and here, shows that you have two children." She must have heard Crystal's sharp intake of breath. "No, not two. It's one child. You *had* two."

John placed a hand on Crystal's shoulder, she leaned her head against it.

"We *did*." His wife told the woman.

"Ahh, there is your tragedy." The old woman declared as if she'd known all along. "I am so sorry for your pain." She pulled Crystal's hand closer, squinted at it with screwed up eyes. "I see the shortened line for the pain, my dear."

You're full of it, lady, John thought to himself, and then hoped again that Gypsy Rose wasn't reading his mind.

"I can see your child in this one." Gypsy Rose studied a crooked line that traversed Crystal's palm. "This one is a strong, steady line. It -"

She paused, staring at Crystal's upturned palm, the color draining from her wizened face.

"What is it? What do you see?" Crystal's voice sounded a little shaky.

"Your daughter." There was a tremor in the old woman's voice that hadn't been there a second before, her phony accent all but forgotten. "God save us all." She sounded terrified.

"Addison? What is it?" Crystal insisted.

"The face of an angel – "

The words hung in the cloying air like an early morning fog as the old woman Gypsy Rose reached beneath her little table and calmly pulled out a small, snub-nosed revolver.

She raised the gun to her temple and pulled the trigger.

The blunt report was dulled by the musky cloths that draped the room; the flash from the muzzle startled John's eyes and they clamped shut.

In that instant, John could see his daughter in his mind's eye, feel her presence seeping into his brain and creating dark, shadowy corners there. He saw Addison's cold, dark eyes and along with that vision; the unholy commotion in the church, Charlotte beaten to a pulp and rotting in an asylum, the gas explosion and decapitated sitter, Crystal's father laying stiff and pale in his casket, a kid blinded in one eye by a yellow pencil, myriad inconsequential things that suddenly compounded to make perfect, terrifying sense. He saw Declan at the bottom of the stairs, eyes glassy and unmoving, an ugly knot in his neck where knobbed bones had snapped out of place and John felt – knew – that far from being the harbinger, his daughter - his beautiful Addison with her wispy, summer-sun hair and darker-than-brown eyes - was the cause.

Gypsy Rose slumped without ceremony from her chair and hit the floor with a dull, wet thud. As she fell, the gray slop of her brain oozed from the quarter-sized hole above her left ear and a scarlet rivulet of blood flowed from her nose.

Crystal Johnson turned to her husband with a sad look in her eyes. "Oh no," she said, "not again."

THE END

James hails originally from Yorkshire, England having relocated with his family to Houston, Texas in 2010. He has an honors degree in Zoology and a background in sales, marketing and business. Relatively new to the writing arena, his writing style and storytelling have already been compared to Stephen King, Dan Brown and Robert Ludlum.

An Affiliate Member of the Horror Writer's Association, he has, to date five novels published, with another and an anthology due in 2017 - in addition to three novellas and eight short stories dotted about in various anthologies.

James also writes screenplays and currently has three under option (a spine-chilling horror, a Tarantino-esque crime caper and an animated family movie). In 2014 he was commissioned by Spectra Records to write a biopic feature on the early life of Bob Marley, and in 2015 was writer for hire on the Kenyan sitcom '*The Samaritans*'.

As if that weren't enough, James has written and directed a bunch of short movies, winning Best Director in the 2013 *Splatterfest* film competition and Remi awards at Houston's *Worldfest* Film Festival in 2012, 2014 and 2015.

James' writing style has been described as uncompromising, unique and entertaining; he combines highly original ideas with brilliant vocabulary and highly effective yarn spinning in which the story always comes first! Be warned, his work does have a tendency towards the dark side – usually with a rich vein of humor – and there is always a delicious twist at the end!

www.jameslongmore.com

THE NEW RECRUIT

By
Toneye Eyenot

So… You want to know a little of what goes on here? Oh, come now! Don't play dumb with me. You know exactly where you are. This, my friend, is Hell. As a new Citizen, you are going to be here for a very long time. Forever, actually. It would be in your best interest to pay careful heed to what I tell you. Your level of attentiveness will determine the quality of your time spent in your new home. No, I am not Satan. I am merely a representative. His welcoming committee of one, if you will.

Firstly, allow me to express my welcome and tell you how pleased I am to finally meet you in person. Yes, we have watched you for quite some years. Grooming your soul for an eternal stay with us, you have never ceased to entertain with your various blasphemies and debaucheries. In fact, we are quite honored to have you amongst us!

The goings on in the world you have just recently left behind are of great interest to all here in Hell. We watch you all as you lose your way and urge you to continue along your chosen paths. Our Hell scouts are sent to reel you in and there is an arena in which our Citizens and Demons alike may watch in anticipation, as you and your ilk fumble your way through your miserable lives.

There isn't a whole lot of difference between this world and the one you previously inhabited. The terrors are just as real, both here and there. Only, where on earth injustice is hidden behind the veneer of a 'lawful' and 'just' society, we here in Hell make no such pretense. Here, there is no law. Here, you are free to do as you please. There are consequences though. They are also just as real as on earth yet much farther reaching. You are here for eternity, after all... Ok.... There is a clause, a loophole... a 'get out of Hell free card', so to speak. Alas, I am not at liberty to divulge. That is something you must search for on your own accord.

You may have noticed the feeling of pain, loss, suffering that has been needling your mind and soul since you arrived. Surely the quote, "as above, so below" is familiar to you? Well, as above, you were a right royal bastard, weren't you? Not an ounce of consideration for those poor souls who handed you their trust, only to have that trust so unscrupulously trampled underfoot for your own selfish gains. Their consequential suffering because of your heartless antics is what you are now being subjected to. I advise you to get used to it... fast. We don't take kindly to complainers down here. You reap what you sow and there are multitudes in Hell who will be more than happy to remind you of this.

Anything you want, you can find here, for a price. We have a unique bartering system here in Hell. We deal in suffering. You personally have been credited with quite a substantial wealth of said currency. Like I have informed you, we have watched and we have liked what we saw. What you have been told in your previous life about this place could not be further from the truth. Hell is, after all, a state of mind. It is not actually a place, per se. In the grand scheme of reality, you don't even exist. The religions of that world were set in place as an instrument of control and nothing more. Remember back to your childhood now. Do you recall Father Peter and his ranting Sunday school sermons of fire and brimstone, set aside for all you naughty, naughty children? Well, he has been here with us now for some thirty of your earth years, enduring the fire and brimstone of his lies and deception inflicted upon the young, malleable minds of countless children. Oh, we have them all here. Ignorant fools!

Never underestimate the cunning of Hell's inhabitants. We here, have the benefit of foresight. We know you well, my friend and soon, you will know many of us just as intimately. Whether that be for good or ill, once again, depends entirely on you. The thriving of the wickedest is how it is played here and rest assured, many scores of depraved souls have spent countless centuries here, mastering the art of manipulative persuasion. You can be taken immediately and left with naught for millennia if you drop your game for even a moment. Manipulation and deception being your forte, however, I see you'll have no problem fitting in here and subsequently charging up through the ranks. There isn't much more I can tell you really, except that you create your own reality. Be careful what you wish for or strive towards, as what you reap...yes, you will surely sow. That is the one "unwritten law" you would be advised to adhere to.

Just treat it as a game throughout your stay. As in all games, there is plenty of opportunity for shrewdness and cheating. Don't get caught and you will do just fine. The wrong move with the wrong inhabitant, be it Citizen or Demon, will have you regretting your choice for longer than you would care to imagine. That's another thing you will find... The course of your stay is to be unbelievably immense. Time will both drag along excruciatingly and at the same time, fly by so fast that you will be loath to seek respite, should you miss even the slightest opportunity that passes by in the eternal blink of an eye. This is a fast-paced existence and either you keep up or fall beneath the scores of stomping feet, aching to feel your crushing bones beneath them.

There is one more thing before I must bid you adieu and tend to this rapidly growing crowd at the gates. Allow me to be the first to say, my friend... Welcome to Hell.

©Toneye Eyenot. Sept. 12, 2014

SON OF MEPHISTOPHELES

By
James Richardson

Sweat beaded down her brow as the pains of her labor grew by the hour. Now was the time, now was the hour, for the world to meet the being that will either damn it or save it. Her cries pierced the cold night air as his head began to crown. She could feel the power swelling in her breast as the child's shoulders passed her birth canal. Smiling wickedly, knowing that their pact would soon be complete as the dark figure stood within the shadows. She slumped back in exhaustion as the child's cries filled the moonlit air.

"My lord I present to you, your son," the she-demon said, kneeling in front of her lord. His red, blistered hand breached the shadows, running over his son's blood and birthing fluid-covered body, feeling his energies coursing through his tiny body.

"Our pact is complete," Mephistopheles' voice hissed like flames flickering off his snake-like tongue. "Enjoy your reward," snapping his fingers, a blue spark of flame jutting into the air.

"Yes!" Euphoria filled her body as unholy might bellowed in her lithe frame. "I live to serve Hell, Mephistopheles!" Vile laughter bubbled forth from her beautiful face, eager to lay waste to those that wronged her.

"Come, bring the child," Mephistopheles commanded, his blood-red cloak bellowed out around him as the silver rays highlighted his crooked form. His twisted, ebony horns ran parallel to his scalp before sharply turning upwards, their ends capped in gold. Fine silver chains dangled from the gold housing, softly reflecting the light. The souls of his victims screamed in silent horror within the depths of the blood-red diamonds that encrusted the chains. "It is time for my son to know the pleasures of his home," Mephistopheles smiled cruelly.

"My lord, has the child survived the birthing?" Aheile asked, her antler-like horns awash in the light of Hell's flames. Her bone-segmented tail whipped and thrashed the air as she rose from her throne. The blue-green glow of her eyes burned brightly as she heard the cries of the young child. The finger-bone necklace resting in the cleavage of her blood-covered bare breast clinked with every movement. Her ivory skin felt flushed in the brimstone-laced air as she neared her husband. The yellow aged skull adorned the three-inch strap of cloth soaked in the blood of the damned, teasing the obsidian stone. Her leathery bat-like wings were folded tightly against her back as the she-demon approached. She could smell the drying blood that still clung to the child's body. She watched as those tiny arms reached out, exploring the tips of the chin horns of the demon that held him.

"As you see, it did," Mephistopheles smiled, moving off to his bone-strewn throne.

"Give me the child," Aheile demanded, taking the child into her awaiting arms. "Come, young Prince, you must be hungry," she cooed, stroking his head as he began to nurse. Smiling as he groped her breast and drank his fill. "My lord, what shall you name him?"

"His name is of no import to me," the master of the eighth circle said, resting his chin in his hand. "The child is only a means to an end. Name him what you will until he has grown and serves me. Only then will I deem him important enough to speak his name."

"Nomen Nesio," Aheile whispered, her needle-like fangs peeking out as her ruby stained lips curled into a smile, her husband's maniacal laughter trailing after her as she headed deeper into their palace.

Nomen grew and learned as he watched from the shadows of his father's realm. He knew he wasn't like those that served his father, that was painfully obvious to him. Yet, as his ruby-hued eyes looked down on the circle that his father governed, it felt like home to him. However, something else within him knew it was wrong to enjoy the suffering he heard as he knelt on the balcony.

"There you are, dear brother," Ungui said with a sneer. Her talons gleamed wickedly in the raging inferno out in the distance. If it was up to her, she would have drained his virility the moment he was brought into their realm. She didn't see why her father thought to father the half breed. She and her six sisters could easily breach the vale between this world and the mortal one. The thought of such a lowly creature walking the halls of their grand palace was so repugnant to her. "Father wishes to speak with you, Nomen," Ungui said, smiling at the true meaning of his name.

"There you are, boy," Mephistopheles voiced without looking at his son. "The time has come for you to learn from the one that birthed you," his red glowing eyes burning into his son's body. The stench of the boy's human half filled his broken, bulbous nose.

"What do you mean, father?" Nomen asked, looking towards Aheile. It was she who taught him how to tap into his demonic energies. To twist the will of the subjects of their domain, bend the fabric of reality to his will. Which, for the most part, Nomen found stimulating, yet he knew there more just laying beneath the surface.

"You need to learn how to tap into that human soul of yours, and she is the only one that can teach you," Mephistopheles hissed, his blistered hands gripping the armrest of his pale throne. "Before you venture into that cold realm, seek the weapon smith," he said, waving the boy off.

Nomen stood along the banks of the gentle river as the gateway closed behind him, leaving him trapped in a world he knew nothing about. Instantly, he felt his skin chill without the heat of his home. The bastard sword felt odd as it bumped against his leg. The evilness that was infused into the blade seemed to sing to him. Coating him in its vile lullaby, whispering sweet nothings into his mind.

"There you are, half breed," Mara's sweet, taunting voice drifted in from behind him. "Come along, boy, the stench of your arrival will draw unwanted attention," she said, turning around not waiting to see if her bastard son followed after her.

A century had passed since he stepped foot into the world of man. Every day, the voice of the sword grew louder, demanding to be set free. To drink from the blood and soul of a certain witch. Nomen knew the time was coming when Mara would no longer be useful to him or his father.

"*The time has come, my son, destroy her,*" his father's cruel voice echoed in his mind. Nomen crept through the shadows as his father's influence flowed through him. Blinding his human half to what he was about to do as his hand crept down to the sword on his hip. The red glow of the blade as it crept out of its sheath washed the frescos painted by people he cared nothing for. Mara had prided herself on the works of art that she had garnered throughout her long life. Bloodlust clouded his vision as his sinews became taut as his grip tightened around the hilt of his sword. Nomen had learned long ago the art of silence, and Mara was too preoccupied with her own vanity she failed to notice that her life was at an end. That was until she saw the blade protruding from her chest, the cold feeling engulfed her as her soul was absorbed into the metal body. Not a word ever escaped her lips, no pleas for mercy, no curses upon his manhood, no questions as to why he had killed her.

Nomen pushed her cold, lifeless body off the blade as it began to crumble to dust after years of prolongation. Something seemed to snap within Nomen as he stared at the pile of dust that was all that remained of his mother. He finally understood why he was given the blade in the first place. He could feel it burning within him to open the way for his father to enter this realm. To allow him to roam this land, unabated, free to feast upon the untainted souls. What Nomen also realized was that once he did open the pathway he was expendable and his father wouldn't hesitate to render his body to ash. Looking down at the blade as his mother's blood dripped steadily onto the marble floor, Nomen knew that no one, not even he, should ever wield the blade knowing the consequences should the sword ever be set free again. He hid the sword in the one place his father would never think to search, coating the weapon in a spell that would shield it from his ever-watchful gaze. Knowing the spell would maintain its hold so long as he lived. Nomen just had to ensure he would survive until the time he faced his father once again.

Three-hundred and fifty years had passed since he had broken away from his father. Oh, he could hear his voice in his head poking at what weakness he could find in his disobedient son. Nomen had spent his time hunting down demons that had broken through the vale.

Absorbing their essences as his handcrafted blades made from the horns of Abaddon class demons after he ended their foul lives, making their power his own, all for the day he would undoubtedly face off with his father. He knew his father would use everything in his power to achieve his goals. No one would ever hear Nomen say he was a hero, he didn't care for such titles, he simply did what had to be done. He wasn't about to become a pawn for his family. That was until the fateful day when all his planning was put to the test.

"Do we have a deal," Nomen asked, as the child whizzed on the ventilator. "Ten years of your life to restore your daughter to perfect health?" This was how Nomen had sustained his human half throughout all those long years. He would never trade souls that would only help his father, which for once, he found repugnant. Yet for him to use his powers in the human world a deal had to be made if it wasn't against another demon; and what parent wouldn't trade a few years of life to save their child.

"How do we know this will work?" The brunette woman asked her hand taking hold of her daughter's.

"Listen, you summoned me, not the other way," Nomen sighed the rolled parchment tapping against his leg. "If you don't want the deal that's fine, there are others that do," he spoke, tilting his head waiting for their answer. "Whether you share the ten years or one does it alone, it matters not to me. Now do we have a deal?" Nomen asked as his skin began to crawl, feeling her close to death.

"If we do this she will be fine?" the father questioned, his weary eyes falling on his comatose daughter.

"As I have said, she will be in perfect health what she does after this is up to her."

"Where do we sign," they said in unison, nodding to each other. Wincing as their thumbs were pricked by the shard embedded into the parchment. Blood was always a part of the contract, blood never lies, never negates on their word, it's the ultimate binder. Nodding as the two droplets graced the dotted line, Nomen placed his hands over the center of their chests as he began feeling the years flowing into him. He didn't have to do this any longer, not with the horded years he had stashed away, however, one can never be too careful. Not when Mephistopheles was chasing you and who knew what he would send after you.

Resting his right hand on the girl's forehead and his left over her heart, bending the fabric of reality around them, repairing the injury that had caused her condition in a matter of seconds. Feeling her life force surging as his work came to completion.

"Now, I'll take my leave," Nomen said drifting towards the door as the girl was crushed in her parent's embrace. The concept of human families was so alien, so foreign to him he just couldn't wrap his mind around it. Nomen had always been taught emotions were a weakness and he had seen them break many men and women alike in his long years of solitude. Though he had to admit some of the human inventions held him in wonder as the elevator cab slowed as it reached the ground floor. He wouldn't shadow-walk back towards his sanctuary, at least not in a building full of humans. That would raise questions upon questions and draw unwanted attention to him. Attention that would surely get back to his father and Nomen wasn't ready to face him just yet. He headed towards the rear exit so he could vanish without much concern of being seen.

"Really!" Nomen exclaimed, looking up, feeling the devil's trap tugging at his body. "Haven't you learned by now?" he sighed shaking his head.

"Be silent, you demon!" Michael cursed as he held up his cross. Nomen rolled his eyes; the symbol meant nothing to him. He had no fear of it, that sort of thing only worked on lesser demons. Nomen just couldn't see why they thought such foolishness could hurt him. "Katherine start the rite while I hold him down."

"Nomen if that is truly your name I send you back to the pit in which spawned you," Katherine said, thrusting out her hands.

"Again I must remind you fools I'm only half demon," Nomen said flinching as he broke the seal of the trap. Even if he was only half a demon, it still pained him as he breeched the seal. The two magic-infused .9mm pistols flew out of their holsters as they thought to attack. "Now, I'm tired of having to tell you this time and time again," he said pulling back the hammers of his handguns. "It's bad enough you made me think you actually cared for me," Nomen said his eyes narrowing as he looked down the sights of his pistol as Katherine took a dry swallow. Seeing the blue veins of energy glowing along the engraved grooves of his weapons. She knew just how deadly those weapons truly were even though they usually only worked on demons. Katherine could only assume at that close of a range it wouldn't matter. "The audacity to think a simple explosion would kill me," Nomen said shaking his head. "You do realize there were two innocent souls still left on that demon infested oil rig when you blew it up."

"Don't listen Katherine, demons always lie," Michael growled, yearning to send the fiend back where it belonged.

"True, they normally do. Yet that's when they have something to gain from said lie. I, however, do not. Not when I can smell their deaths engraved upon your own souls."

"You can't know that," Katherine whispered.

"Oh, but I can. As you so like to point out, I'm a demon," Nomen said shrugging his shoulders. "We can smell an innocent soul a mile away. Would you like to see how they died," Nomen said with a flick of his index finger sending the images straight into their minds. "Now, who's a demon that allows innocence to die just to kill one half-breed," he said sneering into Katherine's ear. "Now, maybe you should stop casting stones in your glass house," Nomen said leaving them to the nightmares that tormented the men before they died on that oilrig.

Weeks had passed since their encounter in the hospital. Nomen had hoped he had seen the last of

Katherine, yet those green eyes of hers always seemed to haunt him. Resting in his apartment, he just couldn't fathom why she was always on his mind. Her betrayal had stung him to the core, yet that was a fact of everyday life in Hell. Was his time among the mortals finally getting through that cold exterior that he had built to survive in that realm? Nomen sighed when his own mind failed to give him answers. Then he felt the tug, the pull as someone summoned him, by name no less. He could outright have refused the consumption of the magic that taunted him, yet the fact that someone called him by his name, that was too intriguing to pass up.

Shadows danced along the blades of his swords, their ebony sheen flashed menacingly as he breeched the shadow gate. Their cruel nature rippling as they felt the faint energies of one of their own. His flaming red hair was pulled tight in a ponytail tucked into the back his jacket. Whoever had called him, he wanted to at least seem presentable when he met the summoner. But that was when he saw her. Instantly his hands were at his weapons thinking they had set a trap for him.

"Nomen! Thank God it worked!" Katherine said letting out a breath. She truly didn't think it would. "Please, Michael needs your help," she pleaded noting how his eyes moved around the room.

"There a reason I should?" Nomen asked coldly, his ruby eyes shimmering in his rage.

"Please Nomen, you have to save my brother!" Katherine said, kneeling before him offering whatever he needed to save her only brother.

"Again I ask, why should I?" Nomen growled, his nostrils flaring, catching the scent of something he had experienced in years. "Where is he? Quickly!" Nomen said, with all urgency, taking Katherine by the shoulders.

"In the other room," Katherine said, pointing through the rotten, plastered wall. Standing silently as his hands moved over her brother's body.

"What is that you want from me Katherine, I need specifics," Nomen said yet his attention seemed to be elsewhere.

"I want you to heal my brother," Katherine stated plainly.

"A year I will take," Nomen said, walking up to her. There was no time to write up a proper contract not if she was near. Nodding that she understood the moment their lips touched feeling the ancient bond formed and seal. If she was already damned, she didn't see the fault in calling Nomen to save Michael. Yet she didn't think the old emotions she had buried deep within her would come roaring back to the surface. Katherine fought herself not to give in, yet she couldn't stop her arms from moving on their own. "Now, once he's healed leave quickly. I won't be sticking around," Nomen said as he worked quickly. If she was in this world he could only assume the others had crossed over as well. He wasn't about to face off with them not if he could help it, his weapons alone wouldn't be able to put down an archdemon class, which his sister's fell into. No, he needed something more that could cleave their immortality as well as their bodies. That was the one weapon he was hesitant to release back onto the world.

"Now go!" Nomen urged them as he approached the nearest shadow so he could escape towards his home. While his home offered protection from lower class demons, it wouldn't hold off his sisters for long. Just long enough to hide him while he made the preparations to retrieve the sword. That was the plan before he felt the heat from the floor below them; he tossed Katherine and her brother into the other room as the floor exploded lifting him off his feet crashing through the crumbling wall. Fire pillars erupted as Rusan rose through the air, her black leathery wing's silently flapping as she hung in the air. Bone earrings dotted along her elf-like ear's, her horns charred black from her eons in servitude to her father. Her ebony hair streaked with brown highlights floated around her as her silver eyes caught sight of her wayward brother. The blue thin cloth strips did nothing to cover her phenomenal, voluptuous breast. Only her brown areolas were barely contained by the fabric. Her shapely hips were draped in the same blue material that scantly covered her womanhood. Multiple leather belts wrapped around her slender legs, each housing its own dagger.

"My, my! Look at what I found!" Rusan cooed as her red succubus energies arced along her raised arms. "Father is very angry with you Nomen Neso," her giggle was anything but friendly as her eyes glowed red hot. "Here I thought I teach those foolish humans what it means to tangle with the daughter of Mephistopheles," her tail striking the scattered broken boards. "Never did I think I'd meet you here," her hooved feet clacking along the worn aged boards, coming to a stop she stood over her brother. "Now, come along, Nomen. I shall not harm you if you come willingly," she said reaching down to grasp the nape of his neck. "Nomen!" Rusan cried out as Nomen rolled over, emptying both clips of his hellfire bullets into his sister's chest and pushed off the rubble to gain enough space to escape from his sister.

"Katherine get out!" Nomen yelled, knowing the bullets had only phased her for a moment. "Now, Katherine! I won't tell you again," Nomen shouted drawing his swords. Pushing off the floorboards with such force as to weaken the already unstable flooring. His ruby eyes flaring, his own demonic energies surged as his ebony blades pierced her chest. Sending bone-jarring tremors up his arms as Nomen impaled his sister onto the load baring post. Holding his sister in place as he heard Katherine escape out the window.

"Nomen you're a naughty boy," Rusan snarled as she tried to break her brother's hold. "Is that human whore worth defying your sister?" her talons clawed at the air, trying to reach her brother.

"No. None of them are," Nomen said matter-of-fact.

"Then why Nomen? Why betray us? It's not too late Nomen, all will be forgiven if you just release me," Rusan cooed seductively, washing him in her lustful voice.

"No sister it will not, nor will I be made into a pawn," Nomen said running towards the nearest window. The ancient glass shattered, cutting his flesh as the deadly shards flew. Nomen couldn't risk shadow-walking; not with his sister so close. It would only take a momentary lapse and she could slip into his gateway. That was something he just couldn't afford to chance. As much as he had grown, in his humanoid form, he was no match for Rusan. Groaning in pain as his shoulder was wrenched from its socket, he caught hold of the fire escape.

"I will find you, Nomen! You will serve your purpose!" Ruslan's cruel voice filled the night as columns of fire jutted out of the windows of the old apartment building.

"Fuck!" Nomen hissed as he forced his shoulder back in place. Sweat beaded along his brow as he held his hand to his left side. Feeling his warm blood coating his hand cursing himself for not keeping an eye on her tail. He had to change, he needed to tap into his other form to repair the damage his sister had caused; yet if he did that it would leave him to vulnerable while he heals the wound. Bracing himself on the brick wall, he made his slow way through the alleyway. He could feel Rusan's poison sapping his strength the longer he remained in his human form. He threw up his hand as a pair of lights blinded him, the squealing of the tires rang painfully in his ears.

"Nomen get in!" Katherine yelled, throwing open the passenger side door. "Come on, Nomen this is no time to protest your rescue," Katherine commanded, not letting on that she saw the growing red blotch. "Go, Michael," she said, patting her brother's shoulder. "Nomen, what happened to you?" Katherine asked, trying to stop the bleeding.

"It's the poison she keeps in her tail, it's deadly to humans, at least my human half," Nomen winced in pain.

"You know this how?" Michael asked, peering at the man in the rearview mirror.

"Because she and her other six sisters are the daughters of Mephistopheles... And I am his son." Nomen's breathing became swallow as the poison slowly spread. "What were you thinking taking her on? She's not some low-level demon. Your chants and crosses mean nothing to them, archdemons cannot be exorcised," Nomen said, knowing he could no longer deny the inevitable. "Look away Katherine, I don't want you to see me," he whispered.

"Nomen… you just saved our lives, I think we can deal with whatever it is," Katherine said, lightly resting her hand on his arm.

"I have to change Katherine it won't be a pretty sight," Nomen said wondering why her expectance bothered him so.

"Yea, yea just get to it," Michael growled not wishing to admit they owed their life to him. Frost began to creep along the windows, the chill of fear filled the cabin of his borrowed car. Unholy howls bellowed out of Nomen as his body succumbed to the pain of the change. Yet as Michael consulted the rearview mirror he didn't see the eyes of a demon looking back at him.

"Head north on I58 for eight hours, there's something that needs to be reclaimed," Nomen said, drifting in and out through the waves of pain. "That should be plenty of time for me to heal myself," he said, resting uneasily against the door.

"Nomen Nesio. That's what she called you," Katherine said studying his bright red skin, his pale ivory horns that curled into a loop, just inches away from his temple. "What does it mean?"

"It means I have no name Katherine," Nomen said looking out the window. "I was raised by demons, they're not all that interested how one feels about being called no name. Then again after a millennium of being called that it just seemed to become my name. It's better than being called half breed all the time."

"What about your mother, surely she gave you a name?"

"My mother was a witch only interested in her own power. Hence why I was born to serve Mephistopheles' dark plan for this world. But Mara shouldn't be a concern of yours."

"Why," Katherine asked, gently squeezing his hand.

"Because I killed her," Nomen said matter-of-factly.

"Good. If she served the devil, the world is better off," Michael said, nodding in approval.

"Mephistopheles isn't the devil; just a very powerful angel that fell to Hell. Or that was what was written in the ancient text I was forced to memorize. But yes, she had to die; her sins outweighed anything good that came out of her... even me," Nomen said darkly.

"Nomen, don't say that. You're a good man," Katherine spoke in his defense.

"No, Katherine, I'm not. At one time, I would have willingly served my father. Opening the portal to this realm so he could have his way with this world. I don't even know if mankind is worth saving," Nomen said, looking over at her. "Can you say the souls of every human on this world is worth saving? All I see with these eyes of mine is sin, after sin, after sin, etched into your blinding souls that I must walk amongst. Knowing I would never be accepted into your world, as I'm not in my own, only tolerated given what my purpose is. After this they will be hunting me. Rusan has my blood; they will wait for my return. However, this time I won't be unprepared for the battle to come," Nomen said, knowing his father would most definitely be making an appearance. He was growing tired of the endless chase. Maybe, just maybe, oblivion would be a welcoming.

"Oh Nomen," Katherine said in a low whisper. She knew the moment they met he wasn't normal, her own fear had overruled her mind for the past five years.

Yet, she never took the time to see his pain of what he was forced to be.

"Kat, wake him up. We're nearly there," Michael said checking his watch.

"Nomen, Nomen, we're here," Katherine said, gently shaking him awake.

"Ah," Nomen said running his hand along the newly healed wound. Feeling the scar that had formed. "Pull over here," he said feeling the energies swirling through the forest. This was the closest portal that led to the broken realm of Limbo.

"Nomen, why are we here? Shouldn't we be asking the church for help, not walking through the forest?" Katherine asked as she pushed through the underbrush.

"Because your church thinks simple words can defeat high level demons that might be if they were possessing somebody. They are here in their physical forms, no mere words will harm them, and this world doesn't have a weapon that can kill arch demons. That is why we are here, Katherine," Nomen said, stopping in front of the gateway.

"Ok, so what can we expect once we cross over," Michael asked, checking his weapons.

"You can't come," Nomen said placing his hand on the gateway.

"Why not?" Michael asked, crossing his arms, looking at the man with concern.

"Because you're still alive," Nomen said looking over his shoulder. "However, I can fix that if you like," he said with sinister smirk.

"I'll wait here," Michael said moving off towards the fallen log to wait for his return.

"Nomen, where are you going," Katherine stepped close to his back.

"Limbo the only place my father wouldn't look for the blade," Nomen entered the gateway. The floating landmasses of Limbo rose and sank along the ebb and flow of the ethereal currents of the realm. Purple lightning streaked across the gray over-casted sky. Trees, large and small, dominated the landscape in their dead corpses never able to return to the earth of the realm. Beings from elementals, to the djinn, to the souls that choice to walk a different path dwelled within that silent realm. No one paid any attention to him as he walked through their realm. To them, he was nothing more than a wraith as they were to Nomen. He didn't belong to their realm any more than they did in his. Yet they made no move to stop him as he transverse the shattered realm. He placed his hand against the stone hiding the blade that started it all, crumbling back into the ether from which it was spawned. It's evilness washed over him after its long years of confinement. Calling to him like had done all those years ago, however, he was no longer that ignorant boy that had slain his own mother.

No, he had become something far more dangerous in the passing years. The soul of his mother hissed in his ears as his hand wrapped around the hilt of the sword, infusing the blade with his own energies as he sought to bend its will to his own. Nomen stood there for what seem like eternity as he fought for control, never moving, never drawing breath as his own demon did battle with what laid within. Until suddenly the sword hummed underneath his fingers, the dormant energies rippling along the blade waiting for the command of its master. Wails of the denizens cried out as his sword slashed through the air, sending a ribbon of red energy through the realm, striking the nearest landmass shattering it with ease sending the fragments rocketing throughout the lonely realm.

Unguis stood wanting his return eager to be back within her own realm. Savoring the screams of those that had fallen so far in their mortal lives, longing to have her talons sinking into the flesh of the damned as she sated her own wickedness upon the unfortunate. Having said mortal souls servicing her to her heart's content, feeding off their misery as they toiled in their damnation. Yet here she stood waiting on the half-breed that should have been slain the moment it was born. Her finger tapping her forearm as she stood before the gateway, with that ever-present sneer on her face. However, she didn't know that Nomen had felt her presence long before he had breached the gateway. Shock and confusion set in her cold black eyes as the cold metal of his sword cut through her being, cleaving her in two, spraying the surroundings in her green ichor as Nomen's sword cut upward. Wisps and wraiths poured out of Unguis's mangled body as its vile stench rose around him, swirling around his feet in a green eerie mist, traveling up his legs, along his solar plexus, before engulfing his whole body.

Power coursed through his body as Unguis' powers soon became his own. Her memories flooding his mind, knowing they had taken Katherine and her brother. Knowing that it was a trap waiting for him to comply with their demands. Yet he was still outmatched and outnumbered, yet he had to try even with Unguis' powers, the other six would be hard to put down single-handedly. However, as Michael always like to remind him he was a demon and with a wicked smile doing what demons normally did: betrayal. Exiting the shadows of the ac unit on the roof of the building that overlooked the intersection. Where

Rusan and the others stood over their captive charges, once their treacherous brother had shown himself then the hostages were no longer needed.

Thinking they were supreme in their own power they never thought to look to the sky as Ruslan's head spun in the air, along with two others' that shortly joined his fallen sister's. Streams of hellfire shot from the palms of his hands striking those remaining in his budding powers. Nomen needed to absorb the last of his sister's essences if he thought he had the chance to stand against his father. He could feel himself becoming more than just a half-breed as the last of his sisters fell at his feet.

"Katherine, you need to flee as far as you can," Nomen said, cutting the ropes at had bound them. "Soon it won't be safe here at least not for mortal life."

"Why, what are you going to do?" Katherine asked taking hold of his arm.

"My father is coming, they forced the gate open. Soon Mephistopheles will enter this world," Nomen said, pushing her into Michael's arms. "Take her and go," he said, before turning around walking towards the spot he was going to ambush his father.

"Nomen!" Katherine called out as she struggled in her brother's arms. "Nomen what are you planning to do?!"

"I'm going to kill my father or we kill each other," Nomen said, turning slightly as the wind tugged at his body. "Goodbye Katherine," he said before dashing off, leaving Katherine screaming behind him as he raced to meet his fate. Nomen narrowed his eyes as he looked through the glare as the gateway crackled and hissed as his father approached. Batting off the arcing energy that sparked from the event horizon. His left hand tapping against his leg as he became impatient, his sword hummed with excitement, wishing to be plunged into its foe. Razor-sharp talons gleamed wickedly in the sunlight, brimstone filled the air greeting the mortal world before his father did. The pavement cracked and heaved as his father's giant hoof sank into the manmade stone.

"So many souls," Mephistopheles hissed his acid drool hanging precariously from his disfigured chin. "So much torment just begging to be released onto their mortal coils. I smell the scent of one not of this world," he bellowed, shaking the foundations of the storefronts that surrounded the portal. "Boy! You traitorous cur! You dare show yourself before me after you failed to bring me forth!" Two mismatched ebony horns rose just above the edge of Mephistopheles forehead, while overshadowed by the two giant twenty-foot-thick twisted ebony horns that rose out the middle of his head. Pale green irises were surrounded by pitch-black sclera as Mephistopheles' true form was revealed to the world of man. The tip of his nose cut from his face during the battle for heaven, leaving only two grotesque holes marring his face. His blackened scarred face, reminders of the wrath of his most hated foe, Raphael. His elf-like ears protruded at odd angles from his head. His once soft lips that were sung of by the maidens he had lain with were cut from his face for his defilement of God's law. Allowing all to see those shark-like teeth that tore at his flesh if he foolishly forgotten what was taken from him. Once pearl-white feathers, now nothing more than black tar covered spikes that had been thrusted into his immortal body.

"No father, this world is not yours not now, not ever, not while I stand before you," Nomen said, rising his blade as he rushed his demonic father.

221

"You think some foolish half breed can stop...." Air rushed out of his chest as his son's might propelled him backwards, bricks crumbled, screams filled the air as his giant bulk crashed into the buildings behind him. Mephistopheles' wail of horrific pain vibrated the glass fiercely, shattering every window within a ten-mile radius. Golden ichor seeped out of the wound as Nomen's sword absorbed his immortality. Drawing upon his own unholy might, racing up his father's chest dragging his sword behind him. Cutting through his once immortal flesh with ease, dodging his father's attempt to grasp him in his crushing embrace.

"That's the problem with you, old man, you always thought you were untouchable," Nomen said, hacking through the tree-trunk thick ribs that protected the fallen angels heart. "You should never have forced my hand Mephistopheles, then maybe you would still be the ruler of your own realm," he said as the pale glistening muscle beat frantically. "For I am now and forever more Malum Peccavi!" Nomen cried out as his sword led the way as he disappeared into the cavity of his father's chest.

"Nooo!" Mephistopheles' voice grew weak and no more as the once general of Lucifer's army became nothing more than a faded memory. Nightmarish screams filled the air as Nomen's skin melted from his body as Mephistopheles' blood ate away his mortal form. There on that still, eerie street nothing remained of those that were nothing more than fiction. Not even the fates whispered the names that died on that fateful day, yet Hell must have a ruler, its greed and lust must be held in check by those that tread those unholy halls. Towering walls loomed in the distance guarding the only entrance, as the giant skulls of the once great

Nephilim that once walked among man. Poured out the torrents of blood that flowed from their gaping mouths, that fed the mighty rivers that flowed to the depths of the underworld. The shadow palace of the fallen Mephistopheles reverberated as the new Lord of the Eight circle approached his new throne. His black feathered wings sparked as his power arced between each feather. His red skin heated as the fires roared in the distance, announcing the new ruler had arrived. Demons and the damned scurried from the wrath of their one-time plaything; fearful they too would meet the same fate. The three rows of ivory horns nestled in the nest of his red flaming hair shone in the red orange light.

"Greetings my lord," Aheile smiled triumphantly as her new King took his throne. "I knew you be the one to win and rule over this realm," she said looking out on to the eight circle.

"Indeed, Mother," Malum said as his chin rested in his hand.

The End.

I'm mostly a fantasy author who dabbles in the horror section. I started out little over a year ago with the release of Twilight City: Edward the silver werewolf. Now I have finished my fourth novel, which is the second book in the Sons of Cain series, titled Twilight City: The Awakening. Where I believe will be a six-part series, at least that's where I believe my books are leading me too. But, like all authors our stories take on a life of their own, we just happen to have the privilege to tag along on the journey.

https://m.facebook.com/#!/jamesrichauthor/

amazon.com/author/james_richardson

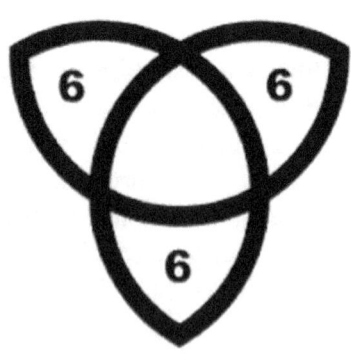

TAINTED REVENGE
By
Lori Fontanez

Willow was not a typical teenage girl. She had better things to do other than have a phone in her face, or have sleepovers with friends. She was a loner and liked to things to occupy her mind.

She was standing on the corner by her neighbor's house, waiting on the city line bus to transport her to favorite bookstore.

She always got off the bus a few blocks away from her original destination.

Willow knew that people judged her for the way she looked. Most of time she dressed in black; it matched her deep purple hair. She chose that color only because her mother died two years earlier from Crohn's disease.

She mourned in her own way, staying distant from her father. He didn't mind, he threw himself into his job, which resulted in him staying home less. He had no idea what his only daughter was into. He had even thought about sending Willow to boarding school, until she threatened to run away. He tried to explain it wasn't because he didn't want her; it would help her socially and she would get better care. She told her father that she was fine the way it was. Her father mostly dropped the subject, but he just couldn't resist bringing it up every once in a while.

The bus stopped and Willow jerked herself back into reality. She got up and grabbed her messenger bag, putting it over her shoulder as she started toward the front of the bus. The bus driver was bitching at her for taking her sweet time. She just laughed at him and when she was off the bus, she turned and flipped him off. She looked at him and said, "I hope you suffer!" The bus driver mumbled a few words then closed the door and drove off. Leaving her at the curb alone.

Willow kicked a couple pebbles as she walked down the sidewalk. She was window-shopping on the way to the bookstore. Once she arrived, she saw the sign posted on the door saying: *at the bank, be back in fifteen minutes.* She shrugged it off and sat on the cold cement stoop.

She opened her backpack and pulled out a book that was on the reading list in her English class. Willow was a smart girl; she just made bad choices. After an hour of waiting, the clerk opened the door and found Willow leaning against the wall fast asleep. The clerk shook her arm lightly; she didn't want to startle the poor girl.

The clerk knew her from her weekly visits to the store. Willow's father left money on the table every morning before he left for his job. Willow jerked as she woke up, dropping her book, losing her page and that frustrated her.

The clerk said, "I'm sorry, I didn't mean to startle you."

"It's okay," Willow replied. She stood up and brushed the dust off her jeans and walked inside the store. She basically knew where everything was.

Willow found the book of spells she wanted and laid it on the counter. She had enough time to catch the last bus back home, before her father arrived back from work. The clerk rang her purchase up on the antique cash register and read her the total. Willow opened her message bag and took out her wallet.

That's when she noticed the clerk's necklace for the first time. It had a red, glowing center that appeared to be thumping as if it had a heartbeat. This was intriguing her, so willow instantly asked the clerk about it.

The clerk said: "The owner brought it in this morning and was only asking twenty-five dollars for it. He had found it in a building he was tearing down in the city."

"I'll take it!" replied Willow without any hesitation.

She whipped open her wallet as the clerk asked: "Do you want to wear it, or do you want me to box it up?"

Willow replied," I'll wear it, thanks."

Willow hurried out the store and back to the bus stop. The necklace began to work on her. She felt the necklace center humming with the same rhythm of the blood pumping through her small built body. Willow began to change; she passed the bus stop and headed north. It was a place she had never been, as it was a rough area. She was badass, but would be out of place.

The more she walked, the more she began to change into someone else. She felt the changes occurring, but couldn't stop them. Willow wasn't herself when she entered a nearby apartment building.

She touched the up button on the elevator. When it opened, she went to the third floor and took an immediate right and knocked on the first door.

The voice behind the door said, "Who is it?"

She didn't reply. She continued to knock harder until the voice opened the door.

He was shocked to see who was standing there.

Willow said: "Oh, you look as if you saw a ghost!" She walked into the apartment.

He followed her in and closed the door, saying, "Let me explain!"

Willow, not being herself, said: "Explain what? How you killed me and shoved my body into the river?"

He was shaking as he asked, "Where did you find that necklace?"

"Don't worry about the necklace, you fool!"

Willow walked into the kitchen and grabbed a knife off the counter. One of those cheap sets, probably from Wal-Mart, that had five knives and kitchen scissors. Willow grabbed the sharpest one. He walked into the kitchen, careful not to follow directly behind her. He hurried to the living room when he saw what she was after and grabbed his burner phone and started to call one of his buddies.

His back was turned to her, but she still heard him on the phone. She hurried into the living room and stabbed him until he fell to his knees. She saw him take his last breath, then fall flat on the floor.

Blood flew everywhere as it splattered up the walls. It was all over her clothes. The person on the other end was screaming his name. Willow picked up the phone and said, "You're next!" and pushed the red end call button.

Willow turned toward the victim and decided not to clean up her mess, deciding only to make sure that he would rot in hell for all eternity.

She looked all over the house for stuff to use for him. She found everything she needed in a drawer in the bathroom. Willow returned to dead body to prepare it for its final trip.

First, she sewed his mouth and eyes closed and cut off both of his ears. She knew that the man had enough gauze for the next step, because he was a paramedic. She found his stash in a closet in the bedroom. She wrapped it around his body leaving his eyes and mouth unwrapped.

She stuck all the knives in different areas of his body as she made him into a human voodoo doll. She tried like hell to tie him up by his arms, but the man was too heavy and, quite frankly, she was getting bored with it. She put him back on the couch.

She was into Wicca and decided, at the last minute, to cast a spell on him. As she walked out the door, she could hear him muffling around trying to break free. With all the knives shoved into his flesh and his eyes and mouth sewn shut, he could feel the pain and would die again in agony. Like he did the first time.

She hit the elevator button again and once inside, she hit the main floor button. The doors closed slowly. When they opened again she walked back onto the sidewalk and began walking. She still had no idea where she was, or who she was.

Half way back into town she began to change as the necklace stopped glowing. She wondered why she had missed the bus.

As she looked down at herself, she noticed the blood on her clothes and shoes.

She hurried back to the bookstore, but it had already closed. "Great, now I have to call my father for a ride," she said out loud not caring who heard her.

She knew he would ask too many questions that she couldn't answer. She pulled her phone out of her messenger bag and noticed another phone in her bag. She ignored it for the moment and dialed the number.

He picked up on the first ring, "Dylan Hawker. Can I help you?" He didn't even look at the caller ID.

Willow said, "Dad, it's Willow. I need a ride home; I've missed the bus."

"Missed what bus? Where are you?" he replied.

"One question at a time." Willow said abruptly. She added:" I'm in town, I went to the bookstore and got lost in the books and lost time." She thought to herself, *he doesn't need to know what kind of book store.* "Are you coming to get me, or do I need to call a taxi? She finished with attitude.

Dylan said, "Well, I've had a couple beers, but I can come anyway. Text me your location."

"Whatever!" Willow walked across the street to the Circle K and asked the clerk for the bathroom key. He seemed hesitate, but gave it to her and said, "Don't do any drugs in there either."

Willow walked back to the counter and leaned in, the clerk backed up slowly. She said, "I don't do fucking drugs, asshole." Willow threw the key back at him. He ducked and it hit the glass window behind him. Glass shattered which caused the alarms to charm. The clerk threw his hands in the air and screamed: "Great! Now, I'm going to lose my job."

"You shouldn't have pissed me off," replied the steaming mad Willow.

The cops showed up a few minutes later and the clerk pointed in the direction in which Willow had taken off.

The faster she walked, she felt herself changing again. Before she knew it, she was no longer Willow. The police pulled up beside her and rolled down the window and asked if she had saw a girl pass by.

"No," she said, "I'm waiting here for my boyfriend. I haven't seen anyone walking or running."

The officer said: "Thank you, have a good evening." They drove off slowly, looking for Willow. After a few minutes, she calmed down and she began to change back.

She said to herself, *how the hell did I get over here?* She was going back to the circle K, when she saw all the police cars. She kind of remembered what happened and turned to go to the location where her father should be by this point. Her father was there, waiting for her and asked: "Where in the hell did you go? I've been sitting here for a few minutes."

"Oh my God!" Willow said, "I went to the damn bathroom, calm down."

"Don't tell me what to do," he said.

They drove the rest of the way in silence. Then, he turned off the radio and said: "I'm driving through Wendy's; do you want anything?"

"Sure, I'll take a burger and fries," Willow replied.

He said and "what to drink?"

"I want a chocolate shake"

He turned into the parking lot and pulled up to the drive-through, he gave his order and the clerk said, "Pull up to window, sir." He looked over at his daughter and said: "I don't know why you can't be nice and polite like that kid."

Willow began to push her lips together and took a deep breath. It didn't help. The necklace began to pulse, she ignored it and blurted out: "You know what, Dad? Fuck you! Fuck your food! Fuck your ride! Just go fuck off." Before he could stop her, she was already out of the car. They weren't that far from the house, she was walking fast, cutting through yards, not giving a shit if she was trespassing.

The necklace had changed her and she didn't even notice this time. When she arrived at her destination it wasn't at her house. She was at another apartment. She walked in without knocking, catching the tenant passed out on the couch.

This was going to be easy, she thought. Willow woke him up and the wide-eyed man sat straight up, looking at her.

He blurted out, "I had nothing in it."

She said, "Burt, you were always a liar and a cheat."

Willow whacked him in the head, over and over with the baseball bat she found behind the door. There was brain matter, and blood on the backside of the couch. This kill was as important as the other one.

She found that she had hit him so hard one of his eyeballs fell out of his skull and landed beside his foot. She found a big knife in the drawer of the kitchen and decided that smashing his head in wasn't enough this time.

She raised the knife and slammed it down hard enough to take his head completely off. She picked up his head and took the broomstick out of the closet in the kitchen and stuck the head on the broomstick. She wanted to catch him on fire, but chose to open the patio door and take the flag down that was nailed to the side of the door. She raised the broomstick and added him to the flagpole.

It was an accomplishment, she thought to herself. She felt sorry for Willow, taking over her body and making her do these things, but it seemed that they were a lot alike in ways.

Still, she wanted to stay and kill Willow's soul so she could take it over. She decided that she would wait until she got all the revenge on her so-called friends. She had a mental list who would die by Willow's hands.

She walked into his bathroom and turned on the shower water. When it was hot enough, she got undressed and climbed in and washed off. She turned off the water and grabbed a towel and went into his room to get dressed. Apparently, she had had clothes in the closet and drawers as she had lived there from time to time. She changed into jeans, tank top and grabbed clean shoes. She put the soiled clothes in a bag, picked up her messenger bag and walked out of the apartment.

When the cool night air hit her, she wished she would have grabbed a long-sleeve shirt. When the necklace let her change back Willow didn't know where she was this time. She found herself looking at street signs and googling them on her cell phone. She had a few missed calls and texts from her father. She listened to the messages as she rolled her eyes; it was the same blah, blah, blah. "Come home; we'll talk about it." The next message said: "Where in the hell are you?", the last message said: "Okay, Willow, get your ass home, now!" Dylan's words became more slurred with each call.

He had a few more drinks of the much harder liquor hiding in his office. When Willow finally realized where she was, she knew a shortcut to the house. She knew not to go in the front door, and decided when she got there to climb the tree beside her bedroom and crawl in through the window. It was something she did from time from time to avoid any contact with her father.

She noticed she wasn't wearing the clothes she had on earlier and wondered where she had picked up the change. It was totally blowing her mind that she kept disappearing. She was a block away from the house. She couldn't wait to get there, so she could take of the hideous clothes she had on.

She took hold of the necklace with her hand to hold it still as she jogged slowly the rest of the way. She felt the necklace pulsating against her skin. She instantly let go off the necklace as if it burnt her hand.

When she finally made to the house, she climbed up the tree, one limb at a time. She reached her destination and opened the window. She climbed in and threw her messenger bag on her bed. The bag opened and the bloody clothes appeared. Willow freaked out.

She grabbed them in a panic and ran to the bathroom. She had no idea what was going on. She looked at herself in the mirror and saw that her hair was matted with what appeared to be dried blood. Willow was scared and thought to herself, *what is going on?*

She turned on the shower water, not even waiting until the water was hot before she yanked off the different clothes that she picked up somewhere and grabbed a towel. She hurried into the water to wash the blood off her and began washing her hair. She looked down at the drain as she was rinsing her and hair and noticed not only blood, but also pieces of what looked to be brain matter rinsing down the drain. Willow was grossed out.

When she finished washing her body and hair, Willow stepped out and dried off. She put her pajama pants on and a long tee shirt.

She unrolled a wad of toilet paper and wiped out the drain, flushing the evidence in the commode. She had no clue where she had been.

Willow walked back into her room and picked up the soiled clothes and saw all the blood and pieces of human flesh on them. She knew washing them at this point would be pointless and hoped that no one witnessed her acts. She grabbed a pair of scissors and cut the clothes up in many pieces. She went downstairs and grabbed a Wal-Mart bag from the pantry and stuffed the pieces of material in them.

Then, she went to the basement and opened the bag, throwing the clothes in the fireplace. They always kept a small flame in the fireplace to keep the upstairs floor warm. She stood there watching it burn, not paying attention. Willow's father came down stairs and was watching her.

She was startled when he bellowed: "What in the hell are you doing, Willow?"

She hurried with a lie; she was good at it. "I hate these clothes and so I'm burning them," she replied.

"Kids these days, have no respect. I'm not buying you anything else, if you're just going to throw it away."

She didn't want another scream match and ended the conversation with, "They were too small, anyway."

Dylan turned and went back upstairs, not wanting her to kill his buzz.

The necklace began to glow once again and she felt it. It was not the first time she felt the pulsing of the necklace. She wondered why she just didn't take it off. The necklace had Willow right where she wanted her. It kept her on task on what it wanted. Soon, there would be no more Willow. The necklace would take over her soul. There were a couple more people that needed to die, though, so she could live.

Willow went back upstairs and got ready for bed. She was exhausted and didn't know why. She opened the book she bought at the bookstore. She wanted to remember to call or go the bookstore and get some information on the necklace she bought. The necklace didn't like that and got hot, leaving a mark on her chest.

Willow grabbed the necklace, but when she tried to take it off, it wouldn't budge. The necklace didn't have any other choice but to proceed in taking Willow's soul and replace it with hers.

Willow was quickly transformed into Candy. She knew it wasn't the right time, but since Willow was going to ask about the necklace, the clerk knew too much about it.

The next person she needed to take out was the clerk, but why? Because she was the girl who had taken her place with her husband. Sweet revenge and Willow would go down for all the murders and she would move on to another victim. The necklace was a beautiful piece. Candy knew it; it wouldn't take long to get another host.

Willow had gone to bed and when she woke up, she felt dazed and confused like she had a hangover, except she didn't drink. She pulled the covers back and sat up, stretched and stood up. She went to the bathroom where she happened to look in the mirror/ It was not her face, the face of Willow, but a stranger's face. Her hair was the same color, but she felt differently, she thought differently, and wondered what was happening.

Candy let Willow have little parts of her life at times. Not very much of her life would ever be the same. Willow looked closer into the mirror and noticed lines around her eyes, as if she aged overnight. *Damn,* she thought, *what the hell is going on with me?*

She walked out of the bathroom and grabbed her spell book. Maybe a spell could reverse the weird shit going on in her head.

Candy wouldn't let her focus on that weird shit, and decided that a new kill would have to happen. Willow's stomach began to growl and she went to the kitchen to grab some junk to eat. However, Candy loved food and could really cook. She overpowered her decision and opened the fridge and grabbed some eggs and ham. She got out a skillet and whipped up a cheese omelet.

Her father got a whiff of something cooking and drifted into the kitchen. "When did you learn how to cook, Willow?"

"I have been cooking for years, Dylan. I mean, Dad," she replied.

Dylan was unsure of why his daughter didn't bite his head off and asked if he could have whatever she was having.

"I guess I can make you one."

He said, "Let me know when it's ready."

"Okay!" she replied.

Candy knew this was the moment she needed; she could poison him and make it look like an overdose, or wait until he was drunk again and take him out that way. Then, she remembered that Willow was a teenager and couldn't live alone. Candy dismissed the idea of taking his life, only because of Willow's age.

Over time Dylan noticed Willow changing. He figured that she was growing up, only Candy was now in full control over Willow.

She did try to do things that Willow would have done. She went to the bookstore and spoke to the new clerk. She asked about the previous clerk and was told that she was missing. Candy said, "Wow! That is unfortunate."

The clerk looked at with a displeased look and asked," What the hell does that mean? Do you know something?"

"No, why would I know what happened to her?" replied Candy.

The clerk walked away mumbling under his/her breath. Candy knew she shouldn't have asked anything. She did see more of her things in the case at the checkout line. Candy wanted them back and told the clerk that she was robbed and those earrings and bracelet were hers. The clerk told her that the person that the items she was talking about belonged to a woman that was murdered.

Candy had to leave it at that. She couldn't fight the feeling that overcame her when she thought about someone bringing her jewelry here to a bookstore.

Candy left the store and knew where she was going. The next to last victim. She loved her new young body. She took the bus over to the South side of town. It was a better neighborhood than the others that she had been to lately. This kill would have to be fast and hot.

It would be in broad daylight, much easier to get caught.

She was sly, though, and had the ability to change herself into different people. She walked up to the house she knew too well. It had a white security gate.

She had the code to enter and did it with pride. Candy took the Molotov cocktail out of the messenger bag, lit it, and threw it through the glass window, and ran. She got a block away when she heard the explosion. She knew her victims were in there.

Candy said, "Rest in hell, bitches," and laughed the rest of the way home. She loved her new way.

Candy was a walking time bomb, she created chaos everywhere she went and followed innocent people home just to start a conflict and slaughter them in their own beds. She often fought with herself over her bad upbringing. Both of her parents had been alcoholics. She got sick of the smell of them and caught their house on fire when she was only six-years-old. They proved the house had faulty wires and determined it was accidental, killing both parents as they were passed out in bed. She had no remorse for killing anyone in that matter.

She had always been on the bad side of the law. She spent most of her juvenile life in out of different foster homes. She brutally murdered the last foster parent. She got into ghost hunting, which led to Wicca, and then sold her soul to the devil. She was sneaky like a snake and this snake was on the loose; no one was going to stop her. She wanted revenge on the weak, the strong, the young and the old. She could manipulate easily.

Candy went back to Willow's house and took a shower, Dylan knocked on her door and asked if she wanted to go eat. She said: "No, I'll make myself a sandwich or something."

"Whatever you want," Dylan replied.

He staggered away from the door. He already had too many beers. Candy knew he had to go, so she opened the door and followed him outside to the patio.

He started to sit in one of the iron chairs he bought at a yard sale. It had a glass table and umbrella attached. He liked sitting outside beside the pool having a few cold ones.

Candy walked silently behind him and pushed him into the table, he fell forward fast and couldn't stop himself. The table flipped over from his weight, instantly shattering the glass. A large piece of the glass stabbed him in the windpipe. She watched blood squirt out of his eyes and ears. She watched him take his last breath and didn't call for help.

She walked back into the house.

She found a map of the area and set out the next day. The only thing Candy took from Willow's house was a book. She had a mission.

No one would be safe as Candy went slithering around lurking for her next kill.

The End

Lori is a wife and mother. She lives in North Central West Virginia. She loves writing in the horror genre. Lori does crafts, sewing and knitting. Her Boston Terrier Millie is her sidekick.

She can be found on her Amazon author page, and her Facebook author page.

https://www.amazon.com/Lori-Fontanez/e/B014JKGO4M

https://m.facebook.com/Lori.A.Fontanez/

THE THRESHOLD OF HELL

By
Marcus Mattern

"Time keeps on slipping; slip - slip - slip - slip - slip,"

The first thing he knew, Michael Door was punching his CD player. It was a gentle punch, strong enough to get it to change, but soft enough to say *I'll love you when this is over*. The rest of the song played without interruption.

As he drove to the next freshly red stoplight, he started to think about the last clear memory he had. There was a vague recollection of getting out of bed, throwing on a t-shirt and jeans, putting coffee in a to-go mug, starting his faded orange Ford Mustang, and pulling out of the parking lot. If you told him all of that happened to someone else, he might believe you. Until he'd hit the CD player, his mind has been on autopilot. Not the I-can't-fail awesome kind of autopilot you feel when you're nailing every shot in basketball or every combo in Mortal Kombat. It was the awful, tedious I-can't-stand this autopilot you feel when doing the same thing you've done a million times.

Naturally, Michael was driving to work.

The next thing he knew, his hands were loading a heavy filing cabinet into a dolly. The usual, playful morning banter had been replaced with an uncomfortable silence. Was it something he said?

"Careful, now China Shop," a lady barked from behind him. Michael had been steady, but jumped at sound of his boss's voice.

"I will be if you don't sneak up on me, like that," Michael said as he strapped the cabinet into the dolly. The office had yellowed walls and a sad, coffee-stain grey carpet, fitting for a business that was closing shop after 40 years.

"If any of this shit gets so much as scuffed, it's your head! We're all sick of your attitude!" Cynthia's round face had grown beet red under her frizzy yellow hair.

Michael shook his head and tightened his grip, then grunted out "Yes, ma'am," and began carting the filing cabinet toward the front door, and the truck beyond.

What the hell was her problem?

Whatever it was, it was catching. His coworkers gave him a wide berth as he loaded more office furniture into the truck. He couldn't remember them ever reacting to him like this, but it was also hard to imagine them acting any other way. Bright sunshine on the windless day stung him harder every time he stepped outside. His breaths were growing heavy and strained.

The next he knew, Michael was screaming, "I am in hell!" as Cynthia stood next to him, arms crossed, in the dark of a closed, empty office room. He flung the door open and headed for his car.

What had even made him this angry? Words and hateful faces swarm in a formless circle of melting memories. It didn't matter who told him to go to hell or when, it was time to leave. His shift wouldn't end for another four hours, but he was done.

Relief washed over him as he slammed his car door shut and started the engine as music began to blare from the speakers. "Irresponsible!" was the word shouting in Michael's mind, in Cynthia's voice, from somewhere in his memory. As the heat in his hands dissipated and his shoulders relaxed, Michael figured this was the most responsible thing he'd ever done for his boss.

The next thing he knew, Michael was staring at the open door to his apartment from the parking lot. This was a break in. A faded beige and brick facade surrounded the street-level entrance. He worried the intruder might have a gun, but the thrill he felt at the chance to use his fists far outweighed any fear.

Creeping in through the open door, he heard his girlfriend Stasia talking in the back bedroom. The front room was ransacked, with the sofa upturned and the TV missing and Xbox missing. Then Stasia giggled, driving a spike of anger into Michael's head.

Was she cheating on him?

Michael clenched his fist and trudged through the messy floor and the burnt cigarette smell of home.

Before he made it to the bedroom door, a large man burst out, carrying a heavy duffel bag and bull rushed him. His sight went dull as his head smacked into the ground.

The next thing he knew, Michael was standing over Stasia as she cried and covered her face, slumping against the wall. The knuckles on his right hand burned from the impact. The red sheets of the bed behind him were half torn off and drawers had been pulled from the wooden dresses and scattered across the room.

He just hit her?

"Leave!" she pleaded as blood dripped down the edge or her chin. Her curly blonde ringlets hid the rest of her face, but the shuddering and sobbing told Michael everything she felt.

His hands dropped open at his sides and he pulled back, horrified at what he'd done. Then he remembered the sound she'd made and hate shot out of his throat.

"No! I'm already going crazy enough without coming home to this bullshit. Who the fuck was that? Why's our shit all torn up? And why the fuck were you laughing about it!"

"I already told you," she said, hugging her knees to her chest.

Is that why he hit her?

He couldn't remember, and as badly as he needed a place to be, anywhere was better than here.

"Fuck this!" he shouted and walked out the room, down the hall, and into his car, leaving the front door open.

The next thing he knew, Michael was parked in front of the police station, cradling the steering wheel with his arms as he cried.

Why was this happening?

Looking up, the police station seemed like a shelter in a storm. The fortress of white bricks and tall windows promised order to a life unraveling in chaos. Maybe not the kind he wanted, but maybe just the kind he needed. Something heavy and sick in the pit of his stomach made him look away as he wiped the wetness from his sodden face.

Was he really just going to turn himself in?

Across the street, he glimpsed the marbled stone and dazzling stained glass of the downtown church. A sign in red and gold proudly proclaimed 'WE SAVE SOULS.'

As with most things, Michael couldn't remember how old he was when he stopped going to church. Younger than thirteen, certainly, but any guess behind that was just as good. He remembered the feeling of wonder, grounded and safe. His father would take him there, when he was alive, and the strength of his hand when they joined in prayer was more certain than anything he could remember thereafter.

The next thing he knew, Michael was stepping through the tall, arched wooden doors of the church, holding his breath. He stepped through the rose-hued entryway and into the main hall. Gold and red light streamed through the stained-glass windows as the afternoon sun bathed the church in color.

This is where he was meant to be.

"Can I help you?" a white-haired priest asked from across the aisle. His red robe featured a series of gold crosses down the center. Michael looked at him and stumbled forward, knees weak, then braced himself on one of the wooden benches.

"Can you?" Michael asked. Doubt swelled, making a lump in his throat. All of the sudden, he realized how he must look: sweating and crying with clenched desperation in his face.

The priest's wizened face dropped into a serious yet gentle look of concern.

"You're here for a reason. Whether I'm a part of that reason is for you to say. Speak now."

Michael wiped the wetness from his face and grunted, then looked up into the stained-glass motif of Jesus rising into heaven.

"You ever-" Michael started, then coughed and swallowed.

"You ever walk into a room and forget what made you go there in the first place?"

"Yes," the Priest answered with some hesitance, and began approaching. "It's quite normal. Nothing to be distressed about."

"I f - I feel. I feel like that *all the time,*" Michael replied, looking at the priest with alarm. "Like there's something there, taking me over. And whenever it needs a break, it just drops me off in some kind of room, doing some kind of thing, and I don't have any clue what the hell I'm doing there. Even now…"

Michael lowered himself into the wooden bench and slouched, looking at his open hands. The priest approached cautiously and took a seat across from him, still listening.

"I know *why* I'm here. I saw the sign out front. I decided to come here. But I don't know *how* I got here. If you asked me where my car is parked, I couldn't find it. But swear to God, if I walk out that door, I'll blank out again and wake up in the fucking car - pardon my French."

Michael turned to the priest as his enthusiasm grew.

"Maybe I'll wake up at home, or at work, or in a crash! I'm sure I was thinking something or listening to song, but I just - I just don't know where my mind goes!" He didn't know why he was smiling so much.

The priest looked away, then frowned. Then he took a deep breath, "Son, as I said, it's normal to forget sometimes where you are or what you're doing.

It's actually important. If you never forgot, you'd never question if you're in the right place, or if you're doing the right thing."

The priest looked up and gestured toward the light "I believe you are in the right place, and I believe you are doing the right thing. The question I have for you…" his eyes widened and locked with Michael's. "Is what takes you over when your mind wanders off. Is it God… or the devil?"

Michael blinked and looked away. Then he glared at the priest, and then he looked away again. His eyes returned a last time, welling with tears and his crumpled lips sputtered out "Or…" and then he buried his face in his hands, sobbing.

The priest stood, and Michael felt the gentle warmth as a hand touched his back.

The next thing he knew, Michael felt holy water splash his face. The priest was chanting something in Latin and walking in a circle around him as he whipped the decanter of holy water through the air. Another, black-haired priest was on his knees against the back wall of the church rec room, praying.

He couldn't believe it was happening so fast, though he wasn't sure how long it had been. His throat was parched and hoarse from screaming and he had rashes across his wrist from struggling in the chair. It could have been hours since he was last aware. Why was he back now?

Did this mean it was working?

Michael breathed deeply, trying to slow his racing heart rate. The thought occurred that he had no way of knowing when this was over.

"I think… I might be healed… You can stop now."

No response.

The priest continued to chant. The younger man rose from his spot against the wall and turned. He pointed at Michael with ruinous hatred and screamed "Defiler! You do not belong in this world! Release Michael Door now, or you will be cast down into the hell from whence you came!"

"Uh," Michael answered, "It's just me, chief. The name's Michael, you are?"

The man in the black cassock raised his finger, ready to declare something else when his white-haired partner interrupted.

"It's alright, Michael," the old priest said. He placed a hand on his shoulder. "You're going to be well again. Daniel and I can help you. You're going to feel like yourself for the first time in a long time - too long. You need to relax now and accept this for the healing to be begin."

"Don't listen," the Daniel commanded, addressing only the priest. "You are not to speak to this thing again until we are through. It will try to endear itself to you - to bring you down with it. It is only through righteous domination that the impurity will be purged!"

Michael grunted and spat on the man's feet. "I will lay a righteous fist across your mouth if you keep talking like that. I never fucking invited you anyway!"

"Silence!" the young man commanded, raising a silver cross. "Father Mateus has neither the youth or experience to wage warfare on your kind alone. By the light of God, I'm sworn to aid his charge until you have been purified!

"Pray therefore the God of Peace, crush Satan beneath our feet!"

Father Mateus begin flinging the holy water once more as he chanted and walked in a circle around

Michael. Daniel continued his liturgy and the screaming sounds of prayer melded together into a meaningless stream of vowels.

Michael's eyes rolled into the back of his head as he suffered the first seizure of his life. Pain gripped his body, his muscles twitched and tremored as sweat rolled down his forehead. His frozen eyes remained fixed on the searing overhead lights.

He lost consciousness.

The next thing he knew, Michael was waking up, still tied to a metal chair as moonlight streamed in from the basement windows above him.

On his left, he saw Father Mateus on a cot, sleeping peacefully. A wooden cross was clutched in his hand as he rested it on his pillow.

His mouth felt dry as ashes and his skin was greasy from the sweating he'd done over…

How long had he been here?

He couldn't tell the time, and he wasn't even sure this was the same day he arrived, although it felt like it. The hours of his memory bled together into one chaotic stretch of searing pain. As he blanked out the painful memories, a tense pang of hunger spiked in his stomach. He couldn't remember the last time he ate.

Were they just going to let him die here?

Michael scrutinized the gentle breaths of father Mateus as he slept at his side. He trusted him, even though he didn't know him, but he didn't trust the company he kept. He wasn't sure what Daniel was trying to draw out of him. At this point, driving it out was more of a risk to his health than keeping it in.

Moving his fingers around the slick cords that bound him to the chair, he found a knot. Michael closed his eyes and concentrated on pushing the knot through itself, widening the loops, and finally hooking his finger around one, he pulled it free.

He wanted to shout in joy as he brought his free hand to his face, but he was wary of waking Father Mateus.

His hand wasn't worth celebrating anyway. Apart from the scars and callouses peppering its surface, his wrist was caked with dried blood from where he'd tried to tear himself free.

Worse than not remembering the struggle, Michael didn't even feel the pain of his wrists until just now.

Slow, but determined, he worked his other hand free and then both feet, stopping every time he heard Father Mateus snore.

Finally, he stood. Breathing in, he stretched his legs and let his hands fall to his side. Father Mateus was still fast asleep. He heard no one else in the church. The moon lit the room brightly and could guide him out of here and back to freedom.

This was the last thought in his mind as he stepped forward, collapsed to knees and blacked out.

The next thing he knew, Michael was fading in and out, struggling to stay awake long enough to find out what had happened. His restless head thrashed against the white pillow of a rigid bed. His wrists and ankles were bound in large, cushioned restraints. In the distance, he heard a quiet voice and cried just before remembering who it was.

"Then you can take him and never give him back."

It was Stasia. The venom in her voice was unmistakable. Michael's eyes fluttered toward her blonde locks in dim awareness. She had a bandage over her left eye. The unharmed eye was cold and resolved.

"I…" Father Mateus was struggling to muster a defense. "This isn't your responsibility. No one deserves what he did to you. What I'm asking you to accept is that you're not suffering alone. Michael is willing to get better. If he has the support of someone close, this will happen sooner. You will not get anything out of this, but you will get to be part of something greater than yourself.

"This-" Father Mateus shook his head, "- being together allows us all to heal faster than any one of us can heal alone."

"Then you don't want me here," Stasia snapped. "I don't want him to get better. I don't want him saved. I want him to feel everything he's done to everyone, every fucking second, forever. So don't call me again unless you want me drag him to hell myself."

"Stasia," Michael called out through a weak, raspy voice.

Her eye glared. Stomping with a clack from her heal, Stasia turned and walked out the door, slamming it shut behind her.

"My, my…" Father Mateus said shaking his head, then turned and looked down upon Michael, "What are we going to do with you?"

The next thing he knew, Michael felt a pressure on his chest as if someone was sitting on it. He felt a warm drip across his forehead and eyes, then he heard the breathing above him.

He opened his eyes and saw Daniel waving a hand over his forehead in the dark of the star-lit room. "It's alright, Michael. I'm going to squeeze the devil out; you won't have to worry about anything once I'm done. It's almost over."

His breathing was strained, and after a day without food or water, Michael lacked the strength to heave Daniel off of his chest.

"What are doing?" Michael asked. He suddenly felt the slick metal of a scalpel as it dug deeper into his head.

"Why don't you want to die, you miserable creature?" Daniel asked wistfully as his hand continued with care and precision.

"We make it so easy for you. We open every door, and you shut them all. Even when you know there's nothing for left you here, you won't move aside. Do you know how selfish that is?"

"Get, the fuck... the fuck... get the fuck off me!" Michael twisted in the bed and Daniel's knees slipped, then he fell. The blade slashed across Michael's temple before it dropped out of Daniel's hand and clattered to the floor.

Daniel snickered as he crawled over to pick it up, then slowly rose from the floor. "Perhaps it's for the best then," he said. "There's tougher than you out there. And I'm not going to stop until we get them all."

Hot breath drew across Michael's ear as Daniel leaned in to whisper. "This world doesn't belong to you. It was ours before you got here. And it will be ours long after you're gone."

Daniel drew back, and then gestured to the white and wood furnishings of the church rec room with a grand smile, "You're welcome for our hospitality."

Scalpel in hand, he walked out of the room whistling *This little light of mine.*

The next thing he knew, it was daybreak. Father Mateus was praying over him in some language he couldn't fathom, holding a torn piece of fresh bread.

It smelled heavenly.

As the priest finished, intoning and drawing out the last syllables, he looked down upon Michael and smiled.

"The host is ready," he said, and presented the bread.

Desperate, Michael tore in as soon as the piece drew close to his mouth. He bit his tongue in the process, but he didn't care. The soft, buttery taste flooded his senses. A soothing relief washed over him as the bread slid down his throat with satisfaction. As he took the last bite into his mouth, he paused. He savored it. For a brief, glimmering moment, he felt whole.

A loud clapping shook him out of the moment. He looked back behind Father Mateus to find Daniel, grinning ear to ear as he approached from the back wall. Michael said nothing, and finished eating the bread without tasting it.

Maybe if he didn't argue, they would let him go.

"You're one of ours, now," Daniel said. He approached closer and placed a hand over Michael's belly. "The life inside you is part of a new world."

Michael blanched. His bloodshot eyes darted toward the priest.

"He's already glowing," Father Mateus said, smiling.

"What the fuck did you do to me?" Michael asked.

"You're part of the Newborn now," Mateus explained. "A new kind of human, developed as a host body for our kind. You can call us demons or aliens or anything else. We don't care. We just need a place to live."

"What-what what the fuck was inside that bread!" Michael demanded. "A parasite!"

Daniel giggled, placing a gentle arm around Father Mateus' shoulder. "Of course, not silly. There's no *matter* where we come from. What you just ingested is closer to…" Daniel snapped his fingers and pointed as he finished the sentence "An idea!"

Father Mateus smiled indulgently and continued. "Your body is like a tree. And your thoughts, like termites, eat away at your consciousness until one day, you realize you're never aware of where you are or what you're doing."

Father Mateus leaned in to divulge the secret, "but nothing in nature is never wasted. All that empty space and all those bugs are providing an ideal home for beings of pure consciousness with no body to call their own."

Daniel grasped Michael's hand to the point of crushing it as he looked down upon him and said, "We are the songbirds. And we are here to make use of the precious life you have so tragically squandered." Daniel placed his other hand down on Michael's stomach and gazed into him with burning delight "until now."

Michael lurched toward his free hand and began gagging himself. He wasn't ready to be a host for whatever inhuman thing was inside him.

Both Daniel and Mateus reached out to stop him, and Michael jerked back and buried his face in the pillow while driving fingers into his throat.

That's when he heard the Velcro tear.

He hadn't realized these new restraints were not tied or locked.

Mateus pulled the hand out of his mouth and Michael started tearing the Velcro free with his teeth. He pushed his arm up through the weakened restraint and opened it the rest of the way. Swinging his free arm out, he pushed Father Mateus down to the ground and reached over to grab Daniel's neck. His grip intensified as he brought Daniel's face in closer.

"I want my body back!" he screamed, pushing Daniel into the wall. He heard a crack as Daniel's skull bounced off it and quickly worked to free his other hand, then his feet.

Father Mateus stood and raised a hand, not in anger, but with caution, "It won't be easier for you out there. There's a reason you're here, a reason for all of this. And if you open that door, you're going to let in something *worse*."

Michael dragged his feet and flared his eyes. He walked up to Father Mateus and drove a fist across his face. A loud snap sounded and the old priest slapped against the tiled floor.

"I'll show you worse."

His eyes darted to the door and he ran out in a flash.

Heart pounding, he ran past a blur of strange hallways and startled, confused people. Finally reaching the stairs, he shot up to the top and burst through the double doors across the hall.

His eyes took a moment to adjust to the stinging sun of the cloudless day. The grass of the fenced-in yard was green and freshly trimmed. He was standing at the side entrance of the church, dressed in the white cotton gown of a choir member.

Looking to his left, he saw the tall, white walls of the police station on the other side of the city street. The faded orange of his Ford Mustang shined below, in the parking lot, waiting for him.

Standing on soft grass, he took the first few steps toward his freedom and stopped. A deep sickness swelled in the pit of his stomach.

He realized he had still ingested the host.

The next thing he knew, Michael was on a bed, huddled against the bars of a cell, trying to rouse his tired mind from the tempting blankness of sleep. The light around him was grey, as were the walls. The other prisoners were quiet, many mumbling to themselves and each other. All were dressed in their street clothes.

He couldn't remember how he'd gotten here, or what reason they'd had to arrest him. It didn't matter. Something about this place felt permanent. Not in the sense that he'd never leave, it was like he'd never been anywhere else.

Barred, basement windows above him allowed the only sight of what he'd left behind. He stood, then approached the windows and stepped up on the toilet to gain a better view.

Behind grey clouds, the sky above was baked in the orange light of sunset. Looking up, he saw the crescent flight of a Golden Eagle as it slipped across the sky.

With grace, it landed on the cross atop of the church steeple and stood. For a moment, time didn't seem to matter. If you had told Michael he could spend the rest of eternity watching this bird of prey, he might believe you. Its head scanned the surrounding area. It spread its wings and took off.

The eagle flew over the rooftops and into a sunset Michael would never witness.

"It's not my fault!" Michael screamed as the bird left his sight. "They put something inside me!"

The last thing he knew, Michael fell to the floor and crumpled on the ground as he recoiled from the gut-punch of shame. It was a gentle punch, strong enough to get him to change, but soft enough to say *I'll love you when this is over*.

EYE OF THE NEEDLE
By
Lance Tuck

Mark opened his eyes, his head throbbing like his skull was on fire. His vision was blurry as he strained to remember how he got here. He knew his name was Mark, and worse, he knew in general what was happening. He just couldn't remember why he was being pursued by these people. He could hear them closing rapidly as he struggled to catch his breath. Mark knew he had been running like hell for quite some time. His throat was raw and felt like it was on fire, but there was nothing here in this unfamiliar urban wasteland that might provide some relief. If there were a fountain or pool (or even a rancid puddle at this point) his pursuers would not give him the time to see to his needs. They were hell-bent on running him into the ground.

He didn't even know who they were, and had only a cursory notion of why they were after him. He was on the wrong turf, with no embassy, no parley. Alone. This was his dream...his nightmare. He had always wanted the thug life, but it just wasn't where he came from. He listened to the music, spoke the lingo, wore the clothes...all the right styles, all the right labels. Downtown, at the club, that was enough to get respect. That, and a big roll of money. No one questioned his bullshit stories, no one tried to test him. He told them he was from New Orleans, that he was an original gangster from the Big Easy, and that was why he had such a funny accent.

The truth was that he was born in Oklahoma near the town of Bochito, a far cry from New Orleans. When he was five, Mark's mother sent him to live with his great-aunt, a recluse who lived off her own mother's wealth. In those days, that woman, Mark's great -great grandmother, still clung to life in the upstairs of the huge mansion nestled back in the deep woods at the edge of a black and nameless lake. She spent the days listening to old records of her long-lost love, the famous composer and mathematician Maestro Mercutio Helmholtz, never venturing from the deeply perfumed apartment, her meals and fresh laundry brought to her daily by his great-aunt Melody Singer. Mark was a welcome addition to the household, but it was made clear every day that he was not one of them. His mother had birthed a bastard, with a man of no consequence to anyone in her family, and her son bore the burden of that outsider's name. He was not a Singer.

At school, it was the same. He was treated with deference, even a sort of grudging respect for his musical talents, but there was always a back tone of derision when they said his name, like it was a dirty word: Mark Yaron. He didn't know his father, and that side of the family wanted nothing to do with him. Hell, his mother's side barely wanted him, except to run errands and lift heavy furniture. He was a live-in handyman who worked for room and board and the privilege of riding an hour each way on an ancient school bus to attend public school every day, year after year. It was wearing him down. That was why he left when he turned seventeen.

He loved music, and he definitely had the family talent for it. Mark had learned all he could at school, his skills out shined even his best teachers. He went to Atlanta to try to break into the club scene. He could write and arrange better than most people ten years his senior. Everybody who heard his beats and mixes knew that he had an ear for good music. He suffered from one major weakness...his lyrics sucked. Really bad.

He wanted to do hard-ass cutting edge hip hop, but his words were fucking ridiculous. He had no real experience with thug life, the gangsta lifestyle, or urban living, so he drew from the films and television shows he had watched to while away the hours back at his great-aunt's house in Louisiana. Mark was getting attention all right, but some of it was from hostiles who called him a tourist, a poser. Some of them were no more legit than he was, manufactured name, manufactured game. Some of them were truly hard and felt disrespected by his perceived misappropriation of their culture. To them it was not a lifestyle choice, but *the life*. They took it very seriously.

"Where are you, little gangster?" one of the pursuers howled.

"Ready to earn some street cred, you piece of shit?" The raucous trio's taunts were accompanied by menacing howls and forlorn cries from the towering buildings that formed the maddening urban labyrinth that confounded the young man. If he could just remember who they were...how he got here... what he had done to deserve their wrath! Was it Atlanta? His pursuers were getting closer.

As Mark ran, he tried to put together what had led up to this life or death struggle. His head felt like an eggshell about to burst from within, throbbing with the effort of concentration. It was the city, he knew that, but which one? They all seemed the same to a lost country boy...maybe it was Miami. But the sky was black, shrouded by a weird smog. It felt like a storm was just about to break. He could see movement in the windows of the buildings, fleeting glimpses of individuals oblivious or indifferent to the struggles taking place beneath them. He couldn't escape the sense that his progress was being watched with great interest, like a rat running in a maze.

It had to be the man who was after the needle that had set this in motion.

The needle was the only thing of value Mark ever got from his family, and that only at a tragic cost. Well, a tragic cost to them. He had been working at a refrigerated warehouse just outside of Atlanta when he got the letter telling of the fate that had befallen his great aunt and great-great grandmother in his absence. Mark Yaron was the sole beneficiary of their wills, and there had been a matter of taxes to which he needed to attend. He had to survey the property with an assessor from the insurance company and determine the value of the remaining property after the fire.

It seemed to have started in the kitchen and quickly consumed the main house. His great-great grandmother's upstairs had been spared the flames, but his aunt's room, the wine cellar, the antique furniture...all destroyed. Mark had hoped to be able to sell some of the furniture or clothing, but it was a total loss. It looked like he was in for one hell of a tax bill with no means to pay it off. His music career was going to be seriously derailed by this unexpected expense. He would have to work all the overtime they would give at the refrigeration plant to settle the taxes. No one would want to buy a ruined house...perhaps the land had some value, but he didn't have the expertise or money to broker a fair deal.

His great-great grandmother's apartment was miraculously untouched, and its contents turned out to be his salvation. The downstairs, once a familiar prison, was now a charred skeleton of a home, absolutely alien to his memories. But the upstairs apartment had always been forbidden. Seeing it now was a sort of revelation. All the sounds and smells that had drifted down from the lofty heights were finally laid bare, their guardian dead, her secrets exposed. He was like an archaeologist prying into the tombs of the dead for profit.

He knew his great-great grandmother had once been a figure in the public eye, if not actually famous. The letters and photographs that were now scattered around the abandoned living room told a far more compelling story than he had ever heard. The old woman named Aria Singer had once been the toast of the town, the belle of the ball. She was young, brilliant, beautiful. She had married a powerful European banker who was mostly absent, leaving his young bride alone and bored in New Orleans with an effectively limitless bank account. It was a recipe for corruption.

Her tastes had always been somewhat exotic, and she had taken interest in certain esoteric arts that were practiced in the South. She acquired a circle of friends with similar interests, and together they had indulged in certain experiments, which according to her letters and journals seemed at first to be miraculous. Later writings were far less optimistic in their characterizations.

They had been a diverse group of well-to-do's, artists, actors, musicians, scientists, mystics and dope fiends. Hashish, opium, solanacea, banisteriopsis...a veritable pharmacopia of consciousness-altering substances flowed freely at their parties. Secure in the deep woods, the Singer house had seen more than its fair share of such festivities; Mark had found a set of photo albums that had a visual record of what could only be called orgies in the familiar architecture that now lay blackened and ruined. He had never imagined.

Apparently, neither had her husband Gabriel. The man had heard rumors of his wife's indulgences in his absence and returned from Europe without warning. There were few photos or news clippings from that time, and it was clear that Gabriel Singer had put an end to the festivities. This precipitated a vicious divorce highlighted by a very public paternity dispute that was ultimately resolved in Aria Singer's favor. This was what gave the family their impressive wealth, but the hostility severed any contact between the two lineages. Maestro Helmholtz was conspicuously absent in any of her later diary entries, as if he had abandoned his young lover to the tender mercies of her raging husband. Left alone, Aria retreated to her bedroom and her opium dreams, listening to the old records that had been the soundtrack to her youth.

That was what he remembered most about her...the music. She always listened to those old records, and always on that ancient phonograph she kept in her boudoir. It sang out at all hours of the day, creeping into his mind, filling it with visions and emotions that seemed almost alien to him. That was what had inspired him to write his own music. If he was honest with himself, he had to acknowledge that some of his original music, stuff he wrote himself, was actually derived from the phantom melodies that still echoed in his mind from his childhood exposure to Aria's collection.

As Mark looked through the bureau drawers for cash or jewelry, he couldn't get the old songs out of his head. He hadn't come here for the music, but now it called to him. He dumped the top drawers onto the sumptuous mattress (carefully avoiding the sinister black stain that had penetrated deep into the fabric.) There was a fortune in rings and bracelets now tarnished from years of disuse. Bundles of personal letters and photographs also spilled out, along with business cards and pawn receipts long forgotten.

"Jackpot!" Mark said aloud, ignoring the little balding man with the thin mustache and thick glasses that was writing down everything he saw. The assessor was eager to record all of the heirlooms and works of art that might be of some value when it came time to settle the taxes. The rest of the place was a total loss, but just the jewelry from the first drawer would be enough. The clothes...the elaborate ball gowns and hand-made shoes...they would be worth a fortune on their own as well.

Mark took photos of the furniture and light fixtures, to facilitate sale on some Internet auction site. He had no romantic attachments to any of this crap. He wanted to sell everything.

That is, until he found the old phonograph player.

It wasn't a common gramophone...it was more advanced than that. More advanced than Mark would have expected for such an antique. He had pushed aside the thick, plum-colored velvet drapes that shielded the upper parlor from prying eyes. On a black ebony table with five ornately carved legs, the device seemed to glow in the dim light. It was gilded with gold and platinum, elaborate geometries inscribed into the almost paisley patterns of metal on pure ivory. The horn was silver, now tarnished black, crafted by a master silversmith. It was absolutely priceless.

"Oh my!" the assessor exclaimed, sweating. "This one alone might be worth enough to pay your taxes and rebuild the house!" He seemed to be on the verge of drooling as his eyes bulged behind his comically thick glasses. His odd, waxy skin was slick with Louisiana sweat, sticking to his fancy grey suit jacket as he wrung his hands, staring at the prized possession.

"You've gotta be fucking kidding me," Mark said with open disgust. The only thing he wanted to do less than move back to Louisiana was sell that phonograph player. Once he set eyes on that antique turntable, he knew it had to be his whether he was a Singer or not. "That's my birthright!" he added. "It ain't for sale!"

After the assessor was finished tabulating the property and its estimated value, Mark Yaron was left alone in the fading light of the afternoon. He knew he needed to get the valuables out of there before someone happened along and stole them. But his priority was the phonograph. He searched the parlor for any of the old records. He found a deck of old tarot cards wrapped in a red silk bag in a drawer in the weird ebony parlor table. At the very bottom of the bag was a small brass key.

Mark searched frantically for the lock that fit that key, but it was a losing proposition in the dying light. He loaded up what loose jewelry he could into the heavy calamander chest Ariel had used to store her party gowns. When he tried to lift the chest, he realized that it was a two-man job. The damned thing was big enough to keep a body in! All he had done was moved the heavy black and ivory box from the spot it had rested for years. But there, in the floor beneath it, Mark saw the lock assembly he had been looking for. He had found a hidden chamber in the floor!

The howling pursuers laughed aloud, untroubled by the notion that Mark could hear them coming. They knew where they were, knew where they were going...they had a purpose. He was running for his life, but he had no idea where he could run to! He didn't belong here, and now he openly admitted it. Still, he remembered through the haze and pain...he remembered the music! It drifted into his mind, and called to him. Uncertain if it was a hallucination or a sign from God almighty, Mark focused on it now...followed it deeper into the dark recesses of this nightmare. He remembered the song...it was one of his own. One he had "appropriated" from the old records his dead great-great grandmother listened to...and it had given him his heart's desire.

He remembered the song, and now he remembered how he must have come to this godforsaken place.

The heavy chest had covered a locked crawlspace that appeared to have been undisturbed for years, but now, with the key in hand, Mark stood poised to see what treasures his family had hidden away. The key clicked in the old iron lock and thunked loudly as he turned it. The wooden door opened easily revealing a delicately carved box of blackest ebony, about 16 inches square, inlaid with a large ivory star and a number of what he recognized as Hebrew letters, but he had no idea what they meant. His father may have been Jewish, but Mark never investigated his own heritage. He was far more interested in being a street thug. That instinct propelled him as he carelessly unsealed the wooden vessel with no regard for why someone might take such pains to secure its contents.

His eyes lit up as he discovered the secret cache of records that had been deposited in the crawlspace. He ignored the elaborate geometric painting on the inside of the crawlspace door, something he might have recognized as a vodoun veve if he had known his great aunt any better. He was transfixed by the antique discs that had been hidden away here and had against all odds survived the fire unharmed. As he read the handwritten titles inked black on the paper wrappers, Mark could hear the ghostly strains of the songs his great-great grandmother used to listen to...he could almost see the grand parties they held, in their fine clothes...

His mind was suddenly flooded with images he had attributed to his own fevered imagination, some old Vincent Price film about an old Edgar Allen Poe story or some such...but in light of the photos he had seen and the letters he had read, the flashes of debauchery and sexually charged rituals now held a very different meaning. The whirling colors and delightfully stimulating contractions of muscle and flesh flowed easily in rhythm to the music that he knew was contained on these antique hard wax discs.

He *needed* to hear them. *Now.*

As darkness settled in, Mark lugged the box of recordings out of its hiding place and over to the phonograph. He slung the stylus up and over, roughly removing the last disc his great aunt had listened to, some old crooner named J. Favorite, tossing the priceless recording aside as he selected one of his newfound treasures. He placed the thick wax plaque on the turntable, lowered the needle, and listened like he had never listened before.

He was transported by the sounds, experiencing vivid images as real as memories, as if something in the recordings was speaking to him directly. The faces now had names attached to them, and contexts...he felt a sense of joy, of fulfillment as he listened to the songs composed by his great-great grandmother's long dead lover. He felt the man's presence, felt his love. It was uncanny.

Each recording produced a different set of memories, a different sensory barrage, and he listened to them deep into the night, only stopping when the light of the rising sun reminded him of where he was. He knew that he had found his ticket.

There were two additional photo albums in the crawlspace, and they contained the rest of the story about Maestro Helmholtz and his fate. Mark wished that he had read those accounts sooner. If he had realized what he was dealing with, he wouldn't have wound up where he was: Lost.

Mark took his trophies back to Atlanta, and with the money he made selling off his dead relatives' legacies, he was able to purchase some equipment to start recording his music. With the help of his family's magic records, he was producing music. Real music, stuff that people wanted to buy. He was poised to make a career change, right on the precipice of real change. But his ego wouldn't let him do it. He didn't want to be a "poser" or a "sellout." He wanted to be legit.

He wanted to be a gangster.

Right now, with the psychopaths stalking him through the dark streets and alleys, he didn't feel like a gangster. He wished he did. He just wanted to be able to sing his songs, to have some street cred. He didn't even know what those words meant, but in his terror, he was learning. In the darkness of the bleak alleyways he had been herded into, Mark was losing hope. There were fewer and fewer avenues out, less and less light to see by. He rested against a strangely hot building, black stone walls that seemed to sap his strength as he struggled to breathe in the thick, stinking air.

His head was swimming as the foul stench of sewage rose all around him. His eyes blurred again as he heard his pursuers whoop with angry delight.

"Making us work too hard, asshole! Gonna make us mad!"

Another bellowed out, "Give it up, wannabe! Come out and take what you have coming, you chickenshit little monkey!" Bluish light flickered from the direction of the sounds.

Mark looked around in a panic...there was nowhere left to go! The cramped alleyway was littered with old trash, cans and detritus in a hundred different strange languages, but there were no doors, no access ways, no way out. The huge basalt building towering over him seemed to be the end of the world. But through the haze and confusion, he heard it still...the music! It was coming from beneath the trash...a grate or manhole! Mark scrambled to his knees, digging desperately to find any means of escape from this nightmare of his own devise.

Through it all, his tormentors never stopped. "Gonna get you, homey! Gonna come and give you that street cred!"

"Brother, you gotta get some street cred or nobody is gonna take you serious!" Daffy was trying to be helpful, but his incessant prodding was well past annoying. He was a low-level thug, a small-time hustler with a knack for rhymes, but no real musical talent. He had been helping Mark with lyrics, but seemed more interested in using Mark's music contacts to get into nicer clubs than he would normally be allowed.

"No lie, my man...real gangsters can smell the bullshit on your Nikes! You don't have the real-world experience with the life, you just another jack-off joker," Kush said, exhaling a small fogbank of high-grade hydroponic. "Now, Daffy and me, we know the people who can hook you up, y'all know what I'm sayin'? We can get you in good with some hard ass O.G.'s who will change your worldview, you get me? You just bankroll the excursion; we do all the rest!" Kush was a facilitator, whatever the hell that was supposed to mean. Truth was that Kush was an instigator, and right at that moment, he was trying to play multiple angles that were against him into a way to get back in good with some very bad men he had double-crossed.

Daffy was in on Kush's hustle. The plan was to deliver dumbass Mark down to some serious players who felt disrespected by his feeble efforts at writing about the gangster life. They figured that they would drain the boy's bank account, take whatever he had of value, and leave him robbed stripped and shot in the hood...that would show him what real gangster life was about! And the guys he had in mind were borderline psychopaths anyway. Daffy figured that this offering would at least generate some goodwill from the real hardcore gangbangers.

The words echoed in Mark's mind. He wondered now how he could have been so stupid...how he couldn't see through their ruse. All those assholes did was smoke his weed, drink his liquor, and go to the clubs on his dime. Why would they want to help him? As his filthy, bloody fingers gripped the cold stone grate at the lowest part of the forgotten alley, he remembered meeting with the real gangsters. He yanked with all his might, pulling the grate free.

They were right on him, only a few yards away. Mark slithered into the filthy drain headfirst, plunging down into the darkness, away from the maniacs who would not yield in their chase. He hit the reeking filth, which was mercifully invisible to him in the sulfurous blackness.

As his head cleared from the ringing of the sharp impact with the sewer floor, he could hear the music still calling, tantalizingly close. As he oriented himself, he saw a greenish glow emanating from his soaking clothes. Bioluminescence? Some weird glowing bacteria? It didn't matter. The eerie glow was just bright enough to show a corridor that led deeper, under the huge basalt towers above. Mark willed himself not to see the horrible living clots that splashed in the fetid waters and, he knew, must be crawling on him as he worked his way toward the passage...toward the music that had always driven him.

"I can't stay out all night, guys...I have to get back to talk to Thor about my turntable!" Mark was practically pleading with Kush and Daffy, but he knew it wouldn't matter. Daffy was driving, and he knew every little out of the way hole in the wall club in the South. Mark would never be able to find his way home from most of those joints. Hell, without Daffy, he'd have never been able to find them to begin with.

"Yo, calm the fuck down. Don't be a little bitch, we'll get you home before your mama freaks out." Kush's tone was decidedly nastier, more condescending than usual. Mark should have realized something was amiss.

"Serious," Daffy added contemptuously. "You gonna die from ulcers if you keep being such a whiney baby."

"I'm not being a fucking whiney baby," Mark whined, "I just have some really important stuff that I need to get done, and Thor is the best electronics guy in town! I don't know when he can get time to help me out with this again if I fuck up and miss it." He couldn't explain it to these two. They wouldn't believe him if he told them about a magic phonograph player.

Oh, at first, he thought it was the records themselves. Mark presumed that his great-great grandmother had worked some wild spell to record the events of her wild parties right into the music they reveled to, somehow allowing whoever listened to experience the memory of being there. The first time he tried to listen to one of the wax discs on a modern turntable, he realized that the magic was not in the recordings themselves. It only worked on the ornate phonograph.

Just for fun, he listened to some of his modern vinyl on the old phonograph, and he found himself transported by the experience. Not all music had that effect. Some songs evoked a sense of malaise and boredom, more than when listening to them on a standard turntable. It had taken some time before Mark realized that the phonograph's power was to make the listener feel what the composer felt when writing and performing the piece.

Now, he was hoping that Thor would be able to figure out how it did it.

Thor wasn't just an electronics and sound man. He was well known in occultist circles as an alchemist. He wasn't whipping up Philosopher's Stones or anything, but he was well versed in the mystic and scientific properties of a broad variety of materials and substances. Mark had entrusted Thor with access to the phonograph in hopes of learning a way to harness that power.

His music was selling. He was so close to making it big. That night would change him forever, as Daffy and Kush's stratagem unraveled around the three of them. That was the night they took him to meet Croc and Chango.

Were they the ones chasing him? His mind was clearing, his memories coming back into focus. Mark was out of options. He had run as far as he could now, nestled into the deepest darkest crevasse of this urban hell, praying that his pursuers would finally just give up. That had not happened. Now, he tried to hold his breath, but his body screamed for air, his tortured lungs spasming, drawing in scorching gulps of methane-thick sewer gases, his trembling limbs weak with fatigue. How long had he been running from them?

Their voices boomed and echoed as they laughed to one another. "Where is he? He has to be here - I can practically smell him!"

"Over this stench? I didn't even know these tunnels existed...and I know every inch of this place. Your boy has some chops...I guess he deserved that 'street cred' after all!" This was followed by volleys of sinister laughter.

Mark tried to remember what he had done to bring this on himself, but above that, he realized something: the bastards chasing him had *walked past his hiding place!* They had missed him!

"He's gotta be here somewhere...nobody gets away," one of the booming voices asserted, the sounds growing fainter as the three moved further away.

Street cred...that was the load of crap that got him into this. He remembered the club where he learned what it meant to be an O.G., the club Daffy and Kush insisted he go to. A meeting with destiny awaited him, but he had no idea.

It had looked like a broken down old strip club from the outside, a failed business among liquor stores and pawn shops. Mark thought it was a joke.

"Are you fucking with me? What the hell is this shit?" Mark was outraged. In this neighborhood, he knew that it was likely they would be robbed, carjacked, beaten...dealer's choice. He had money. They could afford a better place to meet these guys, Croc and Chango. "This place is a fucking dump!"

"Don't be dumb, man. This is a private club...invitation only!" Daffy smiled as he maneuvered the gleaming mustang into an impossibly narrow alley. From the shadows, gangsters in black seemed to coalesce around them. "Gonna need that cash...that's the invitation!" he added as a heavy chrome pistol rapped gently at the tinted glass, motioning the driver to lower the window.

"Gentlemen, perhaps we can help you find your way?" the gunman said in a smooth bass voice.

"No, my man...we know exactly where we goin'...tell Croc that Daffy has his membership dues."

The driver handed over the roll of money with a knowing smile. The hired gun took the money, but remained, staring at Daffy as if there was something more. Daffy looked back at the man, then added, "Tell him we have that other thing, too. The one he asked about."

"Daffy? Shit, is that you?" The burly, bald gunman leaned down to look in the car. "Hey Kush...hey youngblood!" His teeth seemed to almost glow as he smiled broadly in the darkness. "Good to see you on board. My kid sister loves your shit." There were audible snickers coming from the lookouts and soldiers in the shadows. This was not a compliment. After a few tense moments, Mark was relieved when a runner spoke to the gatekeeper. The huge bald man smiled again. "Just follow Lowball there...he'll take you inside." He opened the door. "Leave the keys. I'm the valet parking." The gleam in his eye made it clear that this was not a suggestion.

The three of them got out of the car and walked along behind the short young fellow in cornrows that they called Lowball. He trudged forward with a pronounced swing in his step, giving him a very distinctive walk. Almost a lurch. He seemed to be sensitive about it. When he noticed that Mark was watching him, he answered back sharply, "Got shot in the hip by a drive by...it ain't some show, asshole." Lowball never even looked at him as he guided them into the club.

The doors were dark, with not a hint of light escaping from within. Past the first set, there was a doorman and three bouncers, all simply strapping in their builds. Muscles rippled as the men moved aside in the dim light. "Croc's been waitin' on you, Daffy. 'Bout fuckin' time you showed back up to pay your bills," the doorman said as he noted their faces. No stamps or wristbands here. It was all personal. Lowball led them through the dim corridor, through a second set of black doors.

A short corridor led to the entrance, the gateway to another world. Lowball chuckled as he opened the doors, escorting the trio in. "Welcome to your new home, kids. Dad's waiting." He pointed across the club to the far corner, away from the runways and the dance floors where the ladies paraded their virtues for any who would pay. There was an alcove there, very private. That was where Croc conducted his business.

Croc was called that because of his scarring. His brother had been killed by a shotgun blast to the head, and the buckshot had lodged in Croc's face, necessitating surgical removal of the lead pellets. This produced a corrugated pattern, not unlike traditional tribal scarification. Croc went with it, adding more scars to his body as decorations in celebration of achievements. Each line, each shape represented a victory, a foe vanquished by the relentless gangster Croc. He had become addicted to the knife, to the rush produced as the flesh yielded to steel in exquisite patterns of laceration. So he conquered ever more foes to justify his own habits. Now, his body was a mass of texture and depth, heavy keloids rising up like armored scutes, a testament to his ability to endure pain as he dispensed it.

His lieutenant was Sean Gobel, a vicious businessman from Trinidad, who went by the name of the vodoun god Chango. He had connections with major studios, and was considered a surefire way to make it in the music industry, but he was a silent partner. His "discoveries" owed him, always, no matter how big they might have become. And Chango always got was owed to him. Croc saw to that.

As the three-man made their way across the club, a dozen beautiful women danced across their path in varying states of undress. This was a private club, so there was fully nude dancing, and no particular hurry to cover up as long as the money kept flowing. The entire spectrum of flesh was on display here for all tastes, beautiful examples of a variety of body types, each with its respective merits. Mark was terrified. He had no idea what his friends had gotten him into.

What he had gotten himself into; by pretending...by wanting so much to be something he was not. He should have been content with being a musician. But he wanted to be more. A singer. A gangster. Things he knew in his heart he wasn't. But here he was, about to face his dream. The emcee called out, "Alright, y'all, give it up for Lilly-Two!" as a naked dancer who had performed with a snake was leaving the stage.

"Let us do the talkin', y'hear? These guys are bad motherfuckers...you don't want to cross them," Daffy said in a low voice, barely audible over the booming bass. "You fuck up with them, you only do it once. We straight?"

"Yeah...we straight," Mark replied, his guts beginning to boil with anxiety. He wasn't watching where he was going as he trotted along, trying to keep up with Kush and Daffy. He bumped into one of the ladies, a flawless, deep coffee-skinned goddess with startling ice blue eyes...perhaps lenses, but so overwhelming! She was just leaving the stage, carrying her money and her scant clothing in her hand, a large constrictor snake draped over her shoulder. She had been trying to don a velvet robe of a midnight hue that glittered like a starry midnight, but his careless impact knocked the beautiful garment to the floor.

He apologized as he bent to pick it up. "Excuse me, I am so sorry," Mark said as he rose, robe in hand. He stopped as he came face to face with her snake companion. The python was motionless, staring directly into his eyes as he stared in terror. The snake's tongue flicked out gently, licking Mark just between the eyes as the serpent's mistress smiled.

"Why thank you...that's very kind of you." She smiled as she accepted her robe. "He likes you. That's a good thing. Serpents have impeccable taste." The dancer winked at him playfully. He could feel the intensity of her body heat, this close to him. He understood why the serpent clung to her in this place.

Mark stood and helped the dancer with her robe. Kush jabbed him angrily, gesturing for him to follow back to the alcove. "Dumb motherfucker...good way to get yourself killed! C'mon!"

The three of them stood in front of Croc and Chango, as the gangsters seemed to be judging them. Croc shook his head in disbelief. "So, this is the talent?" Croc asked roughly. "Don't look like shit to me."

"No-no, I see it. Yeah. He's got it. He's definitely got it." Chango smiled and nodded as he looked Mark over. "He's got solid musical skills. I listened to the demos, to the beats he's written. I think that he will do just fine. Once he gets his street cred."

Croc smiled malevolently. "Alright, Daffy. Looks like you paid your debt. But Kush...I told you I didn't want you bringing this snitch back around no more."

Kush's jaw dropped. "Wait a minute...I only did it cause of the money it'd bring ya! I did it to help y'all out!" Mark froze as he sensed the danger. Croc shook his head as he pulled out a heavy chrome automatic pistol, pointing it directly at Kush, not hesitating as he fired six shots into the terrified man's chest. Blood sprayed Mark as Kush dropped. He couldn't move if he wanted to.

Croc pointed the pistol at Daffy, and without another word, emptied the clip into the stunned "gangster." More blood, as the only other person that Mark knew in the place dropped dead. He pissed his pants as he stood motionless, waiting for what seemed to be the inevitable.

"Shit man. Looks like we gonna call him Deejay Peepee!" Croc said, smiling, still pointing the smoking weapon at him.

"Aw, leave him alone, Croc. He's good people." Lilly-Two, the dancer, was there now, in spite of the shooting. "He's one of ours. He always was." She slithered up to him, put her arms around his skinny shoulders and kissed him lightly.

"Alright. Alright," Croc said. "Standard contract. Chango, lay it out for him."

"This is what is: your music belongs to Croc, now. You gonna sign this contract, and you gonna sign your rights away to your music in perpetuity. In exchange, we give you your street cred...we hype your shit, make sure it gets play. Your ass is ours, now...y'hear me? In return, you stay alive, as our bitch."

Mark understood. He belonged to them now. But he still had an ace up his sleeve that they could never have expected...

He still had the phonograph.

Mark didn't remember how he got home from that club. He signed whatever they told him to. They kept his car, he assumed. He never saw it again. He couldn't remember leaving the club...he must have been drugged, he reasoned. He wouldn't have dared to refuse, that was certain. As the foggy curtains of unconsciousness parted, he found himself at his home. He had missed his appointment with Thor. Now, he feared he might never know the secrets of the record player.

Mark Yaron walked groggily through his home, already regretting whatever he had done the night before. He had trusted Thor with the keys to his home, and he was relieved to see that the man had brought the phonograph back to him. And he had left a report of his findings.

As Mark read through the analysis, everything seemed normal. The device was of the highest quality, much of it handcrafted, but there was no overt sign of anything magical in the horn, on the armature, the spring...but the stylus was another matter.

It was made of an unknown material, but magnification seemed to indicate it was secreted, like casein, but much stronger. It was too dense to get a sample for spectroscopic analysis, but there appeared to be a maker's mark engraved on the needle. Thor guessed that the mark was made during the hardening process, there was no other good explanation. The symbol appeared to be an open mouth with an eye in the middle. It did not correspond to any known maker's mark.

The deeper, metaphysical analysis was incomplete. Thor had definitely experienced the psychic effect Mark had noted, a participatory hallucination, but he needed to do a bit more research before he was prepared to suggest a mechanism of action. He advised Mark to use the device with caution, if at all.

Mark ignored the warnings. His mind was racing with adrenaline; his near-death experience had opened up something in his mind. He needed to exorcise the horror from his mind, so he wrote about it. The ride there. The club. Croc and Chango. What happened to Kush and Daffy? Each event inspired him to tell the story, changed, veiled, altered to make him look less like the selfish chickenshit he knew he was. He had been moved by what happened, and he finally understood the ultimate truth of the life: the life is death.

He used the music he had written based on what he heard on the phonograph as a foundation, and after a week of furious, no-sleep mixing and editing, Mark created his first serious gangster rap album. His experiences had gestated into a powerful work of art, something that was bound to be noticed.

His new agent, Chango, agreed. He immediately sold the rights to the songs, giving Mark a pittance from the royalties. His boys "convinced" Mark's old agent to release him from any contractual obligations, so everything belonged to Chango and Croc, the only way out an impossible buyout option: ten million dollars. It was hopeless.

As Mark cowered in the darkness, he felt an even greater hopelessness. As his mind cleared, it still pulsed with pain from dehydration and concussive trauma. He suspected he had been drugged, like before. This had Croc and Chango's fingerprints all over it. But he wasn't going to take it anymore. The pale luminosity still persisted, glowing dimly from his chest and forehead, providing enough light to see the length of pipe attached loosely to the maddening waterworks in these infernal tunnels.

If he could wrench it loose, he would have a weapon! With the last of his strength, Mark jerked the black pipe free with a terrifying shriek. His eyes went wide with terror as he realized that his pursuers had to have heard it. They would be coming back. And now he was ready!

How had he betrayed them? What drove them to this? It was the man that the assessor sent...the investor. Mark remembered now.

Thor's inquiries had garnered the attention of a man who had substantial knowledge of the phonograph player and its history. Specifically, the origin of the maker's mark is what brought the two together. Thor had published images of the mark on an occultist's website and learned that the symbol was an ancient representation of the spirit of knowledge. As you look at the world, you are consumed by its complexity, and it consumes you with the need to understand more...an endless cycle of consumption, one form of understanding devouring another, digesting it...the Ouroboros was a polite representation of the serpent of understanding. But the devourer was older than that...possibly older than creation itself.

The man who told him about this ancient mythology, a Mr. Graver, had offered a king's ransom for the artifact. Ten million dollars, cash, no questions asked. He would deliver the money himself and would exchange it for the needle then and there. But first, he felt Mark needed to know the truth about his family and how the needle came to be in his great-great-grandmother's possession. He had researched the phonograph extensively, and had tracked it down through the tax assessor's reports to the Singer estate. His attempts to contact the Singer family in the past had met with failure. Only after the deaths of the two older women had Mr. Graver been able to move ahead with his efforts to acquire the needle.

He explained that the needle had come into Aria Singer's possession because of a pact she made with the dread Ouroboros to revenge herself and her lover. It seemed that when Gabriel Singer had returned to punish his wife for her indiscretions, he did it by castrating her lover and sending the offending parts to her along with Maestro Helmoltz's final composition, a symphony composed in her honor. Oh, Gabriel assured her that he did not kill Helmholtz. No, the composer took care of that for himself. Aria was beside herself with grief. She was desperate to know his love again.

And that is what raised Ouroboros...an appetite for knowledge...for love...for destruction, all at once. It appeared to her in dreams, as an Egyptian serpent of shadows, whispering terrible secrets to her in her dreams. She wrote down what she learned, and sacrificed both what remained of her lover, and whatever issued from her womb to the coils of the great serpent wrapped around the world tree. In exchange, she was given the needle...a single tooth of the Ouroboros. Its vibrations would let her see and feel her lost love, in exchange for her children's souls.

In the black sewers below, the hunters howled again, scenting their prey. Mark had taken too long. He should have run, tried to escape...there was nowhere to go as the three converged on his final hiding spot. Mark drew back the metal pipe, ready to waylay whoever stuck their head through first...he saw the heavy, scaly features on the face emerging from the darkness. It had to be Croc!

Mark hit the reptilian horror as hard as he could, the pipe making a wet thud as it lay open the skull of its target. Glowing blue ichor spewed forth from the gaping hole in the skull of the hell spawn that had just found its prey. Mark drew back in horror as he realized what was happening.

He had refused Mr. Graves offer. He did it because Croc and Chango had made good on their promises. He was big-time now, rolling in the money. He just needed to shake loose from his masters. He figured the needle was the key. He refused to sell it to Mr. Graves so he could use it to play his songs at his live concert premier. When he played his songs with it, the listener would experience what he had experienced. Everybody listening would know how Croc had screwed him...stolen from him. And he would do it...had done it...on stage at a concert they had arranged. He remembered how the crowd reacted as the needle played his songs...but he had forgotten. The needle wouldn't lie. His words were hard as hell, but his emotions…that was what the needle broadcast.

And that night all he knew was fear.

As the demon bled glowing ichor, it grinned. Its two brothers followed it into the room. Mark tried to lift the pipe up, but his strength was flagging.

"You made us work for this one, ape. We are gonna make you suffer." It licked its terrifying fangs, as Mark realized where he was...where he had been all along. He shook his head as he cringed back into the corner. He raised the pipe feebly.

"No...no, please..." Through his tears of terror, he saw the demonic trio stop in their tracks. There was fear in their eyes, as much as there was confusion in his own. The pale green light he had noticed emanating from himself earlier now shone brightly, illuminating the demons. In the hellish light, he heard one word.

"MINE!"

Space seemed to compact, narrowing the crevasse the demons had followed Mark into. They couldn't retreat now as something massive shifted in the solid darkness behind Mark. The bleeding demon became enraged, its blood igniting with a violet fire as it spoke with fury.

"Ours! Ours by right of the hunt! We stalked it...ran it to ground here!" It flexed its terrible claws and licked its fangs as it repeated its claim. "Ours!"

Mark turned and saw the unnamable horror that was behind him, around them...it was as if they were inside of it. Its eyes glowed a soulless green and flared as it spoke.

"MINE!"

One of the other demons, a lanky thorny creature with dead black eyes shook its head as it spoke. "This is our place...our law! Our claim is valid! You have no right here! No claim!"

"Older than your laws...older than your God," the thing called Ouroboros whispered. "MINE!" it shouted again.

The bleeding demon glared at Mark, then spoke again to Ouroboros. "You have no claws...no teeth. You are weak! Ancient and weak! Brothers! We have claws and fangs...let us show this toothless fool what demons can do!" It sprung forward, attacking with a mighty roar, but it was caught in mid-air by the horrible ripping tentacles issuing forth from Ouroboros's horrible maw. The demon was yanked into entity's jaws where it was crushed in a series of powerful contractions, spraying boiling blue ichor everywhere.

"My teeth are everywhere...they serve me well. Now you shall see what it means to digest for a hundred years in the spiraling guts of the Ouroboros!"

Its baleful eyes turned toward the other two demons. The hell spawn screamed and begged as they were devoured by the nightmarish being. It belched a sulfurous gout of steaming air, adding to the noxious atmosphere.

Mark cowered down in front of the glowing green eyes. He remembered his concert. He thought it would set him free. He couldn't have been more wrong. As his music resonated through the tooth of the Ouroboros, everyone who heard it, live or via electronic media, felt the same terror he felt that night. Some collapsed in a heap from fright. Some ran. Some drew their weapons and opened fire on whatever was closest to them. He remembered the chaos...the gunfire...the feeling of the bullets ripping through his chest. Going cold and numb.

"So this is my punishment...you're going to eat me. This is my hell." Mark sobbed.

The great serpent fiend looked at him puzzled. "Eat you? No. You are mine. You always were." It smiled as its horrible breath suffocated him.

Everything seemed to click in his mind at once. The stains on his great-great-grandmother's bed - she had been dead for a while. His great aunt had locked away the records, she had to have...she was the one listening to the records when the fire started. She had killed her mother and left her to rot. The deal that Aria made..." whatever issues from my womb." Her children...his own mother. All were part of Aria's terrible sacrifice. But not him. Not Mark. He remembered the last memories, before he died. That bastard Mr. Graves was there...he stole the needle.

"My teeth...I sow them in the Earth, and they grow into legions of servitors. Like your matriarch, Aria. Like your aunt. Like you."

"But I'm not one of them! I'm not a Singer!" Mark screamed as his sanity fled him again. He was just beginning to realize the truth.

"You are trapped by names, boy! Yaron means Singer, my lovely little Mark. And you have been such an easy mark, every single time." Ouroboros smiled a bloody, toothless grin.

"How many times?" Mark's fracturing mind screamed as the memories came crashing back through. Of course the serpent wouldn't hurt him...it needed him as bait. Over and over again, til the end of time. Mark descended into a horrible black oblivion.

Suddenly, he was awake. He didn't know where he was, where he was going. His lungs ached and burned as he struggled to breathe. His mind was fuzzy, he couldn't remember anything clearly, except that something was after him.

He heard a howl in the distance. He didn't recognize this place...it was the city, but not one he recognized. Behind him, he saw five silhouettes rapidly closing on him. He stood up to run, trying to remember why they were after him...who he was.

Mark. He remembered he was a Mark. As he ran, he struggled to remember...

THE ARTHROGENS: A NEW BREED
by
L Ashby

Serenity sat at her desk, yawning struggling to keep her eyes open, as she worked the graveyard shift as a tech at the local hospital. The night was rainy and lightening outside, with thunder so loud she didn't know how it was possible for anyone around here to even sleep. She was the only tech tonight due to the weather, but she didn't mind too much because there were only four patients on her end of the hall. No one had beeped their light for assistance in at least a half hour and the night was not going fast by any means. Looking through patient charts on the computer, she takes another bite of her lunch, a peanut butter and jelly sandwich.

Just then a light goes off. It's room 613, Mr. McGregor.

Serenity answers the call light. "Yes, Mr. McGregor, It's Serenity, how can I help you this evening?"

"Yes dear, I need to go to the bathroom and I seem

to have got my gown all caught up, could you please come help me Serenity?" he answers.

"I'll be right there," she replies before letting go of the call button and giggling to herself about him getting caught up. She enjoyed her job and the people but sometimes the situations they got themselves into was the most entertaining part of the shifts.

Serenity enters room 613 and the sight before her is of this fragile old man sitting on the edge of the bed with his gown caught around the bed rails and him trying to untangle it. She goes over to him and begins to help unravel it when something moving behind him catches her eye. The only light she has is from the storm outside but she doesn't want to turn on the lights and hurt Mr. McGregor's eyes. She shakes her head, that's impossible, Serenity get a hold of yourself.

Finally getting him untangled she helps him to the bathroom. As he goes in he tells her, "I could be awhile, if you need to go I can pull the cord when I'm done if I need you again."

"That's okay, it's a good night so I'll just hang around until you're done, if you don't mind. I'll fix up your bed and clean your room a bit until then," she says.

He shuts the door behind him and she begins to go to his bed when something stops her. Movement again. Ignoring what she is seeing, thinking it must be the lightening or something. With that she begins making the bed, bending over to tuck in the corners. All the sudden she feels something come up behind her. She shivers.

"Mr. McGregor, you scared me you know that's not appropriate," and she begins to turn around looking at the old man behind her.

"I'm sorry Serenity, but I'm ok now, thanks for

helping me." He says, getting back into bed.

Serenity nods, "No problem, that's my job." She turns to leave. "If you need anything else just call. I'm about to leave but the next person will be here soon, goodnight."

She walks back to the desk and her relief person is there. Coming back, she grabs her sandwich and takes another bite.

"Hi Serenity, I'm here now so you can go." Amy greets her.

Serenity replies while grabbing her bag, "Thanks Amy, nothing has changed, same patients. Do you need anything before I leave?"

"No I don't think so, I'm all set. Have a nice night and be safe on your way home. It's quite a storm out there." Amy tells her.

Serenity grabs her bag, with sandwich in hand," Sure thing, I'm gonna shower before I head out though, don't wanna take anything home with me if you know what I mean." Serenity yells on her way down the hall. After all the hospital is not as clean as you'd think.

Amy laughs, "Yep I know what you mean."

Serenity goes down the hall and enters the locker room. Thankfully the hospital had this for employee usage. She hated going home with her work clothes still on due to all the germs and no telling what else on her clothes. If she didn't get the chance to shower there, she would usually just strip in her garage and put her clothes in the washer right there before heading inside. But tonight she felt too gross to make it home. Not to mention, as an added bonus it was flu season.

Finishing her sandwich, she notices an odd taste in her mouth. She spits out that last bite and there is a creepy crawly slimy leech mixed in with it.

"Oh my gosh, ewwwww, gross, how did that get in there?" Serenity says aloud, throwing her sandwich bit into the trash.

Shaking off the disturbing image she removes her work clothes. She takes the clothes out of her bag along with shower essentials (including toothbrush and toothpaste) and places them inside the stall. Placing her phone with her things on the outside bench, she hits the play button on her playlist and grabs the toothbrush and toothpaste. She steps into the shower. Getting the hot water running, she holds her stuff and begins brushing her teeth first. She had to get that taste out of her mouth. Next moving onto her hair, she lathers the long tresses, feeling how great it is to finally get a shower in.

Opening her eyes, Serenity spots something moving on the ground. Another leech. Oh my gosh, she thinks to herself and kicks it out. Looking all over her body. She spots suction marks where the leech had obviously feasted upon her flesh. What is going on?

Suddenly Serenity feels a pair of hands come around her waist from behind. And the lights go out from the storm. Serenity's gasps, not knowing what to expect she shivers with the anticipation and awaiting to see what was going to happen next.

The person becomes more aggressive and won't allow her to move, pushing her forward against the stall wall. Not knowing what's going on, all she gets a glimpse of, is a figure with a doctor's mask on through the flashes of lightening coming in from outside window. He quickly turns her face back to the wall and before she can yell for help the person shoves a pair of disposable socks into her mouth, making it so that she almost chokes on the disgusting things.

"You're gonna listen to me and listen to me good. Understand, Serenity?" the voice muffles from within the surgical mask.

She shakes her head yes and tries to calm herself so he doesn't feel threatened at all. His hands begin to work their way down her body starting at her throat. She steadies her breathing as he moves his fingers slowly down her shoulders to her breasts. He squeezes her nipples slightly giving her a sensation, making them erect as the water cascades down the tips. Then he moves his hands down to her waist and rests them there. He begins kissing her neck and slowly running his tongue over her.

"I've been watching you for so long. You think your invisible but I see you Serenity. I always have. Quite the woman but just look at your sexy curves." He moans to her.

Serenity listens to him carefully trying to recognize the voice but can't hear it well enough between the running water and mask. It seems familiar but she can't place it at the moment.

"You should always remember that I will be with you and you should be taken in a way you never have before. And I'm more than happy to do just that." Suddenly he bends her over with her butt out towards him and his hands run down her back. Grabbing the soap, he washes her slowly and she can't help but to become a little aroused at his gentle touch. He then washes her luscious ass and her vagina. She then hears the zipper of his pants come undone and he pushes his hardness against her opening. Washing his erection, he teases her with the tip as it enters barely into her.

She doesn't know why but she ends up replying with a "Yes."

He enters her with a quick thrust and she goes up

on her tippy toes trying to keep herself balanced at their height difference. He holds onto her tight so she doesn't slip. Moans escape her and she can't believe how this man is making her feel. As he comes to a finish and her not far behind him, they both release suddenly and their mixture washes down the drain from her. He turns her around and tells her to close her eyes. Serenity does as she is told and he removes the mask long enough to kiss her deeply. She can taste his tongue; it tastes of something putrid she almost vomits in her mouth. Then he tells her to count to ten before opening her eyes again.

She does as she is told and when she gets to ten the stranger is gone. Was it a dream? Daydream? The lights flash back on and no sign of who was just there, but there is a leech at the drain where all the sin was washed down. Through tears, she finishes her shower quickly looking for anything of indications, marks, anything to verify what just happened. Nothing is there, just the leech, which too has disappeared now along with the suction marks from earlier. Even the feeling of just being fucked isn't there anymore. She rushes to collect all of her things and out the door she goes as soon as she's done, just wanting to get home and fast.

Heading to her car, she hears a noise. Oh no, not again she says to herself and tries to unlock her car as quick as possible. Her car finally unlocks and she enters it. Fumbling with her phone she dials security. Why didn't she think of that before?

Security picks up. "Hello this is Serenity Baker and I'm calling because I think someone is after me. They just violated me in the locker room and now I'm in my car and I think they are outside. I'm really scared; can you please come check for me? I'm scared they'll follow me home."

Security replies, "Give us your location and we'll be right there, ma'am."

Security gets to Serenity's car a few minutes later and they start to get her statement but she feels stupid as none of it makes sense and there is no evidence. Even when they look at video footage of her during that time in the locker room, it only shows her, no one else going in or coming out. And it never shows the lights going out. Even though it doesn't show her in the actual shower stall it does show everything going on outside and nothing looks out of the ordinary, even a bear is in her bag the whole time, which she never noticed before now. Maybe she did just imagine it all. But how is that even possible? Was she having a mental breakdown?

"I'm sorry Serenity but I think you just had a nightmarish day dream, after a long night with lack of sleep, you should try to go home now. You look okay though and we did a search, there was no one around as far as we could see."

"I guess it was just all imagined but it all seemed so real. Thank you for coming anyway, I really appreciate it." Serenity says as she gets back into her car to drive away.

She waves bye and looks behind her before heading home. She starts driving out of the parking lot and onto the side roads she takes on her way home, wondering what just happened. I can't believe I did that. She feels stupid. I probably looked like a big idiot. Great job Serenity. Sighing, she turns on the music to drown out the night's visions in her head. Relieved that she wasn't attacked though, according to all the non-findings, she feels a little better.

As she turns the radio up she looks in her rearview mirror and she sees movement. Leeches on her back window, looking at the wheel she sees they are also covering her steering wheel. Then she recognizes the figure in the back seat. It's him, the guy with the mask. Not again. Before she can yell the thunder drowns her out and the figure comes up with a scarf and grabs Serenity into a choke from behind. She starts to lose control of her car due to the slippery roads and her car skids off the road into a nearby ditch.

"Your mine now Serenity." The voice says.

She finally recognizes the voice. It's her best friend Jesse. But he died two years ago.

"I need you, I want you and now you're going to join me. You know the best things about being reborn? You have no emotions anymore; you just crave lust and fear from others," he says to her.

"No please Jesse, don't do this." Serenity says, "Why are you doing this?"

"Because we belong together, you promised me, remember? So now we can. When I was given the chance to come back, I was told I only had to promise one thing. That one thing was that I would continue to add and build a family of others to change like me. We are called Arthrogens, we are the beings that prey on fear and have insects as our pets, I chose leeches but you can choose anything you want. I see you as a queen myself with killer bees as your choice."

"I promised you what? Anthrogens? Insects as pets? Fear? What are you talking about? I don't understand any of this, why me?" She replies.

"Well you find it easier for people to cooperate when they are in fear, insects intensify that feeling. Almost everyone is terrified of insects. That is why you said yes in the shower, your fear took over and you wanted to survive. Willing to do whatever I wanted to do so." Jesse grins.

Jesse whispers, "And I was told I could choose anyone for my mate, Serenity I choose you, because you understood me and liked me for who I was."

She can see herself start to float above her body and knows that's not a good sign.

"No," she says as she wills herself back into her own body and pulls the scarf from her neck to stop the suffocation that Jesse is doing. "What are you doing, Jessie? Think about it."

"Oh I have. Just die already Serenity, we can be together again, like the old days," Jesse pleads.

Serenity answers, "I'm sorry Jesse, I can't. I've got too much going for me. Stop now. I'm beggin' you."

Serenity starts to lose consciousness and soon she can feel herself slip into her new destiny. Just then the scarf loosens from around her neck and Jesse disappears, along with his pets.

Serenity starts to breathe again and turns off the music. She tries to collect herself taking into account what just happened. Why was Jesse trying to kill her? Was he just lonely? And why two years later? None of this made sense at all. Getting herself back into as much control as she could, she thinks back to the days with her and Jesse.

When Jesse died, Serenity was his best friend. They did everything together and even attended the same classes. After college, they began their own paths and she went into medical, becoming a tech at a hospital and he was going for his major is biology. He was a smart guy, which was one thing Serenity really liked about him. He was kind, sweet and caring but he just wasn't her type, she was focusing on her education even though he made it well known that he wanted more with her. When he died a few years later in a climbing accident, it broke her heart to know her best friend was now gone. She was working that night he came in. She remembered the call of a climber that fell coming in and when she saw his face she knew exactly who it was as they zoomed him by. She was thankful she was not working the ER that night because she wouldn't have been able to keep herself together. She kept checking on his chart throughout the night until it said that he had died and she cried the rest of the night. Now he was back but as a being of darkness, asking for her life. She closes her eyes.

Serenity finally restarts the car and checks her surroundings. It seems to have started to storm again, she better get home fast. So, it wasn't a dream after all, she was being hunted.

As she pulls into the driveway, she hurries inside and locks the door behind her. Setting her things down in the hall, she notices something in her bag. The teddy bear? Where did this come from? She smiles and thinks, Amy must have given it to me to help me feel better. They had teddy bears like this at the hospital when children came in. Taking the bear with her to bed, she goes to her room and turns on NETFLIX.

"I need to get some sleep if I'm gonna make it back in tomorrow," she says out loud after an hour of her favorite show and turns off the television for the night.

After changing into her nightgown, she heads to her bed and lays down, covering up, praying for a good night's sleep and for Jesse to now be a distant memory.

In her dreams Serenity is with Jesse again and they are talking by a tree they use to visit when they were younger. Their initials carved in the bark so they could remember THEIR place. He is trying to tell her something but she can't hear what he's saying. She's really trying but just can't make out the words he's trying to tell her. Leeches come spewing out of his mouth along with black ooze. Then all the sudden his face distorts and she feels him grabbing at her feet. She tries to kick him away but he's too strong and she can't break free. Struggling with him she can't fight him off.

Serenity wakes up and is thrashing around in her bed but she still feels a pull on her ankles. She screams loud and pulls back the covers, realizing it's not a dream anymore. There at her feet is Jesse, with an angry face, clawing at her legs.

"Ah, stop it, stop it, please stop it," she begs.

She grabs a flashlight from her nightstand and looks at her bed, leeches cover the mattress. Jesse starts to move up closer from the bottom of her bed. The leeches are moving up and down, slithering up her body.

"Jesse, I know it's you," Serenity says.

"I told you your mine Serenity and if you won't die for me I'll have to kill you in other ways. You teased me, you lead me on, made me think you liked me, maybe even loved me." Jesse replies.

Serenity continues to fight off the leeches and Jesse who is shredding at her nightgown, "I kept telling you Jesse that I didn't think of you like that. That I wanted to get done with school first and see what happened. It's not my fault you took my actions wrong. I did like you and loved you but as a friend Jesse, I promise I never meant to hurt you."

"Such an ungrateful person you are, you didn't appreciate me or anything I did for you. Well now you will. I'll be the only one you can be with Serenity, the only one, in death." Jesse tells her.

Is there something she should know about what he just said? She can feel the leeches, sucking their way up further onto her, as Jesse gets between her breasts and works his way up her neck. He kisses her and his hand slips between her thighs, ooze from his mouth, dripping like saliva onto her delicate skin, almost burning her flesh. The burning from it hurts and she can smell the smell of death. Jesse's weight is so heavy pinning her down hard. The leeches are lingering there now and Jesse begins to slip a finger into her.

Jesse begins to whisper in her ear, "Your gonna love being like me, are you ready to accept yourself as an Arthrogen?"

Just then she remembers a pair of surgical scissors on her stand and reaches for them.

"Not today, Jesse," she screams.

Jesse then sees the scissors as they go straight into his head. Black ooze and leeches start to pour out and Jessie screams out and backs away in severe pain.

"You stupid little - you will join me," Jesse growls. "You have no choice now."

What does he mean I have no choice anymore? He grabs for her again but misses and she takes the opportunity to get out of bed and grab her keys and purse before running outside. Jesse tries to recover and go after her as fast as he can. By the time he gets to the door, scared for her life, she gets in her car and digs around in the back seat for the extra pair of extra scrubs she always keeps in her car. She backs out of the driveway leaving Jesse standing there with a dumbfounded look on his face, as he watches her leave. She drives back to the hospital. The only place she knew to go at this hour of the night. She needs help and they will believe her, they have to. After pulling into the parking lot, it's so dark, but she pulls her scrubs on and runs into the hospital.

She goes up to her floor hoping Amy is still on shift, she really needed to talk to her. When she sees Amy, "Amy thank goodness you have to help me. My dead best friend just attacked me right now at my house, he's trying to kill me so we can be together. And there are these massive leeches everywhere."

Amy looks shocked, mouth gaped open, "Um Serenity, are you okay? I mean you've been saying some really off things tonight and this is by far the weirdest."

"You have to believe me, please Amy, we have to tell someone I need help. You have to help save me. He's at my house right now. And he's not going to stop." Serenity screams.

"Right, with pet leeches? I mean really Serenity; you expect me to believe this shit?" Amy replies with a worried look on her face.

"Yes," she replies.

Amy picks up the phone and makes a phone call. Good Serenity thinks to herself she's calling the police, someone, I need help with this. I can't keep fighting him off on my own.

Amy gets off the phone and looks at Serenity. "I'm sorry sweetie. But help is coming."

"Sorry for what? That's a good thing." she asks.

"Not that kind of help darling, your sick Serenity but it's all going to be okay, I promise." Amy says.

Two men with a straight jacket come quickly down the hall towards Serenity, she is surprised and looks at Amy. "How could you? I thought you were my friend."

Amy shrugs, "Because I love you and you need help. Trust me I didn't want to."

Serenity backs away and starts to run, the two men

chase her down the hall and security is coming off the elevator. She runs to the stairwell and takes the flights of stairs two steps at a time. She's quick but they are quicker and they place her into a hold, wrapping the jacket around her. She didn't even think they made these jackets anymore. They buckle it and begin to lead her to the psych floor. Pushing through the doors she still fights them but is losing that battle as she can barely move.

"Just listen to me, I'm not crazy, I'm telling the truth," Serenity yells.

The two guys walk her into a padded white room and let her go, causing her to hit the floor with a thud. They hold her down as they unhook the buckles and take the jacket off her finally.

"Well you'll be plenty safe in here young lady," the older of the two says, and then they laugh as they leave her alone.

Serenity and now by herself. She starts to cry.

"What am I going to do?" she says to herself.

Just then she happens to look over and notice the teddy bear from her bag in the corner. She walks over to it.

"How did you get in here?"

Serenity looks the bear over then feels something inside of it starting to move. She quickly sets the bear down. It's still moving. What on earth?

Unsure of what to do she tries to yell out, going to the door window. "Um excuse me? Can anyone hear me? There's something really weird going on in here. I need someone's help. This teddy bear is moving on its own."

A guard yells back at her, "Hush and go to sleep, stuffed animals don't move. After some sleep you'll feel a lot better. The doctor will see you tomorrow. Do you need some meds to help you?"

"No thanks, I don't need any medication."

She backs away from the door and looks at the bear again. Suddenly a bee flies out of the mouth of the bear. A bee? It lands on her shoulder as if saying hello. Oddly enough Serenity isn't scared of the bee and actually allows it to stay.

"Well hello, new friend," she laughs.

Then she remembers what Jessie said. That he saw her as a queen bee herself, with pet bees. Hmm, that's odd. Looking at the bear again, another bee appears and flies out of its mouth.

"Oh no," she says. "I can't be, no, no, no, no, I can't be."

Thinking back, how was it possible? When did he change her? It must have been in the shower when he penetrated her and filled her with his semen. Of course, he inserted himself into her, preparing her body for the change. And then again with the scarf in the car, she must have died after all but didn't know it and was reborn at that moment. Now she knew she has now been changed and joined him.

Jesse appears at her window, "*Shhhhh*, now you know the truth. So come with me Serenity." He opens his arms and the leeches leak from him, consuming the door, evaporating it to nothing.

Serenity approaches him, "I told you I didn't want this. I told you I wasn't ready."

"It's okay we are going to be so great together." Jesse tells her.

Serenity looks at him, "You're not listening to me Jesse."

And he kisses her deeply, running his tongue over her lips, nipping the bottom lip, drawing a little blood. Instinct takes over and Serenity finds herself returning

Jesses' kiss with force and takes his tongue into her mouth as she sucks it as if she was gonna swallow it whole. This time is tasted sweet like honey and lemon, the sweetest tasting kiss she'd ever experienced.

After they break the kiss he begins to lead her out of the room.

"What about the guards? They aren't just gonna let me leave."

Jesse smiles, "My pets took care of them, feeding on their fears, they sucked the fear right into them. They fell unconscious and will wake in an hour or so. No harm done."

He takes her by the arm and leads her closer to the door. She picks up the teddy bear with the remaining bees on her way out.

"I found the bees fitting for you, I hope you don't mind me going ahead and adopting them to your new self. You will find them very helpful and great companions, well other than me of course." Jesse winks at her.

"They are great so far. Not a single sting. They are beautiful and deadly, like me now. I better get used to it huh?"

Jesse smiles, "You will my sweet. I'm sorry I had to scare you to get you changed. I knew you weren't going to do it willingly but now that it's done, I love you and I promise to make you happy."

"I love you too Jesse, I guess it's time to begin our life together. I admit at first I didn't want this but you know? I think we'll be okay and this might actually be a little fun. Like you said I have no choice now." Serenity sighs.

Amy is coming to visit Serenity, when she freezes in the hall. She watches the two head out together, under her breath she says, "She WAS telling the truth." Noticing the pet leeches and bees surrounding the couple. "I'll be damned. I should have listened." Noticing the guards, she dials for help.

Looking back and seeing her friend, Serenity gives her a quick goodbye wave. Amy gives a wave back as she talks to the operator to get assistance for the guards.

Amy mouths quietly, good luck to Serenity and Serenity mouths back thank you and take care.

Heading out the door of the hospital, the only thing Serenity could think of as she and her new partner headed on their new path was: Life is never what you expect or plan, that much is for sure. And as for karma? Well, karma is a bitch.

I DATED SATAN'S GIRLFRIEND

By
P. Mattern

The truck goes where it's supposed to, preprogrammed by tech savvy engineers from the Kingdom of the Damned. Of course, I sit up in the seat and PRETEND to drive, waving and smiling as the shiny truck covered with images and scenes from the circus rolls through well-manicured neighborhoods. The design culminates in a large artistically painted on clown face that utilizes the windows for eyes and the front grill of the truck for a mouthful of white teeth surrounded by big fat red clown lips.

I've gotten great at picking victims. Mr. L. says he has his eye on me.

On one side of the truck is the freezer containing the frozen confections. There are traditional choices like ice cream sandwiches and drumsticks, creamsicles and orange pushups.

Then there are the frozen treats from the new line-some of them contain a gumball inside, others are multicolored popsicles in gradient layers of neon. Still others are frozen éclairs on a stick.

On the other side are the 'special' confections; sweet treats for the ever-increasing ghoul population that Satan himself has planted within the mainly human neighborhoods. They don't eat regular food so they depend on deliveries. They have usually keen hearing, and the soft calliope rendition of 'Shoo Fly, Don't Bother Me' pouring from the twin speakers on the top of the truck alerts them that it's feeding time.

They are well trained. They exit from their safe houses in family groups including the mom and dad and two or three children. They look down to the last hair to be the person they last consumed. They retain the all the memories of their last meal and can carry on all the activities of the no longer living families.

They take time choosing their treats. There are tender frozen finger sandwiches harvested from young children under the age of five, bloody entrails on a stick, eyeball pushups and cones filled with tongues and livers. Everyone walks away satisfied.

It's a living, and 'living' is the operative word here. Though it is a far cry from the luxurious life I was living two years ago, I am grateful to still be breathing. Mr. L. says if I do my job I might even get early release from the sentence I am currently serving.

What was my crime you ask? I dated Satan's girlfriend.

My name is Max Bonem and it wasn't until I got laid off from my position as a Counselor, level five, that I really started to engage in what the Dalai Lama refers to as my 'right livelihood'. Whenever I look back it seems like the best thing that ever happened to me. I finally had time to write.

My wife of 13 years married the guy she'd been banging off and on for over half our marriage and they moved to California without any interference from me. We hadn't had our first child until 5 years ago. Soon after that 'we' had a second boy. Although I never said anything aloud I wondered how two persons of Italian descent could wind up with a set of kids with flaming red hair the color of Bozo's.

I stopped wondering after I met the 'other' man. He was a massively built 6'4" tall Ginger.

At first I didn't know what I was doing. I wrote my first novel and thought that it was pretty good. I titled it 'FAILINGS' because it was largely a memoir and a sort of prolonged literary whining session. For some reason, it must have resonated, likely because we have become a society of whiners.

It took a few weeks but one morning I woke up to discover that it had made the USA Today Bestseller list in Fiction.

I never had to contact an agent—they started contacting me from my author page. Within 7 or 8 months, just when I was running out of 403B money, I found that I was making a decent living as a writer.

Hater can just keep hating—that's exactly what happened.

I moved into an upscale apartment. After several articles and interview by local and national media I had a lot of new friends who knew people that I needed to know, and I had an active social life for the first time in 13.5 years. Gorgeous women who wouldn't have given me the time of day as a Social Worker were giving me blowjobs in the restroom of Private Members Only clubs. I got to be a single, healthy American male again, but this time the experience exceeded my expectations. I was careful not to make the usual mistakes or repeat the wretched excesses of unknowns that Fate had suddenly thrust into the limelight. I politely avoided snorting cocaine or using other recreational drugs, (I said I was allergic), only drank until I felt a good solid buzz and let oversexed young women with barely concealed Daddy issues satisfy my sexual needs.

I kept writing on a schedule, determined to release my second novel before the buzz from the first one died down. Just as sales started to tank, a Top Five Publishing House released, 'INTREPID'. This one was a completely fictional story about an underdog amateur boxer from the wrong side of the tracks who made it big despite many heart-wrenching setbacks including the death of his longtime girl to pancreatic cancer.

This one hit the ground running and was almost instantly a New York Times Bestseller. My future was made, I was on a roll and, despite some critical backlash, it was optioned for a movie.

The first time I noticed Sable it was at an exclusive gathering of New York Times Bestselling authors thrown at the Soho House in New York. It was held on the rooftop where the pool is located on a gloriously warm evening in early summer, catered by their own restaurant and the hippest party I had ever been invited to attend as a guest of honor.

Sable was standing with a fellow author friend of mine, Caleb Barney. She was staring at me over his shoulder as he talked - Caleb is only 5'8" tall. She had an individual sort of beauty that set her apart from the usual perfect blondes I was used to, their various shades of blonde hair the only way to tell them apart.

In makeup, they all looked alike, most from good families with money, most of them smelling expensive between their legs, most of them suffering from some form of eating disorder and chronic vaginal dryness.

That has always turned me off. I figure if a woman desires me she gets wet. I don't think that's my ego talking, I think it's the way nature intended it to be.

Sable, in contrast to the rest of the women floating around the pool wearing clothing that glittered or shone in some way and carrying a drink, was a study in contrasts. Her hair was dark, her skin was pale white and her full lips were rouge red, the sort of red lipstick you'd see the gangster molls wearing in the 1940's movies. Her brows were gorgeously arched and her eyes so dark they seemed to match the depthless ebony of her hair.

Do I sound like a writer? Lol.

She kept sneaking peeks at me. I'm not a bad looking guy—strong chin line and dark good looks from my mother's side of the family. On my dad's side, they bald early, and I still have a full head of hair at 37, for which I'm very grateful.

Finally, I swallowed the last finger of my Glenlivet Scotch and walked toward her. I swear we weren't more than 15 feet apart but time seemed to slow down, along with everything else appearing to be in slow motion. My focus was on her upper half. She was wearing a tropical print dress tied halter style at the neck, causing the rounded perfection of her breasts to be on display. Her skin was pale and flawless and her lips opened slightly as I came toward her.

At last I reached her.

"Caleb!" I said jovially. "Introduce me to your friend, would you?"

Caleb gave me a forced smile.

"Hey Max! Sable Servus, this is Max Arrha Bonem of 'Intrepid' fame. Max, this is Sable, the most beautiful woman at this event, wouldn't you agree?"

"I certainly would," I said, taking her hand briefly. Only it didn't feel like briefly, it felt as though I couldn't let go for a minute.

The feel of her skin against my own was amazing. It was wild. It was like I could 'taste' her with my sense of touch.

The rooftop wind blew her skirt up for a moment, a la Marilyn Monroe over the grate iconic image. She tried to catch it in front but it floated up just high enough to give me a glimpse of her full thighs and a mound of Venus that had been vagscaped Brazilian style.

That happens to be my favorite. I could never trust a girl that was fully shaved. But a well-cared for tuft of hair is intriguing and shows off the labia to full advantage.

It's really about aesthetics.

After just a glimpse of her goodies I was smitten, obsessed, and more attracted than I could ever remember being to a woman.

She came back with me to my penthouse that night. As soon as we arrived I realized that I didn't know much about her. She cleverly had kept me talking about myself the entire evening, which I didn't have any trouble doing, especially since she seemed to hang on my every word.

When we got to my penthouse and were alone at last it was a different story.

"This place is very nice," she said, removing her wrap and laying it gently on the back of my horseshoe shaped sectional sofa," The view is to die for. And who does a girl have to blow to get a drink in this place?"

"Me," I volunteered, pouring some 50-year-old Glenlivet scotch from a fancy decanter into two glasses and handing her one, "I hope you like Scotch, beautiful. I didn't notice what you were drinking before," I confessed.

"Scotch is fine," she said. She took a sip, then a second sip and then set the heavy leaded crystal glass on the bar. I was drinking also, but when I saw her reach behind her and untie the halter-top of her dress with one tug so that it abruptly fell to her waist, I set my glass down and stared.

Her tits were perfect, set up high despite their heft, full and beckoning. She had the largest nipples I'd ever encountered on a white girl too, bigger than silver dollars, a deep rose color and big enough to have been commercial baby bottle nipples.

I am a tit guy, so I was in hog heaven.

I took her hand and led her into my bedroom, and she came along willingly. I laid her back against the bank of pillows on my California King silk sheet covered bed, removing her dress, then quickly shedding my own clothes.

I had the biggest woody I can ever remember having as I climbed on top of her, giving her breasts all my expert attention. She moaned and thrust herself up at me as her full hips moved in slow circles on my bed.

She must have anticipated that I was going to fuck her, because she said," No…wait!" and yanked on my erect penis hard. I had no choice but to follow my cock to her mouth. I was trying to be gentle as I watched my favorite organ disappear in by inch into her warm wet mouth, and she rolled her tongue around it, this way and that as she swallowed more and more of it.

I didn't realize until my balls were resting on her pretty chin that she had swallowed me down to the root.

No blowjob had ever felt as good. Sable apparently had no gag reflexes. Fucking her mouth was like fucking a vagina with a tongue inside to undulate over every vein in my prick. Are you kidding me?

That was the first time I came, and she swallowed every drop like she couldn't get enough.

As if that wasn't amazing enough she flipped me over so that she was on top, and after rubbing her sopping wet pussy over the bottom half of my face, and giving me a good look at it, she mounted me. She was so tight, and the sensation of being inside of her so pleasurable, that it almost hurt despite her natural lubrication.

After the second time, I was ready for a rest. Generally, it takes me a few minutes to recover after the first two bouts of release, but that wasn't what Sable had in mind at all.

We had sex in every way I had ever been familiar with and even some ways I hadn't known were possible.

"Fuck me in the ass darling," she asked, and I did. I was startled to notice that she had a huge pentagram tattooed on each of her fine full butt cheeks, and wondered why they were the only tattoos on her body. Seemed like an inconsequential thing, but for some reason it stuck in the back of my mind.

I wouldn't understand why until later.

She was every red blooded American guy's fantasy...every part of her was imminently fuckable. We had a sixty-nine session in which we came at the same time, and I felt her hot juices blast down my throat.

Well that was a first.

Not once did I think about birth control or protection, and I am careful with those things. I mean I have no desire to spend my waning years going blind from Syphilis like Al Capone, especially since I'd finally tasted financial success, my plan was to hang around a ridiculous amount of years and grab for all the gusto I could get

By the time I noticed the sun coming up I was more than all fucked out. I didn't get the impression that she was, though. When she laid her hand against my cheek and fell asleep on my chest I felt like she was letting ME rest, like she was some sort of sexual automaton that could keep going and going and going.

I didn't know it at the time but my instincts were point on.

I saw Sable often after that, as summer turned into fall. I took her to wonderful restaurants. We saw shows, went dancing at exclusive clubs, and took long walks in Central Park.

The highlight of everything was, of course, the sex.

I had found that I didn't want to be with any other woman. What she did for money was still a mystery to me, but I LIKE mysteries...I even write them for fuck's sake!

The only sour note in this cornucopia of erotic pleasure was the fact that she would disappear for days at a time. Unreachable by cell, she never would tell me where she was staying. Her MO consisted of showing up at my door out of the blue.

My day of reckoning came much sooner than I anticipated.

I was at the local bar on the corner, having a drink after a dismal day trying to finish a short story for Harper's, when out of my peripheral vision I saw a dark-haired gentleman take a seat at the crowded bar next to me. He ordered and then turned his head and stared at me until I couldn't ignore him any longer.

"Hello," I said, turning to face him. I'm sure I had a snarky remark all lined up in my head but I forgot what I had planned to say as soon as I looked into his face.

He had longish hair as black as raven's wings that was slicked back and tucked behind his ears with some kind of styling product. He had perfect facial planes, arched brows and one of those damned hero type cleft chins. And he had really dark eyes. I read somewhere that no human actually has black eyes, just really dark brown ones.

I would have sworn his were black. I couldn't tell the difference between the depthless black of his pupils and his iris.

He was good looking enough to be an actor. I wasn't even sure he WASN'T an actor. I thought I might have actually seen him in something.

"Hello," he answered. "You don't know who I am, do you?"

I shook my head. All the while he was talking to me it seemed as if I could feel a steady trickle of ice water crawling up my spine.

"My name is Luce, but you can call me Mr. L. "

"Max Bonem," I responded, extending a hand his way, but he didn't take it. He just kept staring into my eyes.

"We have business, you and I," he told me, his tone casual.

Again, the ice water crawled up my vertebrae. I managed a perplexed look.

"Business?" I echoed" What business would that be?"

"The sort of business two individuals have when one of them discovers the other has been fucking his girlfriend," he answered smoothly," THAT sort of business."

Against my better judgment I immediately went into defensive mode.

"Sable never told me she had a boyfriend," I blurted, as a felt a thin sheen of perspiration breaking out on my forehead," I don't even know where she lives, straight up man!"

"Oh I believe you," he said, tossing back his drink and holding up a finger for another, "But that doesn't negate the facts that you have been dipping your wick in another man's honey pot. I think you owe me restitution in some way. You're not stupid. Somewhere in the back of your mind you knew she wasn't without some form of male companionship. No woman that looks like her is ever without a companion—can we agree on that?"

I felt like he was playing with me and I started to get mad. Sable had never refused any of my advances. She had shown up several times when I hadn't even called her. I wasn't in the mood to play the 'blame shame game' with some arrogant asshole who was ten time more attractive than I was and probably ten times more successful.

"Maybe not but this conversation is over," I told him, finishing my own drink and standing up as I adjusted my jacket and pulled out a twenty-dollar bill to leave on the bar. I was turning to leave when I felt him grab my left arm just below the elbow. And for a while that was the last thing I would know.

I was shocked awake by a bucket of cold water thrown in my face, and as my eyes adjusted to the spotlight I was under I saw the blur of Mr. L.'s face in front of me and realized I was bound to a chair with heavy chains and fetters. Bound not only by my arms but also at the waist, the ankles and an iron collar at my neck.

I was fucked. And also, naked in some sort of medieval torture chamber. It was windowless, smelled of damp and stone dust, and except for having electricity could have been something from lithographs I had seen depicting the Spanish inquisition.

I noticed other features that didn't bode well— several large drains in the stone floor.

"The bar is upstairs," he told me, peering deeply into my eyes," And we are in the second subbasement under it. I am the owner of course. I was quite drawn to this building because it dates back nearly 400 years to the 1600's. It's not on the historical registry though. It has always been occupied by those drawn to the dark arts. There was a speakeasy in the sub-basement during the prohibition years; no one is sure anymore how far down into the earth the earth the sub basements go.

Some say they go all the way to Hell. Kind of like an inverted condominium if you will. At least that's how I like to think of it. It has a lot of character, don't you think?"

As the water finished dripping from my eyes I could see over his shoulder a massively tall figure standing in one corner of the arched ceilinged chamber. The figure was wearing a metal studded vest, a pair of dusty looking breeches and had enormous feet, which were bare. The most ominous thing about it was that it wore a hood of gunny sack material with no eyeholes., fastened at the neck with rope.

"Oh that is Ire, one of my goons. But I am saving his diverse talents for later. Right now, I want to revisit your affair with my girlfriend for a few minutes. Did you enjoy fucking her?"

"Yes," I said. I hadn't wanted to speak but since I was at a huge disadvantage I decided to keep my answers as short as possible. It was obvious to me that I had been brought here to be punished, and maybe even killed.

I was sorry as hell that I had fucked Sable, but that seemed beside the point.

"Well I think we shall see what you are made of, Max, perhaps layer by layer. First I want you to experience the orgasm of your life—one that goes on and on...one that might remind you not to fuck another male entity's property...

Ready...Set...GO!"

Immediately, although my iron collar kept me from looking downward, I felt my prick rising of its own accord. After a few moments, without any stimulation, I felt physical building up to an orgasm. I was sweating and grunting despite myself, and I felt a rush of blood and heat clear up to my brain before I came involuntarily, saw the hot jet of my ejaculate squirt out in front of me into the air.

A momentary lapse of three seconds and it began again, this time my nerve ending seemed irritable, and the attendant pleasure diminished. It didn't matter. My body responded to invisible stimulus like I was fucking Sable again. This time I came less. My captor seemed to be intently studying my penis during the entire process, although his expression remained neutral.

The third time felt like a maddening tickle gathering force from multiple directions making me feel desperate for it to quit. I had never noticed how painful the buildup was before the explosion, but by the time I had repeated the same process five times it was no longer pleasurable, and I had depleted what sperm had been waiting for release.

"STOP!" I cried out, but it didn't. The rise and fall of pressure morphed into one long painful burning sensation. I got nauseous, and I knew I must be getting dehydrated. At one point, I felt like I would have cut my own package off just to make it stop.

And then suddenly it did. I realized that I'd been crying. I felt beaten, ashamed and defeated.

"There, there," my captor said in a soothing voice," I think that will do. I must say that the offending organ seems quite depleted. I don't think you want to fuck my girlfriend anymore, or anyone else's girlfriend for that matter. Am I right on that Max?"

I barely had the strength, but I lifted my eyes to Mr. L.'s. He no longer had any whites showing in his eyes at all.

"Who ARE you?" I asked, while at the same time knowing that I didn't want to hear the answer.

"I am the Devil," he said quietly," Top Dog, the real deal, and Earth is my turf. No one is coming to help you. You placed yourself beyond any hope of redemption by fucking my favorite human female. That is why you are being punished, and why the punishment befits your crime in so many exquisite ways.

I haven't decided whether to let you live or not, but either way I will clarify your position. I rule the earth with its inherent chaotic nature—it's activities, wars, murders, tsunamis, earthquakes and futilities. Hell is not a place, it is more like a Cartel. I run things. Many evil empires and world rulers dance to our tune.

Do you ever pull your head out of your ass long enough to notice that things are getting worse? Evil in the hearts of men is on the rise, as well as atrocities against the innocent. That's because we are winning, just as we are intended to.

They will miss you in the book world. Rumors, I am sure, will abound. Some will assume suicide, kind of a tradition for writers. Others will imagine you retired from public life to pursue an esoteric one.

He seemed to sense that, even at that point, I had just enough gumption that I might try to plan an escape. Even the thought of Sable made me nauseous. I wasn't finished with my narcissistic author life, though, and so he called Ire over to finish what was left of both my will and my self-esteem off.

Ire, Mr. L.'s goon, had a little mechanism that looked like a small clothes wringer on wheels. He was able to run my testicles through it several times, crushing them to the point of maximum pain without actually causing them to rupture.

I screamed like a woman, mewled like an infant. Ire emitted snorts of laughter from beneath his hood and seemed dejected when Mr. L. ordered him to stop.

I hadn't noticed that there was a circular rise in the stone floor. It turned out to be a cistern, and I was lowered into its depths and then jerked upward just at the point where I was drowning, with the ever-present Ire pulling the ropes.

By the time they got to the Spanish donkey I was incoherent and passed out again. Only to have Ire throw another bucket of freezing cold water in my face.

And then somehow the Devil managed to conjure up my Mother, a woman who I had always condemned to Hell in my mind my entire childhood. Apparently, she finally made it. Thanks to her I had lasting scars from wire coat hangers on the backs of my legs, a lifelong love affair with alcohol and my first fuck had been with the upstairs neighbor woman, a redhead old enough to be my grandmother.

Because Mr. L. Was a Zen Master of torture he took me for a walk down memory lane with Mom, including some humiliating memories that I had repressed my entire life. In between the replayed memories that were so real I could experience them all over again with all five senses, my Mother would launch into a shame/blame soliloquy, her technique so skillful that she could have taught a Master Class in it.

The psychological torture is so much more painful than any physical pain. After the initial shocking pain the body seems to go numb, or you pass out from it.

When the mind is skewered it stays awake through the entire process. When the time came for what would be the grand finale, and Ire pulled off all my fingernails and toenails, I was happy to take the fast train back to oblivion again.

At some point, I drifted into consciousness and agreed to accept an offer to work for Mr. L. My other choice was death. He assured me that if I were to choose death I had led such a worthless self-absorbed life that I would end up working for him anyway, probably side by side with Mom so it was a no brainer.

So, believe it or not, running the Frozen Confection truck is a relief. I've learned a lot.

THE END

P. Mattern is an award winning, Amazon #1 and Amazon Top 100 Bestselling author. She began composing stories in utero and was born with a stylus clutched in her tiny hand. She has written more than 25 books, has appeared in numerous Bestselling Anthologies and currently has publishing contracts with CHBB Publishing, Tell-Tale Publishing and Dark Books Press. She has co-written the Bestselling Full *Moon* Series, *Strident House* and *Forest of Bleeding Trees* with her adult children J.C. Estall and Marcus Mattern and has been nominated for a RONE award for the co-written thriller *Fangirl'* with D. James.

Author Page on Amazon
https://www.amazon.com/P.-Mattern/e/B00MYKZCXY/ref=ntt_dp_epwbk_0

On Facebook
https://www.facebook.com/patricia.annette.3
https://www.facebook.com/FullMoonSeries/

INSATIABLE HUNGER
by
Elizabeth Cash

It appears hunger strikes when you least expect it too. You can be sitting there one minute, enjoying your day, then boom! Your stomach is yelling at you to feed it, and to feed it something good.

My appetite has grown immensely over the past year. The thing is, it's not food I seek. I don't crave the normal vegetables and meat you get from the market. My hunger is driven by something fiercer. More intense and dark.

The way I see it, if I can't sustain this hunger, then people are fucked. Not just one person, but everyone around me and those around them. It becomes an epic feeding frenzy that will land my ass in prison on death row. Or in a mental institution.

Today, my hunger has me on edge and ready to strike. I can hold on for a little while longer. Soon, I will get what I want, and I will be okay. All will be right in my world. Today I'm going to find some food to ravage.

As I walk towards the park, my mind wanders to my ex-girlfriend. *Olivia.* She has been on my mind a lot lately. Her beautiful, round face and almond-shaped eyes. Her pale skin that is delicately sprinkled with freckles. She was breathtaking.

I miss her. I must shake her from my memory. She was a sweet one, but she also hated the things I did. The people I would bring home and never let leave. She just didn't understand me. I still love her, although I shouldn't.

When she left me, she took a piece of me that I can never get back. A vital organ that I need to live. That I needed to feel and be human with. She just ripped it out of me and took it with her. Now, I am nothing. I feel nothing, other than the occasional sting from guilt. But that easily goes away when I remind myself why I do what I do. It keeps me safe. It keeps my mind from eating me alive.

I sigh, telling myself to just let her go. *Easier said than done.*

When I make it to the park, I survey the area and find a nice little place to sit that is shaded by one of the biggest trees in the park. It's an oak tree that has just begun to shed its leaves for fall. I should have brought my camera. Oh well, I'm not here for pictures today. I am here for something else.

It is such a nice day. The sun is shining brightly. Birds are chirping. It's beautiful outside. As I sit down, my eyes lock with his, causing me to still. I'm sure I look like an idiot with my ass suspended in the air, staring at him, but my God, he is perfect.

He shall be mine. One way or another!

After a beat, my ass hits the bench, but I don't break eye contact with him. I need him to know that I am interested. Not too much, though, I would hate to come off as a creeper. Even though I look nothing like one, it is still easy to come off as a predator. Especially these days, when all you hear on the news is about men and women stalking and abducting people.

Oh, wait! The news people hear on television is about me. I let out a chuckle. Knowing that my impious doings are getting the media's attention makes me extremely happy. They have no idea it's me. I plan for them to never find out either. After this one, I will be done in this town and move on to the next.

I finally break eye contact with the fine gentleman in front of me and smirk. Hopefully, he will walk over and strike up a conversation. It will make my work a little easier. I stand up and walk around the oak tree. Examining each piece of bark my fingers touch. Trees are such a treasure to have. Without them, we would die. Wither away into nothing.

A hand touches mine, causing me to jump. I step back and smile after seeing who had the audacity to interrupt my thoughts. My anger dissipates as a smile spreads across his face. Oh, what a smile he has. It stings just a little. Knowing what must be done to him. That's okay though. He will understand after I take him home and begin the process that I need to feel alive.

He has to understand. *Because Olivia never did.*

"Hi." My voice sounds so small, and distant. I am not much of a talker. The only time I say anything is when I am talking to my victims, telling them how much I appreciate their sacrifice. Even then, it's short and to the point.

"Hey."

I smile, wondering if his struggles sound just as sweet as his voice.

"What's your name?" He asks.

"Kingsley. Yours?"

"David. Nice to meet you." He holds out his hand, and I place mine in his. He has a firm handshake, which shows dominance. I like that. Not many people these days will give you such a handshake, you always get a limp arm and sweaty palm. It's immature and disgusting.

I decide to walk back over to the bench and sit down. David follows me like a lost puppy, and that's when I know my job here is done. All I have to do is ask.

"You from around here?" David asks.

I nod. "About two blocks away. Right down the road from the corner store."

I stare at him for a second, feeling the adrenaline kick in. It hits me full force like a freight train. Now is the time to ask, before it dies down and I lose my magic touch. I lean over and place my hand on his thigh, rubbing it gently.

"You wanna get out of here?" I whisper coyly.

"Hell yea." The lust in his voice makes me want to puke, but I manage to hold what little I have in my stomach.

We both stand and begin to walk. I place my hand in his so I can guide him in the right direction. It would be annoying for me to have to give directions aloud. My voice is not something I am fond of hearing. So, I keep talking to a minimum.

As we near the corner store, my heart begins to pound against my chest like a drummer hitting the kick bass at a rave. Each thump hitting harder than the last.

"Just up here," I tell him.

Soon. But not soon enough.

My stomach begins to ache and growl from anticipation. *It knows.* Just as well as the rest of me. My hunger isn't the only thing that gets satisfied when I bring someone home. I never fuck my victims. Ever.

I would hate for people to think so little of me if news ever got out that I was the perpetrator. It would gut me if people thought I would stoop as low as to have sex with these poor souls before they die.

What I truly mean is that my entire body reaps the benefits from eating people. It's like their youth becomes my own. I become younger with each piece of muscle I chew on. I feel stronger with each piece of skin that glides down my throat. My body sheds layers of toxins with each sip of blood I guzzle down.

My victims are my own personal Fountain of Youth. Each one serving a purpose.

"Here we are," I say as I guide him up the walkway. I dig into my pocket to retrieve my keys and unlock the front door. I step aside so David can walk in. It's easier to get the upper hand when you are behind them. They can't see you, so they can't expect anything.

Once my door is locked, I turn around. I'm caught off guard when David pushes me against it and kisses me. It's so sudden that I damn near fall flat on my ass. If his hands, and the door, hadn't been there, my bottom would be bruised from the harsh impact.

I place my hands on either side of his face and pull back, "Slow down. There's plenty of time for that."

He smiles. "What if I don't want to wait? What if I want to rip your clothes off and fuck you right here?"

His carnal words fuel me. He thinks he is so slick. When in reality, he sounds like a fucking idiot! Does he think that his putrid come on will work on me? He wants somethings completely opposite of me.

He wants a quick fuck. What I want? I want to rip his body open and devour him. Bathe in his blood and tear him apart, limb from limb! I am not some piece of candy he can suck on and dispose of when he is finished.

I am Kingsley! I am a fucking goddess!

Some say I am pretentious. Cocky. But I know what I have. My appearance is special to me. I take pride in my looks. Not for others, but for myself. I refuse to be a pig. A slob who lets themselves go. I have one body, and I intend to treat it like the temple it is.

"Well, what if I told you that it's not polite to speak in such a manner when you are in someone else's home?" I whisper, leaning closer to him. I will play along. For a moment. Then I will fuck his world up. He won't know what hit him!

"Wait here, naughty boy." I softly nudge his chest and walk past him towards my bedroom. Once I am inside, I quickly work myself out of my clothes. Taking off just enough to make him think things are going the way he wants them to go.

A shiver runs through me as the excitement intensifies. I take a deep breath, then grab my belt and exit the room. Keeping my little weapon behind me, I walk into the living room. David is still standing there.

I clear my throat, catching his attention. When he looks up, his expression changes from somber, to hungry.

I'm hungry too.

"Well, don't you clean nicely." He pulls his hands from his pockets and begins to walk towards me. I shake my head, giving him a sexy smirk.

"No. Crawl."

David cocks his head to the side, confused. Then it registers with him what I want him to do.

"Yes, ma'am." He drops down to his knees, then leans forward until his hands are planted firmly on the ground. Slowly, he moves forward, not breaking eye contact. I guess he thinks his sultry look is supposed to turn me on. It only repulses me.

As he nears me, I step backward. Each time he moves forward, I move back. Until we are in front of my bedroom door. David tries to stand, but my foot stops him.

"Nope. Stay down, or it will only get worse for you!" I warn. *I mean it.*

I open the door and move aside, letting David crawl inside. Once he is inside, I close the door and walk up to him.

"Lie down on your stomach. Don't turn around. Don't look at me." Each instruction that comes out of my mouth, he obeys. I am really enjoying this. As soon as his body is flat on the floor, I straddle him. It will be easier to this way. That way, if he does put up a fight, I will still have the upper hand.

I drop down to my knees, placing each hand on either side of him, so my head is next to his. He looks over at the belt in my hand, and his body moves when he lets out a chuckle. Please, do find this entertaining. It is for me. Probably because I know what is about to occur. David, on the other hand, poor thing. He is absolutely clueless.

"Are you ready, naughty boy?" I whisper, getting annoyed with the sound of my voice. I usually don't talk this much, but this guy seems to need it. Only a few more minutes and I can have peace. No more talking.

He nods, and that's all the reassurance I need, not that it was warranted anyways. Permission has been granted.

"Good boy," I whisper. "Thank you, for coming here and giving me the pleasure of sustaining my hunger."

Before he can respond, I slip the belt around his neck. I pull on it as hard as I can. David begins to struggle and buck underneath me. His hands are trying to get a good grip on the belt to pull it off, but it's no use. My grip overpowers his because his body isn't fighting to release the belt, it's fighting for air. His mind wants to fight me, but his body wants to bring life back to its lungs. His hands continue to claw at his neck while he gasps for air.

As David slowly begins to fade in and out, I wonder if I should give him a fighting chance. I decide against it when he has one last surge of adrenaline and reaches around, grasping a hand full of my hair and pulling me over. I falter but quickly gain my bearings again. I pull tighter on the belt.

His face turns various shades of color. Pink. Red. Purple. Blue. And once his body gives out from the lack of oxygen, it begins to turn a sickly gray color. I drop the belt, and his head falls to the floor with a thud. It makes me laugh.

I will admit, though, that I am a little disappointed that he didn't put up that much of a fight. I was sure that he would when he shook my hand. I stand up and wipe the sweat off my forehead. My body temperature rises from the excitement every time I do this. It gets hot…

Shit!

I forgot to turn on the oven. I sigh. Dropping the belt, I grab my shirt off the floor and put it on. Then I make my way to the kitchen, so I can do what was supposed to be done when I first got here. Patients will need to be something I acquire within the next half hour, or I will go bat shit crazy and tear into him raw!

I turn the oven on broil, deciding that it would hasten the process and I won't make a mess by slicing him up now instead of on the plastic tarp in my back yard. I love my back yard. It's fenced in, and I have no neighbors behind me. It makes my work a lot easier to clean up and my house won't have to smell like chemicals all the time. Plus, no one can see me hack into these degenerates that are dumb enough to come home with me.

I hum merrily as I stride back to my room. David is still lying there, of course. I grab his feet and begin to pull him down the hallway. He is heavier than I expected, but I venture on. Grunting and groaning with each pull.

This reminds me of when Olivia had passed out drunk, and I had to drag her to bed. It made me mad that she went out without me, but she said she needed the alone time. She wasn't alone, though. She had a "friend" with her.

The same fucking friend she left me for. I wanted to slaughter him for making her fall in love with him. I wanted to skin him alive and make her watch. I didn't. Although, I could still do it. I know where they live. Where he works and his schedule. The times he goes to meet with his mom and when he goes golfing with his father.

I may be a bit of a stalker, but I am low key. No one knows I am there, no one knows what I do or when I do it. Just like no one knows it's me luring people to my home and killing them. I don't do this for sport. I do it out of necessity. This is my life, and I don't plan on changing for anyone. I didn't change for Olivia, nor will I change for anyone who comes after her.

I know it will be hard for someone to accept me for what I am. The things I do. Then again, I don't plan on getting into a relationship with anyone anytime soon. All I need right now is this. I just need to survive on others until I can find a someone worth keeping. Someone worth telling my deepest, darkest secrets. Someone who I know will accept my flaws and the atrocious things I do.

With one last grunt, I shove David out the back door and onto the tarp-covered patio. His body rolls once, then stops, landing him on his back. My back pops when I stand up. I stretch out my limbs, relieving them of their duties, for now. Dragging him down the hall was the easy part. Chopping his limbs off will be the harder chore in all of this.

I will start with his legs, then work my way up. Once he is completely severed, I will cut out my favorite parts of the body, and cook it. It's almost dinner time, and I have worked up an appetite. I walk over to my shed and grab the box cutters and saw.

I set my tools down and then sit down next to them and David. Taking the box cutter, I glide it down the front of his shirt, then continue down onto his jeans until he is naked. I remove his shredded clothing and toss them aside.

A knock on my front door makes me sigh in frustration. Who the fuck dares interrupt me while I am working? I drop the box cutter and stand up. As I make my way to the door, I can see that my living room is illuminated by red and blue flashing lights.

I groan. These assholes better have a good explanation for coming to my door. I unlock the top lock, then the bottom, and open the door.

"Hey, Chris. What's going on?" I ask him. Chris has been to my house several times. He used to bring Olivia home when she would pass out drunk at bars. She got really bad towards the end of our relationship. She said it was my fault. That I tainted her. That my needs haunted her and she needed them to go away. I guess she thought drinking would help diminish the things she knew.

"Hey, Kingsley. We had a missing person's report, and we are following up on it. His name is David Lancaster. His last known location was at Wordly Park down the road. Have you seen him wandering around the streets?" He holds up a photo for me to examine.

I shake my head. "Nope. How long has he been missing?"

"A few hours. But his mom insists that he is never late for dinner and demanded we look for him."

"Oh. Well, I'm sorry I couldn't help." Please, get the fuck out of here. I hate talking!

"Alright, well, you have a nice night." Chris nods then hops off my steps and walks back to his patrol car. I watch as he drives off, then I close the door and secure the locks. *Thank God!* I don't know how much longer I could have kept up that façade.

I spin on my heel and head back to my dinner. My stomach is starting to hurt because I haven't eaten all day. I have been waiting for this moment to fill myself up. This will be a lot more satisfying than a burger or some other pathetic excuse for a meal.

The second my foot hits the tarp, I hear another knock on my front door. This time, anger surges through me. What is with people today? I have never had so many people come to my house in one day! I swing my front door open with a forceful pull and am met with another familiar face. Not one I was expecting to see, though.

"Olivia. What are you doing here?"

"When are you going to stop?" She questions, "Chris came to my house asking about a missing guy. I was kind enough to wait for him to leave your house before coming over."

Oh, fucking hell. I miss her!

"I have no idea what you're talking about." I go to close the door, but Olivia puts her foot in the way, preventing it from shutting. I look down at it, then back to her. "I suggest you move your foot before you take his place tonight."

She doesn't waver. It makes me smile. Maybe she isn't scared of me anymore. I doubt it, though. I would hate to get my hopes up just for her to shot them down.

"I loved you, Kingsley. I did. I wanted to accept what you did, who you were... No, who you are, but I couldn't. I still can't. It's wrong. So, I'm warning you, now. Stop, or I am going to go to Chris and tell him everything."

I laugh. "Then what? You would get into just as much shit as I would. You withheld vital information about the abduction and murder of several people. You are just as guilty as me. Besides, I planned on stopping. In this town anyways. Now, if you'll excuse me. I would hate for my food to fucking spoil!" I kick her foot out from in front of the door and slam it shut.

This is not how I wanted tonight to go! This is bullshit. Like a tyrant child, I stomp back over to David. Olivia always knew how to push my buttons. It pissed me off and turned me on.

I pick up the saw, ready to slaughter David into little bits. I usually have a certain way I go about cutting into people, but I have had enough interruptions, and I can not handle another. Picking up David's arm, I place the saw underneath his armpit and begin my process.

Each tug of the saw if more forceful than the last. Anger driving each slice, making it easier to cut through his skin, muscle, and bone. Before I know it, my body is splattered in blood, and I am holding a severed arm. I drop it down on the tarp and do the same thing to his other arm, then his legs.

I thought by the time I finished hacking this idiot to pieces my anger would have subsided, but I am still fuming. I walk over to my toolshed and grab the hedge clippers. This is something I would never do. Something that I usually would never allow myself to do.

I know that what I do is wrong. On many different levels. That's why I keep simple. Just cut them up and eat them, so my conscience is partially clear. But right now, all moral character has been replaced by rage. I am letting my emotions take over. David will pay for all the shit Olivia has done to me.

I bring the hedge clippers above my head, in one swift, forceful thrust, the clippers are embedded inside his abdomen. I grab the handles and open them, slicing him open like a pig. The only thing that would make this better it hearing his squeal. But seeing how he is dead, that won't happen.

I continue to stab and slice him open until his stomach is in shreds and is just one big gaping wound. Blood pours from his injuries, making my mouth water. I drop the hedge clippers and bend down.

My knees land in the puddle of red, gooey liquid. It feels so good. I place my hands inside of David's wound, coating them. Letting his life soak into my soul. I take my right hand and rub it along my left forearm, covering it in blood. Then do the same with my right arm. Them my legs, stomach, and then my face. Until every inch of my body is soaked in his blood. I would love to see how horrid I look, but I'm hungry, and I am done waiting.

Fuck cooking my dinner, I will dig in raw.

I place my hand inside of his stomach again and grab a hand full of butchered organs and flesh, then bring it to my mouth. The metallic smell causes me to shiver. This is so much better than any drug, than any alcoholic beverage, any piece of fucking ass I have ever had.

Nothing will ever top this. Nothing will ever make me as happy as this does, right now. In this moment. Olivia couldn't even make me feel anything even remotely close to this. Sometimes it hurts to know that this is my only real solace, but this was how I was designed. I accept that. My fate was sealed the first time I ever did this.

My mouth opens voluntarily as my hand approaches it. I bite into the chunk of meat and flesh that is intertwined with my fingers and relish in the flavor and texture as it moves around in my mouth.

I lay down next to David and continue eating what I have in my hand until there is nothing left. Reaching over, I grab another hand full and take a bite. The more I consume, the happier I get.

This is the nostalgic feeling I revel in.

When I'm eating, I feel like a child on Halloween digging into their candy bag, eating every piece of candy their hand touches.

Once my belly is on the verge of exploding, I decided that I have had enough. I better not over eat, or I will regret it later when I am doubled over the toilet. It tastes amazing going down, not so much coming up.

The sun has finally gone down, and I gaze up at the stars. This town was fun. It gave me many memories I will cherish, people I will not forget, and it sustained my hunger. I'm a little sad that my time here has ended, but it is for the best. I'm sure the next place I go to will give me just as much, if not more, things to love. The only thing it won't have is an Olivia.

My Olivia.

She may have stolen my heart and broke it, but I still miss her. I still feel for her. Olivia was an angel who was afraid to live in the dark with me. Afraid to feel the devil's touch.

I, on the other hand, have willingly let the devil inside. He has consumed me and given me the best thing I could have ever asked for. A habit that brings me true joy. I wasn't designed by God to do good deeds. I was made by the devil to live in sin. I will never give this up. As dark as my life may be, I will always be happy with the things I do.

After all, happiness can be found in the scariest and darkest of places.

DARK LAND
Tales of the Horsemen;
The Carnage of Pestilence
By
Bryan A. Tann

July 19, 1995

"Are you nervous, honey?" the man asked his wife as she sat on the exam bed. She wore a stylish, yet plain blue dress. Her slender frame was complimented in style and fit, as though it were tailored for her body specifically. Her dirty blonde hair masked the slight splotches of aged gray, her skin remained tight yet the experience in her eyes revealed that she was nearing middle age.

She smiled to her husband, her nerves evident in the lines of her face. His dark hair, coupled with his own gray, broad shoulders, and squared chin gave him the look of an aging-with-grace warrior that would not give into nature's clutches.

"About as nervous as you are Doctor." She chuckled.

"Well Mrs. Martz, no matter what happens today everything will work out. We will just call the adoption agency like we spoke about." He smiled, patting her leg to reassure her.

"Of course." His wife replied. "I just…"

"I know honey. I know." Her husband gave her knee a gentle squeeze of support.

"Doctor and Mrs. Martz, sorry to keep you waiting." The young looking female doctor walked into the room, after her knock interrupted their moment. Her olive colored skin looked almost onyx compared to the bright white of her lab coat.

'Suppose fertility is a better racket than being a surgeon.' Doctor Martz thought to himself looking at the young woman in front of him.

"It's nice to see you again Dr. Granger. I'm Genevieve and this is my husband David." Mrs. Martz smiled, trying to keep everything cordial. Her marriage to David Martz was met with compliment; since their days as undergrads, she used her free-spirited nature to offset his more rigid mindset. This also included not allowing him to get too big of a head as one of the country's top surgeons.

"Of course. My apologies." The young doctor smiled, feeling slightly embarrassed that she continued to lose the non-formal attitude that the good doctor's wife seemed to insist on despite his wanting to keep it strictly business.

"Dr. Granger." Doctor Martz replied, standing to shake the young woman's hand. She took his hand into hers firmly, refusing to show weakness in front of him.

"Dr. Martz." The young doctor replied.

"Oh David cut it out already would you? Leave the girl alone and let's get our news, shall we?" Genevieve chided her husband, putting an exclamation point on the subject with a firm slap on his backside.

Looking over his shoulder, David Martz gave his wife a gentle smile before giving the younger doctor a polite nod and sat back down in his chair.

"So what news do you have for us?" David asked nervously.

"Congratulations." The young doctor smiled warmly.

"Are you...? Oh, my God!" Genevieve squealed, leaping from the exam bed, throwing herself into her husband's arms. He caught her and hugged her close as she sobbed tears of joy into his suit.

"We are, of course, ready to perform an ultra sound to see what we are working with. I also have to remind you that, with in vitro fertilization, there is a strong chance that this could be a multiple birth."

"Well that's even better!" Genevieve replied.

"Well yes, and no." Granger replied calmly. "There is a chance that, due to your age as I'm sure you're aware, successful carrying of a multiple birth can be quite difficult and is not guaranteed and..."

"And I am sure that we will have a firm plan in place to ensure that this pregnancy is successful. Correct?" Dr. Martz replied in a firm tone, not ready to allow anyone to ruin their moment.

"Of course Dr. Martz." The young woman replied. "I have taken it upon myself to ensure that everything goes as flawlessly as possible. I will be working with you both every step of the way in this.

"I know I am in very good hands Dr. Granger." Genevieve replied with a smile, hugging her husband's arm gently. "So ultrasound then?" she asked.

"Yes. If you want to follow me into the next room, you can get changed and then we'll get to work." Granger smiled warmly.

**

"That girl." David grumbled an hour later. The sleek black Mercedes went down the abandoned road as though it were a king's carriage.

"Oh David she was just trying to ensure that we knew all the facts." His wife chuckled rubbing her tummy lightly.

"I'm a doctor. I'm sure I know what the risks could entail." He boomed.

"Of course you do honey. But it is a lot different when your wife is the patient, than you being just the doctor. You know it and I know it. Calm down Lancelot and just be happy that you're going to be a daddy?" she gave his thigh a gentle squeeze. "Besides your swimmers did a great job with the help of the in vitro. I think someone is going to get a reward when we get home."

"Really?" the darkness of his mood began to lift. "I like the sound of that."

She smiled warmly to her husband giving his thigh another squeeze. Having met as undergraduates and married before their junior year, both agreed to not have children until after he had at least begun his residency. When it was finally time to begin trying in full, they were unable to conceive. Finally, ten years later, after all the stress and pain their dream was finally coming true.

"All this time." He said, cutting into her thoughts. "I can't believe it is finally going to happen." He smiled.

"I wonder how many there will be?" she asked aloud.

"Well at about thirteen weeks we will know for certain if there are multiples. As far as we know right now, there is just the one little bean," he chuckled.

"I hope there is more than one." She said with a smile.

"You do?"

"Of course. If this is our only chance to have a baby, I don't want him to be alone."

"So you want a boy then?" he asked with a grin.

"I would like one of each and then that can be that to be honest. I would love to watch you in the backyard, throwing a ball around. Meanwhile I have a little girl that can…help me cook and stuff. And then not want to talk to me because of boys and things like that." She laughed lightly.

"You have it all figured out then." David purred lightly.

"Of course I do. I may not be a stuffy doctor like some people I know, but I do think things through and have plans. Do I have to remind you about…"?

"The first two years of medical school." They replied in unison.

"Yes I remember. If it wasn't for your planning, we would have been ruined financially."

"You're welcome." She looked to him, moving her hand over his thigh to his crotch. "Although I think that tonight I'll show you how thankful I am."

"You're welcome." He said, forcing his eyes to stay open despite his want to close them as pleasure began to overtake him.

October 21st 1995

"Alright Genevieve, Dr. Martz, let's see what we are working with shall we?" Dr. Granger said with a smile. In the three months since the announcement that she was finally pregnant, Genevieve's stomach began to bulge considerably. After squeezing the cold jelly onto her stomach, the young doctor placed the ultrasound paddle onto the woman's stomach. Instantly the young woman's eyes widened.

"Oh my!" she chuckled.

"What? What is it?"

"Four babies..." David said in awe, a wide smile on his face.

"I can't believe it," Genevieve whimpered as tears of joy fell from her eyes, taking her husband's hand and kissing it gently.

"It looks like there will be three boys and, it looks like, yes! A little girl!" Dr. Granger smiled looking to the couple.

"A daughter? I'm going to have a daughter?" The walls of arrogance and disconnected that had been built around David Martz fell instantly as he looked to the ultrasound screen. "So we have a doctor, an athlete, a musician, and a..."

"Whatever they want to be honey," his wife chuckled patting his hand gently. "They haven't been born yet it's a little premature to start planning their lives, don't you think?"

"So far they look healthy, their heartbeats sound strong, but remember there are multiples there are still risks." Dr. Granger reminded them.

"Yes we are aware," Dr. Martz replied, looking to the younger woman with a warning gaze. "We are prepared, but at the end of the day we are going to enjoy the now. If that is quite alright?"

"Oh David," Genevieve smiled taking his hand and looked to Dr. Granger. "Yes we do understand, thank you Dr. Granger." She smiled patting her husband gently.

"Alright well I will just clean the gel off of you and you can get dressed and then schedule your next appointment. Again, congratulations," the young woman smiled to them exited the room.

"That woman is so irritating!" David growled in frustration.

"What is wrong now David?" she smiled to him patiently.

"She keeps reminding us about the bad things, why can't she just let us enjoy the moment?"

"For the same reason that you remind your patients of possible problems David; because you want to make sure that they fully understand any and all risks. She's doing her job David that is all she's doing. Be nice to that girl will you please? For me?"

"Fine," he grumbled in irritation looking away before finally looking to his wife. The look of joy in her eyes erased the anger toward the younger doctor and he smiled warmly. "These children are going to be amazing people, aren't they?"

"Yes they will," the joy in her eyes infected him and sent tears of joy running down his cheeks as he held her close and kissed her softly.

"I love you Gen."

"I love you too David, very much."

February 27th, 1996

"David?" Genevieve cried weakly as her hand moved gently to her stomach as a sharp pain shot through her core and radiated outward like a rock in the center of a pond with its waves rippling to the shore. "David!" she screamed as the next stab of pain made the first a paper cut.

"What is it?" David asked sitting up quickly, putting his hand to the hand that cupped her belly.

"It hurts!" she screamed loudly as she felt another stab of pain tore through her insides. She fell back to the bed wrapping both of her arms around her pulsating belly. "The babies David! The babies!"

"Okay, okay," he began attempting to calm the two of them. "I'm going to call an ambulance and your doctor and we are going to get through this okay? The babies are going to be just..." he stopped when the smell of copper hit the air. He looked to her lower half and saw the blood between her legs. "*Our* babies are going to be just fine, you'll see!" he reached for the nearby cellphone and dialed.

"This is Dr. David Martz. Yes. Yes. I need an ambulance to my home immediately! Also, put a call into Dr. Chloe Granger. She's my wife's OB. Get her to meet us there. Yes! Hurry! Please?" he disconnected the line and looked to her helplessly. "Okay the ambulance is on the way and Chloe is going to meet us at the hospital. It's going to be alright Gen, I promise it's going to be alright," he said, doing his best to keep the confidence in his voice.

"You're sweet. And a terrible liar," she replied as sweat poured down her brow. "They aren't moving David. They aren't moving anymore," she sobbed. "There was so much activity before I went to bed tonight and even when the pain first started. Now? There's nothing."

"Gen it's going to be…"

"They aren't moving anymore David! David Jr., Jennifer, Martin, Deacon…they aren't moving anymore David," she sobbed.

"No!" he cried as grief tore into him. "No! They aren't! They're going to make it Gen! They have to!"

"I'm so sorry David," she whimpered. "I'm so sorry I wasn't strong enough…"

"That's enough! They aren't dead! Do you hear me?" he shouted, tears pouring from his eyes as he kissed her forehead gently. "You're having some complications. That's all, can't you see? They're just in distress. The ambulance will get here and you will go to the hospital. You'll go in for emergency surgery and you'll delivery four little angels via C-section. They'll be in the NICU for a little while, but they will be coming home. Do you understand me?"

"How do you know?" Genevieve asked as she felt another wave of pain strike her.

"Because I'm a doctor. That's why," he said with the same overconfident smirk that won her heart so many years prior. "I know what I'm…" a sob caught in his throat "I'm right…"

The two rested their heads together as they shared tear filled laughter. He rocked her gently as agony rocked through her body as her body contracted and convulsed.

**

"Alright people, what do we have here tonight?" the lead surgeon walked into the prep area washing his hands vigorously preparing to scrub into the Operating Room.

"Dr. Ryan," the nurse greeted him calmly, "Forty-five-year-old female multiple births having complications," one of the nurses replied as she finished cleaning up. "One of Dr. Granger's patients doctor," she replied.

"Oh, is this the wife of the famous Dr. David Martz?" he asked blandly.

"That would be the one Bob," one of the other doctors replied. John Williamson looked to his colleague as though he were a super hero diving in to save the day. The squat little man with the receding hairline looked to the taller, handsomer man with distinguished salt-and-pepper colored hair with hero worship masked with respect.

"Alright let's make sure we get this done as clean as possible, that smug son-of-a-bitch loves to make trouble for anyone that pisses him off," Dr. Bob grumbled.

"The wife is a nice woman at least," a third doctor replied.

"Yeah she's a peach alright," Bob replied as he began to finish his preparations. "I met her at the hospital Christmas party about three years ago, why she married that prick I have no idea."

"I've heard that he gives poor Chloe Granger a hard time each time they go in for appointments. I'm willing to bet you dollars to donuts that she'll be glad when she's rid of them, just for his presence alone," a fully scrubbed doctor replied going into the OR.

"Let's see what we can do to bring the newest Martz's into the world," Bob replied as he finished his preparations and then stopped to turn on the machine on the wall to show him the film from the earlier ultrasound. "My God…" Bob exclaimed as he looked at to the films that came from the earlier ultrasound. "Is it just me or does it look like…"

"I said the same thing Bob, that's why I called you," the doctor at his side said. "It looks like the smallest one has cords wrapped around the other's necks. It has to be a mistake Bob don't you think?"

"Well, we will have to see once we get inside, so let's get to work ladies and gentlemen," the doctor replied.

**

"Alright Bob, give it to me straight," David Martz replied pacing in the waiting room area like an aggravated caged animal. "You don't let me into the room while you perform the C-Section…"

"Because, Dave," Bob replied with scorn knowing that he used a form of Dr. Martz's name that he hated. "You don't know how to shut your mouth and let people work. While the rest of this hospital and its administration may kiss your ass, I will not. I'm the best at what I do and you know it and I was not about to let you compromise me doing my best to save your wife and your children. Now do you understand that? I'm not Chloe Granger, I will not be intimidated by you."

The two alpha male healers glared at each other, neither prepared to give into the other. The tension between them growing thicker by the second.

"Alright *Doctor*," Martz spat the word with venom. "Enlighten me."

"Your wife is fully stable and will make a full recovery," Dr. Ryan said calmly.

"Thank God," David sighed with relief. "And our children?" When Dr. Ryan remained silent, David looked to him with earnest. "Please Robert? What about my children?"

"I was able to save one of the boys. The others had already passed before I could get in. I am truly sorry David,"

David Martz looked to Robert Ryan closely as tears began to swell in his eyes and then flow down his cheeks.

"I...I would like to see my wife please,"

"Of course. She's in recovery now and your son is in the NICU being that he is nine weeks premature,"

"Of course. T...thank you Robert. Truly," David walked past him quickly to join Genevieve. While he stood in firm place in the empty waiting room, he took a deep breath before heading back to the unit.

"Hey Bob," John Williamson walked up and placed a pudgy hand on his shoulder. "How did Martz take it?"

"About as can be expected for a man that just heard that three of his four children died in utero," Dr. Ryan replied.

"Did you tell him?" Williamson asked in a hushed tone.

"Tell him what?"

"That the little boy killed the others?" Williamson asked leaning in closer.

"No, because that isn't what happened. Its speculation and nothing more, do you understand me John?"

"Bob! We have seen children born with their cords wrapped around their necks, but not like that! He had their cords in his hands and..."

"Jesus Christ will you listen to yourself?" Dr. Ryan hissed in a hushed tone, looking around to ensure that they were alone. "A nine-week-old, premature baby cannot kill anything, do you understand me? We are not sure of what we saw and this is the last time we are even going to talk about this. Do you understand me?"

"But Bob…"

"John please use that melon on top of your neck for a minute will you please? Do you realize how insane that truly sounds? That an infant in utero murdered its siblings? Why would you want to go around discussing this with people? Do you realize how crazy that makes you sound?"

"I know Bob but…" he rubbed his temple with a relenting sigh. "You're right. I'm sorry I just…"

"I know John. I know. It's insane, but if we bring this up at all we are both out of a job. It is best to just leave as the three babies died. It's the most believable situation given her age, and that's the way it is going to be. Do you understand?"

"Yeah Bob. I understand."

June 22nd 2005

"Deacon?" Genevieve Martz called from the backdoor to the massive backyard. She looked past the tire swing that hung from the tree that also housed her son's favorite place in the world; his tree house with the large 'Keep Out!' sign scrawled in red paint.

He could hear his mother calling, but Deacon Martz was involved in an experiment. It had taken him almost two hours to track down the Jefferson's cat Mr. Bip. He was grateful that he had thought to keep a jacket, face mask and gloves in the tree house from over the winter, it was worth being yelled at by his father for losing clothes at school. It would have caused his mother to ask him questions if he had gone into the winter clothes for gloves and a jacket. Her questions would be ten-fold if she saw the scratches that Mr. Bip's struggles caused.

He looked to the crucified calico and smiled at his work. He was proud that he had been able to wrap his hand around the cat's throat and duct tape its mouth shut fast enough to put the first roofing nail just above its right paw, then repeat the process.

The other cats, squirrels, and animals in the woods he'd been able to trap were just practice to this point. He'd never gotten this far before with a living subject. The reminder of his failures made this success even sweeter as the muffled meowing tickled his sense.

"It's okay Mr. Bip. Surgery is about to begin. Sorry I wasn't able to get any anesthetic, but Daddy and Mommy would have noticed and…"

"Deacon Jacob Martz! You answer your Mother right now!" grunting in frustration, he pulled off his jacket, mask, and gloves and lifted the wooden board that acted as a door to his window.

"Yes Mama?" he called in his most innocent tone.

"What are you doing up there? It's almost time for lunch."

"I'm conducting an experiment Mama!" he called back to her with a sweet smile. "I want to surprise Daddy with my findings for when he comes back from his conference in San Francisco!"

"Well finish up and come in for lunch! I've got your favorite ready!" she called out with a wide smile of pride.

"Personal pizza with pepperoni and sausage! Yum!" he said to himself. "Okay Mama! I'll be out in five minutes, maybe ten!" he called back before letting the wood block the light from the window.

"Well, Mr. Bip, I don't intend to rush this by any means, I can promise you that. I don't think you're going to be alive long enough to care one-way or the other though. Sorry." The small boy chuckled as he walked past the multiple medical books he had stacked up in the corner and made his way back to his make shift exam table.

The old surgical tools that his father had discarded over the years made their way to his tree house where he would make them his own. He gripped his wet stone and began to run the blade of his scalpel over it a few times and grinned.

"It's going to be alright Mr. Bip. I'm going to make a small incision right at your throat and then cut down to your pelvis which should be right…here!" he tapped lightly to make the cat wince. "Okay so I'm just going to start here," he sunk the tip of the scalpel into the cat's flesh and cut downward with precision in one fluid motion then secured the flaps of flesh and fur to the wide expertly.

"Now let's see what you have going for you. Hello, what have we here?" he asked himself with a chuckle putting his fingers inside of the cat's stomach. "I suppose they should have named you 'Mrs. Bip'," he chuckled lightly looking at the five fetuses within the cat's womb.

"I guess if I would have waited a little bit longer, oh well it is what it is. I'll be able to get another one no problem. But I am going for lunch, while you six sit here. I still have a lot of work to do," Deacon smiled coldly, kissing Mrs. Bip on her forehead before lifting the trap door to his tree house and climbed down the tree. He licked the last of the blood of the cat from his finger tips and went into the house with a big smile on his face.

"There's my little genius! How did your experiment go honey?" Genevieve asked with a proud smile.

"It went amazing Mommy! I think Daddy is going to be very happy when he comes home!" he said sitting at the table, taking a sip of juice from his favorite 'Fight Force Five' cup that he wouldn't eat a meal unless he had on the table.

"What is this experiment anyway?" she asked curiously.

"It's a surprise between me and Daddy, sorry Mommy it's for doctors only," he said with a wide smile.

"You're not a doctor yet smart guy," she sat in front of him digging into her pizza.

"But I will be!" he said chewing hungrily at his pizza.

Later That Night

"Did you have a good day my angel?" Genevieve asked Deacon as she tucked him into his bed gently.

"Yes Mama. I learned a lot and I'm almost ready for my experiment!" he smiled widely.

"That's great honey! Will I like it?" she asked kissing his forehead.

"Mama, it's going to be to die for," he smiled brightly.

"Well your father will be home tomorrow afternoon so you can show it to us then okay?"

"Okay Mama."

"Good night my sweet boy," she kissed his forehead again, turned off his light and left his door open just a crack so that the hallway nightlight would show into his room like he liked, and departed to her room.

He waited until he was sure that she was asleep and slipped out of his bed quietly. His innocent, bright smile of anticipation plastered on his face. Deacon made his way into the bathroom and opened the medicine cabinet that he had been forbidden to ever enter and found Dr. David Martz's Valium that he'd been prescribed after hurting his back the year prior during a fall from the tree house while making repairs. He unscrewed the top and selected four pills and went to his mother's room and smiled down to her.

"I think you and Daddy are going to love my experiment Mama," he smiled warmly leaning over to put the pills into her partially opened, sleeping mouth then lightly rubbed on her throat so that she would swallow the pill.

"D…Deacon?" she asked wearily.

"Go back to sleep Mama, I'm sorry. I just wanted to give you a kiss goodnight," Deacon smiled, kissing her gently on the forehead.

"Okay honey, get back to bed alright? Good night Angel," she rolled over and was back to sleep instantly.

Deacon exited the room and walked down the stairs, doing all that he could to maintain his patience and calm as his experiment was about to finally be achieved. He climbed the tree to his trap door using the pegs that acted as a ladder and entered his tree house. The smell of Mrs. Bip and her kittens greeted him, along with a large group of flies buzzing on the necrotic flesh.

"Ew, gross!" he chuckled as he claimed his tools and rolled them up in medical tool roll and went back into the house and began to wash the tools in the kitchen sink, being careful not to cut himself on his scalpel. Deacon then went to his father's study to retrieve a stapler and then went back to his tools, beginning to sharpen the scalpel again looking up to the ceiling. He knew that the pills he'd given his mother had to have effect by now.

"Okay Mama, it's time for the experiment," he smiled walking up the stairs to see his mother sprawled out, snoring much louder than usual.

He approached her, and cut off her nightgown with an emotionally detached precision. 'A good surgeon loves what he does son, but he never lets it make him careless. Get the job done, love it later,' Deacon remembered his father lecturing him.

After he cut her nightgown and panties off, he looked to his mother's firm frame and pulled a marker from the tool roll and made a straight line from sternum to her pelvis. He released a small yawn before gripping his scalpel. Deacon looked closely, remembering from his father's books exactly where he needed to make his first incision. He sank the scalpel into her flesh and began to cut downward.

The Next Morning

David Martz exited the cab with a smile on his face, anxious to see his wife and son. The week-long conference had earned his contempt, but all of that was forgotten now. He was proud of how his son devoured knowledge, especially medical knowledge. He'd made sure to get Deacon as much literature as he could so that he could take it to his room, or to his tree house and they would discuss studies at dinner. David loved to explain the things that Deacon didn't know, and he marveled that speaking to his eight-year-old was more intellectually stimulating than speaking to most adults.

Looking at his watch, David knew that with Deacon waking up at eight in the morning when he wasn't in school like clockwork, it gave him time to get a shower and some private time with his darling Genevieve. The thought of it brought a tightness to the front of his pants that brought a silent moan to his lips as his sensitive member pressed against the gentle fabric of his underpants.

He put his key into the lock and entered the house with a slight sigh, thankful to finally be home and looking for some peace and quiet. He put his bags down and, despite hating clutter, made the self-rationalization that he would get them later, he was just exhausted.

He walked up the stairs carefully, ensuring that he didn't awaken his young son. He opened the bedroom door with a smile.

"Gen, I'm home I…" he stopped short, shock claiming his entire being. Blood coated the tender white bed sheets. Genevieve's sightless eyes looked upward to the ceiling, already turning milky white, indicating that she'd been dead for hours. The white bed sheet was pulled over her midriff to cover her stomach.

"No…no…no!" he cried rushing toward her only to step in something on the floor that forced him down to the floor. He looked down to see his wife's stomach, liver, intestines, and kidneys laying on the floor. He pulled himself to his feet quickly, tears streaming down his face. He frantically pulled the sheet away from her and his eyes widened with shock.

Looking to his wife's womb, lay the naked body of Deacon. He was curled up, his knees pulled to his chest, sleeping soundly. He was covered in blood, his Genevieve's blood. He began to stir, David's shouts breaking into his peaceful slumber. He began to groan and whimper gently finally opening his eyes.

When Deacon looked up from a most peaceful sleep inside of his mother, to see his father's panic fueled face. His eyes wide, mouth agape at the sight. He pulled his arm out from the warmth that her body still offered him and rubbed some of the blood from his eyes.

"Hi Daddy! Welcome home!"

***

Known for the Path of Redemption series and the John Baker Chronicles, Bryan also does voice overs and some audiobook narrations. Bryan A. Tann was born in Pittsburgh, PA and has lived in Western PA all of his life except for eight years in New England.

His debut novel "The Enforcer" was first written in 2007 and was originally self-published in 2009 before being accepted by CH&BB Publishing in 2016 and published in early 2017.

Bryan lives a quiet life with his two cats while geeking with his friends. He's got a 1st Degree Black Belt in Kenpo and by day he's a security supervisor. He graduated from Southern New Hampshire University with a Bachelors of Arts in Communication with a Minor in Creative Writing.

He used to sing in R&B groups and a Metal Punk Band. Bryan is also a movie fanatic! He proudly has close to 1100 dvds in his ever growing collection. His favorite shows are The Flash, Arrow, Agents of S.H.I.E.L.D., Legends of Tomorrow, Black-ish, Goldbergs, Lethal Weapon, The Walking Dead, Fraiser, Cheers, Friends and Z Nation. His ultimate goal is to live in a cabin in the woods. Or a Double Wide trailer in the middle of nowhere…so long as he can get Netflix…

And if he can't have those things then he wants to be the weird guy that people politely call eccentric that won't let anyone on his lawn.

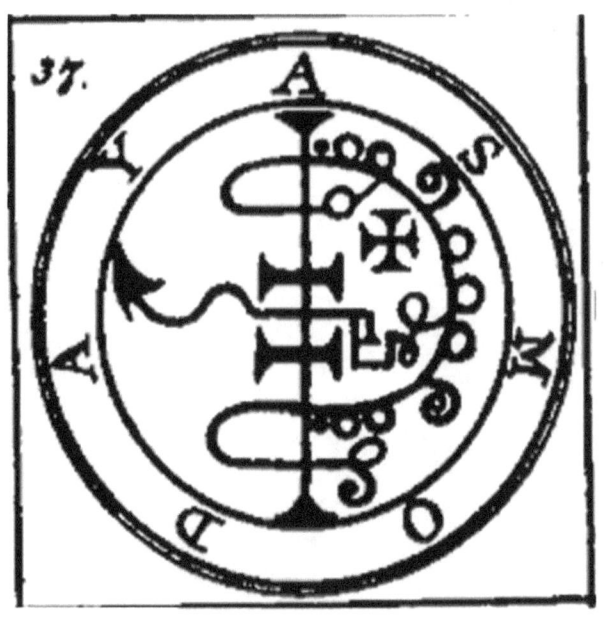

H⊕LTBY
By
Elizabeth Zemlicka

In a cozy little town, tucked away from the lights and noises of a big city, surrounded by thick forests and rolling hills. A town of only a thousand people, most of them related, all of them keeping a secret.

The name of the town was Holtby, named after the first settler in the 1800's, Milo Holtby. Milo built the large house on the hill that overlooks the rest of the town. It was originally a coal-mining town, and in its prime, it was thriving. Now there is a dilapidated wooden sign, dangling from a rusted chain, blocking the entrance of what was once a large, booming coal mine.

Milo started the mine and created jobs and took in quite a profit for himself, hence the 20-bedroom mansion that looms sadly over the town, vacant and in disrepair.

At the turn of the century, Milo Holtby went crazy, or so they say, nobody old enough to have known him is alive today to tell the story. He woke up one morning and his wife and kids were gone, just vanished. Now I know what you are thinking, she took the kids and left in the night and I would agree but she didn't take a thing with her, all her and the kids' belongings were neatly in their places, no food was missing from the home and the horses were all accounted for.

Townspeople had their own theory; Milo killed his family and buried them somewhere on the property.

Not long after this, part of the mine collapsed, killing close to a hundred miners and effectively shutting down the mine completely. The town went from thriving to almost desolate in a matter of weeks and Milo Holtby was never seen again.

The Holtby mansion still looms over the town like a bad omen, nobody dares to try and fix it up. Oh, there have been businessmen in the past who have had dreams of turning it into a hotel, a bed and breakfast even a clinic was talked about, but they never get farther than the first day. Workers would refuse to return and pretty soon there was no one willing to go in there.

At the same time, no one dares to bulldoze the place down.

As kids, we were told it was a part of our history and it would be blasphemy to tear it down. We always accepted that, until the night of our high school graduation. The night we accidentally learned the terrible truth the town has been hiding.

The senior party was winding down close to midnight when my best friend, Andrea, approached me.

"Let's get out of here and do something that's actually fun" she said in a low voice.

I laughed.

"What? This isn't fun?" I teased

"Let's get the guys and go get some food" she ignored my teasing.

I shrugged and followed her to the front door, where our boyfriends, who were also best friends (it's a small town) were drinking keg beer from plastic cups and looking as bored as we felt.

We joined them on the front porch. Noah, my boyfriend, slipped an arm around my waist and said

"Please tell me you guys are ready to blow this joint"

"Yeah Andrea is hungry and I would love to get out of here too so let's go down to the cafe and get some greasy food to go with that beer" I suggested.

They all nodded in agreement and we headed down the street to the only all night cafe/truck stop in town.

We sat down by the window and ordered greasy breakfast food and talked about how we weren't ready to call it a night quite yet.

The table got quiet as the waitress cleared our plates and refilled our coke's. When she walked away, Charlie, Andrea's boyfriend, leaned in toward the center of the table and in a low voice,

"Let's go up the hill and check out old man Holtby's place!"

"Charlie, you're drunk!" Andrea slapped his arm.

"Haven't you guys ever been at least a little curious?" He ignored her.

Noah chimed in

"I should tell you you're crazy and I'm taking you home, but I have to admit, I'm curious"

"Really?" I said to both of them.

"Ok so Andrea and Kayla can stay here and we will go" Charlie said.

"No we will go, right Kay?" Andrea volunteered.

I shrugged.

"I guess we're going, are we walking up there or did you guys have a plan for that?" I asked.

"My brother is home for the summer, he will let me borrow his car" Noah flashed a big smile as he fished his cell phone from his pocket.

"Ok let's do this before we chicken out then" I said

As apprehensive as I felt, I would be lying if I said I wasn't a little curious about that house on the hill.

It was nearing 2am when we piled in Noah's older brother, Parker's car and headed to the edge of town.

"Did you tell him where we were going?" Charlie asked from the backseat.

Noah gave a snorting laugh

"Hell no"

"Why don't you take the old miner road? It at least goes around the mine, no chance of it caving in on us" I suggested.

"If it hasn't caved in by now, this little car isn't going to do it, but now that you mention it, it feels safer to go around" Noah was nodding and flashed me a smile.

There was uneasiness in his smile, like he was having second thoughts but didn't want to admit it. I felt relief that I wasn't the only one with knots in their stomach.

We rode the rest of the winding dirt road in an uncomfortable silence. As the car followed the last curve, the old mansion loomed over us, moonlight danced over the big windows, making it look alive. While the rest of the huge, dark house seemed to gleam in the moonlight.

Noah turned off the car but make no move to exit, we all looked on in an uneasy silence, almost as if we were waiting for an invitation.

Finally, Charlie broke the spell

"Come on, chickens, let's check it out!" He was already halfway out the door. The rest of us followed suit when I asked

"Does anyone own this property now? I know Holtby's are gone but didn't someone buy it a couple years ago?"

"It was foreclosed on after the last renovation plan fell through" Charlie answered, not breaking his gaze from the beautiful but neglected carpentry.

Noah turned to Charlie

"How do you know all this?"

"I researched the history last year for a paper, it's really sad and very edited. I guess I've been kind of obsessed ever since, I mean what are they hiding?" Charlie answered a bit sheepishly.

Noah shrugged.

"Think we will set off any alarms by going in?" Noah asked.

"I seriously doubt anyone has put in any modern alarm systems" Charlie reassured him

Noah looked at me and smiled

"I'll keep you safe, let's go have a look" he slipped an arm around my waist and kissed my head

The four of us made it to the massive oak door with its beautiful handmade woodworking and thick stained glass windows. I lightly ran my fingers over the raised cross-crossed carvings, it's surface smooth.

"It's beautiful" I whispered.

Charlie responded by pulling the iron door handles, slowly creaking the heavy door open. The door creaked so loud it seemed to echo through the trees. I involuntarily held my breath and followed the guys inside.

Andrea reached for my hand from behind me, I squeezed her hand reassuringly.

The foyer was massive, the walls looked hand carved like the door, there were minimal windows and the moonlight was cut off by the slamming of the heavy doors, which vibrated the whole house and plunged the four of us into an unnatural darkness.

"Anybody bring a flashlight?" Andrea asked nervously.

The guys each flipped on big yellow spotlight flashlights, lighting up the foyer and making the carvings clearer. I moved closer to examine the wall.

The name "Holtby" was carved in large, raised letters. Around it were carvings of tall, skinny trees and small funny looking creatures among those trees.

"What do you think these are supposed to be?" I asked without looking away

Andrea stood next to me

"Creepy, why would you want this in your house?" She sounded disgusted.

I shook my head, thinking the same thing.

"C'mon girls!" Charlie yelled as they moved into an open room with a staircase.

"Why do all old mansions have the same staircases?" Noah asked, shining his light up and down the massive, winding staircase. Charlie was already halfway up; we all hurried up the stairs to catch up with him.

"Hey slow down!" Andrea called after him, sounding annoyed.

At the first landing, there was a large portrait of Holtby and his family hanging on the wall, Charlie was stopped in front of it, staring intently.

"What's up Charlie?" Noah asked as he shot me a look with furrowed eyebrows. I shrugged in response.

"These portrait paintings give me the creeps; the eyes always seem to follow you" Charlie said without breaking his gaze.

Just then there was a loud crash from upstairs; we all froze.

"Someone else is here" Noah whispered.

"Guys, we should get out of here" Andrea gasped and moved closer to Charlie.

All of us were frozen, staring at the top of the stairs where the noise came from. It was now silent.

"Think there's a homeless person camping in here?" Charlie whispered finally.

"I bet its old man Holtby, not missing after all" Noah joked.

I elbowed him in the ribs

"That's not funny"

Charlie started up the second flight of stairs to the dark hallway.

"No way! He's crazy, I'm waiting in the car!" Andrea sounded close to tears. She turned and ran down the stairs and out the heavy oak doors.

Noah and I looked at each other.

"What do you think babe? You want to go with her?" Noah asked.

I took a deep breath

"No, she's fine out there, it's Charlie I'm worried about. Someone is up there and that idiot just ran right to them" I said. He nodded and we climbed the rest of the stairs to find our friend.

At the top of the stairs was an impossibly dark hallway that smelled of stale air and a faint flowery smell seemed to linger.

Noah stopped and waved his arm at me as if to say "stop and stay quiet" I stopped and listened for a few seconds, then turned to him and shrugged, whispering

"I don't hear anything"

"Exactly" he whispered back

Then it dawned on me

"Oh my God, Charlie!" I said a little too loud

Noah fished a small keychain flashlight from his pocket and handed to me

"It'll have to do; you check the rooms down that way and I'll check this way...let's get him and get out fast!" He was talking fast

All I could do was nod as I headed down the hallway. The bright white light of the LED shook as I pointed it in each room, each time my voice shook as I called out his name.

Suddenly, I stopped and shone my light down the hall behind me.

Nothing.

Where was Noah? My heart started pounding harder than before, when I heard footsteps approaching behind me.

"Hey guys! There's a secret stairwell back here! Whoa, what happened to you?" Charlie was excited

"Dammit Charlie! We couldn't find you and it's impossible to see anything" I stopped to catch my breath, relieved that Charlie was ok but now we had to find Noah.

Charlie flipped on his spotlight flashlight and lit up the hallway with a brightness that made me shield my eyes

"Ow! You going to signal for help with that thing?" I blinked away the sting.

The hallway was empty. We looked at each other and ran to the other end of the hallway where Noah was supposed to be, we checked every bedroom, I felt panic rise in my throat, I turned to Charlie, he looked concerned but didn't seem panicked.

"He's here, probably just hiding so he can jump out and scare us" Charlie laughed.

I nodded in agreement, although the knot in my stomach didn't agree with him.

We made it to the end of the hallway and still no Noah. We stood silently staring at each other hoping the other would have an idea when we heard a rhythmic thumping sound from one of the rooms. We looked in every room until we reached the middle, Charlie swung open the door to a dusty old bedroom with a giant poster bed, the pink flowered quilt was tucked in tightly, reminding me of how hotel sheets are made when you check in. The dust was so thick it danced in the light of Charlie's spotlight, he had it pointed at the corner of the room, his eyes big like saucers.

"Charlie? Wha-" I stopped when I saw it too.

"Oh my god," I whispered.

In the corner of the dusty bedroom was a little girl, no older than 10, rocking back and forth and ramming her head into the wall behind her. We both froze in fear, but we couldn't look away.

The little girl started mumbling something I couldn't understand and I found myself inching closer to her, Charlie shot a hand out and grabbed for my arm to pull me back.

"Charlie, just a sec I didn't hear what she said, she probably needs help" I tried to keep my irritation out of my voice but I was pretty sure some got out.

I turned back to her and was surprised to see her directly in front of me. I jumped and then let out a nervous laugh.

"I'm not the one who needs help, it's too late for me. Get out before they kill you too" her voice was quiet but I heard the message that time around

I looked at this little girl, all by herself in this huge mansion I felt sorry for her. I turned to Charlie and said

"We better get out of here, hopefully Noah just got spooked and is in the car with Andrea" I suggested

"But wait a sec-" I turned back to the little girl, she was gone, the only way out was through the door we were still blocking.

"Charlie?" My voice cracked

"Yeah I saw that too. Let's go!"

We ran down the stairway and out into the crisp fall air.

"Was – that – a – ghost?" Charlie asked between breaths, as he leaned over, resting his hands on his knees.

"You're out of shape!" I teased, deliberately ignoring his question. Then I looked at the car, 20 feet to our right. It was empty.

I ran to the car, pounding on the windows and yelling

"Andrea! This isn't funny!"

Pretty soon Charlie was joining me.

He stopped and turned to me.

"We have to leave"

"What??!!" I was getting angry

"We have to get in the car and go report them missing, if they send more searchers out here to help, our chances are much better" he calmly explained.

I was angry with him for being so calm and rational. Of course, he was right, but I hated the idea of leaving them behind.

He was already pulling the driver's door open and dropping down into the seat.

Then he froze.

"Kayla?" He called to me

"What?" I asked, a bit harsher than I meant to.

"You don't happen to have Noah's keys, do you?" Panic was rising in his voice and my heart sank to my toes.

"No, Noah still has them, can't you just hot wire it or something?" I asked lamely.

Charlie snorted a laugh

"Sorry, they don't teach that in shop class"

I shrugged and turned back to the house. Now it looked dark like a shadow was cast over it, the windows opaque and the little girl's warning rang in my ears.

"Charlie? Who do you think "they" are?" I asked quietly.

When he didn't answer, I turned back to him. His attention was to the far side of the huge building.

"*Shhh*! Do you hear that?" He whispered.

I didn't hear anything, I stepped closer to the house and suddenly I heard it. It was a low buzzing sound, I held my breath, it was getting louder and louder.

Alarmed, I yelled

"Charlie we need to go now!"

He furrowed his eyebrows and said

"We don't even know what that is, it could be Noah and Andrea"

"Buzzing? Are you serious?" My voice was starting to take on a high-pitched squeal I didn't even recognize.

"Kayla! How the hell do you think we are getting out of here? We can't go anywhere without the keys and I sure as hell ain't walking through that forest so close to an unstable and probably haunted mine. We need to find our friends," he sounded more angry than scared.

I jolted, I had never seen him angry, his face turning a dark shade of red.

"Charlie, why are you do mad?" I took a step back

His face softened a bit "I... I don't know I don't understand what's happening"

Then, almost as an afterthought, "the buzzing is getting closer" he turned back to the house

It was louder, reminding me of a very large swarm of angry bees.

"Let's look behind the house" I suggested.

I was beginning to feel funny, almost like someone else was controlling me. I didn't wait for Charlie, just walked back to the house on shaky knees. I found myself in front of the big oak door and reaching for the iron handles, I could hear loud footsteps crunching on the gravel behind me.

"I feel like we are safer in here" I said without looking behind me.

I entered the foyer and Charlie shut the door behind us, I was studying the beautiful but unsettling carvings on the wall.

Charlie pointed to the creatures

"That's where the noises are coming from" he said in a flat voice

"How could you know that?" I couldn't take my eyes off them but I knew he was right.

"Think we are safe in here?" I added.

We silently stared at the carving for what felt like hours. When a loud voice echoed through the house.

"No!" Was all it said but we froze

"Charlie? Tell me that was you" I slowly turned to see my friend's face white as a sheet as he slowly shook his head.

"Who's there?" He finally managed to call out, his voice squeaking like a prepubescent teenager.

We were met with an electrified silence; the air was heavy, making my chest feel tight. I shone the flashlight around the massive room, dust swirled around the beam but the room was empty.

"Turn that off!" The voice snarled.

I jumped and fumbled with the button

"Where are you?" I asked, my voice low and trembling.

When I got no answer, I asked again, this time regaining some of my composure

"This house is not for sale" the voice boomed this time.

I was beginning to relax; someone was squatting in here after all

"I believe this house is owned by the bank, sir" Charlie chimed in

"This house is owned by ME, I am not selling this cursed place" he boomed again, his voice echoing off the walls, making it sound like it was coming from everywhere.

"Acoustics are pretty good in here" Charlie whispered in my ear, I nodded but had an eerie feeling

"Are you Mr. Holtby?" I asked.

Charlie jabbed his elbow into my ribcage and I waved him away

Silence.

"Way to go Kayla, scare off the squatter" Charlie teased and I shot him a disapproving look.

I was about to snap at him for jabbing me when I saw a faint orange flickering glow behind him

"Hey, what's that?" I pointed toward it

"Looks like a lantern or something like it" he didn't look away from the orange light as it got brighter and brighter.

A shadowy shape materialized behind it and got more and more defined.

"You kids shouldn't have come" the voice was softer now

"Seriously, who are you?" Charlie asked

"I told you, I own this place. I built it from the ground up and I have no intention of letting anyone turn it into anything else" I could make out features now. He was a small man with defined features that had wrinkled with age and his hair was now thinning white whisps where the thick black shiny hair had been. But his eyes were a piercing green, hauntingly beautiful and unsettling at the same time.

"Mr. Holtby" I breathed

He held out a small hand, and I shook it, his handshake was firm and meant business.

"That's not possible, that would mean you are over a hundred years old" Charlie finally chimed in and I realized he was right

The small man laughed "a hundred and fifty actually" his eyes were darting around the room now; he was looking more and more nervous

"Are you a ghost?" Charlie blurred out

"Ok kids, I will explain everything but you really need to come with me, it's not safe here"

Charlie and I exchanged nervous glances and followed this strange old man behind the sprawling main staircase as he unlocked a door and waved us in behind him

"Shut that door behind you, son" he said to Charlie.

Charlie did as he was told and we followed the old man down a tunnel so narrow and so short we had to duck and Charlie, being of larger stature than myself, looked like he was in Willy Wonka's fun house, walking crouched and sideways it would have been comical if we weren't so scared.

The old man stopped in front of a big metal door that could have been a safe big enough for a person to walk into. He punched a series of numbers into a number pad, stealing suspicious glances behind him as he did so, finally there was a loud hiss followed by a click.

"Here we are" Mr. Holtby said smiling, he turned to us and saw our expressions, his smile quickly faded

"Oh this is my panic room, I built it after, uh, they started coming" his face darkened and he quickly snapped out of it and smiled again

"I'm trying to keep you safe, I don't intend to hurt anyone, I know what the townspeople say about me and what happened out here but none of it is true. No, the truth is far more terrible than those silly rumors" he realized he was making things worse and chuckled

"The ones you should be scared of are out there, not this little old man" and he waved us into an impossibly large room with metal walls and a complicated looking panel of electronics on one wall. The door hissed behind us, with the same loud click as when it opened.

Mr. Holtby sat down at a small table and gestured for us to sit with him. We both found chairs folded against a far wall and did as he had requested.

"Did you come out here for cheap thrills? If you did, you are stupid kids!" He spat, his demeanor had changed in an instant it seemed and I felt my face turning hot with embarrassment. It was Charlie who spoke first

"It was my idea, but I made them think it was just for a good scare. I have been researching you, this house and the mine since I was probably 13 years old. I dragged them along because I didn't want to come alone. Now our friends, my girlfriend and her boyfriend are missing and it's my fault"

My mouth dropped in shock

"WHAT!!" I shouted at him

Charlie hung his head mumbling

"I'm sorry Kayla"

I couldn't speak; our friends were possibly dead because of his research project.

Mr. Holtby cleared his throat and spoke softly this time

"Yes that was stupid, but it isn't your fault your friends are gone, son. It's theirs"

"You keep saying 'they' and 'theirs' but who are they?" Charlie finally asked, refusing to look at me.

"Ok kids, I will tell you a story that isn't anywhere in those history books or whatever you were reading. You won't believe a word I have to say and that's ok, because I can show you the truth"

We sat in silence for a moment letting that sink in.

"When I built this place, it was nothing but a one room log cabin, it was all I needed at the time. It was just me, a 20-year-old single bachelor with big dreams. Back then, coal mining was the most prosperous since everyone had a need for it, so I was on a mission." He paused, he was sitting stone still at the little table, no bigger than a card table, his small hands, dotted with age spots and wrinkles, were folded together on top of the table in front of him, he stared intently at his hands as if speaking directly to them. He continued.

"I built this little cabin, right here on this very spot. Then I set out to make my fortune. The town where you came from was there at the time, if you can call it a town. It was more of a trading route; people came in to the small post that was just at the bottom of this hill and would exchange what they had for food or just come to get their news every week. I believe that post is still there, I don't go out much but I believe it is now a historic tourist trap" he cleared his throat and shook his head as if amused "kids, that place was a shit hole, pardon my language ma'am" he smiled as he looked up at me. I smiled back at him and shrugged, I still couldn't speak but I had so many questions.

"You're waiting for the good stuff" he chuckled. "Ok, I'll start with the business man. I would make my weekly trips down the hill myself as I needed supplies and things also, but one day was different. When I entered the little post, there was a man sitting on the porch sipping coffee from a tin cup but he looked out of place. He was very clean and put together, dressed in clean, pressed clothes that I would call 'church going clothes'. He wore an impeccably white shirt under a wool jacket and straight-legged pants, but his hands gave him away the most. His hands were smooth and clean, not the hands of a working man, at least not in these parts. I thought maybe he was one of those bankers they have in the big cities. I thought no more about it and went about my business, but when I came out, he was standing next to my horse, this made me nervous so I yelled 'hey! What do you think you're doing?' He turned to me and smiled. Then he said something that makes my blood run cold even today.

He said 'Milo, I am going to make you rich!' He knew my name, that should have been enough to make me run for home and never come back but I was young and greedy. I listened to his pitch and didn't ask how he knew me," he shook his head "stupid" he said.

"The man told me where to find coal right in my backyard, he told me he would help me get it going and advertise for jobs and that I could run the entire mine and have a wonderful life, he never asked for anything in return. Just a warning that didn't make sense to me at the time, he had showed me the exact spot to start the mine, my mine, but he also showed me a part of the forest and hills that was not to be disturbed no matter what. He said if we dug too far out, the land would take its revenge." He grew silent and still, a quiet little tear began to roll down his cheek.

Finally, Charlie broke the silence

"That buzzing we heard, the mine collapse, you're, uh, family. I'm sorry" he hung his head

"Yes all of that happened because I didn't heed his warning, it's ok son" he reached over and patted Charlie on the knee.

"I'm confused, how are you still alive at a hundred and fifty years old? No offense" Charlie asked

The old man smiled "none taken" and he chuckled

"This is my punishment; I live forever and watch my loved ones die"

"That businessman wasn't a businessman, was he?" Charlie was piecing things together

"No, no he wasn't. I don't know exactly what he was, or is, and I have no intention of finding out"

I finally found my voice and almost whispered

"What is out there?"

His face darkened again

"Something so horrible men have been driven to insanity just by seeing them. But they take many different forms, they live underground and when we dug too far, my men were trapped, I had to listen to the screams for hours without any way of helping them. When they were recovered, half of them were missing and never found, two were still alive but so shell shocked they couldn't speak or function. The ones that died, had bites all over but not from human teeth, those teeth marks were like nothing anyone had seen before. After that the businessman showed up at my door very angry and cursed me and my family. I never saw him again and after that night I never saw my family again either. That's when I built this panic room." More tears began to fall now.

"Those strange creatures that were carved into your wall? Who did that?" I asked

The old man stared at me, perplexed.

"There's no creatures carved into my walls" he stated

"Yes, in the foyer there's a carving that says your name and then a mural type carving around it of trees and weird looking creatures that were small and furry with long fangs, reminded me of pictures of wooly mammoth teeth but they had little tiny legs and gave me the creeps" I explained.

He looked more perplexed. He really didn't know that was there.

"Who carved that if it wasn't you?" Charlie chimed in.

"I really have no idea. I have never seen the creatures myself, I've heard them but seeing what they did to my men, I run and hide like a coward" he dropped his eyes to the floor in shame.

We sat in awkward silence for a few long minutes.

"Maybe one of the construction people who were hired to turn this into a hotel did it" Charlie offered.

"No, it was done by someone with artist talent, those are so detailed they look almost real, someone who does work like that for a living carved that" I replied.

Silence again.

Then blood curdling screaming came from somewhere inside the house, a female, Andrea. Charlie stood up so fast his chair crashed to the floor, he was at the door pulling on the metal handle with everything he had, it wouldn't budge.

"Hey! She needs help! Can't you hear that?" He screamed.

Milo looked up, sadness in his eyes

"There's nothing you can do for her now" he said and dropped his head again.

"What! So, you are trapping us in here to listen to our friends, MY GIRLFRIEND die?" His face was turning a bright crimson and his hands were curled into fists. I could do nothing but watch as he grabbed the old man by his collar.

"You need to unlock that door. NOW!" Charlie was screaming in his face now; Milo's expression was unchanged as he slowly shook his head.

"It's not safe" was all he muttered.

"Here's a thought, why don't YOU go out there and get her? You can't die, right? That's your curse. Maybe you can die and you're too chicken to face these things. I think you are just a coward old man" he spat back at him.

Charlie was such an easy-going guy, he would be the one to make smart ass comments or poke fun, I had never seen him like this before and it scared me.

It prompted a response out of the old man, his face flushed with anger and he pushed Charlie with such force he hit the wall next to me and sat on the floor, too stunned to move.

"Listen to me you little shit!" Milo was on top of him in a second.

"I am greedy and selfish but I am not a coward! I am cursed to stay living, I know this because I have tried countless times to kill myself, bullets bounce right off my head, knives barely leave a scratch and those THINGS won't come near me. Why? I don't know maybe they know they can't do anything to me I never dwelled much on it." He fell back and held out his hand to help Charlie up

"But you're right. I will go out there and find your friends." He added

Without another word, the old man left and locked us back in. Charlie was out of breath but seemed relieved.

"Charlie? I hate to say this but something is very wrong with that man. Not just the obvious, but why would he build this room and hide in here if those things won't touch him? I don't think that is Milo Holtby and I think we are trapped in here and sent whoever that was to get our friends. Did you not notice him throw you across the room?"

I asked, alarmed.

Charlie slowly turned to me as reality dawned on him

"I've just killed my girlfriend" and he dropped back to the floor.

"You didn't know, you were panicked and so was I, we weren't thinking clearly" I tried to comfort him.

Suddenly Charlie looked up at me

"There's no way we are trapped INSIDE, everything is electronic and all the panels are in here." He jumped to his feet and began examining the panels

"I didn't see the code he entered, did you?" I asked

"No but there has to be an override, or if we can cut the power to the door somehow..." he began pushing buttons. I jumped up to help him. In one corner, there was a small, glass-covered box. I ran to it "Charlie, here!"

He ran behind me and smiled.

Charlie flipped the glass up and pushed the big red button, we were plunged into darkness and hear the familiar hiss and click of the door.

"Did you hear that Kay? We're free" his hand fumbled over my shoulder and down my arm

"Take my hand!" He added.

I grabbed his hand and let him pull me in the direction of the door. There was a loud metal scraping and a crash

"Ow!" He called out. "Watch out for the chairs" he added sheepishly.

We made it out to the narrow tunnel.

"Charlie? What do you think he is? He can't be human; I know that sounds crazy but everything that has happened tonight has been crazy" I whispered

"It's not crazy, I was thinking the same thing" he assured me as we slowly squeezed through the tunnel.

"This didn't seem so narrow the first time" he complained

He stopped so suddenly, that I ran into his back

"Ow! Warn me next time!" I cried out

"Shh! I heard something" he hissed

I held my breath and listened in the dark. The longer we stood frozen in that tiny tunnel, the more the walls felt like they were closing in, the air was stale and damp and my spine began to tingle

"Charlie" I whispered "I don't hear any - " just then there was a high pitched, inhuman screech from just outside the walls

He gripped my hand tighter

"Don't let go of me, no matter what!" He whispered.

I couldn't speak; my legs were trembling so hard they felt like rubber. I squeezed his hand back and he slowly led me toward the door.

"What are we gonna do when we get to the door?" I whispered

"We are going to RUN" he replied

He stopped at the wooden door; his breathing was heavy as he stood in front of it.

"Ready?" he whispered.

"Wait a second, do you hear that?" I hear faint noises that reminded me of scurrying mice or rats.

"What the hell is that?" his voice was starting to shake.

"I don't know but its right outside the door, I don't think I want to find out what is out there" I whispered back.

"We have to, Kayla; we can't stand in this little tunnel forever" he sounded more in control and squeezed my hand gently.

I knew he was right but I couldn't shake the feeling that something was waiting for us, that Mr. Holtby or whatever that was pretending to be him had set this trap. He was clearly much smarter than we were.

"Ok, here's the plan." Charlie whispered

"When I open this door, we run for the front doors. Don't look back and don't let go of my hand, no matter what" he finished

I took a deep breath "ok, let's do this" I sounded more confident than I felt, but if we didn't go now, I was afraid I would lose the nerve and break down.

"On my count, 1-2-" he was cut off by a loud bang on the door.

"Help!!!" it was Andrea.

"Charlie, let her in! Quick!" I yelled louder than I had meant to.

He quickly pushed the door open and we were greeted to something that was not Andrea. It was bigger than the carvings made them out to be and what it was covered in was not fur but spikes like a porcupine, it had small feet attached to muscular legs that bent backwards. Its small eyes were a bright yellow and sat above a sniveling snout. Drool was dripping from its large, stained fangs, it made a snoring sound as it inhaled and an overpowering odor of decaying meat almost knocked me down when it exhaled. We stood staring, sizing each other up for what seemed like hours. Then I was being pulled backwards, almost in slow motion, my limbs felt heavy and weak and I barely heard Charlie screaming my name as he pushed the heavy door shut and bolted it.

"Kayla! You've got to snap out of it! I need your help!" His voice was getting closer but still sounded muffled, like he was yelling from another room.

Then a bright light stung my eyes and everything focused at once

"What was that?" I asked finally

"Welcome back" Charlie snorted, sarcasm hung heavy in the air.

He was sitting on the floor, leaned up against the stone wall with his knees pulled up to his chest. He looked sad and defeated.

"We are stuck here" he said flatly.

I sat down next to him and laid my head on his shoulders. I was exhausted. Charlie wrapped an arm around my shoulders.

"What time is it?" I asked quietly.

He paused and sighed deeply.

Moving his free arm to his face, he clicked a button on his watch with his teeth, illuminating the watch face.

"Almost 5:30" he answered.

We had been at that house for three and a half hours, how was that possible? I sat up suddenly.

"Charlie! How?"

His arm that was still on my back tensed.

"We got here at two am according to the dashboard clock in the car, did we lose time somehow?" I added.

Before Charlie could respond, we heard heavy footsteps running overhead. Both of us froze and listened.

"It's probably Mr. Holtby…or whatever that was…coming back" Charlie shrugged it off.

"No, there's TWO sets of footsteps, listen!" I whispered sharply.

Charlie jumped to his feet so quickly that he almost knocked me to the floor. In an instant, he was pounding on the wood door, yelling.

"Hey guys! Over here!"

The footsteps sounded like they were coming down the stairs above us, Charlie continued pounding and yelling louder than before.

Then I heard it, a low snarl just on the other side of the door. I jumped up and grabbed Charlie by the shoulder.

"It's still out there! You will lead them right to it!" I yelled, alarmed.

He stopped suddenly and listened.

"They can't hear us" he sounded perplexed.

"Kayla, why can't they hear us?" he added.

I had noticed the same thing; I could hear my friends calling our names loud and clear as they ran around the big house, looking for us.

I sunk back to the floor in defeat.

"Because, Charlie. They aren't missing. WE ARE"

CAREFUL WHAT YOU WISH FOR

By
M.J. Sutton

"Text message with a demon…? You understand how stupid that sounds, right?" Gina said, still holding a hand over her face.

"Well ok, it's not technically a text message, but it is communication though text… technically"

"What kind of cell service do they have in hell, then?" Gina laughed.

"You've heard of one before, right?"

"Of course I have, Tab. They've made movies about Ouija boards. I just don't think it's what I need to do."

Tabatha stood up from the lunch table, tossing her backpack over her shoulder. "It was just a suggestion, if you want to get back at him then that's an option. I'm a go catch a quick smoke before the bell rings. You coming?"

"I'll pass."

Gina kept her hands over her face until Tabatha disappeared from the courtyard. She took out her phone and glanced at the screen. No new messages. She found herself looking at least every ten minutes to see if Kamron had texted. It had been two days. Gina wasn't trying to let it get to her, but she really couldn't help it.

Most of the girls who lost their virginity that year had a great story behind it, with a boy that they loved and who loved them back. Gina had always had a crush on Kamron, although she was almost certain that he didn't even know that she existed. But that night at the party had proven different. He said that he had always had a thing for her and her baby blue eyes. He took another shot and swore it wasn't just the alcohol talking. He had slipped off her shirt and the two explored their curiosity in the pool house of the host's backyard. But now it was hard to even get him to text her back, let alone talk to her in public. He had told her they had to keep it secret, on the down low. She didn't understand why. If two people liked each other, what did it matter what other people thought.

Gina looked at her phone again, pulling up the messages. "Can I see you after school?" She typed, hovering her finger over the send button until she deleted it and put her phone back in her bag. She sighed, threw away her tray and headed to class.

"I'm just saying, look at the possibilities!" Tabatha said lighting up a cigarette as they pulled out of the school parking lot. "It couldn't hurt anything, except him maybe." She laughed, blowing the smoke out of her nose.

"I don't want to hurt him; I just want him to talk to me."

"Well it's obvious that's not what he wants. I'm telling you, G, this is only going to get worse."

Gina didn't want to believe that, she wanted to believe that what they had was real, and worth continuing. She had eye-fucked Kamron for the past two years, and if he had as well then why the hell not.

"Ah shit!" Tabatha said, dropping her lit smoke to the floorboard. The cop pulled right past them, not even glancing their way.

"You're good," Gina said, watching the police cruiser take a left into the school.

"So, you're telling me you're not even the least bit curious?" Tabatha reached down and grabbed her smoke again, puffing a few times to keep it lit. Gina didn't respond, she was too busy checking her phone, and with a blank screen she drooped her head, keeping her mouth shut.

"What's wrong honey?" Gina's mom asked. "You haven't even touched your plate.

"Huh…?" Gina asked, snapping her head up.

"You haven't touched your food," her mom said.

"Sorry… guess I wasn't as hungry as I thought."

She stole another look at her phone, sighing as she shoved it back in her pocket.

"Expecting something?" her mom asked.

Gina shook her head.

"Well if you're not going to eat put your plate in the microwave, your father will eat it when he gets home tonight."

She didn't even shower that night, didn't feel like she needed it. Who was she going to be seeing anyway? She lay in her bed, staring at her phone waiting for it to ring, or vibrate, or flash, or anything. It remained black, still, and silent for the rest of the night.

The next morning Gina slammed Tabatha's car door shut and walked right up to Kamron. The parking lot held the majority of the teenagers before the day started. Some smoking pot, some taking shots of liquor they had snuck from their parent's counters, and others just standing around listening to their overly loud music. He looked shocked, eyes wide as she approached. Dropping both of his hands he looked like he wanted to run, but with his friends close by he quickly recomposed himself, leaning himself back against the black mustang that his parents had bought him for his birthday.

"Kamron, we need to talk," she said, holding both of her hands to her side.

"About what?" He chuckled, looking over at his friends nodding his head.

She raised her hands shrugging her shoulders. "Please," she said, slapping both of her hands on her fishnet stockings.

"There's nothing to talk about," Kamron said, looking past her as if she didn't even exist. Gina could feel her face start to get hot, but she held her tongue, grinding her teeth. She stood there for a few more moments staring at him as he avoided eye contact at all costs before she spun around and stomped away.

"Crazy bitch." She heard him say to his friends under his breath. They all erupted in laughter.

"You have enough pads, don't you?" Gina's mom asked that evening.

"What...Yes...Why?"

"It's getting close to that time of the month, isn't it?" she asked.

"Yes -Yes I'm fine," Gina said, heading back up to her room.

She had enough pads, but she was also three days late, which wasn't uncommon for her. Her periods jumped all over the place from month to month. It was like throwing a dart on a calendar, where it landed was anybody's guess. But the next morning she found herself hugging the toilet tossing up the chicken noodle soup she had for dinner.

"Holy shit, G!" Tabatha said as they pulled into the parking lot. "You're not pregnant, are you?"

"No... I can't be," she said. "He pulled out, remember."

"Yeah and got it all over your leg." Tabatha made a vomiting sound. "Then don't breathe on me if you're sick. I have to seduce Mr. Fonte today." She put her fist to her cheek pushing her tongue against the inside of her mouth to other side.

"Fucking gross!" Gina squealed, punching Tabatha in the arm. They both laughed as she threw the car in park.

"I'm not sick, or pregnant. It was probably just my dad's cooking. Mom had to work late last night."

Kamron and his group of friends walked casually by the parked car. He took a quick glance in the cabin then immediately looked the other way.

"Oh Kamron! Oh, Kamron! Fuck me harder!" Tabatha started to make loud moans and sex sounds, sticking her head out of the window before Gina punched her again. Kamron didn't even look back.

Gina wasn't hungry at lunch or at dinner again. Staying up in her room, trying to convince herself that everything was normal. It wasn't until a month later and still no period that she took the test. Tabatha had driven her to the supermarket and bought it for her. Gina being too embarrassed to even be in the same aisle.

"So are we taking it?" Tabatha asked as they pulled up to Gina's house.

"I'll take it tonight," she said.

"Aw come on, let me watch! Let me see!"

"Tab! I will let you know, ok? Can we just… Drop it for now!" Gina slammed the car door behind her, shoving both of her hands into her coat pocket as she walked back to her house.

"Fine - rude bitch! Call me later."

Gina could smell the freshly lit cigarette as she pulled away.

Even just the thought of it grossed her out. Peeing on a stick that she had to hold. Gross.

But with her eyes held close, she relieved herself on the stick, getting it all over her hand as well. She almost dropped the stick into the toilet bowl. She paced back and forth in her room while she waited. It was the longest 10 minutes of her life. Back and forth, back and forth, checking the lines again every 10 seconds. "Please go away, please go away!" She whispered to herself out loud. That night she lay in her bed, small tears welling up in her eyes as she stared at her still blank cell phone.

"Kamron, I'm pregnant." The message said, her finger still hovering over the send button. Only this time she didn't delete it.

The next day Kamron avoided her like the plague. Gina tried to catch him in-between classes, but she always missed him. He made eye contact with her once, and then took off down the hall like he was being chased. In the parking lot after school Gina stormed over to him and his group of friends. As soon as he saw her coming, he tried to get into his car, but Gina had already made too much ground. She threw her pregnancy test at him from her purse, and placed both hands on her hips. His friends looked stunned, and all eyes were on Kamron. He looked at his friends, then looked at the pregnancy test that lay on the ground, then eyed Gina.

"You walked around all day with a stick you peed on in your purse?"

The explosion of laughter that followed was enough to hurt Gina's ears. She took three steps closer and slapped Kamron across the face. His mouth dropped. "Bitch! I don't even know you! Go play your games somewhere else!"

Gina's head started to spin and her face got so hot she thought her makeup was going to melt right off. She stormed off again, where Tabatha was waiting in her car. She slammed the door shut, and threw her hands over her face.

"Fuck him!" Tabatha said, looking into the rearview mirror.

Gina couldn't help it; she started to cry, choking back her tears as best as she could.

"Just go!" she sobbed.

Tabatha threw the car into reverse and placed her front bumper in line with Kamron's group of friends. Her tires squealed sending the car forward quickly, leaving tire smoke behind it. Kamron's group of friends scattered, and Kamron jumped up onto the roof of his car like a scared cat. Tabatha slammed on the brakes, stopping the car inches from making impact, flipping him the middle finger through the windshield before throwing it back into reverse, leaving Kamron speechless on top of his car.

"Let's do it." No more than five seconds had passed after Gina sent her the text message that her phone was ringing.

"You're serious! You're really serious, right?" Tabatha was almost yelling.

"Dead serious."

Gina could hear a rustle of boxes on the other end of the phone, as if Tabatha was getting everything together right then and there. "Ok, Ok I'll be over in – "

"Tab… Not right this instant, I'm about to go to bed!" Gina said, not being able to help the smile that crossed her face. "No school tomorrow, and its date night for my mom and dad, let's do it then, ok?"

"Ok– Ok–" Tabatha said, breathing in deeply to calm herself. "But you can't back out, ok?"

Gina giggled. "Ok, Tab, I promise."

The wind shook the windows, and the clouds covered the moon leaving in its wake a night consumed by darkness. The door nearly flew off its hinges when Gina answered it to Tabatha at 9:00 pm.

"When will they be back?" Tabatha asked, pushing the door shut again with both hands.

"My parents? Late, probably past midnight."

"Perfect," Tabatha said, unslinging her backpack on the couch. "11:00 it is."

Gina had done her research, and honestly wasn't convinced that this was even real. But Tabatha seemed to think it was legit, and if it was going to pass this boring night away, then what the hell.

"Want a shot?" Tabatha asked, pulling a small bottle of vodka from her bag.

"Pregnant!" Gina said, sitting down on the couch beside her.

Tabatha shrugged her shoulders and tipped the bottle back to her lips, gagging on the bitter liquid.

"So what do we do until 11:00?" Gina asked.

Tabatha smiled and pulled out three black candles, lighting them as soon as they were placed on the coffee table. "Kill the lights," she said.

Gina hit the lights, and then grabbed herself a glass of water, sitting back down on the couch. Tabatha had already pulled out the Ouija board. The room was cold, even though Gina swore she had turned the heater on earlier. The next two hours consisted of Gina watching Tabatha get consistently drunker, and the room getting consistently colder. She checked the thermostat; it read 71 degrees. She ended up wrapping herself in a blanket anyway.

"Put your fingers on the planchette," Tabatha said.

"The what?"

"The pointer, put your fingers on the pointer."

Gina did as she was told. "No not that way!" Tabatha said, spinning the small plastic piece around. "It needs to be upside down."

The two placed their fingers on the pointer lightly after Tabatha took the last swig from her liquor bottle, shaking her head with disgust. "Help me move it," she said. The two started to move the pointer in a circle around the board.

"We call tonight the spirits of the dead," Tabatha started. "In the name of the darkness, the evil and the impure. Is there anyone out there who would like to contact us?" They continued to move the pointer in a circle.

"Again, is there anyone who wants to contact us?" The pointer still moved in a circle, and Gina sighed.

"Sprits of the undead, we call upon you now! Is there anyone who wants to contact us?" The only sound Gina could hear was the scraping of the plastic against the board.

The black candles were now dripping wax onto the table, which Gina knew she would have to clean up later. They continued to move the pointer in a circle. "Spirits of the undead, is there - "

"This is stupid," Gina said, taking her hands off the pointer. "Let's just order a pizza before they close and watch a movie or something."

Tabatha continued to move the pointer around the board. "Spirits of the undead, please show yourself! Is there anyone who would like to contact us?"

"Tabatha, seriously, let's just do something else." Tabatha removed her fingers from the board, leaving the pointer in the center. "I don't know why it's not working," she said.

"Cause its bullshit," Gina murmured.

The clouds disappeared from in front of the moon, casting its light in through the windows directly onto the board, and the pointer slowly moved itself over to "Yes"

Both girls gasped. "Bullshit," Gina whispered."

"Put your hands back, put your hands back!" Tabatha said. Both sets of hands were back on the pointer and they moved it in a circle again. "Spirit, show yourself, we need your guidance," Tabatha said, holding her head upwards toward the ceiling.

"Tabatha stop it!" Gina said.

Tabatha looked back down and the pointer was moving in a figure 8. "I'm not doing it!" she whispered through her teeth.

Gina could feel her heart thump in her chest.

"There's no way this is real."

Tabatha looked back up to the ceiling. "Spirit of the undead, are you there?" The pointer stopped moving, then slowly moved back over to the "Yes"

"Holy shit!" Gina said. "Swear to me you're not doing this." Tabatha ignored her question.

"Spirit, we welcome you into this board. Where are you from?"

The pointer started to move in its figure 8 pattern again, then slowly started hitting letters. N-O-W-H-E-R-E. The figure 8 again. E-V-E-R-Y-W-H-E-R-E.

"Tabatha this isn't funny!" Gina said.

"Spirit, what is your name?"

The pointer stopped.

"Spirit, I demand you tell me your name!"

The scraping sound of the pointer was haunting; Gina didn't want to look but couldn't help herself.

Z-O-Z-O-Z-O-Z-O-Z-O

The pointer started to move faster between the two letters, jumping back and forth with a speed that convinced Gina that Tabatha couldn't have been doing this on her own.

Z-O-Z-O-Z-O-Z-O-Z-O-Z-O-Z-O

"ZoZo! Is that your name?"

The pointer stopped again, then moved. "Yes"

"Who the hell is ZoZo?" Gina whispered.

"Be careful what you wish for!" Tabatha whispered back.

"ZoZo, we seek revenge. We seek your strength and your will to help with this deed. Can you help us?"

"No, No! We don't seek revenge!" Gina said loudly. "Tabatha stop this now!"

"We seek revenge ZoZo! Please help us!"

"Tabatha stop now!" Gina pulled her fingers from the pointer. It continued to move under the fingers of Tabatha.

I

A-M

Z-O-Z-O-Z-O-Z-O-Z-O-Z-O

C-U-N-T

F-U-C-K

B-I-T-C-H

The pointer was moving so fast it was hard to keep track of the letters.

I

A-M

Z-O-Z-O-Z-O-Z-O-Z-O

"Tabatha I'm done!" Gina yelled. "Stop this now!" Tabatha looked back down at the board.

9-8-7-6-5-4-3-2-1-0

"Shit!" Tabatha said.

"What? What?"

Tabatha screamed and flipped the board off the table, knocking over two of the lit candles, leaving the single flame and the moonlight lighting the small room. "Tabatha what the fuck!" Gina screamed.

The room was silent, except for the heavy breathing of Tabatha. "I'm not sure that was good," she whispered.

"What do you mean?" Gina started. "What the hell did we just-?" Gina then screamed out in pain, clutching her stomach, hunching over. She gasped to catch her breath.

"Careful what you wish for," Tabatha whispered.

"I didn't wish for anything! I told you to stop, Tab!" Gina whispered.

Tabatha put the board back on the table, and moved the pointer around again. "ZoZo."

"Stop it!" Gina said.

"Are you still here?" Tabatha continued

Tabatha stopped moving the pointer, it didn't move. "ZoZo are you still here." No movement. The rest of the night was quiet, the moon's light disappeared again, and the two girls held their tongues, having no idea what they had just done.

Gina went to sleep that night convinced that everything was a fluke. Convinced that Tabatha had played the whole thing, and that her stomach pains were just cramps, indigestion, or the fact that she had to take a huge shit. Anything other than a demon jumping out of a board and attacking her. The two didn't even mention the incident that Monday morning on the way to school.

Throughout the entire day Gina received looks of pity and whispers laced with giggles as she walked through the hallways. At lunch, she was quiet, and Tabatha kept her eyes down as if there was something she needed to say but just couldn't.

"The fuck is it Tab?" Gina finally asked

Tabatha shrugged her shoulders. "I know it isn't true."

"What?"

"What they are saying."

"What who is saying?"

Tabatha put her half-eaten hamburger down. "Everyone. Kam' told everyone that you threw yourself at him at the party. That you were out of your mind drunk, almost – *rapey*, I guess. He said he had to push you away."

Gina's mouth dropped open, and her eyes squinted shut. "That's what the looks are for then?"

"I guess."

The bell rang, and Tabatha threw away her tray. "Didn't even get to smoke. Don't let it bother you, G, kids talk. It will die down sooner or later."

"But that's not what happened!" Gina said

"I believe you, and who cares what anybody else thinks."

I do!" Gina raised her voice. "I'm carrying that motherfucker's baby!"

"Just let it die down, G. He'll get what's coming to him."

Gina stormed off to class, with both hands balled into fist. She was so upset that she forgot her backpack at the table. When she realized it, the bell had already rung, and the teacher began his lesson, asking his students to pass in their paperwork.

"Mr. Caldwell," Gina asked, raising her hand. "I left my backpack in the courtyard, can I please go get it?"

The teacher didn't answer at first, picking up the rest of the students' paperwork that lay on their desk.

"Mr. Caldwell, please," Gina said, gritting her teeth.

Two rows up a group of girls giggled, one of them turning around looking directly at Gina. "Better let her go, she may start begging." The group of girls all laughed in unison and Gina balled both of her fists at her side. Staring wildly at the girl. In that instant, the leg of her chair snapped and the girl went toppling over to the ground. A loud noise of flatulence escaped her to short of a skirt, followed by brown liquid streaming down her leg. The entire class let out a noise of disgust as the foul smell consumed the room.

"You've got to be shitting me!" Tabatha said on the drive home. "No pun intended!" She laughed so hard she choked on her cigarette smoke, dropping drool from her lips.

"I don't know what happened, I was so mad!" Gina said.

"Wait… You think..."

"Don't even say it!" Gina snapped. "Don't you dare!"

Tabatha whipped her mouth and lit another cigarette as they pulled to the stoplight. Kamron's black mustang pulled alongside them, his music blaring so loud that it shook the cars around it. Gina peered over into his cab. A blonde girl in a halter-top sat in the passenger seat laughing and slapped his shoulder. When Kamron looked over to see who he was stopped next to he let off the brakes slightly to move forward away from eyeshot.

Gina squinted her eyes, balling her fists and her cheeks flushed red through her white make up. The black mustang suddenly died, the music stopped and the car continued to roll forward. Gina could hear the panicked screams from Blondie next to him and Kamron yell as he tried to turn the engine over again. The car stalled and continued to roll forward. A loud horn blared and an 18-wheeler T-boned the side of the mustang, plowing it right through the intersection, smashing the car into a light pole.

Tabatha choked on her second smoke. "No fucking way!" she yelled.

Gina stared at the wreckage in utter disbelief.

The crash was all over the news. Two students in critical condition at the local hospital after an engine failure right outside the school. It was unclear if they were going to make it.

"Did you know either of them?" Gina's mother asked that evening at dinner.

Gina stared down at her plate. "Something like that," she said.

"Well, you might want to give them extra prayers tonight. The local church is holding a prayer ceremony this evening, if you wanted to go."

"No thanks."

Gina stared into the mirror that night after her shower. She was over a month pregnant now, but she couldn't see a difference. She ran her hand over her belly, patting it softly.

When she lay down in bed, she saw her phone light up. It was Tabatha.

"I know you don't want me to say it but I really think this is ZoZo. Think about it." The message read.

Gina started to type back until her screen went blank, and her phone died. She smacked it against her palm and plugged it in, hitting the power button several times before the light came back on. "That's impossible, Tab!" She wrote back. Tabatha didn't reply.

The next morning Tabatha didn't come to pick her up. Gina waited on the curb in the light mist until her mom asked her if she needed a ride. Gina hopped in and pulled out her phone. "Could have let me know you was going to ditch today," she wrote her.

She didn't get a response and when her mom picked her up after school her face was emotionless. "You OK, mom?" She asked as she closed the door.

Her mom didn't answer until they were back on the road. "Tabatha is in the hospital, baby," she finally said.

"What? What for?"

"Her mom wasn't sure. They think it was a seizure but… The doctors are still running tests."

"Well can I go see her?" Gina blurted out.

"Not yet. Her mom said she will let me know when she is allowed visitors."

Gina's thoughts swirled around in her head the entire ride home. She refused to let herself believe what her mind was telling her. But the next morning when her mom got the call that Tabatha was only getting worse, Gina couldn't help but admit to her assumptions.

After school that day Gina walked to Tabatha's house. No one was home, but the backdoor was unlocked, it always was. She let herself in and went to Tabatha's room. Rummaging through her closet, under her bed and chest of drawers until she found what she was looking for. The black box with the eye on it. She tucked the box under her arm and went home.

The box sat on her nightstand, daring her to open it. It was a little past midnight when she finally gave in and dumped the box open on her bed, the pointer landing upside down on the board. Gina stared at it, not wanting to touch it. Her fingers found their way to the pointer and she flipped it right side up, moving it around the board slowly.

"I'm out of my damn mind," she whispered.

She closed her eyes and looked into the celling. "ZoZo?" she asked.

She felt the pointer move under her fingertips, and her hair stood straight up, she didn't want to look down but had to. It rested right on the YES.

Gina breathed deeply, tears starting to develop in her eyes.

"What do you want?" she whispered.

The pointer moved in the figure 8 pattern until it landed on the first letter.

Y

It didn't move for a long moment, Gina tried to move the pointer but it refused to slide.

O-U-R

Gina held her breath.

B-E-L-L-Y

Her heart sunk, and her fingers started to tremble on the plastic. "You want my belly?"

The slider moved.

NO

Gina swallowed hard. "You're-you're in my belly?"

YES

The tears fell from her eyes now. "Please-please leave - Please?"

The slider didn't move.

"Please?"

Her fingers shook on the slow-moving plastic.

NO

"Why?" she cried

Z-O-Z-O-Z-O-Z-O-Z-O-Z-O

The pointer moved into the figure 8 patters again, until the lights flickered in her room and all motion on top of the board ceased. Her stomach cramped hard, and she flung the board off the bed, crying into her pillow.

She didn't sleep at all that night, and when the morning came she told her mom she wasn't feeling well. Her mom agreed to let her stay home from school; she had the day off anyway. As they sat on the couch together watching one of her mom's soap operas Gina opened up.

"Mom," she whimpered.

"Yes baby?"

"I'm... I'm pregnant." As soon as the words left her lips she broke down into tears, and her mom scooted over to her, throwing an arm around her daughter's shoulder.

"It's going to be OK," she whispered. "Don't worry, it's going to be ok."

Her mother never tucked her in anymore, and for good reason Gina was 16, but that night her mom made an appearance. She sat down on her bed, and took Gina's hand.

"Well… Your father is OK," she said, smiling. Gina couldn't help but return it. The thought of telling her father of her predicament scared her more than the thought of a demon inside her stomach. "What did he say?" Gina asked.

"Not much. Just shook his head and opened up the liquor cabinet." They both laughed softly, Gina whipping a tear on her cheek.

"It's going to be all right, baby," her mom whispered, squeezing her hand softly. "Who's the lucky boy?"

Gina stared down into her blanket. "Kamron," she whispered.

Her mom shook her head in understanding until she did a double take at her daughter. "Hold on, the Kamron that's in the hospital?"

Gina nodded.

"Oh… Wow," she said "Were you two able to talk about it before….?"

Gina shook her head.

Her mom looked down at the floor. "You two are awfully young," she said. "What do you think about the *A word*?"

"Huh?" Gina asked.

"Abortion, dear. It's still pretty early."

Gina felt a stomach cramp, and she winched. Then shrugged her shoulders. Her mom patted her head. "It's a big decision," she said. "We can talk about it later." She stood up and gave her daughter a kiss on the forehead before moving towards the door. "I love you, baby," she said.

"Love you too, mom."

She closed the door behind her, and Gina rolled over, sinking her head into the pillow trying not to cry. She breathed deeply then shot straight up when there was a loud crash outside her door. Then, the sounds of something tumbling down the stairs. Gina flung herself out of bed and tossed open the door running to the top of the staircase. Her mother lay at the bottom, completely unconscious.

"She's in a coma. The doctors don't know why," her father said, the whiskey still lingering on his breath. After the police had questioned him, they were convinced that it was an honest accident, but it still didn't explain the coma. At least to the doctors it didn't. Gina held her stomach tight. Her father breathed in deeply as if he was going to say something then stopped, sighing outward and placing his face in his hands. Gina leaned her head against his shoulder.

With Kamron, Tabatha, and her mom in the hospital, Gina was too afraid to tell her father anything. She was scared to even talk to anyone, at school she just kept her head down, didn't make eye contact and forced her way through the day. She was too scared to even visit them in the hospital. The bastard inside her belly was ruthless, and was out of control. The A word kept creeping back into her mind constantly, but how on earth was she supposed to get one. She knew there was a clinic by the courthouse, she had seen all the protests on the news, but she was sure that she needed to be at least 18 to even consider it. She had a fake ID, her and Tabatha had each gotten one so they could buy liquor three months prior, but even if the clinic did accept it, how much would it cost, and were would she get the money? The questions clouded her mind the entire day that Friday, and by the time she made it home she decided to give the clinic a call.

"$500! That's all?" she found herself asking out loud.

"Um… Yes, ma'am," the voice on the other end of the phone said. "Can I schedule you an appointment?"

Gina hung up before she answered, glancing at the large jar of quarters that sat on the mantle over the fireplace. Her parents had been collecting for over three years now, in the hopes that it would fund a family cruise before Gina graduated high school. The thought of stealing the money made her stomach hurt even more, but if her mom died, there wouldn't be a cruise to speak of anyway. Her father wasn't able to take any more days off, and Saturday was going to be his long day at work, so Gina swallowed hard, hoping that "ZoZo" Wasn't a mind reader as well.

"498…499…500." The lady counted the last dollar behind the desk, which was now covered in stacks of quarters. Three other patients in the waiting room had seen her haul the huge water jug in through the front door and the looks she received where shocking. She was in the building for the same reason they were; she didn't understand the looks.

"I just need you to fill this out Katherine," the lady said. The name didn't register, and Gina continued to stare at the floor lost within her own thoughts.

"Ma'am!" the lady said a little louder.

Gina snapped her head up and grabbed the clipboard, walking back over to the seats by the window. The commotion outside was still loud. One of the protesters had knocked the jug of quarters right out of her hand as she walked through them.

"This is a demon, ladies and gentleman!" the man had said, waving his picket sign of an aborted fetus back and forth.

"You have no idea," she muttered under her breath.

"Gibbs!" the nurse called from the open door. It took Gina a moment to realize that it was her that they were calling. She never had to answer to the name on the ID. There had to be at least another $500 in the jug, probably more, but she left it in the waiting room, and followed the nurse back. After getting her vitals, the nurse asked her some basic question, typing them into her computer before telling her the doctor would be in shortly.

Gina waited. The minute hand on the clock ticked all the way around to where it had started when she entered. Her rear end was starting to hurt from sitting on the hard chair. She wondered what was talking so long. A few moments later, she heard a commotion outside, and then shouting. She wanted to be confused but she felt she knew what it was. She cracked open the door to see two paramedics wheeling out a man in a white coat on a gurney, an oxygen mask over his face.

"Still no pulse?" one of them asked

"Nothing," the other said. A nurse held the door open for them and the doctor was wheeled out.

Shaking, Gina sat back down on the chair; sweat building up on her neck. A nurse opened the door shaking as well, still trying to stay professional. Gina could tell that she had been crying. "I'm sorry, ma'am, but we are going to have to reschedule your procedure." She said, holding a hand over her mouth.

Gina punched the glass mirror in her bathroom shattering it and splitting open her hand. "God damn it!" she screamed at the top of her lungs, sinking down to her knees.

A sharp shard of glass lay in front of her, point directly at her knees. She picked it up and examined it, the blood from her knuckles smearing all over the glass. She slowly stood up and looked at her reflection in the remaining spider webbed mirror. She looked a mess. Resting both of her palms on the sink, she started to cry, then hyperventilate. Then suddenly she took a deep breath, and looked back into the mirror. The sink stuck out several feet from the wall. She clasped a hand on each side and took a deep breath. Another ear-piercing scream left her lips as she rammed herself forward, stabbing the protruded sink into her stomach. She whimpered in pain. Backing herself up she did it again, and again, and again until the pain was so much she couldn't breathe.

Collapsing on all fours she tried to catch her breath, but she felt like the momentum needed to continue. She stood up, turning to the door that was hanging halfway open. She hung herself halfway in and halfway out of the doorway and gripped the handle hard, pulling the door against her stomach as hard as she could. Two, three, four times the door made contact. On the fifth attempt, she leaned too far in and the door smashed into her pelvic bone dropping her to the floor again screaming in pain. Her entire body ached, then her stomach started to convulse. She hurt like it was her first period and a slow red stain started to show through her jeans.

Still hyperventilating she pounded her hands on the ground, trying to breath. When the pain subsided, she stood up. The bathroom was a wreck, but she didn't care. Her eyes glanced into the broken mirror. She tilted her head to the side allowing her mangled hair to drape over half of her smiling face.

"Black eyes…" she whispered

"Nice touch."

***

M.J. Sutton is a horror/fantasy writer out of Texas, currently slaving away in the oilfields of North Dakota. When not writing he is creating art work and polishing up his largest project to date. An illustrated collection of short stories revolving around the apocalypse.

For more information on M.J. Sutton please visit his website: www.DarkRoadFiction.com

ICARUS ASCENDING
By
Thomas S. Gunther

Paul's hands were making him miserable. Just grabbing a mop handle would cause him to grimace. The pain would subside only after he had worked a little while, rubbing the blisters open, and the insides of the latex gloves he wore were smeared with his blood, creating a cushion, however gruesome. It had all started as just an itchy, minor irritation in the palms of his hands, and as the maintenance man of the local burger joint, Paul figured it was just something to do with his job. It was just some reaction to the dirty, burned grease in the fryers he had to clean every day. Maybe it was a combination of things or cleaning chemicals causing his body to react. Regardless of what had caused the blisters, damn near anything made them pop, sting, and ooze watery blood.

He couldn't recall just when he'd first noticed it, though he had been suffering this bloody, crusty-hands-hell for weeks. He no longer cared what had caused it. He just wanted it to stop. His employer was still giving him the run-around on his benefits package, so he had no insurance, and no doctor. Using beer cans for gas money, Paul had hitched a ride to the free clinic where a physician's assistant gave him some penicillin and a topical cream. But it wasn't working, nor was anything else he tried. Everything seemed to agitate it, and cause it to worsen, as if it were some living, thinking thing.

The fear of playing host to a weird bacterial strain, some alien microbe, or some parasitic fungi, like that black mold in the cooler at work, heightened his anxiety of the dilemma. Discarding the topical, he tried Benadryl to dry up the blisters, but this only intensified the burning. So, he used Vitamin E cream to sooth the pain. It worked, for a while. Then the blisters would spread. He employed a cornucopia of balms, lotions, and creams. Everything failed. His hands, cracked cakes of raw hamburger, always hurt.

But it wasn't his hands and the stinging blisters that were keeping him up so late. The oppressive mugginess of a hot summer night didn't help, but that wasn't it either. There was something nagging at him, gnawing away at his thoughts like whatever was eating away at his skin, and Paul was forced to confront it. *"If thy hands offend thee, cut them off..."* His father had written these words in a letter. They were from the Gospels, and tied in with the whole *"idle hands are tools of the devil,"* thing, an analogy from which his father had drawn thirstily. The cliché, repeating itself in his father's voice, cut through the numbness Paul preferred, despite the beer.

So, he stood on the balcony of his second-floor apartment, absently contemplating a serene view of all his downstairs neighbor's neglected crap. Broken plastic toys, a rusty, useless grill, and empty booze bottles littered the narrow strip of dried grass that bordered the edge of the woods. Bathed in the pallid, combined light of security lamps and the moon, these eyesores contrasted starkly with the natural beauty of the trees, the only pure thing Paul had left to cling to. He wanted to clean it all up, and throw it in a dumpster while screaming and verbally assaulting - smacking - the offending neighbor. But the compulsion only reminded him of work, adding to his phobic discomfort. Seemed like he spent his whole life picking up after callous slobs. His co-workers were the worst. Kids, they were all guilty of making his job twice as hard.

Ignorant, lazy, and fat, they were clueless lummoxes that were always in his way. Every day he wanted to tell some of the fatter cows that maybe if they moved a little faster they might actually lose some weight. He worked his lower lip between his teeth, noting his rising hostility. At the same time, he subconsciously became aware of a faint humming, like a bee buzzing his ear.

Paul had grown to hate his job, and while there he spent most of his time hiding in the dumpster corral where he nursed his hands, smoked cigarettes, and daydreamed. Early morning, when it was still dark and cool, was the ideal time. In this sanctum, he could kill an hour looking for giant green Luna moths or the occasional feral cats he would feed. But mostly he spent his time fantasizing, spinning new versions of favorite reveries. He loathed having to go back inside, clean toilets, and smile at people. His voyeuristic daydreams served as a crutch to get him through the job, especially when he was forced to work indoors, though he'd be the first to admit they'd been waxing morbid. Yet he took exceeding pleasure in passing the time by visually raping his younger, cuter co-workers.

He envied their youth, could almost taste it, and envisioned taking the girls repeatedly, brutally, and without guilt, to make them pay for his misery.

The introspection snapped him out of his blank, staring state, and he forgot about the vibration between his hand and the beer can, pushing the sensation to the back of his mind in favor of a mental debriefing. He hadn't cross-examined himself in a long time, and when he considered his own character objectively, he was shocked.

Noticing drool on his chin as if he'd been asleep, he wondered how long he'd been leaning so precariously against the balcony railing. "They're just kids, for Christ's sake," he snarled, "just babies!" He threw his half-empty can of warm, pissy beer into the copse of trees, instantly regretting his own trespass against a love for nature. The can bounced through shadowy branches, disturbing unseen birds that shot out from their roost, their wings beating a feathery rustle in the dark. Paul avoided looking into the darkness any longer. Retreating into his kitchenette, he slapped the screen door shut, trying unsuccessfully to block out the perverted images and the lure of the dark.

The air was still, sultry. He had to get up early for work, but sleep in this relentless humidity, with his bloody, throbbing hands, was impossible. The air conditioner - probably full of roaches - didn't work, and the manager had been as elusive as the sleep Paul coveted. Television was out of the question. He didn't own one. He had hocked it and the computer for drug money long ago. So, he kept drinking, sitting in the dark at his tiny table in front of his tiny, oscillating fan that labored to push hot air around his tiny, cramped apartment. Cast in ghostly moonlight that streamed in from the screen door, a library book about Greek mythology lie open on the table. Tucked between an illustration of Icarus and one of the chick that had sex with a bull, folded neatly in thirds, was the source of Paul's insomnia, fluttering lazily each time the fan clicked through a cycle.

It was the letter from his father.

The last time Paul had seen it was the last time he'd seen his father alive. The letter had been written out of deep concern for a son who had traded his career, his wife, and common sense to pursue drugs, whores, and other, baser things. When Paul's phone was disconnected, and he stopped responding to his father's letters, the old man had chosen to deliver this one personally. He had skipped Mass, driving a hundred miles or better in a blizzard. The door had been unlocked and Paul, high and wearing headphones, never noticed his father's presence. The man found his son sitting at his computer, perusing Internet porn, and trying to burn the last brown glaze of speed off a burnt and blackened foil. Paul's father never said a word. He simply laid the letter on a pile of books on the kitchen table and left, tears welling in his eyes.

Paul cried as well, after reading the letter. It was a plea to return to his wife, to the Church, and to God. Later that evening, when a state trooper showed up at his door to inform him his father had died in a head-on collision, Paul *wept*. His father had been driving on the wrong side of the freeway.

He sat cross-legged, his chair pushed out, away from the table, both hands close to his body. For a while Paul was content just to stare at the letter from a distance. He had always wondered what the hell had happened to it. It had never dawned on him that he had left it in the very same library book. And there it was still, right where he'd left it, untouched for almost a year since his father's death. The idea that someone may have checked out the book and read the letter was weirdly unnerving. The idea of someone reading the letter and leaving it in the book was worse, yet. Paul didn't want to think about that, or the last time he had seen the cursed parchment.

He worried a nickel-sized blister in his right palm instead, absently squishing something that felt like a pebble inside it. Swollen with pus, and threatening to pop, the blister hurt worse than ever. Relieved by the distraction, he made his way to the bathroom. He muttered curses at the roaches that scattered when he turned on the light. Probing the blister with his thumb caused it to split and eject the pebble in a spurt of watery pus. Stinging pain was instantaneous, so he thrust his hand under the tap, turning on the cold water. But the water was tepid, and it only made him itch like crazy, so he increased the heat, turning it up in stages. He did this until both hands were red with heat.

Reluctant to examine the pebble, whatever the seed-looking thing was, he picked it up with wadded toilet paper, and tossed it into the trash bin. After cleaning up the sink, he dabbed his face and hands dry on a threadbare towel. Then he wrapped the palms of both hands with fresh gauze. His hands felt better, but the experience had left him feeling slightly woozy, and he was already sweating again.

He turned off the light, and returned to his claustrophobic kitchen. Fetching himself another beer, he sat back down at the table. Icy cold, the brew tasted wonderful, and dispelled his dizziness while the chilled aluminum cooled his hands. The respite was short lived, however, and Paul was once again overtly aware of the letter, a pungent layer of sweat covering his body, and his stinging, tingling hands. Impulsively he reached for the letter.

A commotion emanating from the bathroom startled him. He stopped, and the noise stopped, but apprehension prevented him from moving again. When he heard nothing more, he turned on the overhead light above the stove and went to investigate. There wasn't much to see, though. The little trash bin by the toilet was tipped over, and wadded-up bits of bloodstained tissue were strewn about. But there was nothing else to see. "Great," Paul mumbled as he picked up the mess, "now I probably got rats to deal with, too." He killed all the lights, favoring the dark.

As he rummaged through the fridge for another beer, he could have sworn he saw something out of the corner of his eye. A blur of shadow, just outside of the refrigerator's dim light, seemed to move across the counter. Sweat stung his eyes, but he held his position, holding the door ajar with one leg so he could use both hands to open his beer. Taking a big gulp, he scanned the darkness earnestly, but there was nothing else to see. The only movement he was aware of was the rustling of the trees outside, stirred by a mellow wind. Letting the fridge door close, he leaned over the counter and turned on the blue night-lite of an otherwise useless Riddex unit.

He lit a square, sat back down, and waited, savoring smoke and beer. He guzzled the liquid feel-good, still trying to drown his somber thoughts while he hunted a specter in the dark. Maybe it was a ghost, or maybe he was just seeing things. What-if scenarios ran through his head.

Perhaps he had managed to nudge the trashcan just

so when he exited the bathroom, causing it to lean momentarily before it succumbed to gravity. Perhaps the cockroaches had gathered upon it, he mused. Maybe they were having a cockroach party, celebrating his demise, and pulled it down in their excitement with their combined weight, as if it were a goal post at a big collage game. Accustomed to this paranoia he associated with drinking alone, Paul was inclined to dismiss it all - nothing more than tricks of the mind, the result of being drunk.

Another cigarette and the beer was pulling at his eyes. According to glowing green numbers on the stove, it was after three in the morning. The letter, a wraith in the moonlight, flapped insistently. He fought down the urge to just snatch it up and tear it apart. But he didn't want to touch it. He didn't want to read those words about his sins again. Paul didn't want to read about God, much less think about Him. *Where was God when you died, Dad? Or when Mom died? And where was God when the damn truck died, and I had to ride a fucking bicycle to work every day?* He had no use for God.

He passed out at the table, and dreamed strange dreams. There were centaurs and minotaurs, endowed with swinging, club-like erections, taking turns with a woman in a cow costume. There were whores of Babylon, singing a backwards litany. He saw the mark of the Beast in his hands, and in his mind, bleeding and oozing. Emanating from nowhere and everywhere was a metallic humming, like a tin can vibrating impossibly fast that steadily grew in volume. While he soared joyously through the air on waxen wings, a strange lover met him. The embodiment of all his hunger and desire, she wrapped him in long arms he could not escape, pulling him tight against soft, giant breasts. A siren with sparkling goat's eyes, she cooed. Then she released him, and he was falling, falling, spiraling to the earth on melting, flaming wings.

He woke with a start, falling out of his chair. He smacked his chin on the floor, causing pain to shoot through his teeth, his head, and make a sickening feeling in his gut. "Ouch, fuck!"

Collecting himself, he acknowledged the familiar pain in his hands, and that they stung with sweat, noting that now his left palm was tingling and seemed to have one of those pebble things in it. Reality, and a sense of responsibility, returned, unwelcomed. It was still dark, but he knew he'd overslept. He checked the time on his cell phone. It was after six. He was supposed to have been to work at five. His head pounded, but he forced himself up. Then he noticed the letter.

Something had pulled it from the book and had ripped it to shreds, which had been strewn about by the fan. The scraps looked like something had chewed them up to make a nest. Rats, maybe? Roaches? Bits of the sundered letter stuck to the table in stale beer suds from an overturned can. Paul stared in disbelief, wondering at what looked like little footprints circling the whole mess.

His stomach suddenly wretched. Stumbling to the garbage can, he vomited. Rib-wracking chills took him, and he flopped on the couch where he normally slept, cocooning himself in a dirty blanket against the hypothermia. He was freezing and couldn't stop shaking. *The flu*, he thought. *It has to be the flu.* But he knew, somehow, it was his hands. *It was his sins.* Then he looked at his hands and almost screamed.

They were bleeding, soaking the gauze. He held them up to see. Slick and glistening, crimson trickled down his arms, tracing rivulets that weaved around congregations of newly formed pustules. Some were more like boils, swollen with yellowish pus. They had spread from his hands up to his elbows. He sat up, looking for his phone, but instantly regretted it as the uncontrollable shivering took him again. Swaddling his bloody arms in the folds of the blanket, he held them tightly to his chest and curled into a fetal position.

His mind raced in horror. *Oh, God! What's wrong with me? What have I done? What have I done, Lord, to deserve this? I'm trying to get it right, ain't I? I'm trying to get straight! Oh, God, help me please. Help me!* As he prayed the pain in his left hand became unbearable, and he pulled off the bloody gauze so he could see. The pebble thing was moving, vibrating inside the boil. It popped, spattering his face. He fainted.

Time moved in surreal changes of light coming in through the screen door. Paul slipped in and out of consciousness, murmuring fragments of the Rosary as his eyes fixated on the box-like outline that framed the door. His eyes wouldn't focus. It was like an acid trip, some of it beautiful as sunshine. One moment the box was invisible, gray and opaque. In the next, it glowed as a golden gateway. His stomach churned and writhed in endless waves of nausea, as if he'd really ingested rat poison. His skin burned, and he knew his body was covered in boils. The blanket was wet with sweat, pus, and blood. He tried to vomit repeatedly, heaving till his ribs hurt, but nothing came up. His face contorted in the effort, and tears flowed from his eyes, falling pitter-patter to the carpet in dark, circular splotches. They were mixed with blood. He marveled at his hallucinations, wondering if he had somehow really been poisoned, and if he was going to die. The kaleidoscope visions extended to his hearing, as well, and he listened in earnest, trying to discern if he really heard what sounded like Munchkin-like gibberish and giggling, and little feet plunking across the carpet.

A rumble of distant thunder broke his feverish speculation. It was dark again. He had lost his phone, and he had no idea if it was day or night. A flash of lightning momentarily illuminated the apartment. Paul could see the wet discoloration of the blanket and inky black goop dripping down the front of the couch. It was pooling on the floor. Paul knew it was his own blood. He knew it was oozing from big boils all over his body. Lightning flashed again. He thought he saw little lumps in the puddle in the carpet. Some of them looked like they were moving. They looked like roaches squirming around in the bloody issue of his body. Forcing open the blood-crusted slits that were his eyes, he strained against the darkness to determine just what he was looking at.

There were dozens of them, and he recognized them as the pebble-things like the ones that had come out of his hands. Some pulsated, or jiggled around like Mexican jumping beans. Some looked like cracked eggs. Wind howled through the screen door, and as clouds parted outside, silvery moonlight illuminated the macabre scene inside Paul's apartment. That's when he saw the hatchlings. That's when Paul screamed.

He could just make out their stunted, diminutive shapes. They were on the floor, on the edge of the puddle, and on the back of the couch, surrounding him in a ring. Their beady eyes glowed purple in the moonlight. Paul gawked in disbelief. The ones looming over him from their perch on the back of the couch were too close. The grotesque, misshapen silhouettes stared back. They bobbed and weaved with a nervous energy Paul felt in his spine. They were small and squat, with disproportionate arms and legs that tapered into long, clawed fingers and toes, and they had the whip-like tails of rats. Their heads were too big - wide, leering grins full of nasty teeth that came together in a Halloween jack o' lantern sort of way. One of them, standing in the middle of the dark puddle, was holding up his cell phone. It was open, and its screen was shining light on the creature.

"Oh, dear God," escaped Paul's lips, and he began to pray. "Hail Mary, full of grace, the Lord is with thee..."

"Paul, Paul, why do you persecute us?" The voice was coming from his cell phone.

What the... They're fucking talking to me? Why are they misquoting scripture?

"You will be born again, Paul. Not to be afraid of the Dark, no. We will help you." Sounding tinny through the phone's speaker, the voice was one, yet many. It was singular, but combined. It didn't sound helpful at all. Hoarse, grated, it sounded more like Mickey Mouse had just gargled with broken glass and a healthy helping of Ajax. Paul covered his ears with bloody hands to shut it out. But the voice was in his mind, in his soul. *Wasn't it?* It splintered, like the shatter of a breaking mirror, becoming multiple voices and myriad fragments of thought, all talking at once. A babbling cacophony of screams, sniggers, and whispers, soft, sweet, and horrifying, tore at his soul from the inside out. "He will not help you... He does not listen," said one voice. "You can have them all," said another. "Not to be afraid of the Dark." *You can take all the pretty ones... Taste your dreams. You have served the Master well.*

Thunder crackled, then boomed in an explosive crescendo that shook the earth. A flash of sizzling lightning illuminated the apartment in searing-white radiance. Neon purple arcs of electricity snapped and popped visibly all around him, and Paul, in a nightmare sensation of falling - as if the earth had rushed away from him - was whisked into an even stranger world. He was no longer on his couch, in his apartment, or even in reality. He found himself walking along a dusty road in a desert, alone in a Biblical wilderness. A giant, fiery red sun beat down upon his head, his skin, and the cracked ground beneath his blistered feet. Hot wind blew biting bits of sand in his face. In his fist, he clenched his father's letter. But it wasn't that letter at all, it was the opposite. It was a scroll, a letter of mark. It was a letter of hatred against the followers of Christ. *I am Saul. I am Saul, traveling from Jerusalem to Damascus, to persecute Christians.* The wind whirled into a violent dust-devil, and he smiled, welcoming the grains of sand that stung his lips and filled the gaps of his teeth. The sounds of dogs fighting, and something unseen and inhuman howling lamentations, made his ears bleed.

The noise stopped and the preternatural interlude ceased, and Paul was back on the couch, though still surrounded by the ghoulish trolls. Using its tail like a cat to balance, the one with his cell phone jumped on his chest. It paced back and forth, speaking through the phone again, as if it were a megaphone. "You want this, Paul. It's what you've always wanted." Holding the phone in front of its face, it dialed three digits with a stabbing claw, and then it turned the phone so Paul could see an image on the screen. The image moved, like a video. Paul recognized himself. He was on top, copulating with the goat-eyed dream woman. Her stygian eyes opened, and she gazed at him from the screen. She raked her claws down the back of his other self, drawing blood. Disturbed, he clenched his eyes shut.

"No," he rasped. "You're not real. This isn't real." *Was it? Was it too late to cut off his offending hands?*

"But it is, Paul," the thing retorted with luciferous validity, snapping the phone shut. Paul reached for it instinctively, but the troll tossed it to the black-stained carpet. Some of the other trolls hurried to gather around it, falling to bony knees and hands as if worshiping an idol.

"What were you going to do," the leader taunted, "call 911?"

Paul lay down in resignation. The trolls spoke in unison again, incanting, "We are your dreams manifested. You are becoming. Now your dreams will be true," they croaked. "One of the lucky ones, yes. Chosen."

Was it possible? Was it possible for all of his sins, all his acts of depravity, all the years of ignoring God and right from wrong, and his sick fantasies to manifest themselves right out of his pores? It's not real! It's not real! But it is! This is the pot of gold at the end of the apathetic rainbow. This is what you get. This is what you want.

"The Master favors you, yes. He has seen your vision. You become!" At this, the leader, the one that had been walking around on his chest, tilted back its head and bellowed out a deep, booming laugh, then suddenly burst into flames. Before Paul could react, another troll did the same thing. Then another, and another, each minion blazing into an animated torch that ran about howling in pain. A staccato of malevolent laughter reverberated off the walls. Trolls, burnt sacrifices, scattered the fire. The flames spread quickly, igniting the couch, the curtains, and the walls. Paul was surrounded in a ring of fire.

Panic pumped adrenalin through his veins, and he jumped up to stand on the part of the couch that wasn't burning. Nausea washed over him as he did, and he reeled dizzily, but managed to keep his footing. Overwhelming him, the heat of the fire was unbearable. His clothes were steaming. He could feel his flesh singeing, and the fluids under his skin begin to boil. Simultaneously he was aware of the anguish of the trolls. Engulfed in flames, they still rolled and wriggled about the floor, howling madly, though their phantasmagoric chanting continued. *Burn the flesh! Cleanse the soul! You will taste all the pretty ones!*

The apartment was ablaze, and filling up with black, choking smoke. The thunderstorm raging outside pushed cold air in through the screen door, trapping the roiling smoke inside. Paul was girdled in a twisting, snaking vortex of hissing flame. His hair caught on fire, and he screamed, trying to beat it out with his hands. His clothing blazed. *God forgive me, God forgive me! I repent, please Christ, I repent!* He screamed in fear and pain, calling out in vain for deliverance, but the voices, the ones not screaming with him, declared he should welcome the cleansing. The remaining blisters and boils on his body began to pop and spurt like hot grease.

Seedlings shot forth like popping corn, immediately bursting into flames. Paul held up his burning hands, and stared at them numbly with swelling eyeballs. Before his eyes burst he witnessed the skin of his fingers, hands, and arms split and peel away, exposing what he thought must be his bones. They looked weird - new. New bones. It was the last thing Paul saw. It was the last thought *Paul* ever had.

Hours later, when the pyre had been put out, tired firemen walked through the charred, steaming corner of the building, examining the aftermath with minds grounded in a world of facts and cold reality. They smoked cigarettes, and spoke quietly, sifting through embers that refused to be extinguished, glowing like chimeric rivers of molten lava when prodded or trodden upon. None of them could identify the crispy corpse. No one knew what to think or say about the strange holes and gaping craters that riddled its body. None of them dared even breathe any comments about spontaneous combustion, though all of them were thinking about it. It was clear, though, that the inferno, for whatever reason, had emanated from somewhere around what was left of a sofa, where they had found the burnt, crumbly man. As far as they knew he was the only victim, and all the other tenants had escaped the blaze. A thick cloud of toxic fumes hung in the twilight pall as they tried to determine a logical cause for the fire. There seemed no obvious, earthly reason for it.

The tall, bluish creature standing in the smoldering corner could have told them, though he wouldn't. He remained hidden, wrapped in the cloak of his leathery wings. Through purplish eyes he observed the bumbling mortals bemusedly, but tired of the scene quickly. This world bored him. It no longer served him. Marveling at the strength of his new body instead, he flexed muscles that rippled beneath his skin, and stretched out his powerful wings.

One of the firemen, who couldn't stop gawking at the bizarre, charred body, felt the chill of a shadow pass over his back. He craned his neck slowly, guardedly, to look behind him, though reason assured him there was nothing to see. The cherry of the cigarette hanging out of his mouth glowed intensely, then exploded like a firecracker. The man emitted a strangled squeaking sound, and spit out the burning square. He backed away from where it landed, and made the sign of the cross. Someone, something, had whispered his name.

Watching the victim of his muse, the blue demon smiled a leering, reptilian grin that was cryptic and knowing. He beat his great wings, rising from the ashes of his old life and into the morning dusk. Laughing triumphantly, he climbed higher and higher, out of the hell that could no longer hold him, ascending into the orangey-gold of the rising sun on wings that would never melt.

End.

Eternally obsessed with the macabre, Thomas S. Gunther continues to write weird tales from his home in Kalamazoo, Michigan. When not writing or running errands for his beautiful wife, he whiles the days away working on a tree farm or attending classes at KVCC. He has a few kids, a bunch of grandkids, and one spoiled Pit Bull that enjoys eating Mrs. Gunther's flowers.

COVEN OF IGNORANCE
by
Feind Gottes

A light summer breeze rattled the leaves of the maples like a thousand children crushing pieces of crepe paper into balls to throw at each other. The gentle sound barely noticed as Dylan stepped out into the warm summer evening to join his friend for a smoke. Dylan pulled his pack of Marlboros from his dingy denim pocket shaking one out for his friend, Alex, before plucking one out for himself. He slid the pack back into his pocket while his nimble fingers retrieved his Zippo lighter. Dylan popped the top flicking the old Zippo to life holding it out for Alex to light his cigarette before lighting his own. He flicked his wrist dousing the flame with a metallic pop then slid it back into his pocket. Neither said a word as they inhaled the sweet tobacco smoke deep into their lungs blowing it out to float on the light summer breeze gently rustling the maple leaves high above.

After a long moment Dylan broke the silence, "So what's this ritual Travis wants us to perform? I mean we could be out pounding some brews, picking up chicks right now!" He bumped Alex's shoulder with his fist.

"I'm telling you this is gonna be epic, man! Besides Morgan is bringing a friend and booze. Relax I promise this is a night you'll never forget!" Alex assured him.

"If they bring some pussy ass schnapps I'm the fuck out, well… unless Morgan's friend is hot! What's her name again?"

"Russue. She's smokin' just a little on the shy side but after a couple drinks all will be well my man!" Alex patted Dylan on the back.

"If not… threesome?" Dylan winked at Alex.

Alex punched Dylan in the shoulder, "You wish, asshole!"

"Alright, alright but we'll see what Morgan thinks. She's been after my man meat for years!" Dylan laughed, receiving another punch.

"In your dreams pal! Wait, no, as a matter of fact don't even be dreaming that shit or I'll come Freddy Krueger your ass!"

"Good thing I'm an insomnomaniac! Good luck, Freddy!" Dylan laughed rubbing his shoulder.

"I think the word you were looking for was insomniac, Dildo." Morgan said as she approached with her friend Russue at her side.

"It's Dylan."

"Oops my bad I get sooo confused." Morgan shot him a sarcastic snarl.

"Uh huh. How about you introduce me to the beauty you brought with you?"

"Dildo…" Dylan shot Morgan the evil eye, "Oops I mean Dylan." She laughed, "This is Russue. Ru this is Dil… Dylan and you already know Alex."

Dylan stepped in front of Russue, "Sir Dylan of Silverburg at your service ma 'dam," he greeted her with a grand bow.

Alex bumped Dylan out of the way, "Don't mind him Ru. As you can clearly see he's brain damaged." They all burst out laughing, "Now you, my sexy sweet, I hope you brought something good!" Alex greeted Morgan with a deep French kiss making Russue blush.

"Get a room you two!" Dylan yelled.

"Jealous much?" Morgan responded.

"Funny you should ask; we were just discussing a ménage à trois tonight." Dylan said with a wide smile that faded quickly as Alex charged at him.

"Well maybe if you play your cards right," Morgan yelled out stopping Alex in his tracks, "I'm just kidding ya big galoot. Y'know this slice of heaven is all for you." She wiggled her hips at him.

"Damn right!" Alex said returning to her side.

The group gathered on the back deck of the abandoned house Travis had picked out for them. Morgan pulled out a bottle of whiskey, two bottles of vodka, a jug of iced tea and another of cranberry juice to use as mixers. Alex immediately snagged the bottle of whiskey taking a long swig then passing it to Dylan. Dylan pulled out his cigarettes offering one to Russue who reluctantly took it awkwardly inhaling as Dylan lit it for her. He lingered a moment taking in her beauty. Morgan was a typical Goth girl with long raven black hair, milky white skin and purple contact lenses hiding hazel eyes while Russue looked more bohemian. Her skin was as pale as Morgan's but she had a glow making her the spring to Morgan's winter. The sun hanging low in the sky created an aura of her auburn hair. Her bright blue eyes seemed naturally electric. Both girls were petite but where Morgan appeared almost sickly Russue emitted robust life. In that moment Dylan was glad he had come.

Once everyone had a smoke Dylan broke the silence, "So Russue what's your story? Are you a witch or just interested?

"Umm just Ru is fine. I'm seventeen like Morgan and I live over in Rosedale." Her meek voice barely audible to the group.

"The commune? Don't think I've ever met anyone from there. I've heard it's a little strange," Dylan said.

"I know there's lots of rumors. It's mostly spiritualists but some, like me, are Wiccan. There are some folks who will read your palm or your aura but mostly it's just simple, normal folks who wanted a place where they were free to worship as they wished. We know most don't understand that's why Rosedale was created."

"I apologize for my ignorance, Ru. I didn't mean to be rude." He winked at her, "Obviously, none of us are devote Catholics. Speaking of heathens, where is Travis?" Dylan asked as Ru smiled at him.

"He'll be here soon, have a drink," Alex said, passing him the bottle of whiskey.

"What's he like? Travis, I mean," Ru asked the group.

"He's one cool motherfucker, Ru!" Alex exclaimed.

Morgan rolled her eyes, "He's short and scraggily. Kinda looks like Frodo, y'know from those movies?" Ru nodded that she knew The Lord of the Rings films, "Typical Short Man Syndrome, what psychologists call Napoleon Complex. I will say he knows his shit."

"Ha! Short Man Syndrome!" Dylan chimed in, "Didn't Hitler have that?"

"Shut yer fuckin' mouth, Dylan! Travis knows what the fuck he's doing. He'll conjure up a demon to rip your pathetic little pecker off!" Alex burst out at his idol being insulted.

"Cool your jets man!"

"Don't insult him. I've seen him do things that would blow your little mind," Alex spit out.

"Calm down sugar." Morgan said, "We're all here to change the world tonight."

Morgan took Alex's head in her hands kissing him while Dylan took a drag on his cigarette and a swig of whiskey.

To break the tension Ru asked, "So how old are you Sir Dylan of Silverburg? Did you graduate with Alex?"

"Year ahead, I'm nineteen. He's just a babe of eighteen," Dylan answered nudging Alex with his foot. "You said you're Wiccan? Ever cast any spells?"

"Not really. In our tradition, my family's I mean, we pray to the Great Goddess for good harvests and things like that but no real spells." Russue couldn't seem to help blushing every time she spoke.

"I can picture you dancing around a fire chanting." Dylan winked at her, "Hell, who knows maybe that's what Travis has planned!"

"What do you know about this ritual?" Russue asked.

"All Travis told me was that he found some special spell book and wanted to perform a ritual he found in it. That's really all I know. You know how mysterious he likes to be, right Morgan?" Alex did his best to answer Ru.

"Secretive is more like it," Morgan answered.

"Whatever!" Alex shot back.

"I'd prefer mysterious, Morgan," Travis' deep voice boomed through the back door.

"Travis!" Alex beamed.

Travis grabbed the bottle of whiskey from Alex taking a long swig before handing it back. Travis stood barely five feet tall but with everyone else seated they all had to look up to him, something he enjoyed immensely. He scanned their faces intensely as they waited for him to speak. He savored the moment slowly pulling out a cigarette, lighting it and inhaling deep.

Finally, he took Russue's hand kissing it softly, "And who might this lovely little flower be?"

"Russue but just Ru, please." Russue blushed a deep red.

"Ru it is then. Travis Reynolds, pleased to meet you," he said softly, "Did these miscreants tell you why I've gathered this little coven this evening?"

"Only that we'd be performing some sort of ritual. That's all anyone seems to know," Russue answered meekly.

"Correct!" Travis let go to address the whole group, "Who wants to summon a demon?" he said vociferously with a wide wicked smile showing through his shaggy beard, "Well, come inside and take a look."

Travis led his motley coven inside the abandoned house. Dry leaves crunched beneath their feet while tiny feet scampered away from the noise. Travis led them into a large room, which had been the family room when the house was still full of life. Sunlight through grimy, cracked windows gave the room an eerie glow. The room was barren aside from a thick layer of dirt and the leaves on the floor.

Travis moved to the center of the room to address his coven, "This is where we'll set up. If you girls would be kind enough to begin clearing the floor I need the boys for a minute. Okay?"

"Don't lollygag we ain't yer fuckin' maids!" Morgan voiced her disgust.

"I promise. Back in two shakes, Morgan."

Travis led the pair to his old, beat up van that had seen its best days at least a decade ago. Dylan imagined a clown popping out the back asking boys and girls if they wanted some candy every time he saw the thing. Dylan was willing to humor Travis' ego for the experience but he saw Travis as little more than a Manson wannabe. He had to admit the van's contents piqued his interest.

"Where'd you get a fuckin' chicken?" Alex asked excitedly.

"A better question would be, is that a bucket of blood?" Dylan added.

"Always on point Dylan." Travis slapped him on the back, "First, Alex, that is a rooster and second, we need it for the ritual. This ritual requires a sacrifice. A human sacrifice would be better but I didn't think you guys would be up for that."

"You thought right... and the blood?" Dylan persisted.

"Ahhh, the blood! Sorry Dylan that answer needs to wait until we're back inside!" Travis excitedly slapped him on the back once again.

"Whatever." Dylan threw up his hands, dejected.

Dylan sped ahead while Alex lagged behind with Travis trying to pry the secret of the bucket out of him. Dylan was annoyed almost wishing he had taken a pass on tonight until he saw Ru's hips swaying back and forth as she swept. He stood frozen until Morgan caught him.

"How about you give us a hand instead of standing there getting a hard on?" Morgan said, annoyed.

Dylan instantly blushed turning deep red as Ru turned around, he was busted.

"Ya can't kill a guy for admiring the view!" he exclaimed, shrugging his shoulders.

Ru blushed though she was flattered. Dylan set the brown paper bag he had carried down grabbing a broom to help and get closer to Ru. She was still blushing but didn't protest.

A moment later Alex entered with the caged rooster holding the door open for Travis with the bucket of blood. Morgan shot him a perplexed look to which Alex could only shrug confessing his ignorance. Travis stretched happy to be free of the heavy bucket then grabbed a pair of brooms handing one to Alex. With all of them working it only took a few minutes to clear enough space. Travis collected the brooms handing them to Alex asking him to put them back in his van. Alex protested but Morgan grabbed his arm leading him out for a few minutes alone.

Travis wasted no time grabbing the sack Dylan had brought in rummaging through its contents. He pulled out a wooden dowel with a piece of chalk tied to the end of a string wrapped around it. He unraveled the string asking Dylan to hold the dowel while he pulled it taut marking a circle on the floor. Travis wound up the string but pulled out the chalk before tossing it in the sack and retrieving several candles.

"Would you be so kind as to light these and set them off to the side for now?" Travis asked Dylan.

"Sure."

While Dylan lit the candles, Travis drew a pentagram inside of the circle then unfolded a piece of paper adding odd scribbles inside the circle. Dylan figured Travis would explain eventually. Alex and Morgan returned, more flushed than when they exited, as Travis finished with a flurry.

"Okay, that's set so I guess you're expecting me to explain what we're doing here."

"That'd be pretty fuckin' nice!" Dylan expressed his impatience.

"Ahh Dylan, ever my precious little, impatient skeptic! I said we'd be attempting to conjure a demon tonight though I assume you don't believe such a thing is possible Dylan?"

"No, not really but I think it'll be hella cool to try!" Dylan answered.

"It certainly will! Now the boys were super curious about the rooster and the bucket." Travis pointed to the items which the girls had failed to notice.

"Fuck! Is that blood?" Morgan asked both curious and repulsed.

"Pig's blood to be precise! As for the rooster - I think you can guess why it's here."

"No, you're not - gonna kill it, are you?" Ru asked, covering her mouth.

"Ru, was it?" Ru nodded, "In order to raise a spirit I'm afraid a blood sacrifice must be made, there's no way around it. If we don't then we're honestly all wasting our time."

"Fuck no! Let's do this!" Alex emphatically chimed in.

"I know you're in Alex. Anyone want to back out, now is the time." Travis gave them all a stern look daring anyone to back out, none did, "Excellent! Now to explain the bucket."

Travis retrieved the bucket careful not to spill any of the pig's blood inside. Then he pulled a towel and rubber gloves from the sack. He carefully laid the towel on the floor then pulled the rubber gloves on slowly enjoying all the eyes fixated on him. He dipped his gloved hands into the bucket grabbing hold of whatever was inside pulling it out even slower than he had pulled on the gloves as though the object weighed a ton.

A thick coat of dark crimson dripped from the object as Travis held it over the bucket letting the tiny rivulets drip back into the pool from which they had come. After a few seconds the red waterfall slowed to a few streams then finally to slow, steady drips like a leaky faucet. As the drips slowed the group realized that Travis' secret was a book. He laid it gingerly on the towel as though setting down a newborn baby proceeding to carefully pull off the plastic it had been wrapped in. He tossed the plastic then removed his gloves tossing them aside as well.

"Ladies and gentlemen, I give you The Gowdie Grimoire." Travis smiled at them like a demented game show host.

"The what? A bit elaborate for a five-dollar book you found at the Goodwill, doncha think?" Dylan felt like a kid who finds out the fortune teller at the fair is a fraud.

Alex punched him hard in the shoulder, "You shut your fucking mouth! Travis ain't a fraud!"

Dylan cocked his arm back poised to knock his friend into next week. Morgan and Ru started yelling though their words became an instant cacophony of indecipherable noise. Dylan swung forward but his arm stopped well short of its target as Travis grabbed him in a bear hug from behind.

"Dylan calm the fuck down," Travis said calmly in his ear, "Alex, cool your jets before I finish what you started and girls, please shut the fuck up! Now Dylan if I let you go can you remain calm for a moment?" Dylan struggled but relented, "Good." He let go, "Now if you'll all calm down I'll explain what this book is but first, Alex do me a favor and grab that bottle from the back deck. We're all gonna have a drink and calm the fuck down. Understood?" Heads reluctantly nodded in the affirmative, "Alex - alcohol."

Alex stomped out with Morgan following while Ru tried to comfort Dylan. She placed a hand on his shoulder sliding it down gently rubbing his back. The soft comfort of her touch soothed his anger, which he tried to convey with a forced smile. It faded when Alex and Morgan reentered.

"Now Alex apologize to Dylan and hand him the bottle." Travis ordered.

"Sorry bro, you know I'm an idiot." Alex said holding out a bottle.

"Yes you are. I love ya but hit me like that again and we're going outside to settle it." Dylan grabbed the bottle, took a long swig then handed it back.

Alex took a long swallow himself while Dylan pulled his cigarettes and lighter from his pocket. He lit one, handed it to Alex then lit another for himself.

"There, now that we're all friends again, please sit and I'll try to convince Dylan that this is no cheap thrift store tome."

They did as Travis asked, sitting cross legged on the far side of the pentagram. Travis moved in closer lighting a cigarette of his own before sitting. He sat there a moment as if lost in thought before he began.

"Have any of you ever heard of Isobel Gowdie?' Travis asked.

"Wasn't she burned as a witch or something? I think there's something about Satan in her story, isn't there?" Ru asked.

"She was executed in 1662. How she was executed is up for debate though. Some say she was burned at the stake, others that she was hanged but the story I believe is that she was hanged and then burned for good measure. There are even some who believe she was never executed at all, they say the church was afraid to kill her in case her story was true. There are many stories of Isobel and the truth is no one knows the truth.

She is called the Queen of Scottish Witches but over the last nearly four hundred years her true story has been lost and parts of it were never known at all. There are two things that are consistent though.

First, Isobel was one of the weirdest people to ever live and the church/religious folks were scared shitless of her. Another thing that seems to be absolutely true is that Isobel was happy to tell inquisitors her tale. I think that's what frightened them so much, she actually wanted to confess. Torturing poor women who were maybe just a little different to make them confess to witchcraft was the norm in those days and for centuries but here was Isobel who said, 'Yeah I'm a fargin witch and I walk with Satan so fuck you!' Whether it was true or not she told them that she had met Satan in a church. Those old bastards had to flip their lid at that!"

Travis saw he thoroughly had their attention, even Dylan, the skeptic. Who doesn't love a good witch and Satan story, he thought. He took a swallow of whiskey before continuing, "I think she was a little bit crazy, a little bit a blasphemer but most importantly I believe she was a powerful witch! Now what you need to ask yourself is: was she crazy and hallucinated what she said or did experiencing the things she said she did drive her mad? Honestly, I believe the latter."

"Wait. Wait. What is it she said exactly? And do you actually know or is this some campfire story to scare the kiddies?" Dylan asked trying to stay wary of bullshit.

"Ahh there's my skeptic! See I need you Dylan, to keep me on the straight and narrow. Now to answer your question no this isn't some kiddie campfire story. Isobel's confessions were well documented at the time though if you want to read the full transcripts I'm afraid I can't help you. I don't know if they still exist but if they do they're most likely locked up in the Vatican library where plebs like us would never be allowed. What information is available should be scrutinized since Isobel has been the subject of numerous works of fiction through the ages. This is what I know to the best of my knowledge and you'll have to decide what you believe for yourselves." He paused before continuing, "Again, Isobel said she first encountered Satan in a church where he convinced her to make a pact with him.

To fulfill the pact, she had to renounce Christianity then he bit her on the shoulder leaving his mark. She said he sucked her blood, baptized her with it giving her a new name, Janet. I know Janet doesn't sound very satanic but hey, that's what she told them. This is where it gets crazy…" He paused as Morgan burst out in disbelief, "Okay crazier. Isobel claims she would fly to meet her coven killing any Christians she encountered along the way unless they were quick enough to bless themselves first. She said Satan himself would attend their gatherings whipping them if they displeased him.

Unfortunately, Isobel named some of her coven though I'd prefer to think she gave up names of some pretentious cunts the world was better off without. Sorry, I mean no offense to you two ladies. Isobel really went off into Crazytown telling the inquisitors that she regularly had tea with the King and Queen of the fairies or with elves under the hills. She told them it was the fairies that had taught her how to fly by climbing up beanstalks yelling out, 'Horse and Hattock, in the Devil's name!' Can you believe that shit? I think she was just taking the piss with that stuff to fuck with them.

More interesting, to me, though is that she also told them she was a shapeshifter capable of turning herself into small animals like rabbits and cats. She even told them she could control the weather. So, was she the devil's disciple or was she just suffering from a mental illness?" Travis scanned their faces, lingering on Dylan's waiting for the doubter to speak up.

"It definitely seems she was crazy but like you said, mentally ill or driven crazy by what she experienced?" Dylan asked.

"Honestly, probably a bit of both, Dylan. Obviously, I've been fascinated with Isobel Gowdie for a long time. I've done a fuck ton of research and what I can tell you is I believed for a long time that she was purely mentally ill or at best a woman with an extremely vivid imagination who wanted to blow the minds of the small minded religious fucks who were the terrorists of their time.

We all know most of the poor women they slaughtered were mentally ill, lesbians or, god forbid, intelligent and outspoken. Women were forced to conform or burn for a millennium or more, at least in European culture... but they were 'civilized' or so they claimed. Anyway, my search for information about Isobel has lead me far and wide ending in the discovery of this book. I believe this is the book that Lovecraft was secretly referencing when he wrote of the *Necronomicon*. This is Isobel Gowdie's Grimoire, her book of black magic that precious few have set eyes upon. I can't make any of you believe it's real by merely talking about it, especially you Dylan, and that's why I wanted us to gather here tonight. If we can summon a demon with this book even Dylan won't be able to deny that all I have told you is true."

"Hell, why not just conjure Satan? I mean go for the gusto, right?" Dylan's sarcasm disguised his growing belief.

"I thought perhaps a rooster would suffice for our first time unless you four are up for a little murder. Satan requires a human sacrifice," Travis answered in calm seriousness.

Dylan swallowed hard finally relenting, "Human sacrifice is above my pay grade."

"Shit you should have said something earlier Travis! Come on Dylan, you can't tell me you wouldn't gladly sacrifice Monica Snyder. We all hated that bitch!" Alex proudly proclaimed prompting a quick smack from Morgan, "Ow! Just sayin' no one would miss that withered up old cunt!" Morgan smacked him again though she was giggling.

Ignoring his ignorant friend, Dylan asked, "How exactly did you find this thing and what's with the bucket of blood?"

"Some secrets I have to keep Dylan. Obtaining this book was far from easy and I'd prefer to keep the 'how' to myself. As for your other query, I was told when the book was not in use it must be kept encased in blood at all times, no exceptions. I do not know what would happen if it wasn't but if this spell is successful tonight, proving its authenticity, then I suspect I wouldn't want to know." Travis answered.

"Fair enough. So, what now?" Dylan asked, looking around for agreement.

"First, everyone grab a candle and set it at the point in front of you plus one in the center." The group did as instructed with Travis placing the center candle, "Now Alex sit at the point on my left, Dylan on my right then Morgan next to Alex leaving the final point for Ru. Make sure you are outside of the circle completely, do not breach the line or the consequences could be dire." The group arranged themselves as instructed. "Good. Now when we begin, join hands."

Travis moved the rooster within reach then retrieved a knife from the paper sack. He set the knife on the floor in front of him taking his place at the top of the pentagram reaching back to retrieve the Gowdie Grimoire. He set the ancient book gently across his crossed legs flipping it carefully open to a page he had marked previously. He scanned the page slowly double-checking his markings inside the circle were correct. Travis closed his eyes as if meditating for a moment before addressing his small coven.

"We'll begin in just a moment. If any of you want to back out this is your last chance. It's imperative that each of you participates of your own free will." He scanned each of their faces slowly pausing longest on Ru and Dylan but saw no reluctance, "Once we begin this ritual we must see it through to the end. No matter what you hear or what you see, you must not stop or break your linked hands. No matter what happens, you must hold on to each other and repeat the phrase I give you until the ritual is done. It may sound simple and it very well may be or it may not, so I ask you one final time, does anyone wish to leave?"

Again, he scanned the faces of his coven finding no reluctance, "Good. Now we can begin. One final suggestion to all of you, once we start close your eyes tight and concentrate on nothing but the words I give you. Repeat them over and over until the ritual is finished. Understood?" They all nodded, "Okay. Once I begin speaking you begin this chant: *Ave satanas sublimis patre nostro.*"

Travis turned to Alex making him repeat the words until he had them correct then worked his way around the circle ending with Dylan. They all felt a little awkward at first but Travis acted like a father patiently teaching his son to ride a bike for the first time. He didn't yell or get frustrated even as Alex fumbled the words several times before getting the phrase correct. Travis gave them all one last solemn look before beginning. The candles cast them in an eerie glow now that the sun had completely set.

"Ready... and begin." Travis' coven of four broke into their chant, a Latin phrase meaning "Hail Satan, our majestic father," as he began the words of the ritual set down by Isobel Gowdie, "We hail Satan, *uile-athair. Tha sinn a 'gairm air an Tighearna an Fodhasaoghal. Hear dhuinn Tighearna Satan. Tha sinn ach iriosal seirbhisich do d 'chumhachd. Hear dhuinn Oh Tighearna! Gheall sinn ar dìlseachd don thu Tighearna Satan. Cuir a mach Minion gu harken agad tighinn. Send mach teachdair. Send mach diadhaidh olc. Cuir thugainn leanabh teine. Gheall sinn ar beatha. Tha sinn a 'gheall ar n-anaman shiorruidh. Ann an Deamhain ainm guidheamaid. Ho Satan!"*

Travis' first utterance of the words was slow and deliberate lacking his full confidence. There was an electricity in the air raising the hair on his forearms as his coven continued their chant. Travis smiled beginning to feel the power of the ritual as he repeated the words in English, "We hail Satan, the all father. We call upon the lord of the underworld. Hear us Lord Satan. We are but humble servants to your power. Hear us Oh Lord! We pledge our allegiance to you Lord Satan. Send forth a minion to harken your arrival. Send forth a messenger. Send forth divine evil. Send us a child of fire. We pledge our lives. We pledge our eternal souls. In the Devil's name, we pray. Hail Satan!"

The electricity in the air grew as the ritual continued. Travis began to feel power coursing through him with each word spoken of the repeated verse, first in Gowdie's native Scottish Gaelic then in English. The candle's flames seemed to grow as the ritual rolled on. The coven's chant grew louder with each telling, holding hands with their eyes shut tight.

After Travis finished the English verse for the third time he opened the cage grabbing the rooster. Grabbing the knife in front of him, he set the book to the side standing to begin a fourth telling. Once he completed the saying in Gaelic he lifted the rooster over his head as if offering it up to heaven then lowering it back down as he began the verse in English. Kneeling he pinned the bird to the floor beheading it with one swift slice. He held the torso toward the circle letting the blood spurt across the encircled pentagram drawn on the floor.

The house began to shake threatening to blow apart. Travis had to shout then the front window burst sending shards of glass flying inside and out. Wind instantly whipped through the room like a freight train followed by sharp cracks of lightning so close they could taste the ozone in the air. The coven continued their chant louder matching their leader's shouts as the wind and thunder roared.

Travis yelled out, "- we pledge our eternal souls. In the Devil's name, we pray. Hail Satan!"

With the words still hanging in the air lightning shot through the window striking dead center of the pentagram blasting the entire coven backward breaking their hold on each other. The wind, rain, thunder and lightning were gone as quickly as they had come. The abandoned house was finally still and quiet as the dead.

"Holy fucking shit!" Alex shouted.

"Shhh" Travis was staring up in concentration.

Dylan waited a moment before asking, "So, did it work?"

They looked to Travis for an answer. He was staring intensely into the circle, his head cocked slightly to the side. The coven followed suit but saw nor heard anything. The only sign that anything at all had happened were the shards of glass strewn across the floor from the shattered window. They all looked completely bewildered including their leader.

"Something definitely happened, we can all agree on that, yes?" Travis' question was met with affirmative nods around the circle.

"Shouldn't whatever we summoned have popped up in the center of the pentagram?" Morgan asked.

"This isn't some Hollywood shit show about faggots playing with a Ouija board. We just performed a ritual that was set to paper four hundred years ago! I'm positive it worked but the entity could be anywhere in this house. In a sense, we turned this entire house into a conduit straight to hell. What I do not know is how big our demon is, it could be tiny or a giant. I just don't know." Travis' calm had been overtaken by frustration.

"So what now?" Alex asked meekly.

"We split up and search this house. If you see something do NOT approach it, understood? Until you name a demon it is loyal only to Satan himself. In other words, it will probably kill you so come get me. The grimoire contains a spell that will force the demon to state its name. Once I say it aloud the demon will obey my every command." Travis seemed to beam at that last part.

"Why you? I can command a demon!" Dylan protested.

"Who brought you here? Who went to great lengths to obtain the grimoire? Who conjured it? End of discussion. Aside from that I'm the only one that can read the spell unless one of you have become fluent in Gaelic in the last thirty seconds," Travis huffed letting frustration fuel his anger before taking a deep breath, "My apologies I shouldn't snap at any of you. Thank you all for helping me perform the ritual. I couldn't have done it without you. Now, I suggest we split up and search. I'll take the basement, Alex and Morgan you search this floor and Dylan and Ru take upstairs. Okay?" Nods greeted him again, "Good. Again, I can't stress it enough: if you see anything don't approach it, come find me."

Travis didn't wait for any replies retrieving the plastic from the corner where he had tossed it, wrapped the book and set it back in the bucket. The task complete, he grabbed a candle, lit it and a cigarette and headed off to find the basement door.

"Well I guess it's you and me up, up into the dark," Dylan said smiling at Ru who returned the smile.

"How about you light us a couple of candles Hormone boy?" Morgan shot sarcastically at Dylan.

"Sure but I doubt it'll be enough to find Alex's pathetic piece of man meat," Dylan shot back.

"Wanna another fresh one, pee wee?" Alex replied.

"Shut yer yaps and just light some candles already," Morgan cut the juvenile insults short.

Dylan lit a candle, passed it to Alex then lit one for Morgan stepping into the circle to hand it to her.

"Don't step in there!" Morgan yelled at him.

"What? It's a little chicken blood, who cares? Either of you want a smoke before we split up?" Both nodded, "Here you go." He flicked a couple of cigarettes from his pack which they used their candles to light.

An unnoticed disturbance rippled the pool of blood an inch from where Dylan had stepped into the circle, something wriggled in the coagulating fluid. If any of them had been looking it was doubtful they would have noticed anyway. The ripple was no more than a pinprick but the moment Dylan set his foot down something sprang into action. It made an unseen beeline for his shoe just as Morgan chastised the owner for putting it there.

It was the size of an amoeba but moved with malice of forethought unlike its single celled twins. It crawled up Dylan's shoe slowly making its way up drawn by an urgent desire for flesh. Inch by slow inch it worked its way up the shoe, across the rubber sole, up the worn leather side, across a peeling swoosh logo, finally working its way to the top and the fraction of knit cotton marking the end of Dylan's sock and its journey. The single cell reared back opening a ferocious circular mouth lined with needle sharp teeth then lunged forward opening a hole and instantly sliding itself inside to swim its way to the top. Dylan never felt a thing.

Dylan held his elbow out to Ru, "Shall we?"

Ru blushed taking his arm, "Just make sure the stairs are the only thing that rise, mister."

"I will try but alas I can't promise I'll be able to acquiesce to your request." Dylan stated trying not to laugh.

"Oh my! Let's go so we can get out of here." Ru lowered her voice to a whisper, "To be honest this place gives me the heebie jeebies."

"I'd guess you're not alone in that feeling," Dylan whispered back.

Alex and Morgan moved off into the kitchen searching high and low for they really didn't know what. Dylan and Ru could her the clicking of cupboard doors as they started up the staircase not really knowing what they were looking for either. The stairs creaked loudly beneath their feet but seemed sturdy enough to hold them. They tried to keep one eye on the stairs and one eye looking for any movement.

As they rose the stairs Dylan felt himself getting uncomfortably warm until a bead of sweat broke out on his brow. At first he blew it off to hormones since he was a happy, healthy nineteen-year-old with a wonderfully attractive young woman on his arm. By the time they reached the top of the staircase though he could feel sweat breaking out all over and his throat felt as though it were closing shut. He stood a moment teetering on the last stair feeling dizzy with a sensation of vertigo which he had never experienced before. He took a tentative step forward so he wouldn't fall backwards down the steps breaking his neck then broke out in a fit of coughing.

"Are you alright, Dylan?" Ru asked out of sincere concern placing a soft hand on his back.

Dylan brushed her off trying to talk through his hacking, "I'm… fine. Go on ahead… I'll catch up."

"I don't really want to be alone. Are you sure you're alright?"

Dylan coughed hard, "I'll be fine… just gimme a second."

"Okay." Struck with fear she backed up a step.

"Right behind you. I swear." Dylan tried to assure her before doubling over with another coughing fit.

Ru turned away hesitating to move at all. She had experienced several Wiccan ceremonies with her family but nothing at all like tonight. She was used to ceremonies to ask for a good harvest and things of that nature not summoning a spirit from the underworld. She had thought Isobel Gowdie to be just another woman caught being eccentric in a male dominated world where such things were unacceptable. She didn't consider herself any expert but she had read numerous accounts of women being hanged or burned at the stake for being witches when all they really seemed to be was outspoken or lesbians in a world that accepted neither. Never once had she come across an account that seemed to be an actual witch. She now questioned everything she had ever known. These thoughts flooded her mind as she took a deep breath and took a step forward into the dark while Dylan continued to hack away behind her.

Dylan finished a coughing spell feeling like he was on fire from the inside. He leaned back against the wall trying to catch his breath a moment but it seemed an impossible task. He was learning how an asthmatic feels during an attack. He closed his eyes trying to calm himself but it felt like he was being strangled while his blood boiled in his veins bringing him to the verge of an all-out panic attack. He felt terror welling up from deep within only worsening as he became paralyzed. Dylan's eyes rolled painfully back into his head as his body shook in a full grand mal seizure. As he was about to blackout a voice spoke to him from inside his own head, *"Frui Infernos! Ave Satanas!"*

The demon stretched out his arms straightening his back to get the feel of his new body. He couldn't believe how good it felt to be out of hell for the first time in years beyond number. He smiled so broadly he looked like a mad clown on the verge of a killing spree.

"Dylan, are you alright? Are you coming?" Ru's voice broke the momentary joy the demon was feeling.

"Coming!" He yelled out in his strange new voice.

Ru had stepped into the first room on the left at the top of the stairs. She stood at the edge of a dusty mattress shining her candle this way and that. The demon walked up behind her placing his hands on her shoulders pressing his body into hers. The move took Russue by surprise and she spun around to face her search partner.

"Dylan, please let's just find this demon," Ru said, though her cheeks were flushed in a rush of her own hormones.

The demon ignored her words leaning forward kissing her hard forcing his tongue deep into her mouth. Ru struggled against the advance to no avail quickly turning her rush of lust to panic. She smacked Dylan across the face, which finally made him disengage.

"Dylan you're scaring me! Let me go!" she yelled in panic.

The demon looked at her with a wicked smile. "I can smell your cunt."

Ru greeted the crass remark with an even harder slap across Dylan's face. Already she felt like she was burning up. Her throat started to close making it difficult to breath. Her eyes began to bulge as she struggled for air.

"What... did... you do... to me?" She struggled to get the words out.

The demon looked at Russue with blackened eyes. "Only that which is in my nature."

The demon shoved Russue onto the mattress sending up a cloud of dust. She raised the candle still in her hand only to see the flame reflected in jet black eyes that were no longer Dylan's. Realization flooded in like a tsunami, this was the demon they had summoned. It began to undress as her consciousness faded. She felt him crawl on top of her sliding her dress up and her white cotton panties down.

"Frui Infernos! Ave Satanas!" he whispered in her ear as he entered her body as she exited it.

Travis wandered around the basement, which seemed to be where all the unwanted odds and ends of the house's previous owner had ended up. There seemed an infinite number of places for anything to hide and since he didn't really know what to look for or expect it made the search that much slower. He had learned that a demon can appear in almost any form once summoned out of hell. He had read accounts of demons being conjured as small as ants and as large as an elephant. There really seemed to be no rhyme or reason to it. It seemed to all depend on which of the thousands of demons came to the surface. All he had found so far were a couple of rats and a buzzing gnat that was annoying but no demon. He began to wonder if they had conjured anything at all but he continued to look unwilling to give up now.

Alex and Morgan weren't having any better luck on the main floor. They had searched all the cupboards high and low not managing to see anything other than a few scampering bugs. There was nothing in the family room where they performed the ritual, nor in the coat closet,
nor anywhere else it seemed. Alex was more interested in Morgan than the search.

"Why don't we slip out to the van and have a little fun," Alex begged tugging at the waistband of Morgan's pants.

"Don't whine, it's unattractive. Besides how can you think about sex when there could be a demon running around in here somewhere? You really are a complete idiot, aren't you?" Morgan teased though the smile on her face and the hand rubbing his crotch gave truth to the lie.

"Just a fool for love my darling."

"Well you're definitely a fool I'll give you that," she laughed.

A lack of any place left to search led to their teenage lust taking hold. They started out kissing but soon Alex's hands were rubbing Morgan's nubile form all over. Morgan was no less passionate as she held him tight to her with one arm wrapped around his lower back while her other hand rubbed at his growing erection. Unable to control themselves they fumbled with buttons and zippers until finally their pants fell around their ankles. Alex pushed Morgan back against the wall lifting her up with his hands under her soft buttocks until he could feel her warmth sliding down around him. They were lost in their own lust oblivious to anything else in the world. Their pure carnal lust was all they cared about.

The couple was lost in the throes of their passion. Morgan had her eyes shut tight while Alex put every ounce of effort into thrusting his hips. Neither noticed the extra massaging taking place between them. Both began to feel a heat building inside them like nothing they had ever felt before. Alex was so intent on thrusting himself deeper and harder into Morgan he didn't notice the pressure coming from behind him at first. Morgan was moaning loudly as they both began to boil in their skin. Nearing orgasmic euphoria neither noticed that they weren't just breathing heavy but gasping for breath. Alex's eyes popped wide open as the demon entered him from behind matching his thrusts into Morgan. Alex wept as his vocal cords failed him. The demon thrust deep and hard into Alex threatening to split him in two. Morgan's moans ceased as her throat closed. She and Alex stared into each other's bulging eyes as the demon thrusted harder and harder until it tensed lifting Alex off his feet with its own powerful climax. Finished the demon stepped back letting the two lifeless bodies slump to the floor.

"Frui Infernos. Ave Satanas!" The demon spat the words, "Enjoy Hell. Hail Satan!" down at the dead couple.

The demon looked down at the still connected pair as though pondering his next move. He saw humans as weak insignificant beings to be wiped away. The denizens of hell suffered constantly for all eternity while weak humans wiled away their lives without a care. His only desire was to wipe them from existence though he knew he couldn't do it alone. He needed to raise Satan who would surely reward him as His right hand. Humans may be ignorant but they had somehow managed to summon him, he needed to know how. The demon could smell another filthy human in the house. Smiling he decided to greet him in style. The demon grabbed the fresh meat piles below him by the hair dragging them into the dark room in which he was born.

Travis reached the end of his patience finally giving up in frustration. He wanted to check with his coven now that Alex and Morgan seemed to have finished their extracurricular activities. Perhaps his little skeptic and the shy one had had better luck upstairs. He plodded up the basement steps loudly trying to give ample warning to the young couple in case they were still naked. He didn't hear any frantic scampering or hushed voices so he assumed it was safe. He reached the top of the stairs opening the door back into the kitchen seeing it empty. He passed through into the doorway with no sign of the young lovers.

"Alex? Morgan? Are you decent?" he called out but there was no reply.

He saw no flickering candles aside from his own. He passed by the family room paying no attention to it since it was dark. He walked to the bottom of the stairs calling up to Dylan and Ru but again there was no reply. He began to suspect what had happened. Alex and Morgan could have slipped outside but not all four of them. One of them had found the demon, he was sure of it. Excitement and fear filled him in equal measure.

Travis rushed for the paper sack quickly pulling out another pair of rubber gloves pulling them on as fast as he could without ripping them. Then he rushed to the bucket to retrieve the grimoire. He dunked his hands in carelessly sloshing blood over the sides but his hands found nothing inside. In a panic, he swirled his hands around but it was gone. He fell to his knees overcome with fear. Had one of his foolish coven removed it? He ran to the front door throwing it wide hoping to find the group of idiots dancing around in the moonlight but there was naught but darkness. He stepped back inside leaning against the wall to calm himself and think.

"Are you looking for something friend?" The voice sounded like Dylan but there was something off about it to Travis' ear.

Travis turned toward the voice which came from the family room. He wasn't sure he wanted to see now that Gowdie's Grimoire was in the demon's hands but curiosity forced him. He peeled off the bloody gloves, pulled out his pack of cigarettes lighting one and inhaling deep. He blew the smoke out slowly with a deep sigh then entered the family room.

He stepped across the threshold unable to see almost anything in the dark having tossed his candle away in his panic to get the grimoire. He plucked a discarded candle from the floor bringing it back to life. He wasn't ready for what the dim light revealed. The demon was sitting cross legged at the far end of the room surrounded by horrors Travis had never imagined. The demon had skinned Alex and Morgan laying their empty skins neatly in front of its naked form. It had arranged their internal organs and muscles in pentagrams on the floor encircling them with the bones. It had neatly cracked open each skull placing the brain in the centers of the pentagrams. There was blood splashed everywhere from floor to ceiling. Gowdie's Grimoire lay neatly in its lap as it chewed what he had to assume was the flesh of one of his friends.

"Please, sit." The demon motioned invitingly to him.

Travis could see no point in refusing the request. If the demon wanted him dead it would have done it already, he thought. His mind raced trying to figure out any way to get the book away from the demon wearing Dylan as a suit. It was only then it dawned on him that Russue was missing. He assumed she was dead but her body wasn't here so there was a chance at least. He tried not to look into the demon's soulless black eyes.

"You're the one who summoned me here, correct?" Travis nodded. "Now that creates a little problem for both of us," the demon stated gravely.

"How so?"

"There are rules. You think you can control me if I tell you my name? Sorry, that's not exactly how it works. However, since you summoned me I'm not allowed kill you myself, it's against the rules. Plus, I need you."

"You need me? Need me to do what?"

"We'll get to that. First thing's first we haven't been properly introduced. My name is Namtar. Is my name familiar to you?"

"I'm Travis. I'm familiar with you. Namtar… son of… Enlil and Ereshkigal? God of death, some say you were the inspiration for the Grim Reaper myth. You were a messenger of Nergal and then something about disease. Am I right?"

Namtar seemed genuinely impressed, "Very good Travis! All pretty well spot on, I must say I'm impressed. Most of you humans are complete ignoramuses but you… are not. I command sixty very nasty diseases to be precise, but the truth is only one would be needed to wipe your kind out."

"I don't doubt your power. How is it that I can be of service to you?"

"I need your help with another ritual. We're going to summon Beelzebub, Satan himself! He's also the rightful owner of this little book. It was that Gowdie woman who stole it from him. The Master drove her mad then had your kind do all manner of nasty things to her but that's nothing to the suffering she's seen in Hell. Perhaps returning it will bode well for you." Namtar laughed. "Oops, I'm sorry. You didn't return it, did you? You wanted it for yourself, to control us, to control Him. Perhaps you are more ignorant than these plebes."

Travis searched his mind for any words, "Perhaps I am a fool but you need me. You said so!"

"Yes. I do." Namtar rose motioning for Travis to do the same, "Please, come closer."

Travis shook but could see no options. Namtar held the Grimoire tight in his hands, there was no way he could get it. He had no idea what Namtar had in mind but he was sure he wouldn't like it. Seeing no option, he stepped closer to the demon.

"I'm going to give you a choice, Travis, as a thank you for bringing me here." Namtar handed Travis his own blade caked in blood.

Confused Travis asked, "What am I supposed to do with this?"

"That is choice number one. I want you to sacrifice yourself to bring Satan to this plane of existence." Namtar was smug but matter of fact.

"What's to stop me killing you instead?" Travis tried to sound bold.

"I truly hope you're not dumb enough to think you can kill me. You do have a second choice that will aid your decision. Refuse to sacrifice yourself and I'll infect you with a disease that will kill you so slowly and painfully that you'll beg for death."

"You said you couldn't kill me!" Travis suddenly felt escape was possible.

"I can't… but apparently, you don't know as much about me as you thought. The diseases I carry aren't diseases as you think of them. They are sub-demons who do my bidding. I can't kill you but they can. So, what will it be? Quick and easy or slow and agonizing. By the way it makes no difference to me. Refuse and I'll get someone else to take your place, you're only costing me a little time and inconvenience for which you'll suffer enormously, of course," Namtar said very pleased with himself.

Travis stood in shocked silence seeing no way out. He had gotten his coven killed and now himself as well. He had been obsessed with finding the grimoire. He had killed to get it but all for naught. He closed his eyes resigning himself to his fate.

Travis tightened his grip on the blade. "God forgive me."

"Pray all you want, there is no atonement," Namtar whispered, *"Frui Infernos. Ave Satanas!"*

Travis slid the blade across his neck, beginning his descent into hell.

Namtar knelt amongst the carnage as his master rose from the sacrificial blood. He held out the grimoire in fealty as Lucifer laid a grateful hand upon his head.

End

Feind Gottes is the horror writing, metal loving founder of the website *Thy Demons Be Scribblin*. Feind began writing in 2012 merely to see if he could, soon falling in love with creating so one story became two and so on. Feind has posted several short stories, poems and flash fiction on his website for free. Feind won the Dark Chapter Press 2016 novel writing contest with the first draft of his first novel, which is unpublished at this time.

Feind is also excited to be one of fifteen finalists in **The Next Great Horror Writer Contest** sponsored by **HorrorAddicts.net**. All published works are listed below in addition to the dozens posted on his website: http://www.thydemonsbescribblin.com/feinds-original-scribbles.

Hell Awaits (short story) published in **Kill For A Copy** from **Dark Chapter Press**

Tamed Brute (flash fiction) published in **Flashes of Darkness: Halloween Special 2015** from **Dark Chapter Press**

The Bones of Baby Dolls (short story) published in **KIDS: Volume I** from **Dark Chapter Press**

Known But Not Named (flash fiction) – Winner of **DCP's December 2015 DreAdvent flash fiction contest**.

Harvester of Sorrow (novelette) – **Top 25** (out of thousands of entries) in the 2016 writing contest at Freeditorial (not a horror specific contest). Still available for free.

Cold Heart, Cold Soul (novelette) – **7 Deadly Sins Anthology** from **Stitched Smile Publications** coming late 2017/early 2018

THE RATS
By
Nik Kerry

When I entered Hell, it was cold. I'd tried to complain to management about it but no one took my call. I'd expected as much with how quickly the fog comes and goes in this place but never anticipated Hell to be much more than a few short months of burning before I had to head back to home for school.

I'd blame my father for this one, if he wasn't so eager to take all the credit.

He's one of those drag kind of dudes, to be honest. He's worked the same dead-end job for God-knows-how-long without a raise all because the man won't suck up to his boss just once-and that's the truth.

And when we try anything, he'd make us work for it. Heh, if I'd knew any better, I'd hide his alarm clock and make him work for it then. See how much he likes the treatment. Well, I suppose it's that kind of mentality that landed me in Hell in the first place.

You see, he said I would be gone for a month or two-or until the Miller twins stopped trying to hunt me down for what I did to their older brother. It wasn't anything too bad. He was bullying some school kids so I landed a punch on him. And then three, four, maybe five; I lost count. He fell forward and broke most of his teeth out on the curb. It could've happened to any other bastard who makes fun of kids.

Of course, it wasn't Hell without having the grandparents here to greet me. Grandma, she gave me all the hugs and kisses that she did while my Grandpappy gave me a hug and handshake. Very…gentleman like of him. My dad was quick with the hellos and goodbyes. Thank God he was. Otherwise, he might've asked me to work on something he saw wrong in his own parent's house.

Grandma was nice enough to me; Grandpappy was stern like my father. And cheap. My great-Grandpappy, God rest his soul, was a millionaire worked-from-the-bottom-up kind of guy. Yes sir, my Grandpappy was growing up with a rich man. When he up and died, he gave the kids some money and that's as far as it got down the line as far as I know. We might've gotten a Christmas gift way back when, otherwise we saw no cent from him.

"Your father told us you can't have your phone," said Grandpappy.

"I don't," I lied. "He took it."

Grandpappy studied me like he did those students he used to teach when he taught high school. Nevertheless, he gave me a shrug, a snort from his nose, and headed me up to the guest room on the second floor. The room was large, heh, larger than any room my dad could afford for that matter. The walls were covered with cheap wallpaper, the type you buy from K-mart. An old writing desk from back when Grandpappy used to write sat in the corner nestled next to the window that overlooked the street. A bed sat in the center of the room, right up next to the wall. After I settled and the dust cleared, I jogged down the stairs to the kitchen. One thing I could always count on Grandma for was the best damned cooked meals from here to New York. I don't care what the cooks around the region claim about their cooking. Line them up! Put them on the screen! I'm willing to bet that any man who tastes my grandma's cooking will agree with me. She *is* the best damned cook from Hell to New York.

She tossed a salad from a bag and let me eat it.

"It's for your weight," she claimed, "Father's orders."

The fog settled in a little bit after five. It crawled up from the river, through the streets, coiled like a snake through the forest and up through the houses. Inside, Grandpappy, grandma, and yours truly sat in the kitchen. A steaming pot of clam chowder enticed me like a ten-cent chick.

We had begun to eat when there was a knock at the door.

"Oh that must be Missy." Grandma used the table to help her to her feet. "I could've sworn I told her I wasn't going to yoga today but the woman is so persist-"

Grandpappy's ears perked up at the sound of the girl's voice.

"McKenzie?" His nose scrunched up. "What is she doing here?"

"Who's McKenzie?" I asked.

"One of the local girls. She's a real tough cookie, laid Victor Perkins flat on his ass when he tried to pick on her. Poor boy, he didn't know she had a real mean punch."

Grandma hurried back into the kitchen, clutching a wet note in her hands. She smiled as she usually did, bright and cheerful.

"Sam." She laid the cloth down next to my bowl. "McKenzie brought this for you. You never told me you and she knew each other."

"I don't know…" my voice trailed off when I unfolded the note.

DON'T FEED THE RATS

"Oh my," Grandma gasped.

"The rats?" My voice left me only with a whisper.

"Here, let's get rid of that. Maybe she mixed up the notes." She tried to yank the note from my hand. I pulled away and crumpled the note.

"Maybe it's a prank." I grinned from ear-to-ear. "I know Shaun and I used to do things like that to each other just to freak each other out."

"Here, I can take that from you."

"Nah, I got this, grandma." I tossed the crumpled paper through the air towards the trashcan. The paper danced on the rim, took a bow, and fell into the trash. "Still got it."

By the time night fell, the fog choked the streets and hugged the houses. Grandma, Grandpappy, and me sat in the living room with grandma playing "Minnie the Moocher' on the piano. Grandpa and I sang along with her on the chorus. Afterwards, we said our goodnights and I climbed into my room.

I sat at the desk nestled in the corner, reading the missed texts I got from Alexis. The poor girl kept telling me she would wait for me. She would wait for when I returned to New York.

Alexis...the feel of her feels like a lifetime ago.

I rose, pulling the small charger for my phone from my pocket and plugged my phone into the wall. As I got ready to strip down and turn in for the night, I froze near the window. The fog around the lamppost made the light have a halo appearance. Standing underneath the halo, the girl stood there.

She simply stared at me. She stared at my window, at my eyes, at my body. My feet froze in their place. The girl stood, I thought I saw her mouth moving, either that or it was a voice in the back of my head. Still, I heard the words exit my mouth at a dead whisper.

I'm sorry.

I'm sorry.

I'm sorry.

I pulled the curtains closed, doused the lights and laid in my bed. Stillness filled the air around me. Right as I was about to fall asleep, a strange thing happened. There was a sound coming from the ceiling above me.

Scritch-scritch.

Scritch-scritch.

"Mornin' sleepy head." Grandma welcomed me with a plateful of eggs and sausage in the morning. The fog was gone, leaving behind green trees and blue skies.

"Hey." I smacked my lips. "Where's Grandpappy?"

"Oh he's off running some errands. Won't be back this afternoon. Now around ten, I have a sewing class I teach. If you want to come along, you may. Otherwise, there's not much you can do around here."

"I'll go for a walk," I said.

"Oh how lovely. There are some nature hikes down by the river. If you go down the hill on the street going by the side of the house, you'll reach it. Now don't go too close to the river, ya hear? A boy fell into the river and got himself drowned a few summer's back."

"I won't." I studied the food. "Real food, huh?"

"Yeah. You're a growin' boy, you don't need salads or stuff like that 'til you're my age."

She left and I won my freedom by going on my walk. The air was cool and crisp. I love the air in the Eastern part of the States. There's something about the way nature breathes mystery in these parts. I have a cousin in Utah, I visited him once or twice. There's no mystery, no place to get lost. Everything is so…symmetrical and organized. When I go into nature, I want to go there to get lost amidst everything.

Downtown Monongahela consisted of a small square block of restaurants, old shops, and nothing much more. The street was quiet and the shopkeepers lazily went about their businesses. Outside a small tavern, a group of yellow-bellied old men sat in rockers, talking in hushed voices to themselves. They probably talked about the 'good ol' days' when I passed and saw the youth the left behind.

By the time I got to the river, the temperature had dropped ten degrees. The roar of the currents and the way the few boats tied to the docks bobbed up and down…it was like standing on the shoreline in New York. Heck, I even looked around for Alexis and Paulie. I guess I half-expected them to be there.

"You're new."

Holy crap, this girl! She had the longest gold hair I've ever seen! It fell down her shoulders and reached almost to her waist. She had these emerald eyes that sparkled in the sunlight and rosy red lips that looked like poison.

"Yeah, straight from New York," I said, smugly.

"I'm McKenzie. You must be Sam."

"Uh…yeah."

She smirked. "You don't remember me? Don't remember the playground or us spending hours there at a time?" She blushed and twirled on her heels. "Don't remember *the kiss*?"

"Uh…sorry I don't." I shook my head. "I'm still a bit groggy."

"Bad night sleeping, huh?" She sauntered over to me. "Some folks say the fog brings bad sleep. I think it's a hoc of crap."

I liked this girl.

"So uh…this kiss?" I smirked. "Tongue or no tongue?"

"Wouldn't you like to know?" She winked.

"Maybe a little reenactment?"

"Yeah…you wish." She giggled. She spun, her hair caught me in the mouth. She smelled like peaches and strawberries. "If you remembered then maybe I would give you…something."

"I remember," I lied. I reached out to pull this girl closer to me.

"Uh-uh." She giggled and shook away from me. "Not until you remember me." With one last giggle, she pranced off, making sure I got clear view of the way she walked.

"How was your day?" Grandma asked as soon as she arrived home. I passed the time texting Alexis and Paulie. Paulie asked permission to take Alexis out on a date. I didn't care. They always had a thing, even before Alexis and I started dating.

"Good," I replied, hiding my phone so grandma wouldn't see it. She always told Grandpappy everything. "Walked along the river and had a merry time."

"McKenzie told me you talked to her."

"Yeah…grandma, did I ever visit here when I was younger?"

"Here? Oh, now let me think…we moved from Iowa to this house when you were about five. So, maybe when you were six. Your mother would've brought you if she did because your dad was working nights at that time while going through school."

"Did I ever meet McKenzie before then?"

"I think so. You and she had a play date once or twice. Why?"

"She mentioned we played before."

"Oh her mother tells her silly things like that all the time."

My phone buzzed in my pocket. I yawned and smacked my lips.

"I'm gonna take a nap before supper."

"Alright, dearie." Grandma smiled at me.

I laid on my bed, staring at the text message. Paulie and Alexis were getting back together. I figured. He always had a way of smooth talking girls.

I rested my head against the wall, letting my eyes droop shut.

Scritch-scritch.

Scritch-scritch.

The scratching came from right behind the wall next to my ear. I tried to ignore it but for every second I laid there, the scratching continued. After ten minutes of trying to ignore the scratching, I sat up, swung my legs over the bed, and walked out the room. The walls were three inches thick. I remembered somewhere hearing that rats and mice could contort their bodies to fit into small areas. I figured Grandpappy and grandma had rats.

I laid on the bed again. The scratching was further on up the wall, near the corner of the ceiling. I closed my eyes to sleep…

(*Scritch-scritch*)

…only to pop them open seconds later. The scratching sounded like it was happening right next to my ear.

"Screw it!" I rose again and walked to the closet to grab a jacket.

No sooner did I open the closet door, I froze.

A second, shorter door sat hidden behind some coats. It was strange. I'd been here before, hid in this closet and I never noticed that door. The scratching, now far behind me. I reached for the door…

…it opened to a tiny spare room. A single chair sat next to a fog-glassed window overlooking the street in front of the house. Tiny dust bunnies sat on the floor except near the side of the walls where stacks of books stood. The room was cold and I could feel heat rising through the cracks in the wood flooring. This room must've been over a heat pipe or vent. How else would heat be getting into here? I gazed around the room again, gave a shrug, and walked out into the room.

The scratching had stopped.

"I think you might have mice," I concluded after telling the entire scratching in the walls story during dinner. Grandpappy listened intently, nodding his head ever so often.

"We did have mice before," Grandma told me. "Maybe we might have 'em again."

"I'll set some traps before I go to bed," said Grandpappy. "And I think we might have a few old ones in the basement from the last time this happened."

After dinner, Grandpappy and I retrieved some traps from the basement and walked back up to my room. Around the corner in my room, there sat a plain white door. Grandpappy opened the door and up into the dark attic we ascended. The attic was filled with old boxes and nothing else. We found a rat trap behind one of the boxes. A skeleton of a rat lay in the metal jaws.

"Not bad if I do say so myself," remarked Grandpappy.

We set the traps, walked down to the room, locked the attic door behind us and spent the rest of the night telling stories to each other. When I went to bed that night, the scratching was gone.

I awoke when I heard the scream in the walls.

My eyes shot open at the sound.

SNAP!

The traps! Something activated the traps! I was about to jump out of bed and run up the attic when I heard the wailing. It sounded like a baby wailing far off in the distance. Instantly, my body froze. Something above me moved in the ceiling. Something was dragging…something. The cry fell to a whimper - *Oh God where's grandma and pappy?* - and around four o'clock, silence took over the room. My eardrums rang loudly until the first car of dawn drove past the house.

I tiptoed out of my bed, crossing to the window as I did. I stopped behind the blind and peered out.

The fog was back and there stood a figure near the lamppost. The man was seven feet tall at least, wearing all black, and bald. His face…it looked so familiar and yet…so strange. It was only when I saw McKenzie standing next to the man did my heart stop. Her lips were moving…somehow I heard her voice in my mind.

Beware The Watcher.

I turned again to the old man.

He had vanished.

McKenzie kept saying something over and over again. I already knew what kept saying.

I'm sorry.

I'm sorry.

I'm sorry.

"Grandma, what are you doing with the spare room upstairs?" I asked over breakfast. I honestly didn't have an appetite after the night but I ate anyways.

Grandma gave me a funny look.

"Well, you're staying in it, aren't you?"

"I meant the room inside the closet?"

"Oh that? It's just for storage. Why?"

"Just curious, that's all," I mumbled.

"It's a neat little outlet, isn't it? Your grandfather and I thought so when we bought the house. And the stairs leading up to the attic, if you squeeze in between the wall and the stairs, there's another room behind the stairs. I don't let any of your cousins sit in there because I don't want them to get stuck and have to get them."

"Is that why Grandpappy always locks the attic?"

"Yep. Your cousin Billy almost got stuck in there and we decided to keep it locked ever-" The knocking at the door broke her off mid-sentence. "Excuse me a moment."

She exited the room, leaving me in silence. After last night, every tiny sound I heard sent shivers up my spine. The cars running along the wet pavement, the howls of dogs down the street, and even the blood rushing by my ears kept me on edge.

"Sam, McKenzie's here!"

I froze. My blood ran cold. Not her. Not her!!!!

"Sam?" The gentle voice sent goose bumps running up and down my back.

McKenzie stood in front of me, smiling as she did. I swallowed a glob of spit and looked up. Her eyes were dried from tears and her face was pale as a midnight moon.

"Hey."

"Hey," I mumbled.

"Sam, I…I'm sorry about-"

"Thanks."

She gave me a quizzical look. "I didn't mean to try and lead you on at the river."

"What?" I shook my head.

"Yeah, I have a habit of being too flirty sometimes when I talk to men. I didn't mean to be that with you. You seem like a good guy and all-"

"Wait, what about last night?"

"Huh? What are you talking about?"

I shook my head. "Nothing. Had a weird dream, that's all."

"Oh, okay. May-may I give you a hug?"

I stood up to receive her. When I did, her body felt cold. She wrapped her arms around me. It was like hugging a corpse.

"The watcher is watching," she whispered.

She let go and retreated fast out the door. There I stood in the kitchen, shaking like a rag doll.

The bait in the traps was taken but the traps themselves, except for one, hadn't been sprung. Grandpappy shook his head and stared.

"Damn things are smart," he whispered. He kicked the old trap away.

There was fresh blood underneath.

He never took notice; he simply walked me down the stairs and locked the attic after he shut the door.

That night as I lay down to sleep, the scratching was gone. I fell asleep instantly and dared not to wake until the sunlight hit my face.

June passed by lazily. Grandpappy and me would sometimes go fishing down the river and talk about life, friends, girls. You know, the usual guy stuff. Once, he took me to Pittsburgh and we wandered a classic car museum for some time. Grandma was equally as fun. During one of the most boring days of my life, she took me to her piano and taught me how to play. I learned when I was a kid but with all the free time on my hands, I finally progressed beyond 'Chopsticks' and 'Mary had a little lamb'.

It warmed up to Hellish temperatures. Nineties with humidity, days upon days of drowning in humidity. On those days, we'd go for rides on the hill tops. There, the air wasn't as thick and the heat not as bad. We took the old roads, roads the locals used to claim were haunted. There was this old highway right off the main one that led to a town close to Monongahela called Rock Creek. Grandpappy and grandma told me that in the early 2000s, there was a 'vanishing' of people except for one girl. All the buildings were intact, all the power still worked, all that was missing were the people. We sat on top of a large hill, twenty miles south of where the old town used to lay. The old highway took people to the town; it was blocked off by a large wire fence. The highway also led to an old fairground quite close to Rock Creek, they told me gas fumes made the place unsafe. During the entire time, my eyes were peeled to the highway. An old red truck drove down the highway. When I blinked, it was gone.

The Fourth of July hit the family like a bomb. Once, the house was empty, now the relatives were here to stay. Cousins I hadn't seen since I was a kid were around me playing the piano, old aunts and uncles alike talked about life itself. It was depressing hearing them talk. If growing up means talking about prices and about who married who, then I'd much rather stay a teenager thank you very much. If life starts off exciting and reduces to this, what's the point of life?

At night, we set off fireworks and joined the celebrations around town. They left before midnight and I sat in my room, jacked up on caffeine. Part of me still wanted the celebration to continue. It was one of those celebrations that stick out from the rest, the ones that the 'best days of our lives' are made from.

Scritch-scritch.

I froze. The scratching was coming from inside the wall across from my bed, where the hidden room stood. I didn't know what I was thinking; I swung my legs over the bed, tip-toed to the closet, and opened the hidden door.

The scratching ceased immediately.

I entered the room, bathed by the moonlight. To my left, little higher than myself, scratch marks crisscrossed each other. Tiny slivers of wood stuck out from the wood itself. My eyes darted across the room.

The other door was almost as invisible as the first. It was not that high, maybe up to my shoulders and in the shape of a triangle with a brass knob in the center. I turned the knob, and opened the door. A blast of stifling air caught me in the face.

I stepped into the darkness

And another step.

And

Another

Step taking

Me down a giant

Flight of stairs that

Continued to descend

Down and down into the

Darkness whilst the air grew

Hotter and hotter. Sweat beads

Grew on my forehead and dripped

Into my eyes, stinging them mercilessly.

At one point, I came to a landing where the steps ceased and the walls rose up around me. I

Started

Down another

Even larger set of stairs
That seemed to be made for giants
Until
They sud
Denly beca
Me small again
And almost steep
As before when I first
Started. Down and down I walked

At times
It was

Like

Taking

G

I

A

N

T

S

TEPS

Andatothers,smallstepsthatwerelikewalkingnonmyowntwofeet.

Towered

WallsOver

TheMe

Like a shell, or a vault…or a tomb. The heat rose, my tongue felt floppy and dry.

Scritch-scritch.

The scratching occurred all around me. I desperately tried to find the rats in the darkness, my hands groped the walls, waved wildly around me. The only change was the heat. Even my sweat stopped coming because the heat was so intense it would dry up as soon as it left my pores. The hair on my arms curled downwards against the broiling. I beat my fists against the rough stone and let my legs turn me around.

The door to the spare room stood not even a foot away from me. I stumbled through the door, closing it tightly behind me, and staggered into my room until I collapsed onto my bed. My eyes lazily found the alarm clock next to my bed.

Only a minute had passed.

My legs ached, my muscles screamed. And there I laid in my bed, panting like a dog.

There's no way a minute had passed. There was no way-

Thump.

My head perked at the sound.

Thump.

Somewhere in the attic above me, something heavy dropped on the floor.

Thump.

Crrrrrrrrrrrrrrrrrrreeeeeeeeeeeeeeeeeeeeeeeeeeeeeeeeaaaaaaaaaaaaaaaaaaaaakkkkkkkkkkkkkkkkkkk!

The attic door slowly opened. In my mind, I remembered the last time Grandpappy and I journeyed the attic. He'd forgotten to lock the door.

Now it stood, fully open.

Thu-

I jumped up, racing over to the door with all the strength I had to run and kicked the door shut. Something caught the door right as it was about to latch and tried to push the door open. My heart raced at a million miles an hour when I threw my body weight against the door. Something behind the door growled with a growl so low, I felt it vibrate through my chest. Whatever it was, it wanted in and it wasn't going to take no for an answer. The door jumped forward, sending my heels digging into the carpet. I pressed my back against the door, my teeth grinding against each other as I tried desperately to keep the door shut. The growing grew to a roar and the claws! The claws ripped through the door, attacking my skin.

"Grandma!" I cried. I cried like a little girl.

Suddenly, everything was still. The door closed gently beneath my weight and there I stood, my heart beating inside my head. I opened my cascading eyes. The closest ahead of me was growing. The top lip reached towards the ceiling and then was arching, arching across the room towards the tip of the door. As quickly as I could, I jumped up and ran for the door. I exited, pulling the door shut behind me.

Silence.

Stillness.

I let out a sigh and tip-toed downstairs to the living room. I laid on the couch, trying to sleep.

Scritch-scritch.

The scratching came from the ceiling. I sat up, tears now rolling down my cheeks. What did they want?! What did these things want from me?!

A truck passed by slowly outside and stopped just outside the house. I turned and instantly wished I hadn't.

The red truck that sat outside was the same red truck I saw on the hill, heading towards Rock Creek. Inside the car sat a figure blackened by the darkness. Even though I couldn't see its eyes, I knew the thing was staring at me. It could see me through the blinds and it was waiting for me.

Scritch-scritch.

Oh God, please let this stop.

Thump. Thum-thump.

Thum-thump.

I turned away from the blinds, facing the dark stairwell as I did.

Ding-ding!

The clock struck six and like that, the truck was gone and the sound stopped. I buried my head in my hands and wept like a baby. For a while it took me to realize that it was raining outside. A gentle rain, chasing away the fog as it came down. I turned again to the window.

McKenzie stood under the downpour, staring sadly at me. She was crying, crying just like Alexis cried when Paulie first broke up with her.

"McKenzie!" I ran to the window.

She shook her head frantically as I neared. When she locked eyes with me, it was as if I could hear her voice in my head.

"Look up on the side of the house from the window."

I backed from the window, retreating to a small window on the side of the living room grandma always called, 'the peeping tom' window. It was a small rectangle that jutted out of the wall a bit. I stuck my head as far out as it could and glanced up. Darkness veiled the house. It was only when lightning cracked the sky that I realized what McKenzie was staring at.

The pale faced man, clad in black, was crawling down the side of the house like a spider, his cold black eyes staring straight at me. I yelped and jumped back. I clawed my way through the darkness, somehow finding my way to the stairs and climbing up all the way to the bathroom. I closed the door as to not wake Grandpappy and grandma and collapsed to the floor. I clamped my eyes shut and inhaled sharply. When I opened them, I froze. The pale man's face sat in the center of the window. He stared at me with those cold black eyes. I don't know what got into me but I stared back, I stared at him as if I were watching him. For hours, it seems, we stared at each other. Tears swelled my eyes until he simply vanished in the rain that soaked the glass.

"Sam?" Grandpappy ratted on the door. "You in there?"

I jumped up and opened the door. Grandpappy, up and early, dressed in his pajamas, looked like an angel more than anything. I wanted to tell him everything, everything I could about the night before. For the strangest reason, I didn't.

The scratching became louder and louder and the nights got worse. Even with ear muffs, I heard the scratching within my head. The rats had invaded and were there to stay. I didn't eat, I locked myself inside the house and dared not to go outside. I tried to sleep in the basement, in a closet, anywhere but the scratching continued. By the end of a week, I'd lost ten pounds.

"Sam, you need to eat," Grandpappy told me one night after noticing the black color under my eyes and the fact I hadn't slept a wink in forever it seemed.

"I'm not hungry," I told him.

"Now Sam, let me tell you something," said grandma. She waved her fork at me as she did. "I once went on a diet and I almost killed myself. I wasn't getting enough meats; I wasn't getting enough protein and the doctor told me if I didn't stop I would die. So, I ate. It was hard but I ate and you're going to eat."

I wanted to eat. Deep down beyond the façade that I put up of everything being okay, I wanted to cry, I wanted to eat, I wanted to move back to New York again. I didn't care about what happened next, I wanted out.

Knock-knock.

I froze.

"Oh that must be McKenzie," said grandma. "She phoned ahead to see if you were home."

"McKenzie?" I whispered.

Scritch-

Silence. For a split second there was silence.

Scritch-scritch.

"McKenzie is coming?" I asked.

The scratching stopped.

"Yep, she's here right now," said Grandpappy.

Scritch-scritch.

The scratching continued until grandma answered the door. Like that, silence ensued.

"Hello McKenzie!"

"Hello!" her voice felt soft.

"Yes, he's here in the kitchen."

Suddenly, I was eating. I was stuffing my face like there wasn't tomorrow. My stomach lurched and tried to reject the food but I forced it down.

"Now would you look at that?" Grandma smiled. "Once he got wind you were coming, he started eating again."

"Hi Sam." McKenzie smiled.

"Hey." I swallowed my food.

"Sam…may…may I talk to you in private?"

"Yeah." I rose and led her into the living room. We sat down but, before she could say a thing, I jumped. "What the hell is going on?!"

Tears swelled in her eyes.

"I'm sorry," she whispered. "I'm sorry."

"Stop saying that."

"I'm sorry!" she hissed through bitter sobs.

"What's-what's going on?"

"Do you remember the playground?" she whispered.

"I-what? No! I don't remember anything! All I want to do is get out of here and never *remember* any of this! Why is it that whenever you're near me, all the bad stuff stops but when you're not, it all starts up again?"

"I can't tell you."

"Tell me, damn it!"

"Look into your mind!" she almost yelled. She caught herself and forced her to quiet down. "Look deep into your memories! Please, I beg you. You only have a few more nights before…"

Her voice trailed off. It was then that I noticed McKenzie was wearing the same outfit-she wore the same outfit each time I saw her!

"McKenzie? Do you have any other clothes?"

"Do you know what it's like being trapped?! Can you even fathom what it's like trying to put on a new pair of underwear and knowing the old ones will be back in a moment's notice? Do you know what it's like knowing everyone you love is dead?!"

"…"

"Do you?"

"McKenzie, how much longer do I have?"

"If you can't remember me, you might have until the end of the week."

"I'll get out. I'll leave and never come back."

She shook her head.

"Unless you remember, you'll never leave. The curse will follow you until you're dead and then, you'll be a shell at their command, an actor playing a part."

"What lives in the attic, McKenzie?"

"The Hunger," she whispered, struggling to stand as she did. "And it's getting hungry."

The scratching, loss of appetite, and the nightmares began once McKenzie left. Grandma and Grandpappy left for errands and there I was, alone in the house. Alone in my room. The closet looked like a giant cave entrance into the dark abyss. Hours passed, daylight grew dim, and with the last of twilight fading away, I rose and walked straight into the closet, the spare room, into the odd shaped door.

And I let the darkness take me.

The

Steps

Were sometimes

Large

And sometimes so small that I thought I was walking on pins

Finally, I reached the landing and started forward. The heat grew and grew, grew to the point where I felt any sweat droplets boil off from their pores. After hours of walking, with the heat scorching my skin, I collapsed to the ground, heaving my last breaths.

"I'm sorry," I breathed, laying down on the hot tile. "I'm sorry."

At that moment, I thought my last thought. *I would do anything to get out of this.*

"I'm sorry."

My mother's soft hand brushed against my tear stained face. She smiled weakly but still, she looked like an angel. She had always looked like an angel to a young ten-year-old like me. Even with the IV in her arm, clad in a hospice gown and laying in that bed with family around, she looked like an angel.

"It's okay," she whispered.

"No ma, it's not." I wept. "I-I shouldn't have dropped the milk! If I-if I didn't, you wouldn't have had to have gone to the store and then the driver wouldn't have...have..."

"Samuel," she whispered, "it's okay. It was an accident."

"No!" I ran from her outstretched hand for the hospital hallway. Boy, did I run! I was Jesse Owens in the hallway, running fast and wildly. My father called me from far behind, said it was the last time to tell her I loved her. But I kept running.

When I broke from the hospital and fell onto the recess ground, I thought I was alone. Until I heard the weeping. The young girl in the yellow dress sat on the swing. I perked my head up and walked to the girl in the yellow dress.

"Are-are you okay?" I whispered, choking on my tears.

She shook her head bitterly.

"What's-what's wrong?" I inhaled sharply.

"My parents died," she whispered.

I sat down on the swing next to her.

"What's your name?" I asked.

"McKenzie. What's yours?

"Sam."

I…I remembered.

I remembered the playground! McKenzie and I met on the playground near Bethlehem, Pennsylvania when I was ten. My mother was hit by a drunk driver. She died while I talked to McKenzie. I never even said I love you. There I was, this almost-eighteen-year-old boy staring down my younger self, trying to tell him to go back. I wanted him to go back, I *needed* him to go back!

"I don't want to go to Rock Creek!" McKenzie wailed. "I want to stay in my house."

"McKenzie." My younger self took her hand. "It's okay. I'll protect you."

Tears moistened in her eyes. "You will?"

I nodded and then she did something I wasn't prepared for. She kissed me on the lips.

I've ruined so many things.

I ruined the lives of others. My dad, my grandparents, myself. I ruined the lives of all those girlfriends I treated like dirt. Each one came into my life, taught me things I didn't know and what did I do in return? Slept with them, told them all they wanted to hear and then left them behind in tears. Each one reminded me of my mother. When I had to face the pain and the guilt, I ran and left anything behind. Paulie and Alexis kept to me like glue but even then, I fled with them. I tried to run away from my dad so he brought me out here to be with the grandparents. It was all because when I was younger, I chose not to go back and say goodbye. I abandoned my mother.

Scritch-scritch.

Light flooded into the empty spare room.

Scritch-scritch.

Thu-thump.

"Oh God, what now?!" I jumped up and ran into my room. The smell of bacon and eggs ruminated through the room. I turned my head to the ceiling. "What do you want?!"

Scr-

Thump.

Thump.

Thump.

Thump.

"…hu-hunger…hunger…*HUNGER!!!*" The voice sounded like a squealing animal.

"If I feed you, will you stop hunting McKenzie and me?"

"…hunger…"

"Speak!" I demanded. "Speak and tell me now!"

Then said the rats in the wall, "Hunger."

"Set McKenzie free and leave us alone and I'll feed you. Deal?"

Then said the rats in the wall. "Hunger!"

Scritch-scritch.

Thu-thump.

I opened the door and made my way downstairs. Grandpappy was alone, dipping his bacon into egg yolks.

"Where's grandma?" I asked. (*Hunger!!!*)

"She's out running errands to Pittsburgh."

"I-I think the traps caught a rat."

"Oh really?"

I swallowed a glob of saliva. "Yeah. I heard the trap go off."

"Ah well, I'll go take a look." He wiped his hands on a napkin and stood. "Get something to eat, orders straight from grandma."

I nodded and sat down while he lumbered upstairs.

Scritch-scritch.

Scritch-scritch.

Scritch-scritch.

Scritch-

Silence. I waited for something, a scream, a fight, anything. All I got was silence. When I walked upstairs, the attic door was closed. I put my head next to the door and listened.

It sounded like something sucking soda through a straw.

I hurried from the bedroom and was halfway down the stairs when I heard the attic door open. I never stopped to look back until I was out the door and walking the streets.

Grandma told me he fell down the stairs and cracked his head open. The police said the same thing. I told them I was walking and for once, I had a voucher. McKenzie. She was happy. Happier than I'd ever seen her in real life. But when she looked at me, her eyes said it all. She knew what I did.

Summer ended abruptly when dad showed up for the funeral and then took me home. Paulie and Alexis got together, we three ended high school and I ran off to college. McKenzie? Well…things are going well if you can say so. We got married last June and are moving to a farm house in upstate New York.

But things aren't…normal. If anyone is reading this, if anyone finds this after I'm gone, please don't blame her. I don't think she's in control of herself at all. But a few days ago, she kept on complaining about her hunger pangs. I made her everything I could think of: steak, potatoes, roast. She ate them all and still complained of hunger.

Every so often she'll scratch the table with her nails. It sounds exactly like the scratching in the house. And a few minutes ago, she whispered into my ear, "Come to the bedroom when you're done. I have a surprise for you."

She sucked in air in between her teeth.

It sounded like someone sucking soda through a straw.

<u>Other HellBound Books</u>
<u>For You To Enjoy</u>

All available now in paperback and eBook from Amazon, iBooks, Barnes & Noble, Kobo etc. For full details, visit our official website

www.hellboundbookspublishing.com

Or
Download our App from iTunes / Google Play – or simply scan the QR Code below

The Big Book of Bootleg Horror 2

The second volume in HellBound Books' flagship horror anthology - this one bursting at the seams with even more fantastically dark horror from the cream of the rising stars in today's horror scene!

Featuring: Tracey A. Cross, Elizabeth Zemlicka, Shelby Thomas,

Matthew Gillies,

Spinster Eskie, Stephen Clements, Ken Goldman, Nathan Robinson, K.M. Campbell, Cody Grady, Sebastian Bendix, Leo X. Robertson, David Owain Hughes, Timothy McGivney, Kane Gordon, Todd Sullivan, Mike Mayak, Edward Ahern, Rose Garnett, Jaap Boekestein, Brandy Delight, Stanley B. Webb, D. Norfolk, and Thomas Gunther.

Blood and Kisses
By
James H Longmore

The definitive short story collecting from James H Longmore - an eclectic mix of dark horror, bizarro and Twilight-Zone style tales of the downright disturbing.

Welcome to the long awaited collection from the writer of horror novels *'Pede* and *Tenebrion*; a forword by Richard Chizmar (co-author of *Gwendy's Button Box* and author of *A Long December*), 18 short stories, 5 flash fiction and even a poem - all skin-crawling, soul-shredding tales of terror, of the darkest things that skulk amongst the night's inky shadows, and of the everyday gone horribly awry.

Discover the alternative implication of technology becoming self-aware, enjoy the acquaintance of a charismatic new pastor who promises his flock a brand new place in which to worship his God, and spend a little time in the company of a nice young man who is inexorably caught up in his home town's terrible secret. Then there is Cupid's revelation that personally he has never experienced love, yet we discover that very emotion alive and not so well amongst the ruins of a post zombie apocalypse world, and we bear witness to a childhood innocence forever destroyed in a war-torn city. There is more, Dear Reader, much, much more; for within these pages we have devils, demons and ghosts, lycanthropes and demi-gods, all rubbing nefarious shoulders with vilest of Hell's offspring who have slithered from the netherworld to doff their caps and wish us all the sweetest of dreams…

No Rest For The Wicked
By
Pamela Morris

Every ghost has a story. Not all of them want it told.

From beyond the grave, a murderous wife seeks to complete her revenge on those who betrayed her in life; a powerless domestic still fears for her immortal soul while trying to scare off anyone who comes too close; and the former plantation master - a sadistic doctor who puts more faith in the teachings of de Sade than the Bible - battle amongst themselves and with the living to reveal or keep hidden the dark secrets that prevent any of them from resting in peace.

When Eric and Grace McLaughlin purchase Greenbrier Plantation, their dreams are just as big as those who have tried to tame the place before them. But, the doctor has learned a thing or two over his many years in the afterlife, is putting those new skills to the test, and will go to great lengths in order to gain the upper hand. While Grace digs into the death-filled history of her new home, Eric soon becomes a pawn of the doctor's unsavory desires and rapidly growing power, and is hell-bent on stopping her.

Worship Me
By
Craig Stewart

Something is listening to the prayers of St. Paul's United Church, but it's not the god they asked for; it's something much, much older. A quiet Sunday service turns into a living hell when this ancient entity descends upon the house of worship and claims the congregation for its own.

The terrified churchgoers must now prove their loyalty to their new god by giving it one of their children or in two days time it will return and destroy them all. As fear rips the congregation apart, it becomes clear that if they're to survive this untold horror, the faithful must become the faithless and enter into a battle against God itself. But as time runs out, they discover that true monsters come not from heaven or hell…

…they come from within.

A HellBound Books LLC
Publication

www.hellboundbookspublishing.com

Printed in the United States of America